THE BEAUTY

VOLUME THREE

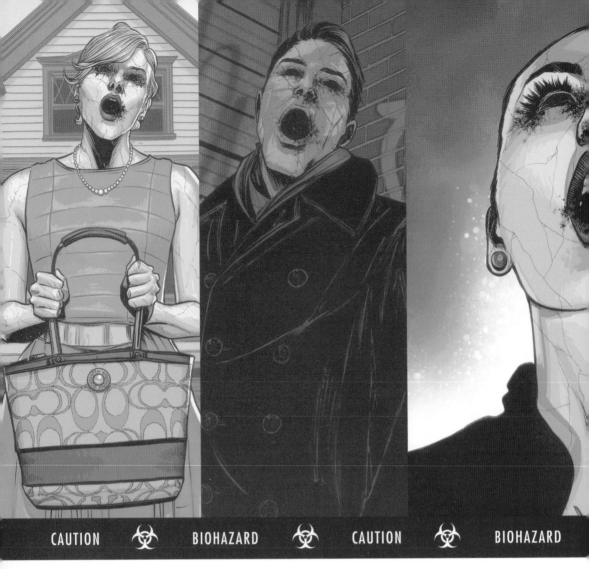

CAUTION ☣ BIOHAZARD ☣ CAUTION ☣ BIOHAZARD

IMAGE COMICS, INC.

ROBERT KIRKMAN Chief Operating Officer • ERIK LARSEN Chief Financial Officer • TODD McFARLANE President
MARC SILVESTRI Chief Executive Officer • JIM VALENTINO Vice-President • ERIC STEPHENSON Publisher
COREY MURPHY Director of Sales • JEFF BOISON Director of Publishing Planning & Book Trade Sales
CHRIS ROSS Director of Digital Sales • JEFF STANG Director of Specialty Sales • KAT SALAZAR Director of PR & Marketing
BRANWYN BIGGLESTONE Controller • SUE KORPELA Accounts Manager • DREW GILL Art Director
BRETT WARNOCK Production Manager • LEIGH THOMAS Print Manager • TRICIA RAMOS Traffic Manager
BRIAH SKELLY Publicist • ALY HOFFMAN Events & Conventions Coordinator • SASHA HEAD Sales & Marketing Production Designer
DAVID BROTHERS Branding Manager • MELISSA GIFFORD Content Manager • DREW FITZGERALD Publicity Assistant
VINCENT KUKUA Production Artist • ERIKA SCHNATZ Production Artist • RYAN BREWER Production Artist
SHANNA MATUSZAK Production Artist • CAREY HALL Production Artist • ESTHER KIM Direct Market Sales Representative
EMILIO BAUTISTA Digital Sales Representative • LEANNA CAUNTER Accounting Assistant
CHLOE RAMOS-PETERSON Library Market Sales Representative • MARLA EIZIK Administrative Assistant

www.imagecomics.com

THE BEAUTY, VOL. 3. First printing. August 2017. Copyright © 2017 Jeremy Haun & Jason A. Hurley. All rights reserved. Published by Image Comics, Inc. Office of publication: 2701 NW Vaughn Street, Suite 780, Portland, OR 97210. Originally published in single magazine form as THE BEAUTY #12–16, by Image Comics. THE BEAUTY, its logos, and the likenesses of all characters herein are trademarks of Jeremy Haun & Jason A. Hurley, unless otherwise noted. IMAGE and the Image Comics logos are registered trademarks of Image Comics, Inc. No part of this publication may be reproduced or transmitted, in any form or by any means (except for short excerpts for journalistic or review purposes), without the express written permission of Jeremy Haun & Jason A. Hurley or Image Comics, Inc. All names, characters, events, and locales in this publication are entirely fictional. Any resemblance to actual persons (living or dead), events, or places, without satiric intent, is coincidental. Printed in the USA. For information regarding the CPSIA on this printed material call: 203-595-3636 and provide reference #RICH–758425. For international rights, contact: foreignlicensing@imagecomics.com. ISBN 978-1-5343-0232-7

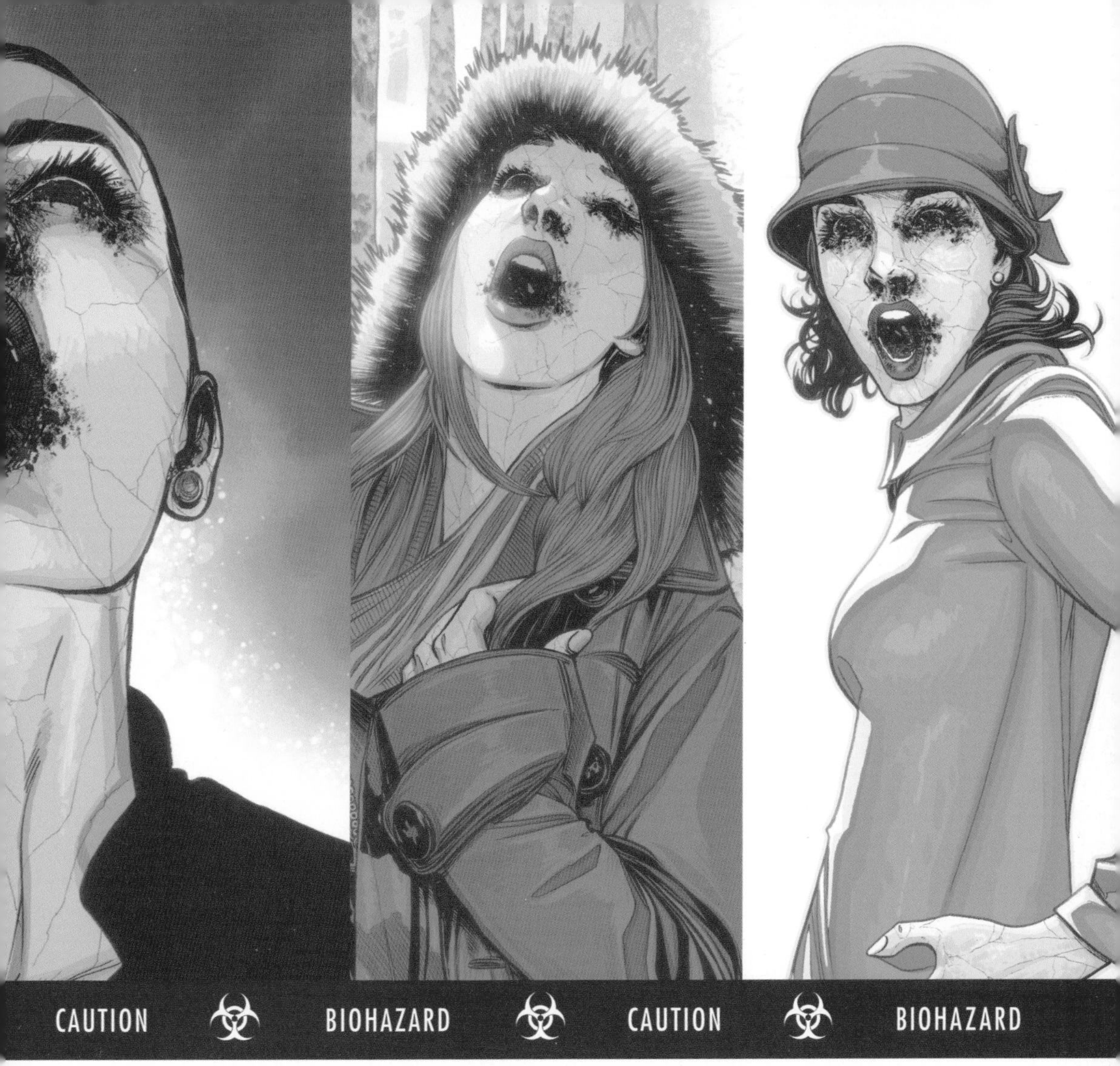
CAUTION
BIOHAZARD
CAUTION
BIOHAZARD

JEREMY HAUN & JASON A. HURLEY
story

JEREMY HAUN [CHAPTER 12]
THOMAS NACHLIK [CHAPTERS 13–16]
art

JOHN RAUCH
color

FONOGRAFIKS
lettering & design

JOEL ENOS
editor

CHAPTER

12

THE WAKE UP

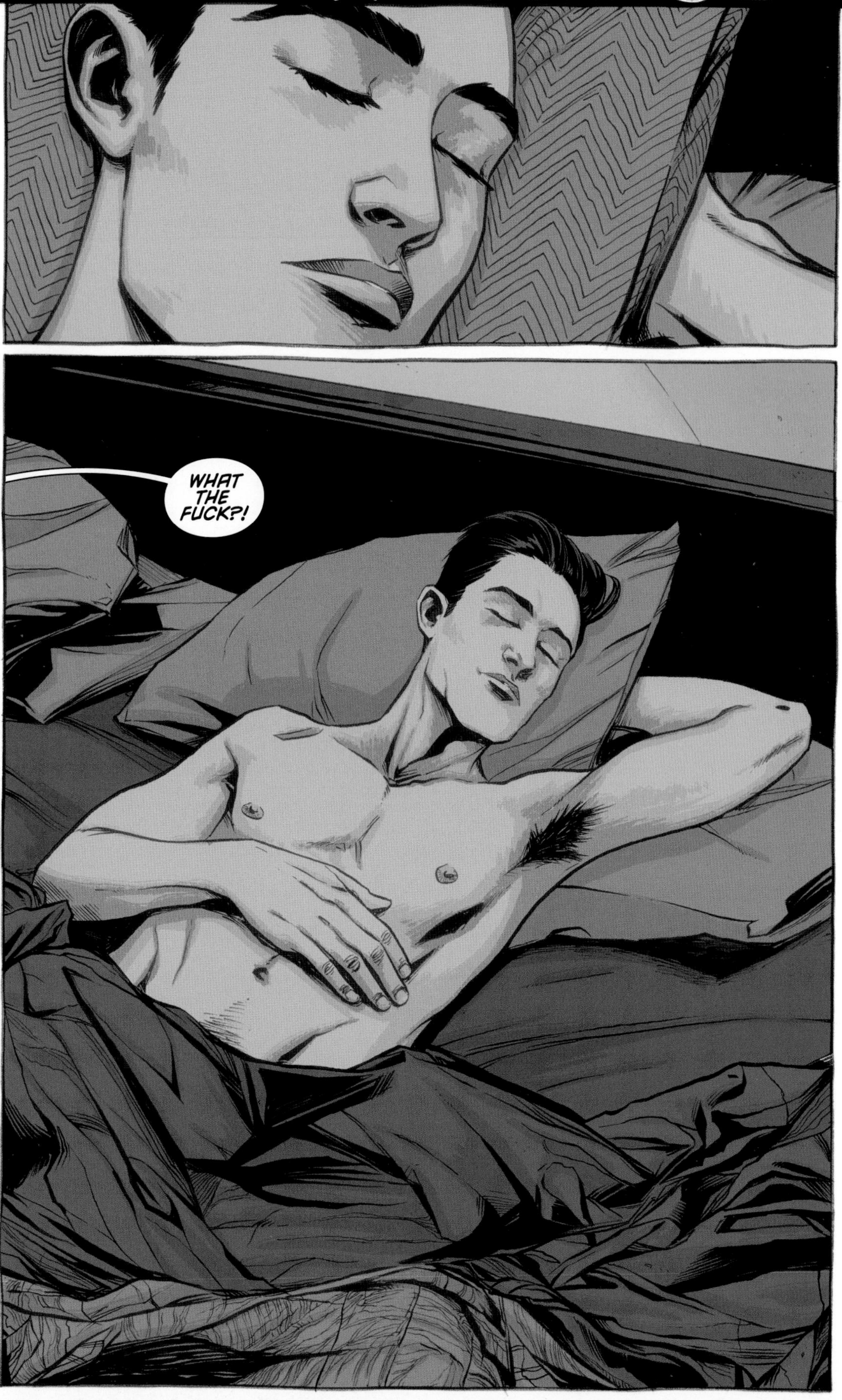
WHAT THE FUCK?!

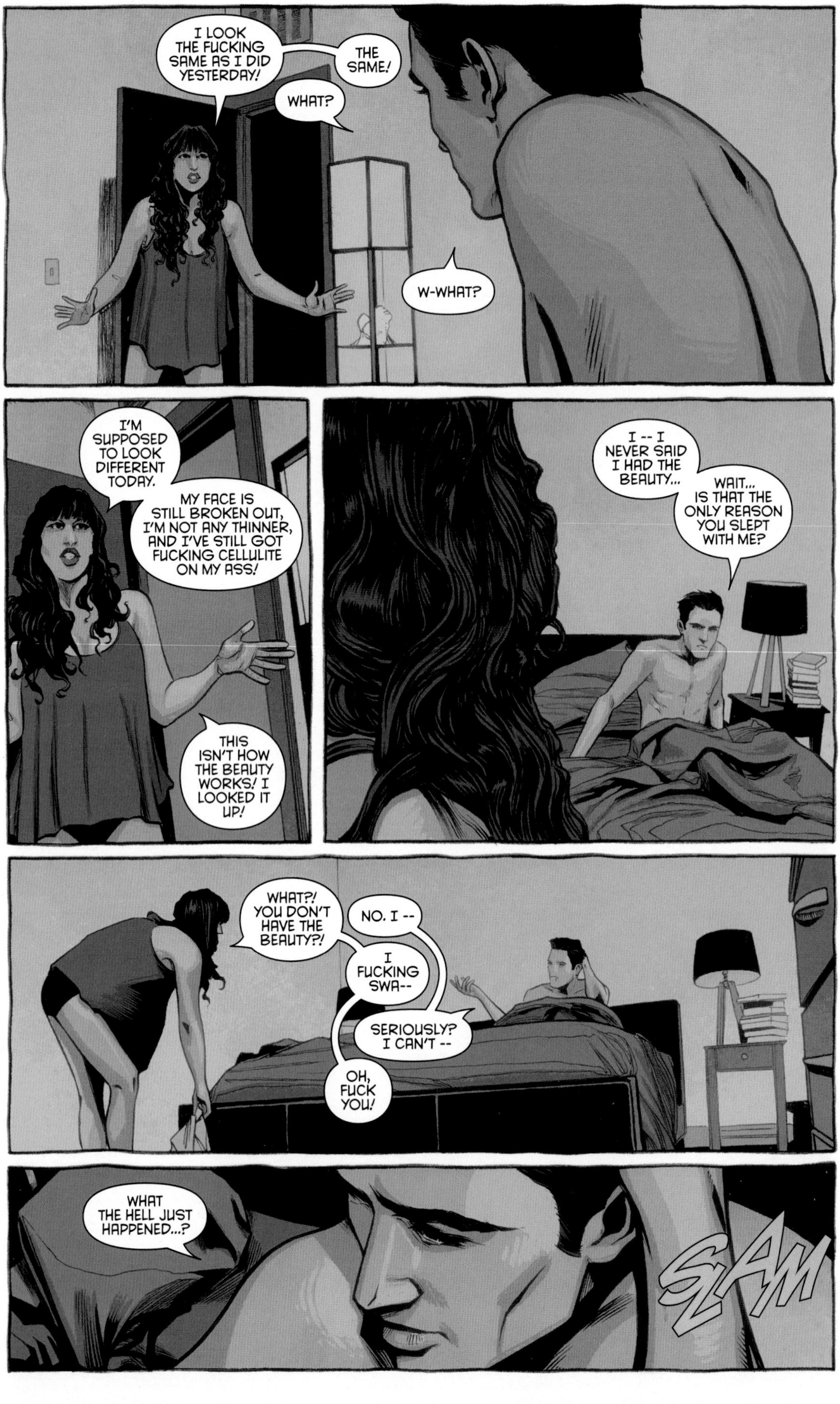
I LOOK THE FUCKING SAME AS I DID YESTERDAY!
THE SAME!
WHAT?
W-WHAT?
I'M SUPPOSED TO LOOK DIFFERENT TODAY.
MY FACE IS STILL BROKEN OUT, I'M NOT ANY THINNER, AND I'VE STILL GOT FUCKING CELLULITE ON MY ASS!
THIS ISN'T HOW THE BEAUTY WORKS! I LOOKED IT UP!
I -- I NEVER SAID I HAD THE BEAUTY...
WAIT... IS THAT THE ONLY REASON YOU SLEPT WITH ME?
WHAT?! YOU DON'T HAVE THE BEAUTY?!
NO. I --
I FUCKING SWA--
SERIOUSLY? I CAN'T --
OH, FUCK YOU!
WHAT THE HELL JUST HAPPENED...?
SLAM

THE SEXY BUG

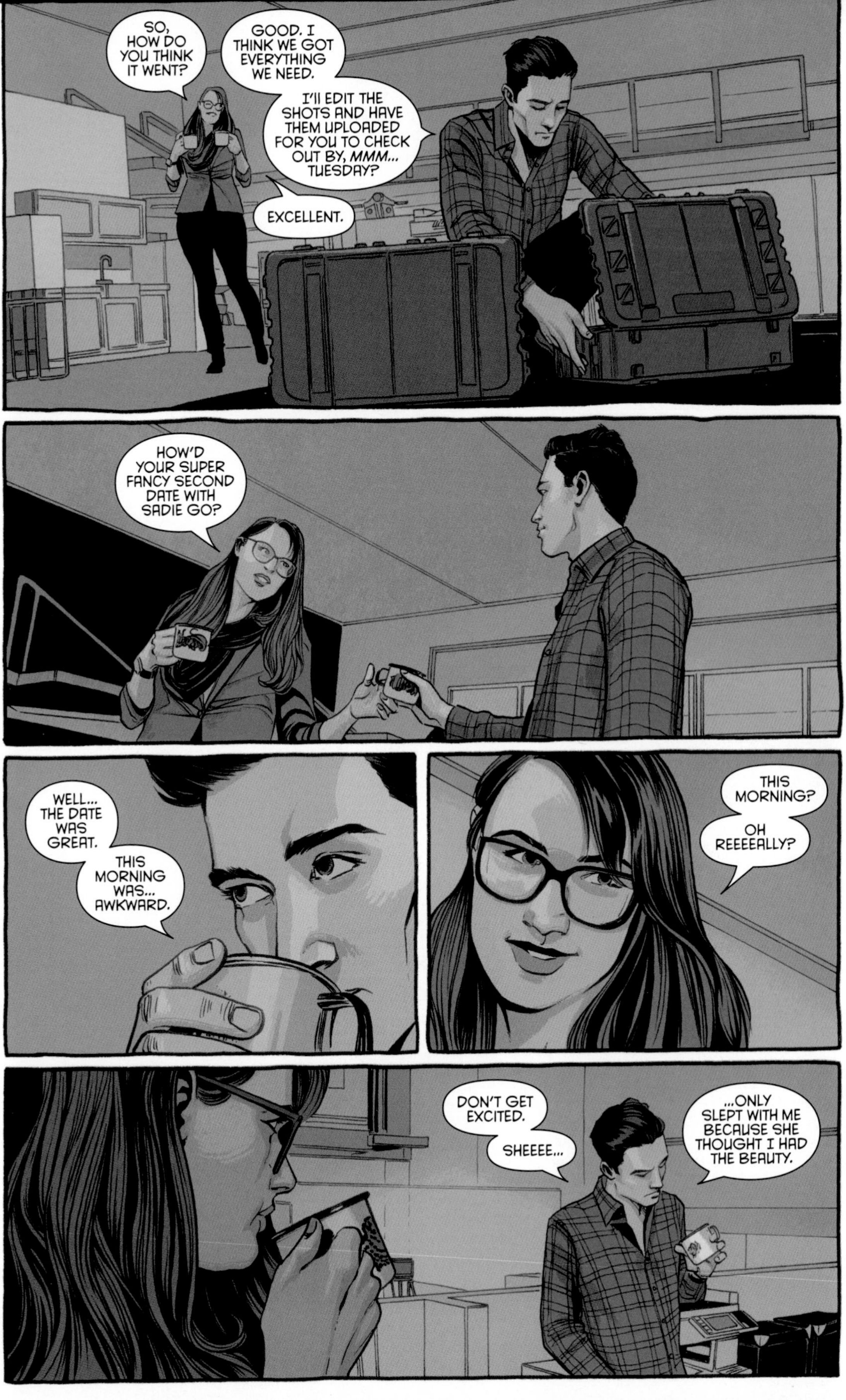
SO, HOW DO YOU THINK IT WENT?
GOOD. I THINK WE GOT EVERYTHING WE NEED.
I'LL EDIT THE SHOTS AND HAVE THEM UPLOADED FOR YOU TO CHECK OUT BY, *MMM...* TUESDAY?
EXCELLENT.
HOW'D YOUR SUPER FANCY SECOND DATE WITH SADIE GO?
WELL... THE DATE WAS GREAT.
THIS MORNING WAS... AWKWARD.
THIS MORNING?
OH REEEEALLY?
DON'T GET EXCITED.
SHEEEE...
...ONLY SLEPT WITH ME BECAUSE SHE THOUGHT I HAD THE BEAUTY.

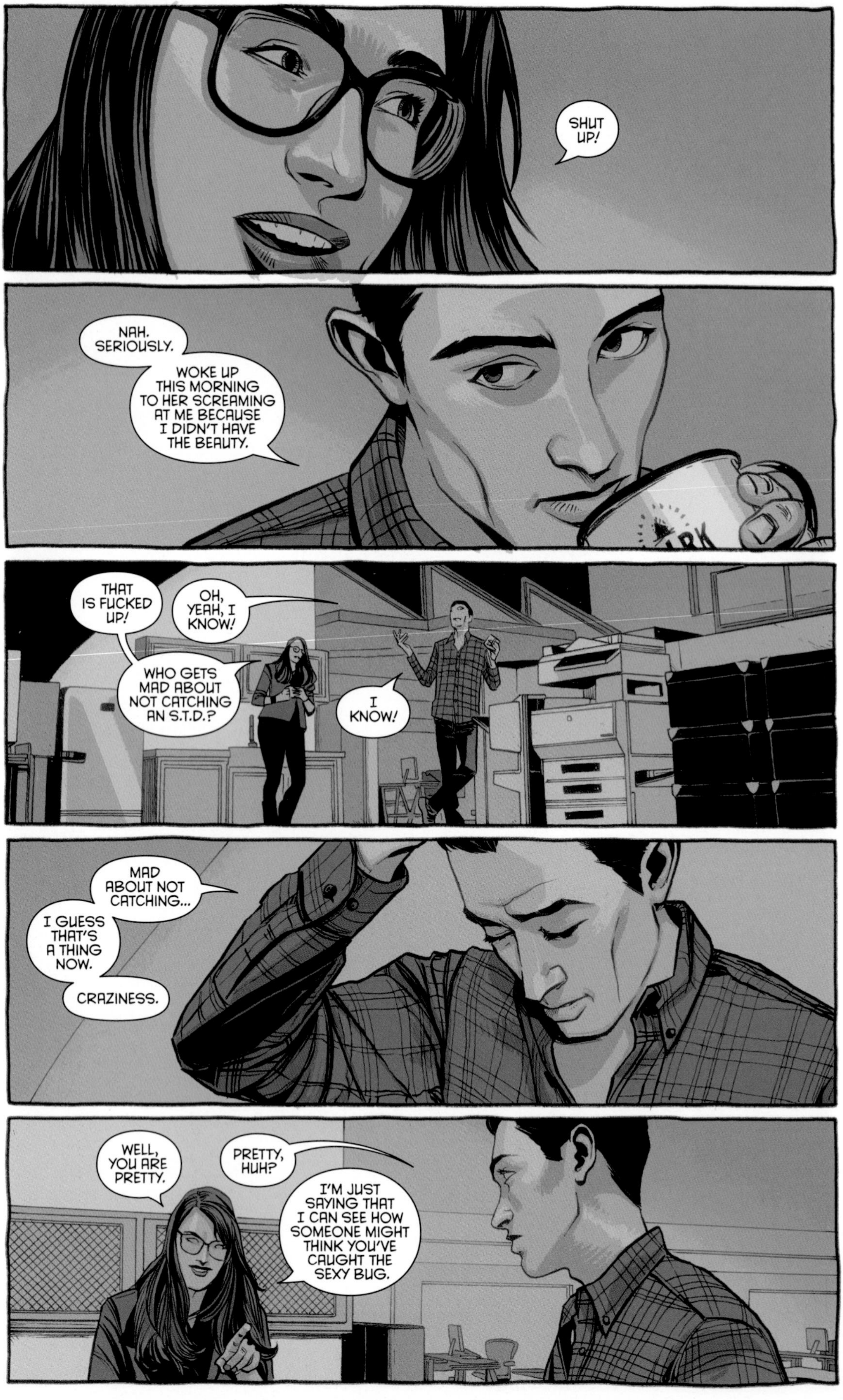
SHUT UP!
NAH. SERIOUSLY.
WOKE UP THIS MORNING TO HER SCREAMING AT ME BECAUSE I DIDN'T HAVE THE BEAUTY.
THAT IS FUCKED UP!
OH, YEAH, I KNOW!
WHO GETS MAD ABOUT NOT CATCHING AN S.T.D.?
I KNOW!
MAD ABOUT NOT CATCHING...
I GUESS THAT'S A THING NOW.
CRAZINESS.
WELL, YOU ARE PRETTY.
PRETTY, HUH?
I'M JUST SAYING THAT I CAN SEE HOW SOMEONE MIGHT THINK YOU'VE CAUGHT THE SEXY BUG.

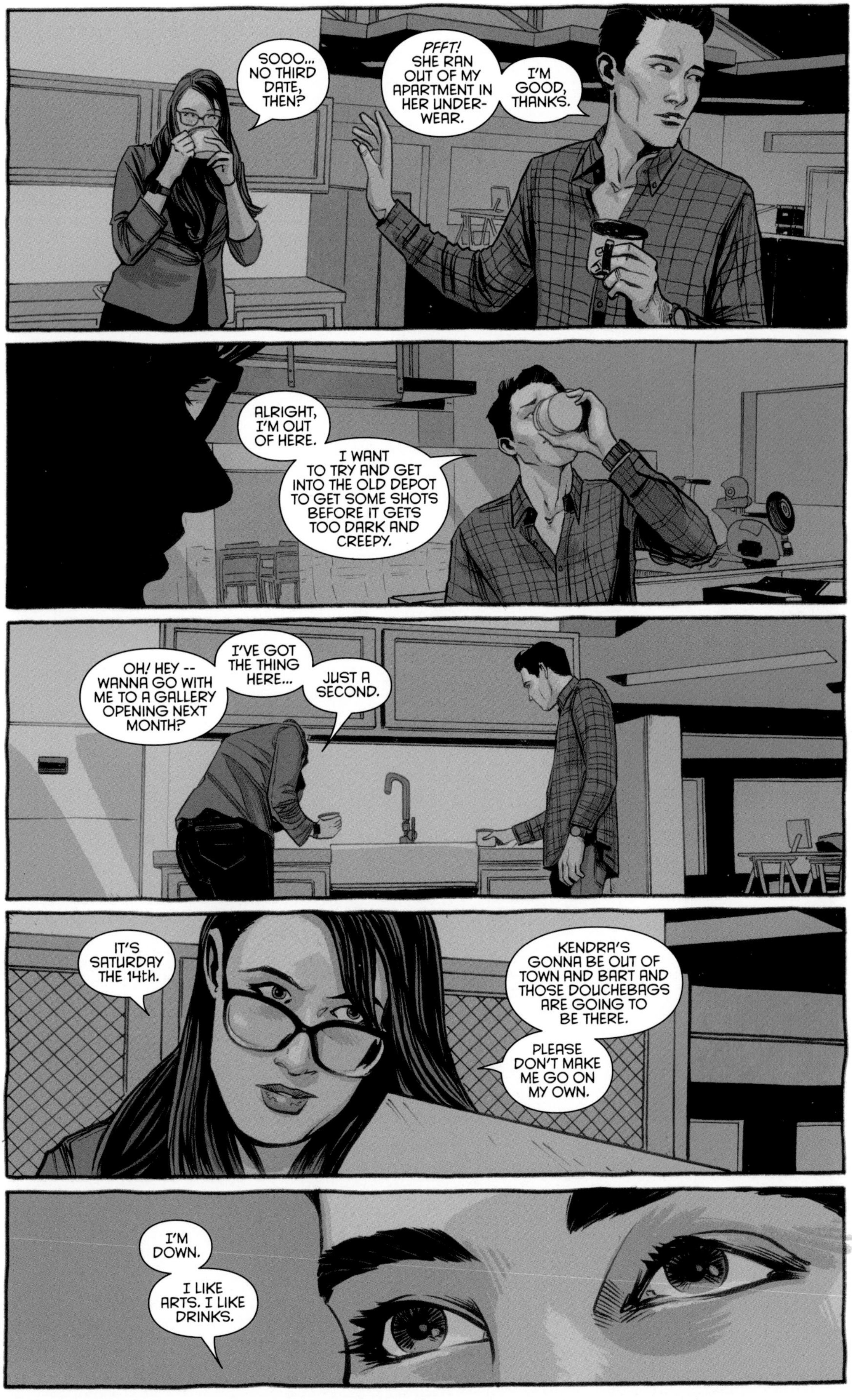
SOOO... NO THIRD DATE, THEN?
PFFT! SHE RAN OUT OF MY APARTMENT IN HER UNDER-WEAR.
I'M GOOD, THANKS.
ALRIGHT, I'M OUT OF HERE.
I WANT TO TRY AND GET INTO THE OLD DEPOT TO GET SOME SHOTS BEFORE IT GETS TOO DARK AND CREEPY.
OH! HEY -- WANNA GO WITH ME TO A GALLERY OPENING NEXT MONTH?
I'VE GOT THE THING HERE...
JUST A SECOND.
IT'S SATURDAY THE 14th.
KENDRA'S GONNA BE OUT OF TOWN AND BART AND THOSE DOUCHEBAGS ARE GOING TO BE THERE.
PLEASE DON'T MAKE ME GO ON MY OWN.
I'M DOWN.
I LIKE ARTS. I LIKE DRINKS.

DATES

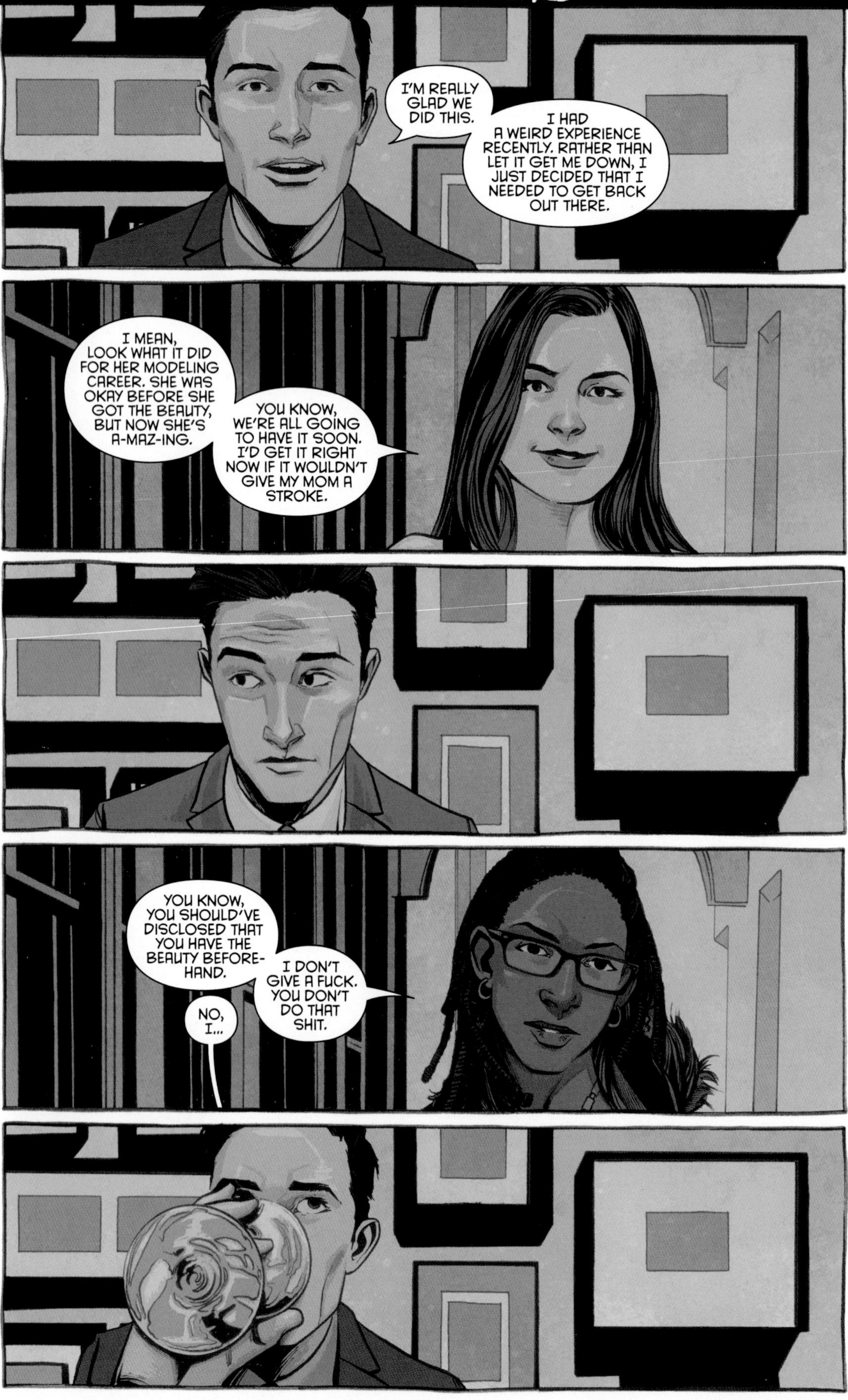

I'M REALLY GLAD WE DID THIS.
I HAD A WEIRD EXPERIENCE RECENTLY. RATHER THAN LET IT GET ME DOWN, I JUST DECIDED THAT I NEEDED TO GET BACK OUT THERE.
I MEAN, LOOK WHAT IT DID FOR HER MODELING CAREER. SHE WAS OKAY BEFORE SHE GOT THE BEAUTY, BUT NOW SHE'S A-MAZ-ING.
YOU KNOW, WE'RE ALL GOING TO HAVE IT SOON. I'D GET IT RIGHT NOW IF IT WOULDN'T GIVE MY MOM A STROKE.
YOU KNOW, YOU SHOULD'VE DISCLOSED THAT YOU HAVE THE BEAUTY BEFORE-HAND.
NO, I...
I DON'T GIVE A FUCK. YOU DON'T DO THAT SHIT.

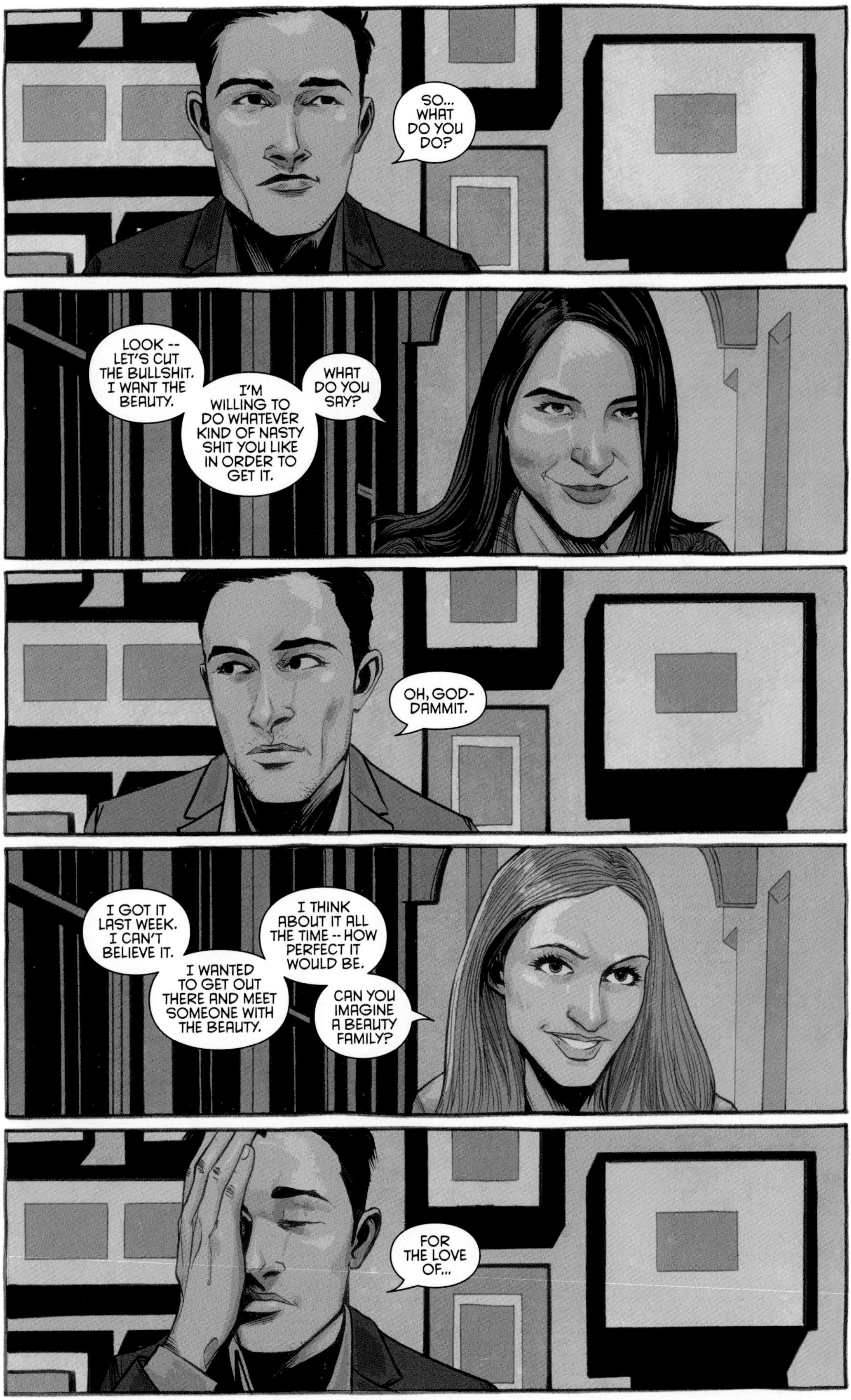
SO... WHAT DO YOU DO?
LOOK -- LET'S CUT THE BULLSHIT. I WANT THE BEAUTY.
I'M WILLING TO DO WHATEVER KIND OF NASTY SHIT YOU LIKE IN ORDER TO GET IT.
WHAT DO YOU SAY?
OH, GOD-DAMMIT.
I GOT IT LAST WEEK. I CAN'T BELIEVE IT.
I WANTED TO GET OUT THERE AND MEET SOMEONE WITH THE BEAUTY.
I THINK ABOUT IT ALL THE TIME -- HOW PERFECT IT WOULD BE.
CAN YOU IMAGINE A BEAUTY FAMILY?
FOR THE LOVE OF...

ADELAIDE

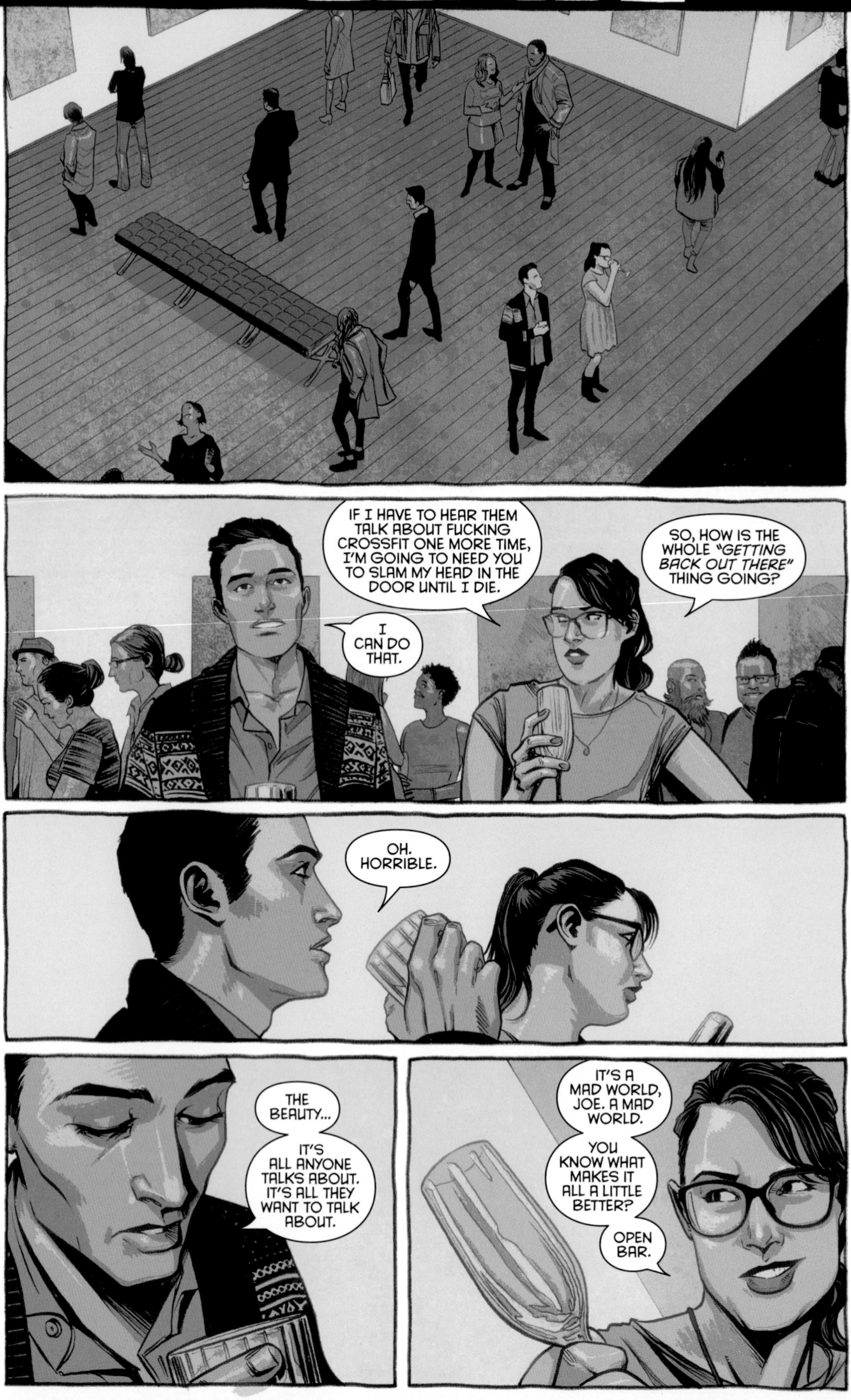
IF I HAVE TO HEAR THEM TALK ABOUT FUCKING CROSSFIT ONE MORE TIME, I'M GOING TO NEED YOU TO SLAM MY HEAD IN THE DOOR UNTIL I DIE.
I CAN DO THAT.
SO, HOW IS THE WHOLE *"GETTING BACK OUT THERE"* THING GOING?
OH. HORRIBLE.
THE BEAUTY...
IT'S ALL ANYONE TALKS ABOUT. IT'S ALL THEY WANT TO TALK ABOUT.
IT'S A MAD WORLD, JOE. A MAD WORLD.
YOU KNOW WHAT MAKES IT ALL A LITTLE BETTER?
OPEN BAR.

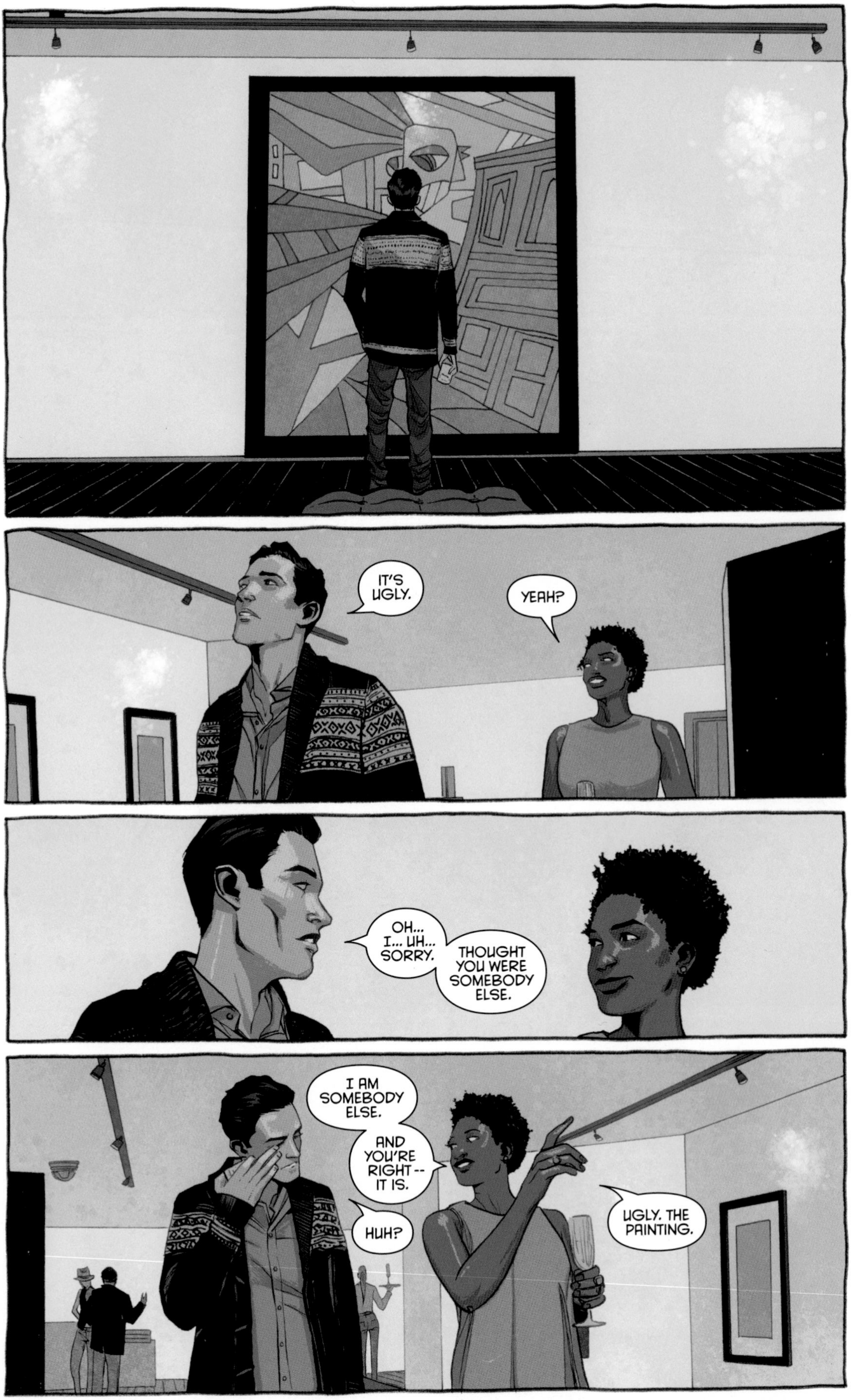
IT'S UGLY.
YEAH?
OH... I... UH... SORRY.
THOUGHT YOU WERE SOMEBODY ELSE.
I AM SOMEBODY ELSE.
AND YOU'RE RIGHT -- IT IS.
HUH?
UGLY. THE PAINTING.

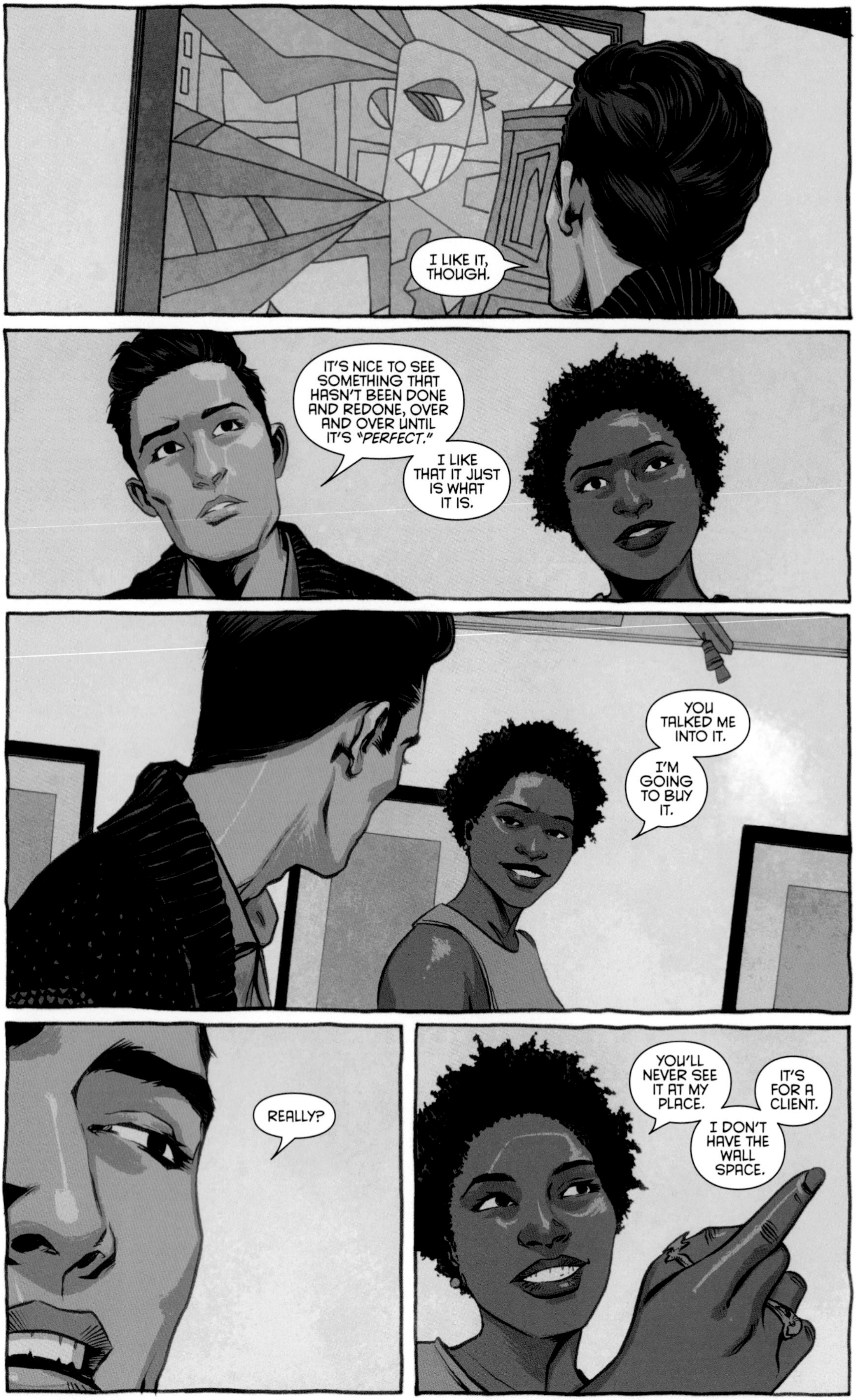
I LIKE IT, THOUGH.
IT'S NICE TO SEE SOMETHING THAT HASN'T BEEN DONE AND REDONE, OVER AND OVER UNTIL IT'S "*PERFECT.*"
I LIKE THAT IT JUST IS WHAT IT IS.
YOU TALKED ME INTO IT.
I'M GOING TO BUY IT.
REALLY?
YOU'LL NEVER SEE IT AT MY PLACE.
IT'S FOR A CLIENT.
I DON'T HAVE THE WALL SPACE.

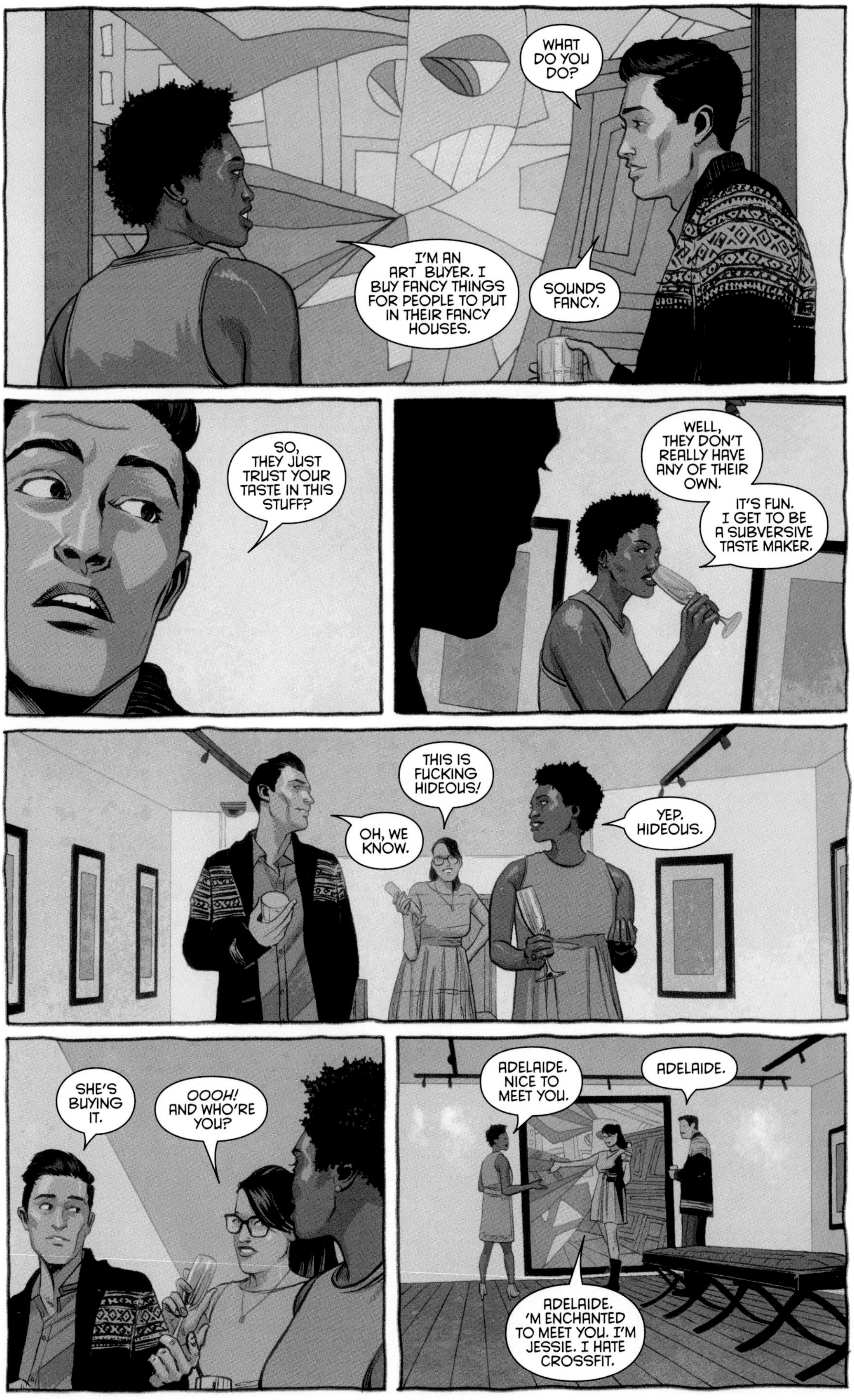
WHAT DO YOU DO?
I'M AN ART BUYER. I BUY FANCY THINGS FOR PEOPLE TO PUT IN THEIR FANCY HOUSES.
SOUNDS FANCY.
SO, THEY JUST TRUST YOUR TASTE IN THIS STUFF?
WELL, THEY DON'T REALLY HAVE ANY OF THEIR OWN.
IT'S FUN. I GET TO BE A SUBVERSIVE TASTE MAKER.
THIS IS FUCKING HIDEOUS!
OH, WE KNOW.
YEP. HIDEOUS.
SHE'S BUYING IT.
OOOH! AND WHO'RE YOU?
ADELAIDE. NICE TO MEET YOU.
ADELAIDE.
ADELAIDE. 'M ENCHANTED TO MEET YOU. I'M JESSIE. I HATE CROSSFIT.

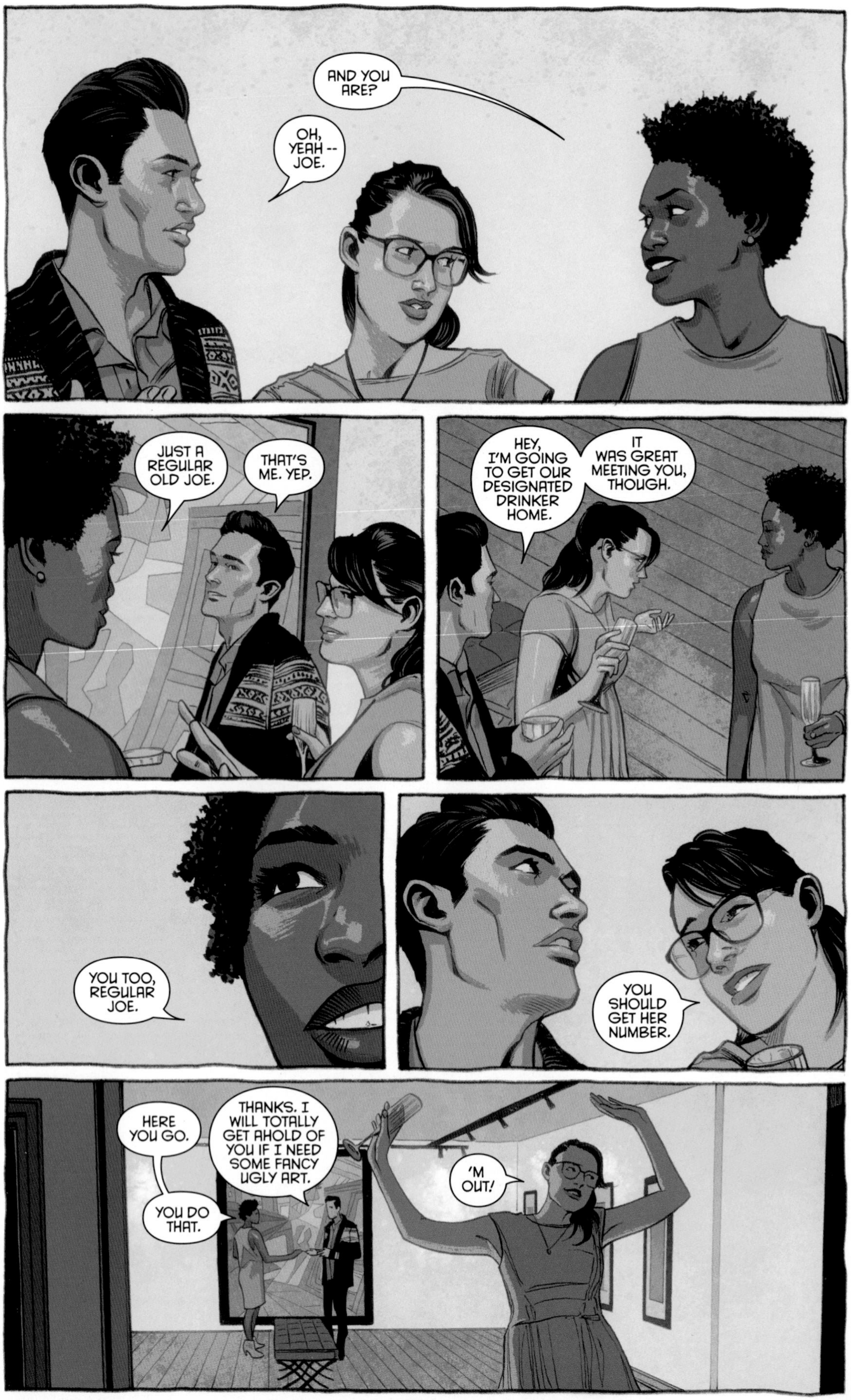
AND YOU ARE?
OH, YEAH -- JOE.
JUST A REGULAR OLD JOE.
THAT'S ME. YEP.
HEY, I'M GOING TO GET OUR DESIGNATED DRINKER HOME.
IT WAS GREAT MEETING YOU, THOUGH.
YOU TOO, REGULAR JOE.
YOU SHOULD GET HER NUMBER.
HERE YOU GO.
THANKS. I WILL TOTALLY GET AHOLD OF YOU IF I NEED SOME FANCY UGLY ART.
YOU DO THAT.
'M OUT!

WAITING GAME

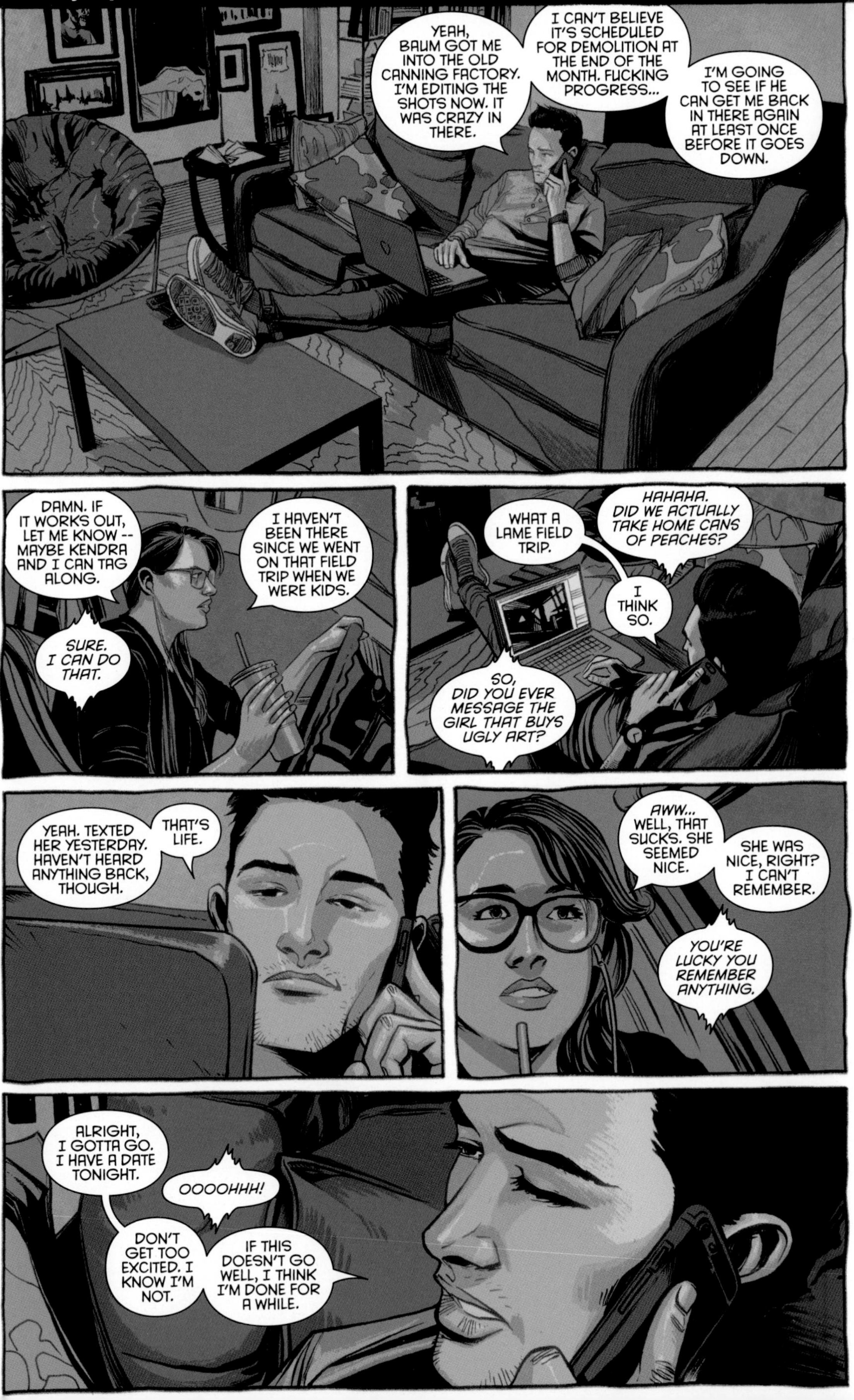
YEAH, BAUM GOT ME INTO THE OLD CANNING FACTORY. I'M EDITING THE SHOTS NOW. IT WAS CRAZY IN THERE.
I CAN'T BELIEVE IT'S SCHEDULED FOR DEMOLITION AT THE END OF THE MONTH. FUCKING PROGRESS...
I'M GOING TO SEE IF HE CAN GET ME BACK IN THERE AGAIN AT LEAST ONCE BEFORE IT GOES DOWN.
DAMN. IF IT WORKS OUT, LET ME KNOW -- MAYBE KENDRA AND I CAN TAG ALONG.
I HAVEN'T BEEN THERE SINCE WE WENT ON THAT FIELD TRIP WHEN WE WERE KIDS.
SURE. I CAN DO THAT.
WHAT A LAME FIELD TRIP.
HAHAHA. DID WE ACTUALLY TAKE HOME CANS OF PEACHES?
I THINK SO.
SO, DID YOU EVER MESSAGE THE GIRL THAT BUYS UGLY ART?
YEAH. TEXTED HER YESTERDAY. HAVEN'T HEARD ANYTHING BACK, THOUGH.
THAT'S LIFE.
AWW... WELL, THAT SUCKS. SHE SEEMED NICE.
SHE WAS NICE, RIGHT? I CAN'T REMEMBER.
YOU'RE LUCKY YOU REMEMBER ANYTHING.
ALRIGHT, I GOTTA GO. I HAVE A DATE TONIGHT.
OOOOHHH!
DON'T GET TOO EXCITED. I KNOW I'M NOT.
IF THIS DOESN'T GO WELL, I THINK I'M DONE FOR A WHILE.

FOURS & SEVENS

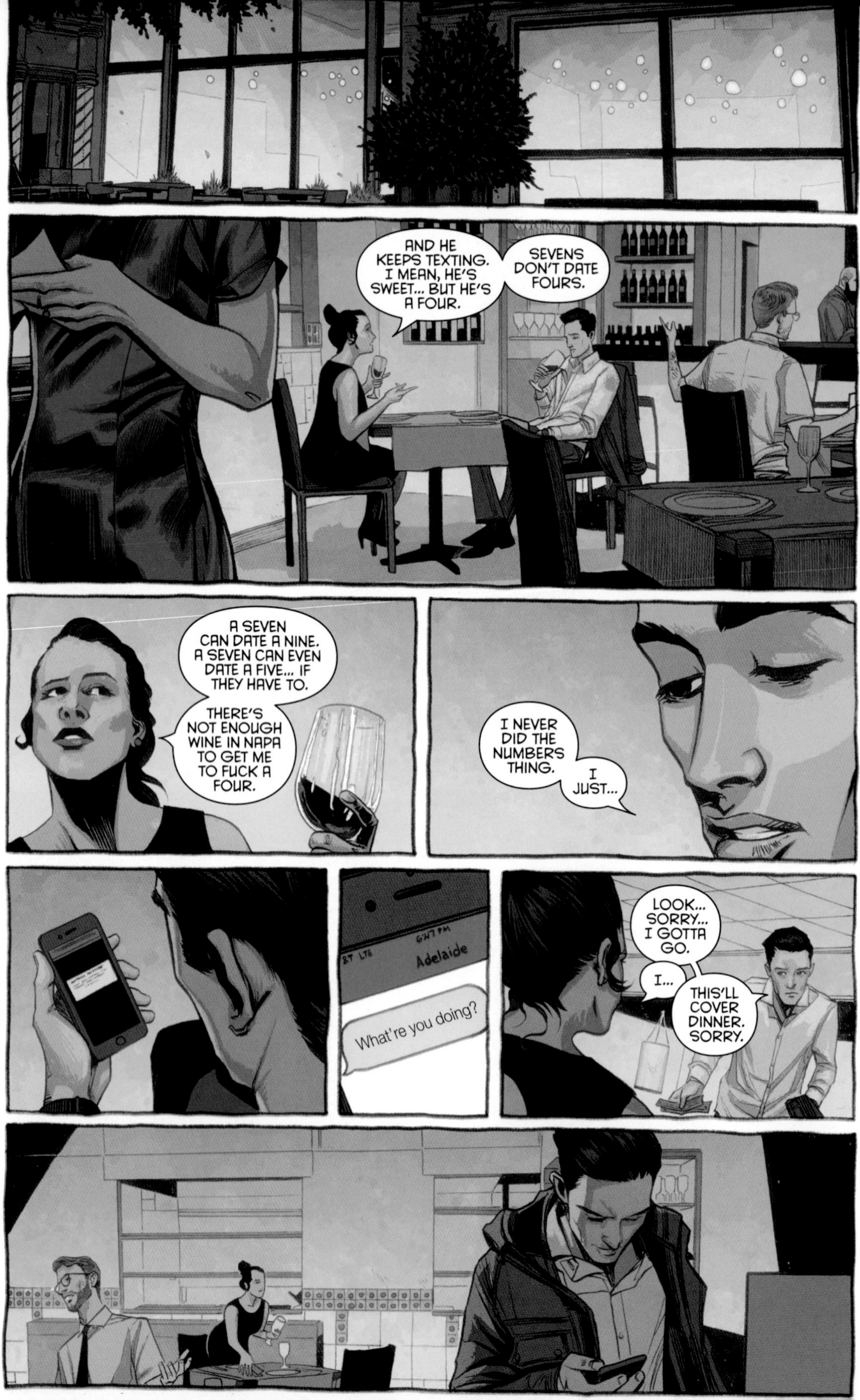
AND HE KEEPS TEXTING. I MEAN, HE'S SWEET... BUT HE'S A FOUR.
SEVENS DON'T DATE FOURS.
A SEVEN CAN DATE A NINE. A SEVEN CAN EVEN DATE A FIVE... IF THEY HAVE TO.
THERE'S NOT ENOUGH WINE IN NAPA TO GET ME TO FUCK A FOUR.
I NEVER DID THE NUMBERS THING.
I JUST...
6:47 PM
Adelaide
What're you doing?
LOOK... SORRY... I GOTTA GO.
I...
THIS'LL COVER DINNER. SORRY.

URBAN DECAY

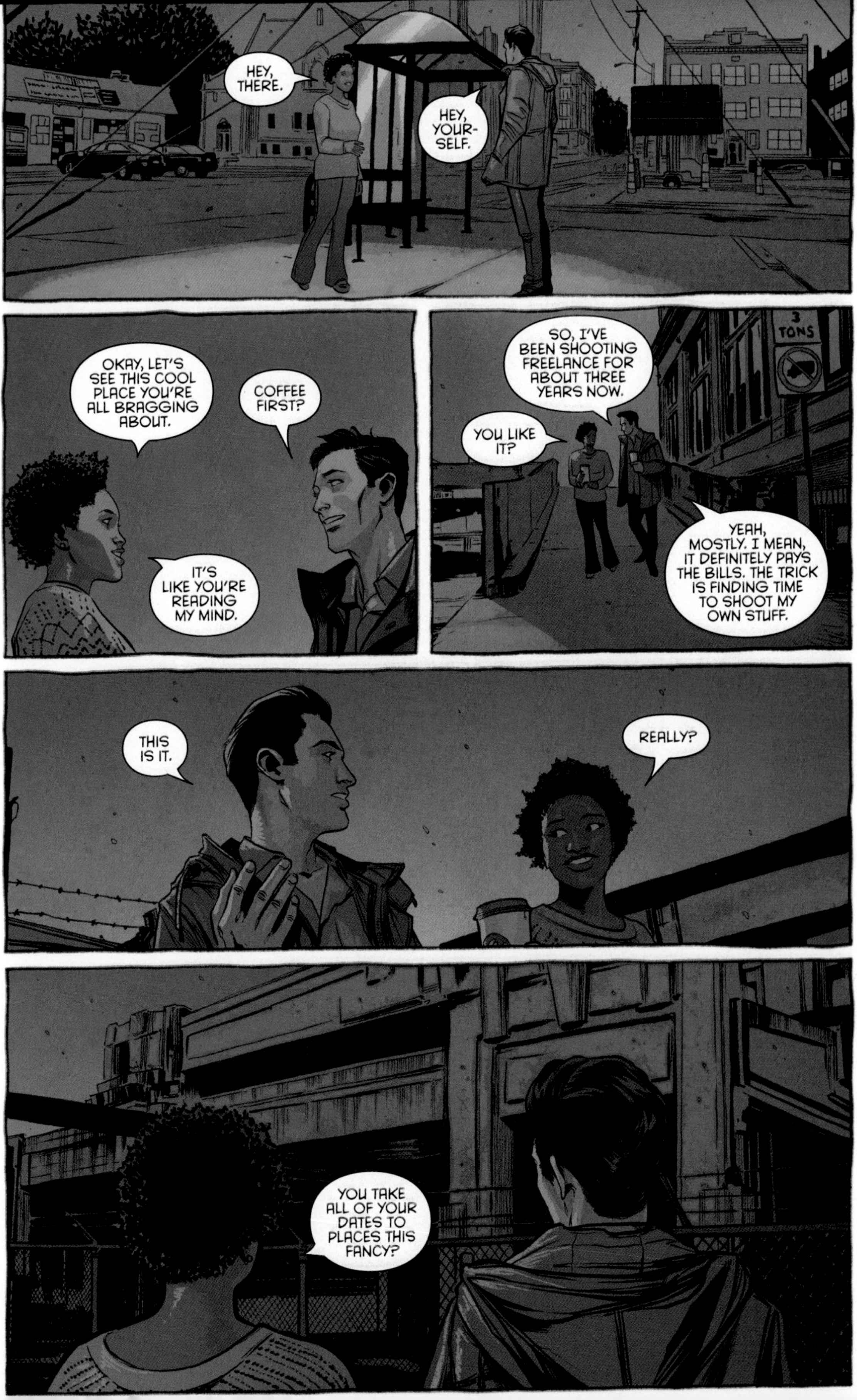

HEY, THERE.
HEY, YOUR-SELF.
OKAY, LET'S SEE THIS COOL PLACE YOU'RE ALL BRAGGING ABOUT.
COFFEE FIRST?
IT'S LIKE YOU'RE READING MY MIND.
SO, I'VE BEEN SHOOTING FREELANCE FOR ABOUT THREE YEARS NOW.
YOU LIKE IT?
3 TONS
YEAH, MOSTLY. I MEAN, IT DEFINITELY PAYS THE BILLS. THE TRICK IS FINDING TIME TO SHOOT MY OWN STUFF.
THIS IS IT.
REALLY?
YOU TAKE ALL OF YOUR DATES TO PLACES THIS FANCY?

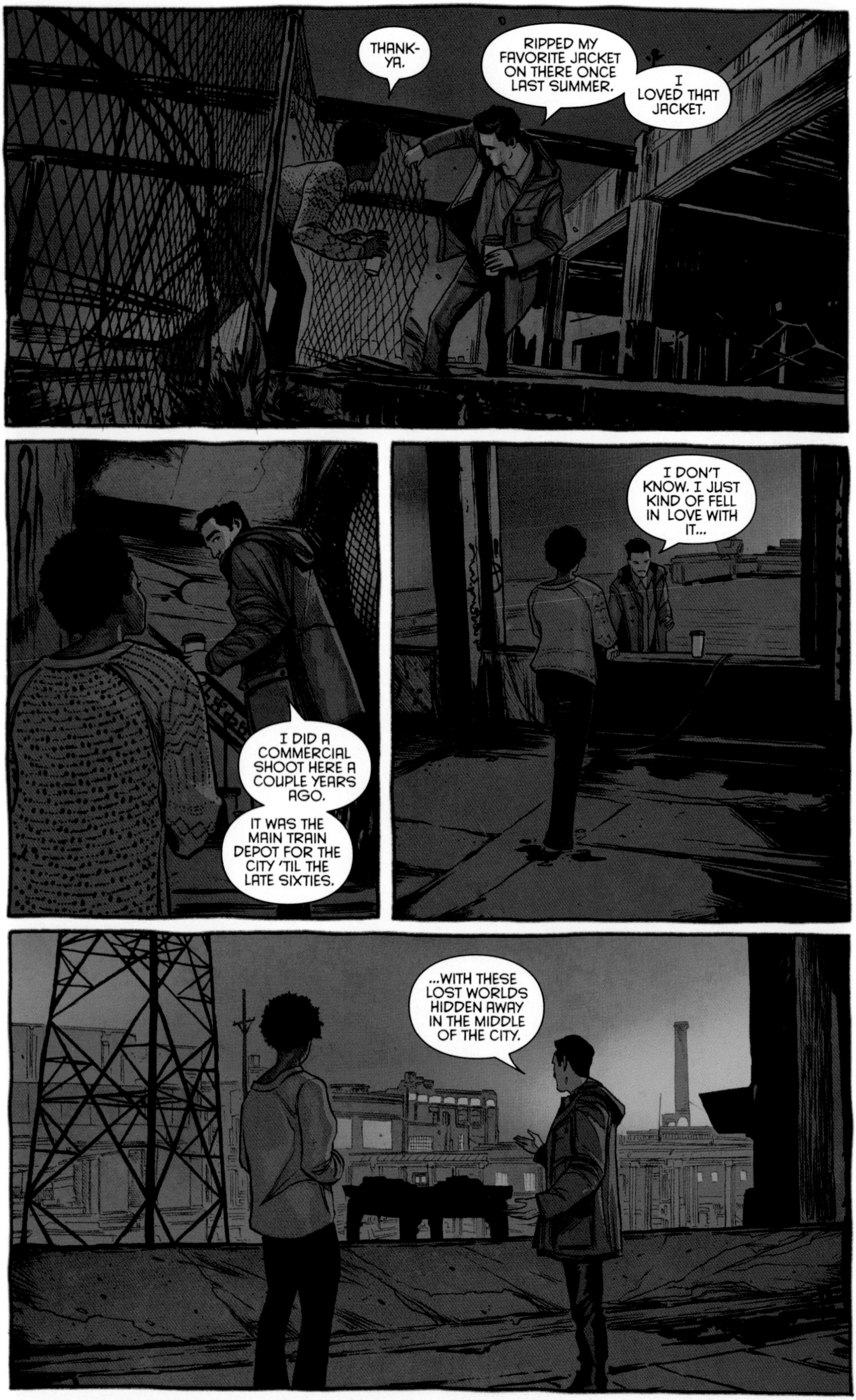
THANK-YA.
RIPPED MY FAVORITE JACKET ON THERE ONCE LAST SUMMER.
I LOVED THAT JACKET.
I DID A COMMERCIAL SHOOT HERE A COUPLE YEARS AGO.
IT WAS THE MAIN TRAIN DEPOT FOR THE CITY 'TIL THE LATE SIXTIES.
I DON'T KNOW. I JUST KIND OF FELL IN LOVE WITH IT...
...WITH THESE LOST WORLDS HIDDEN AWAY IN THE MIDDLE OF THE CITY.

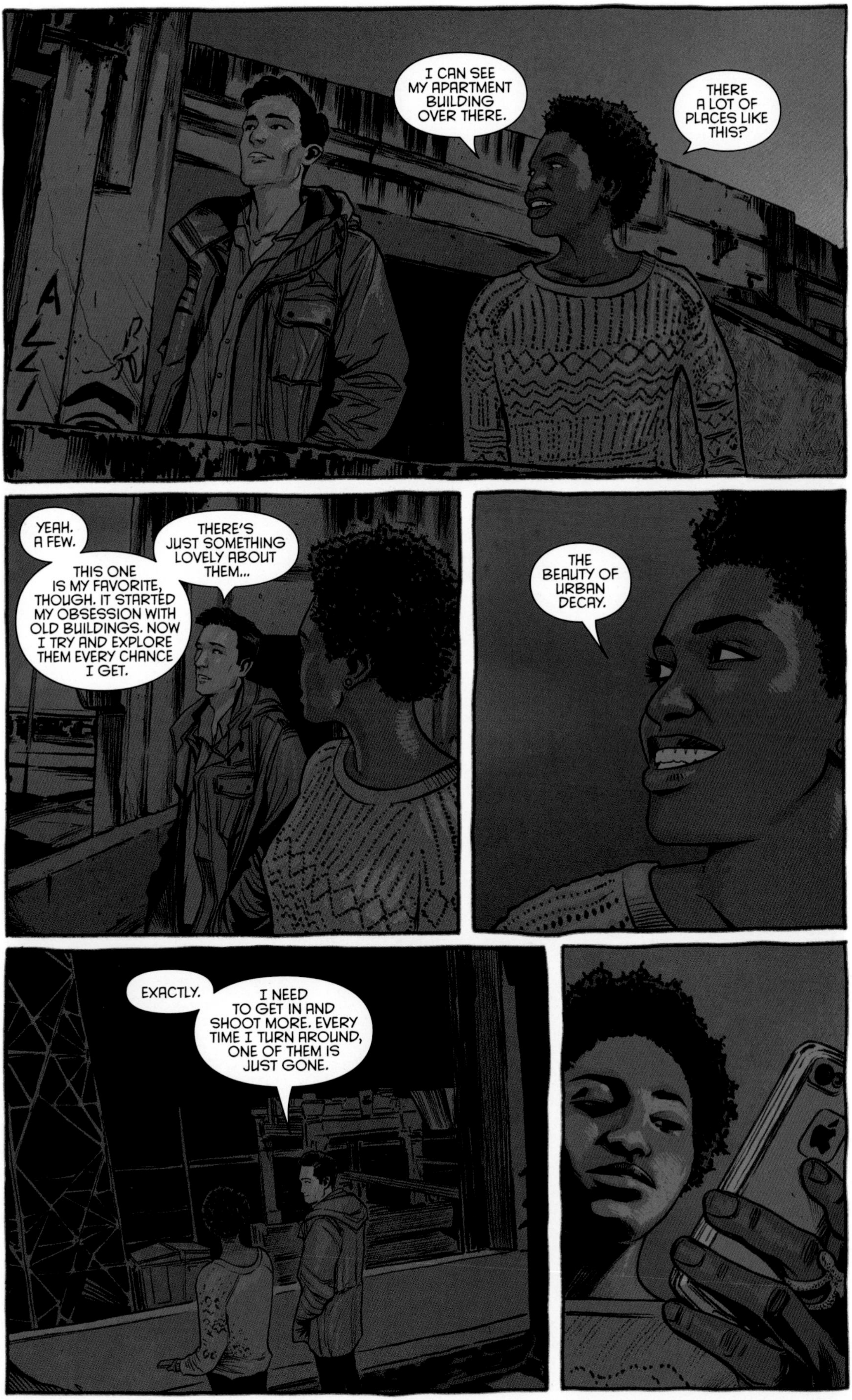
I CAN SEE MY APARTMENT BUILDING OVER THERE.
THERE A LOT OF PLACES LIKE THIS?
YEAH. A FEW.
THIS ONE IS MY FAVORITE, THOUGH. IT STARTED MY OBSESSION WITH OLD BUILDINGS. NOW I TRY AND EXPLORE THEM EVERY CHANCE I GET.
THERE'S JUST SOMETHING LOVELY ABOUT THEM...
THE BEAUTY OF URBAN DECAY.
EXACTLY.
I NEED TO GET IN AND SHOOT MORE. EVERY TIME I TURN AROUND, ONE OF THEM IS JUST GONE.

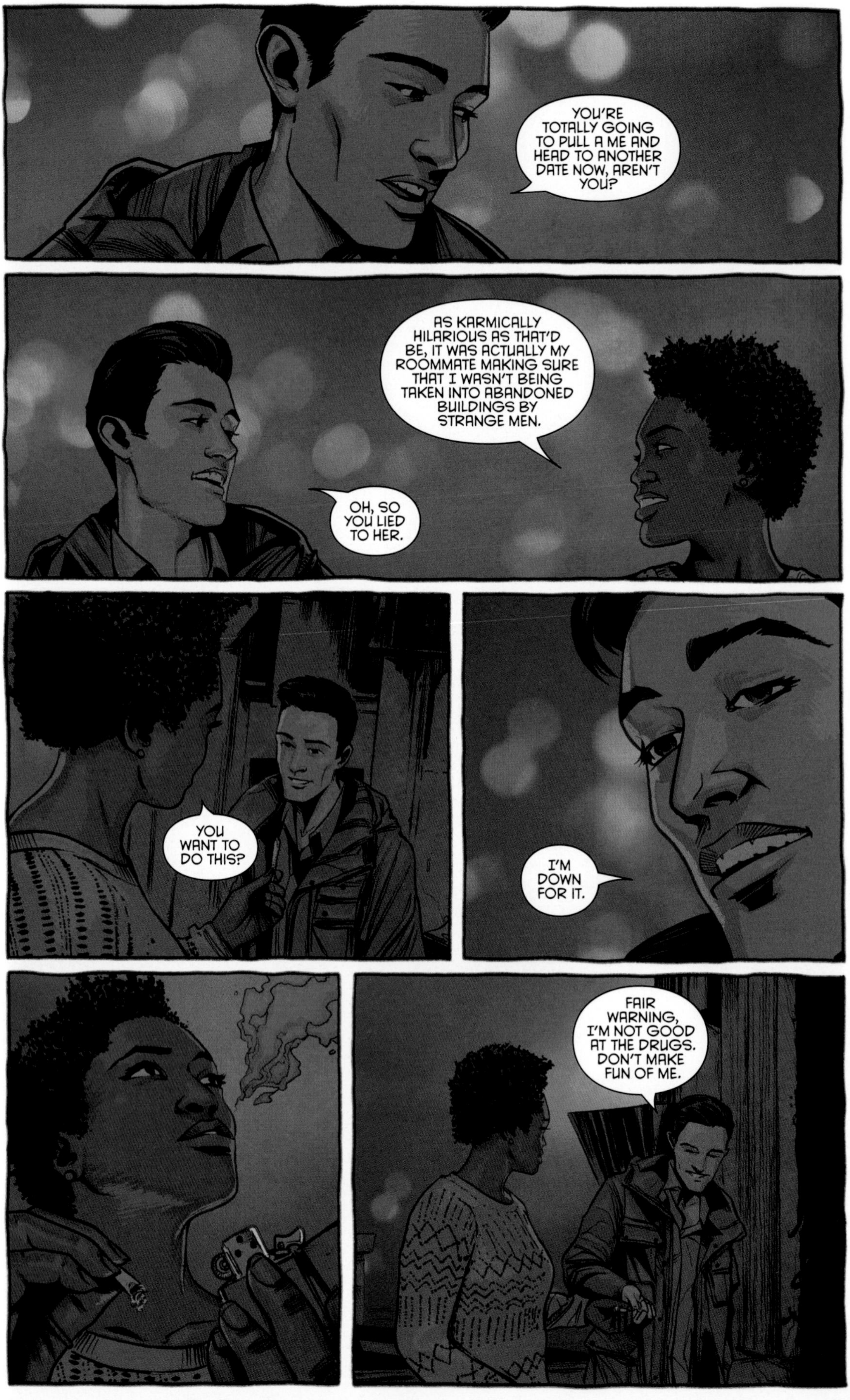
YOU'RE TOTALLY GOING TO PULL A ME AND HEAD TO ANOTHER DATE NOW, AREN'T YOU?
AS KARMICALLY HILARIOUS AS THAT'D BE, IT WAS ACTUALLY MY ROOMMATE MAKING SURE THAT I WASN'T BEING TAKEN INTO ABANDONED BUILDINGS BY STRANGE MEN.
OH, SO YOU LIED TO HER.
YOU WANT TO DO THIS?
I'M DOWN FOR IT.
FAIR WARNING, I'M NOT GOOD AT THE DRUGS. DON'T MAKE FUN OF ME.

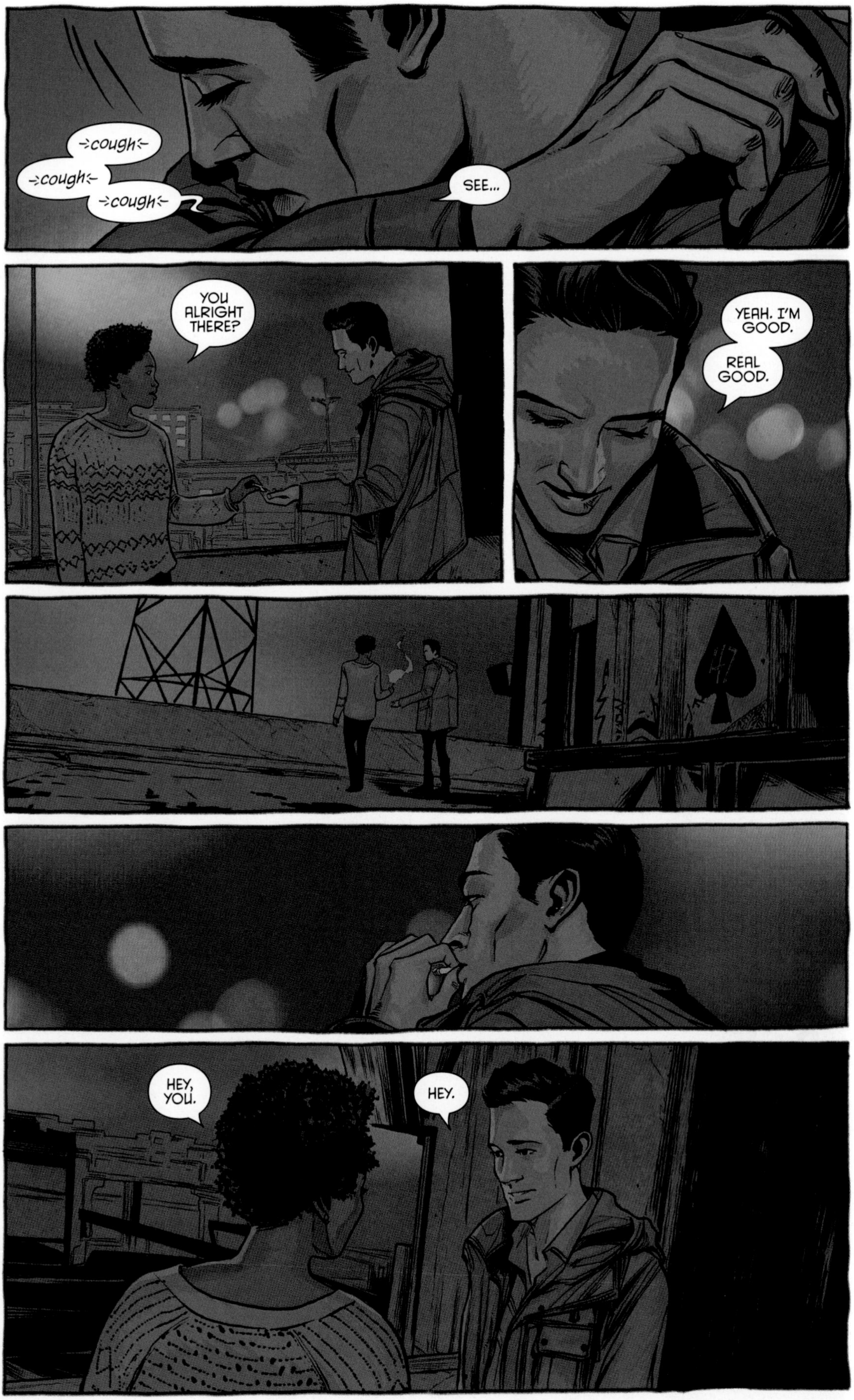
cough
cough
cough
SEE...
YOU ALRIGHT THERE?
YEAH. I'M GOOD.
REAL GOOD.
HEY, YOU.
HEY.

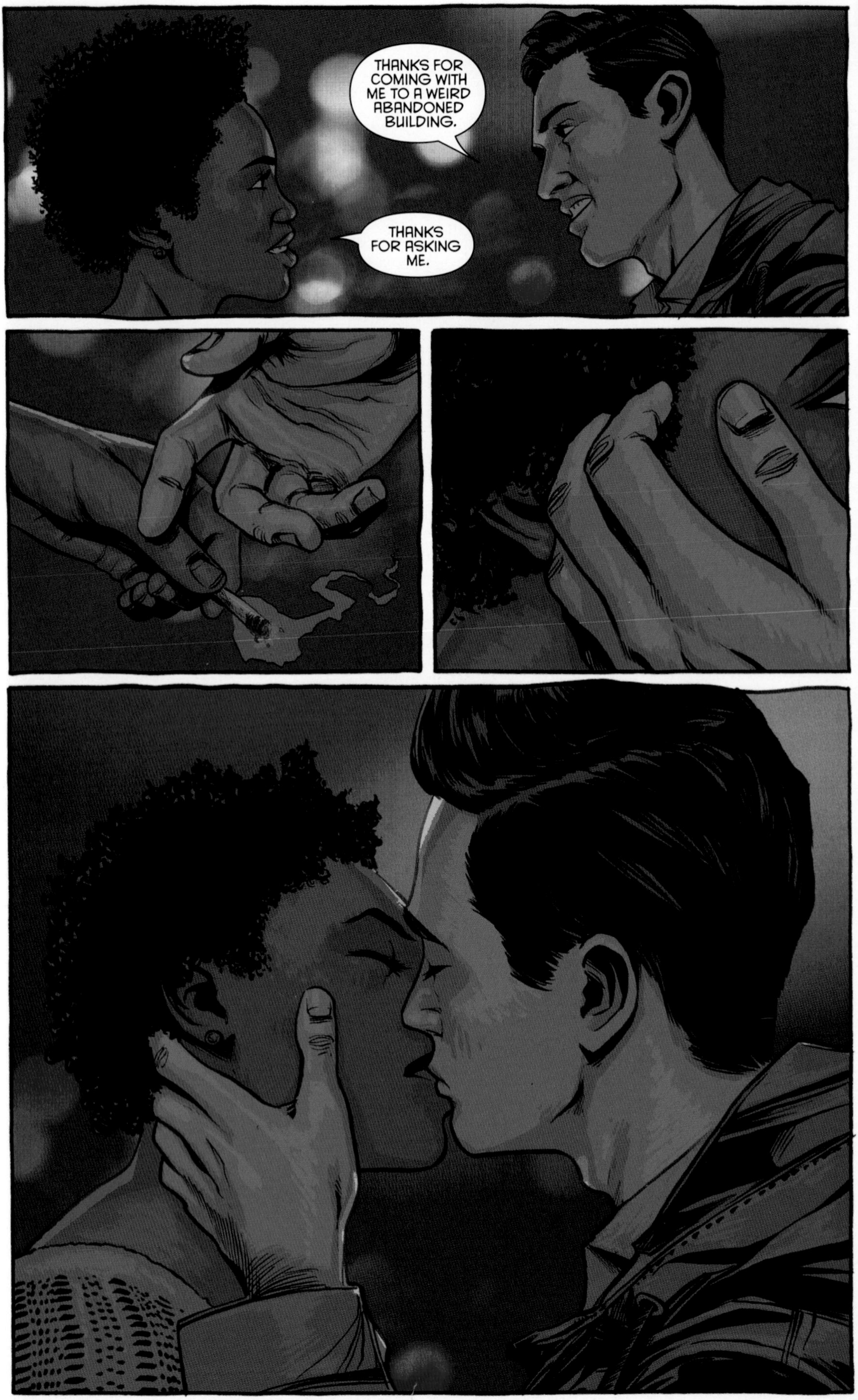
THANKS FOR COMING WITH ME TO A WEIRD ABANDONED BUILDING.
THANKS FOR ASKING ME.

A GOOD PLACE

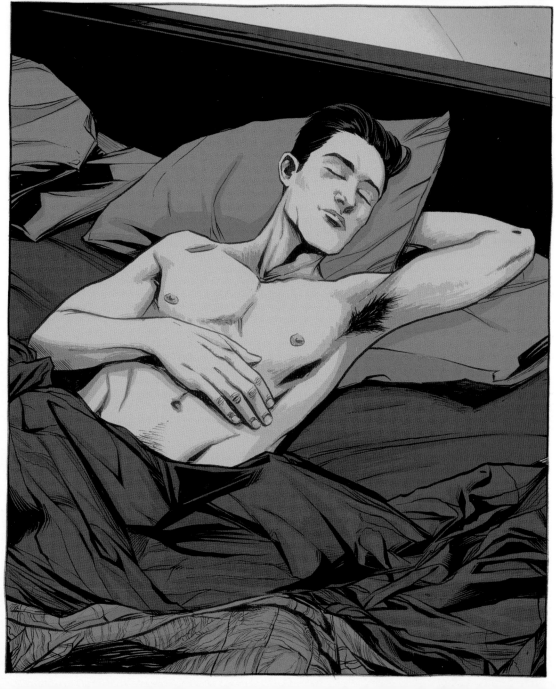

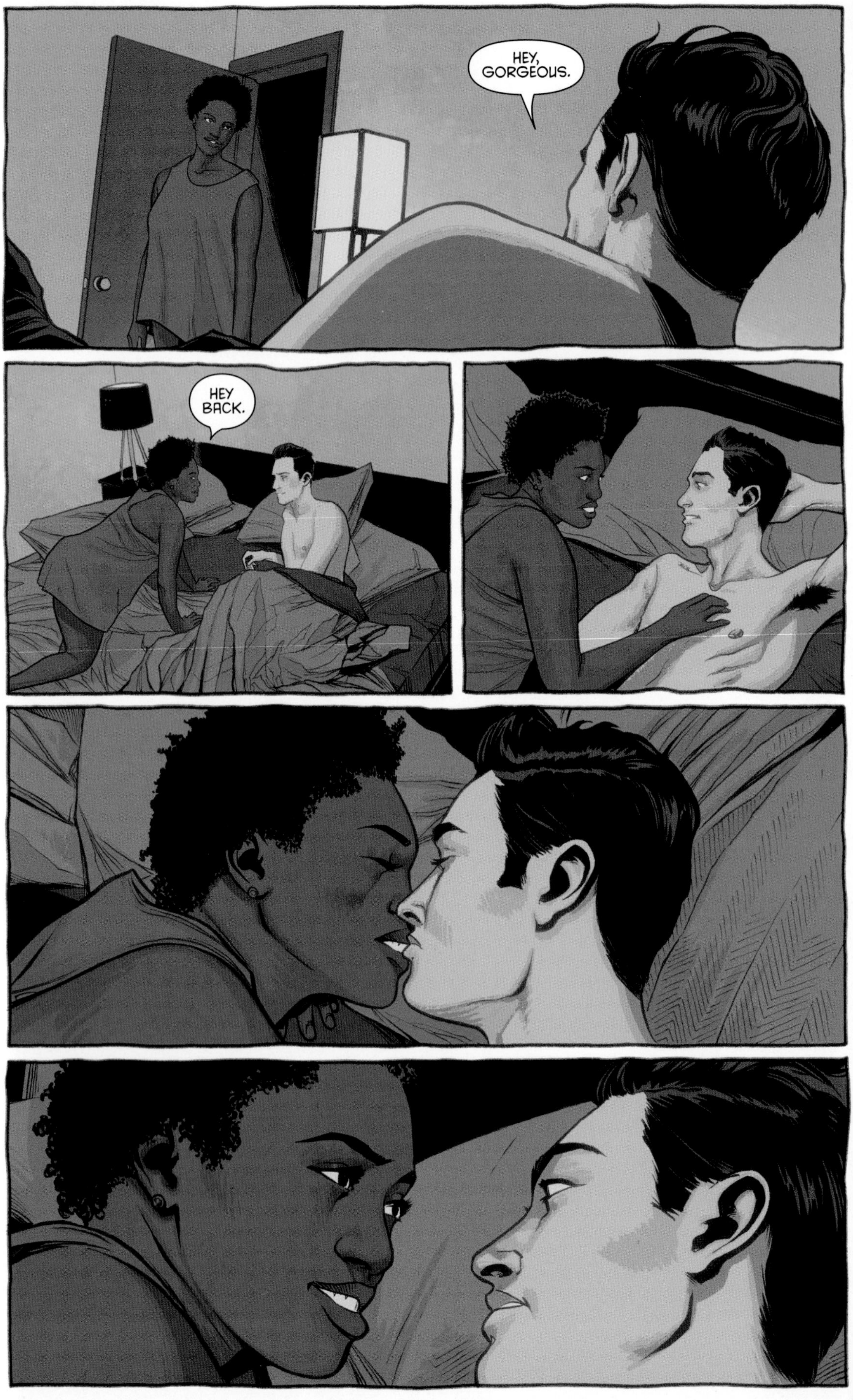
HEY, GORGEOUS.
HEY BACK.

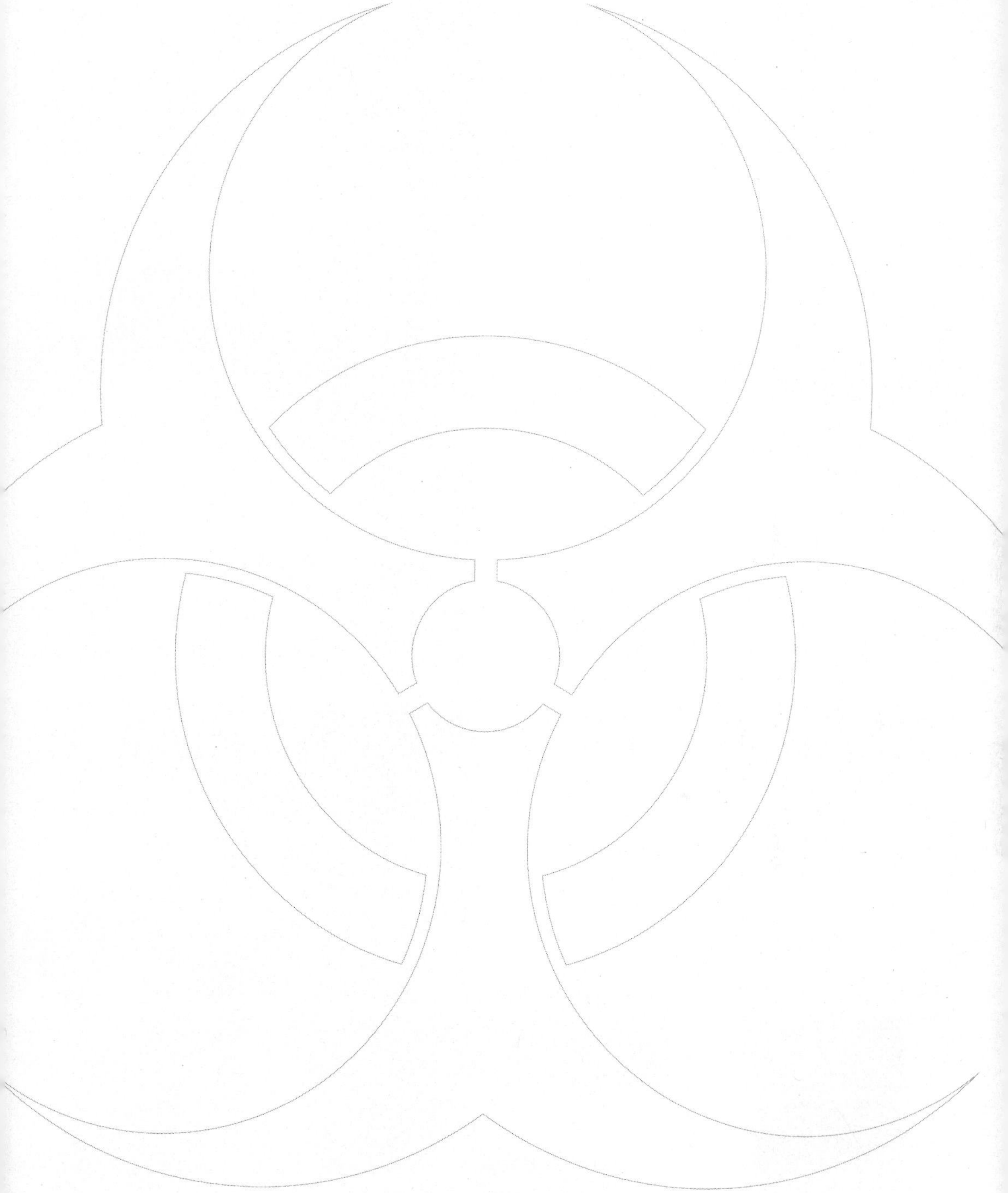

CHAPTER

13

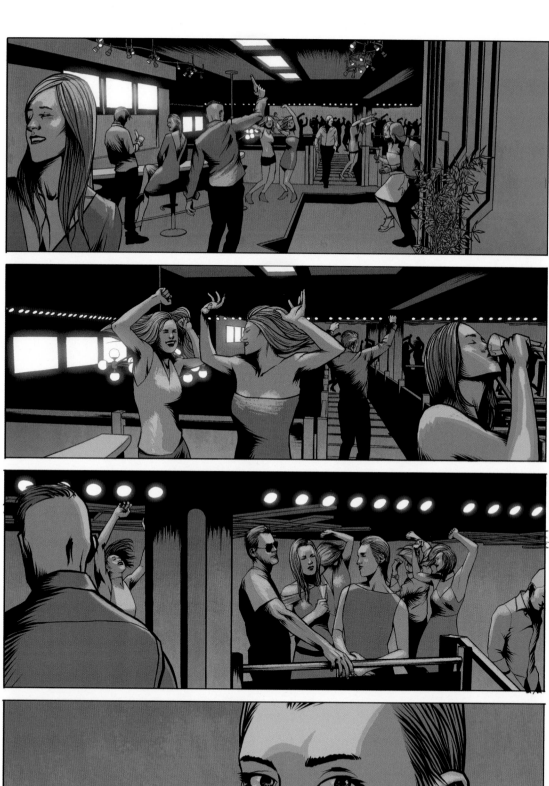

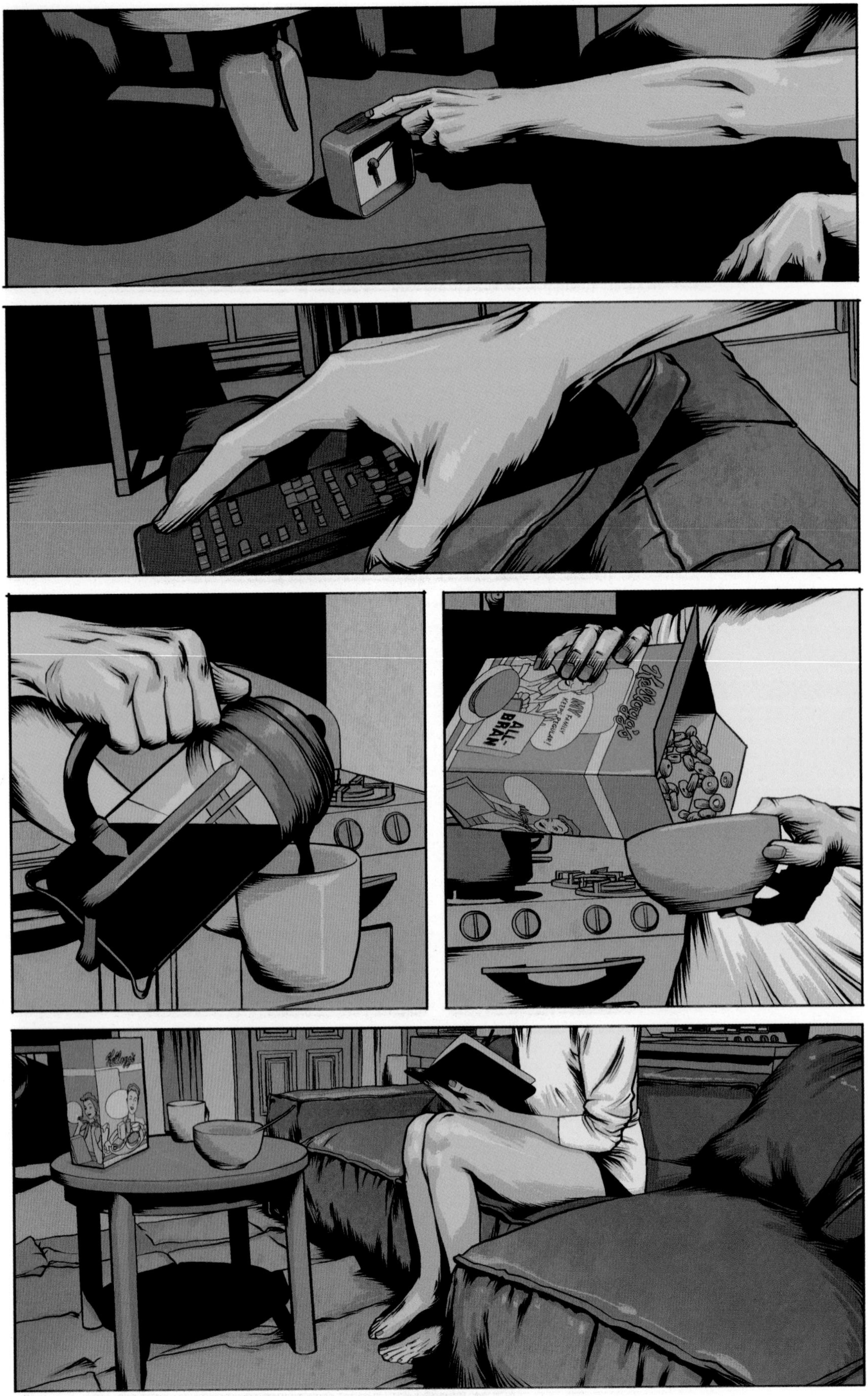
Kellogg's
MY FAMILY KEEPS REGULAR!
ALL-BRAN

OH,
FUCK
YOU.

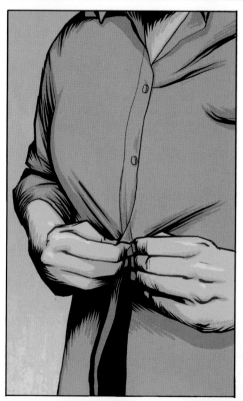

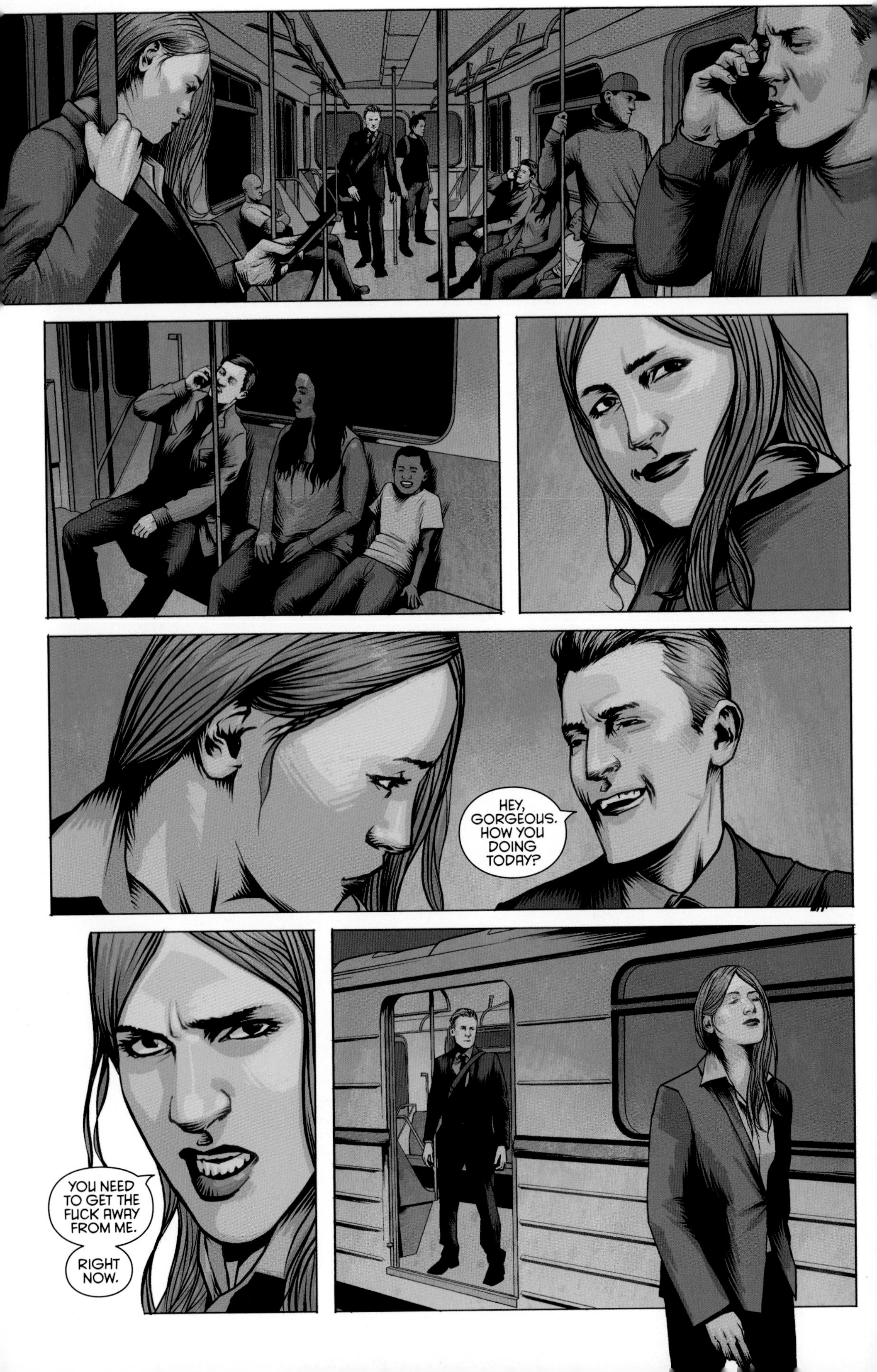
HEY, GORGEOUS. HOW YOU DOING TODAY?
YOU NEED TO GET THE FUCK AWAY FROM ME.
RIGHT NOW.

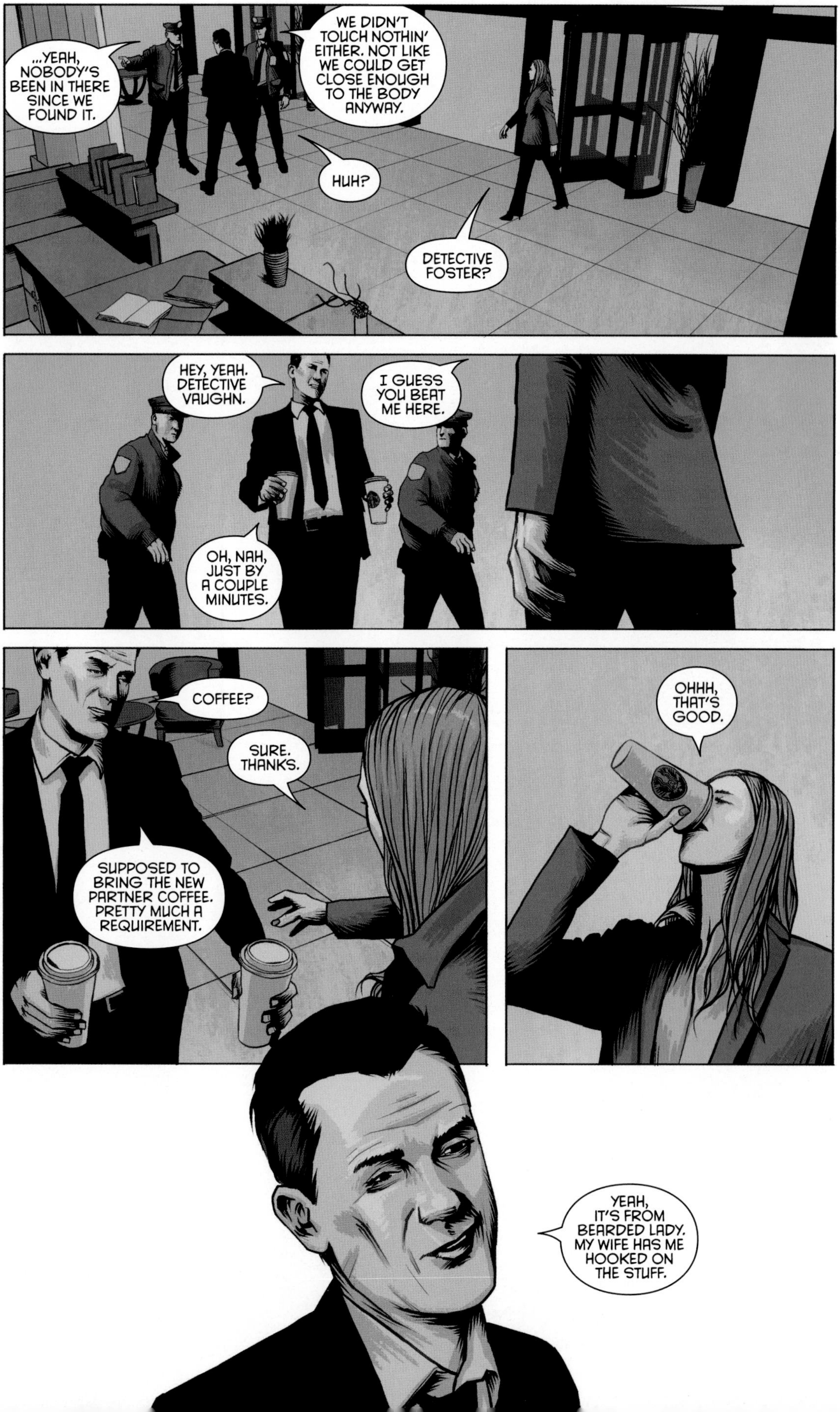
...YEAH, NOBODY'S BEEN IN THERE SINCE WE FOUND IT.
WE DIDN'T TOUCH NOTHIN' EITHER. NOT LIKE WE COULD GET CLOSE ENOUGH TO THE BODY ANYWAY.
HUH?
DETECTIVE FOSTER?
HEY, YEAH. DETECTIVE VAUGHN.
I GUESS YOU BEAT ME HERE.
OH, NAH, JUST BY A COUPLE MINUTES.
COFFEE?
SURE. THANKS.
SUPPOSED TO BRING THE NEW PARTNER COFFEE. PRETTY MUCH A REQUIREMENT.
OHHH, THAT'S GOOD.
YEAH, IT'S FROM BEARDED LADY. MY WIFE HAS ME HOOKED ON THE STUFF.

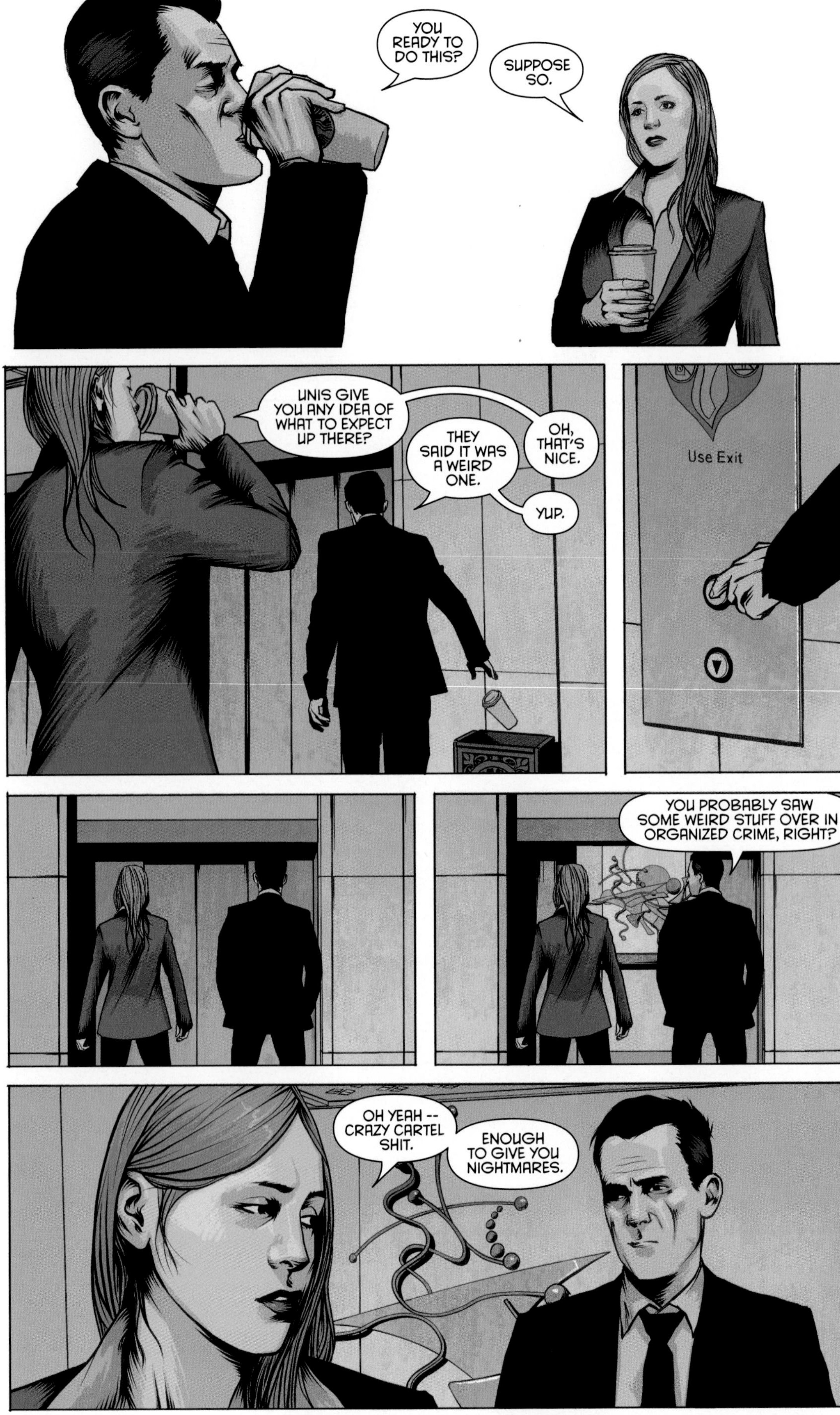
YOU READY TO DO THIS?
SUPPOSE SO.
UNIS GIVE YOU ANY IDEA OF WHAT TO EXPECT UP THERE?
THEY SAID IT WAS A WEIRD ONE.
OH, THAT'S NICE.
YUP.
Use Exit
YOU PROBABLY SAW SOME WEIRD STUFF OVER IN ORGANIZED CRIME, RIGHT?
OH YEAH -- CRAZY CARTEL SHIT.
ENOUGH TO GIVE YOU NIGHTMARES.

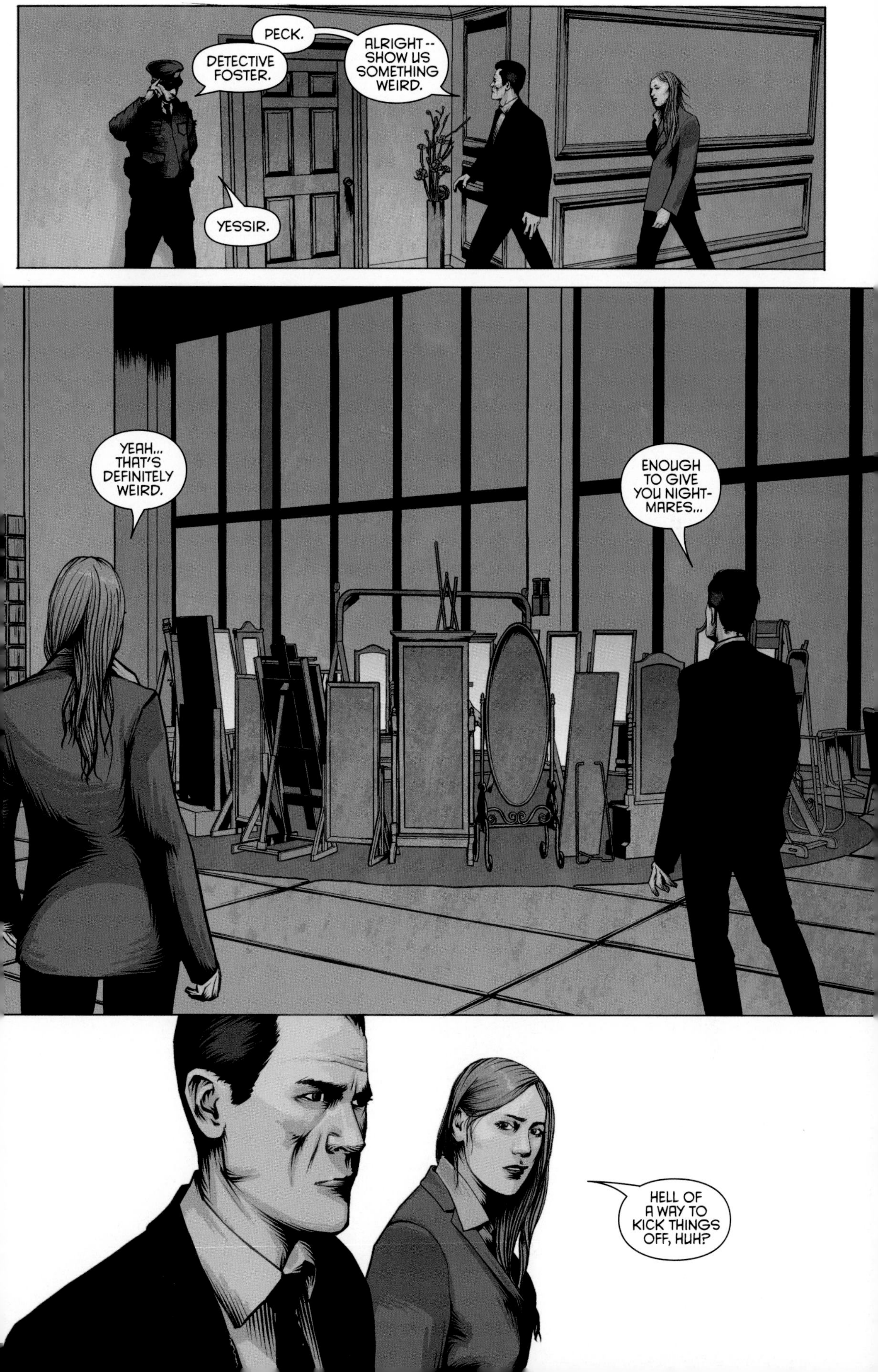
DETECTIVE FOSTER.
PECK.
ALRIGHT -- SHOW US SOMETHING WEIRD.
YESSIR.
YEAH... THAT'S DEFINITELY WEIRD.
ENOUGH TO GIVE YOU NIGHTMARES...
HELL OF A WAY TO KICK THINGS OFF, HUH?

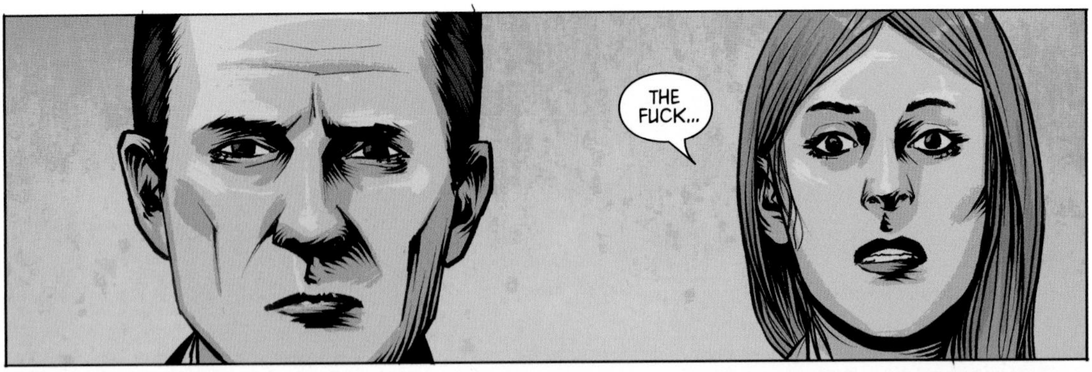
THE FUCK...

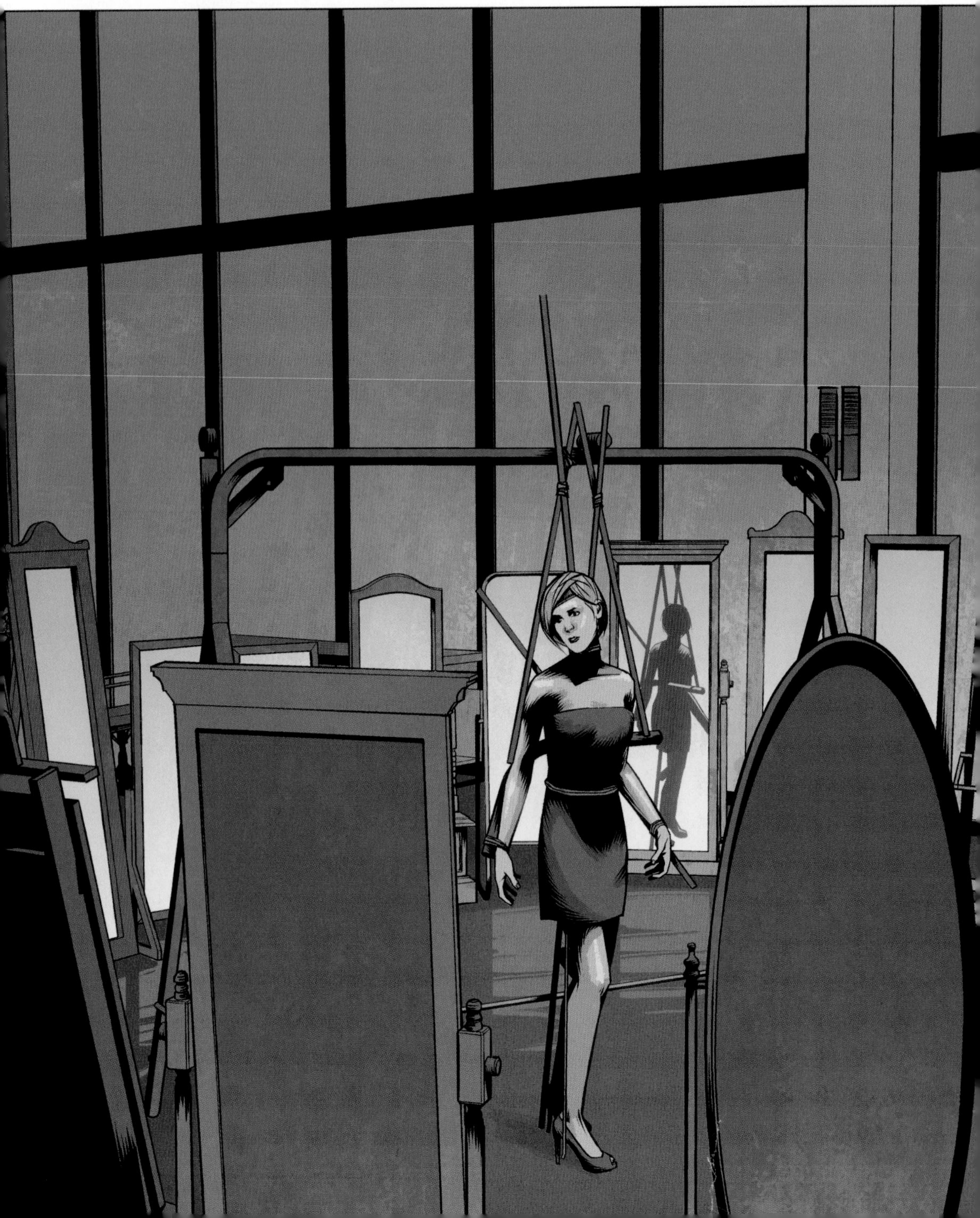

Ahhh... HOW DO WE EVEN DO THIS?

THAT'S A LOT OF BLOOD.

PROBABLY ALL OF IT, RIGHT?

GOTTA BE...

HAD THIS CARTEL KILLING ONCE -- FUCKING HORRIBLE.

WE TOOK AS MANY PICTURES AS WE COULD, THEN HAD TO PUT ON BOOTIES --

-- AND JUST... WADE IN.

WHAT THE ACTUAL SHIT?!

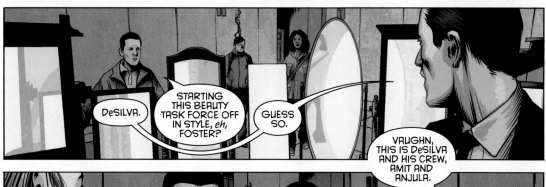

DeSILVA.

STARTING THIS BEAUTY TASK FORCE OFF IN STYLE, *eh*, FOSTER?

GUESS SO.

VAUGHN, THIS IS DeSILVA AND HIS CREW, AMIT AND ANJULA.

HEY.

HOPE YOU WERE LOOKING FORWARD TO GETTING DIRTY TODAY.

THE BLOOD...

I WASN'T... I...

WE'RE FINE.

LET'S GET TO WORK.

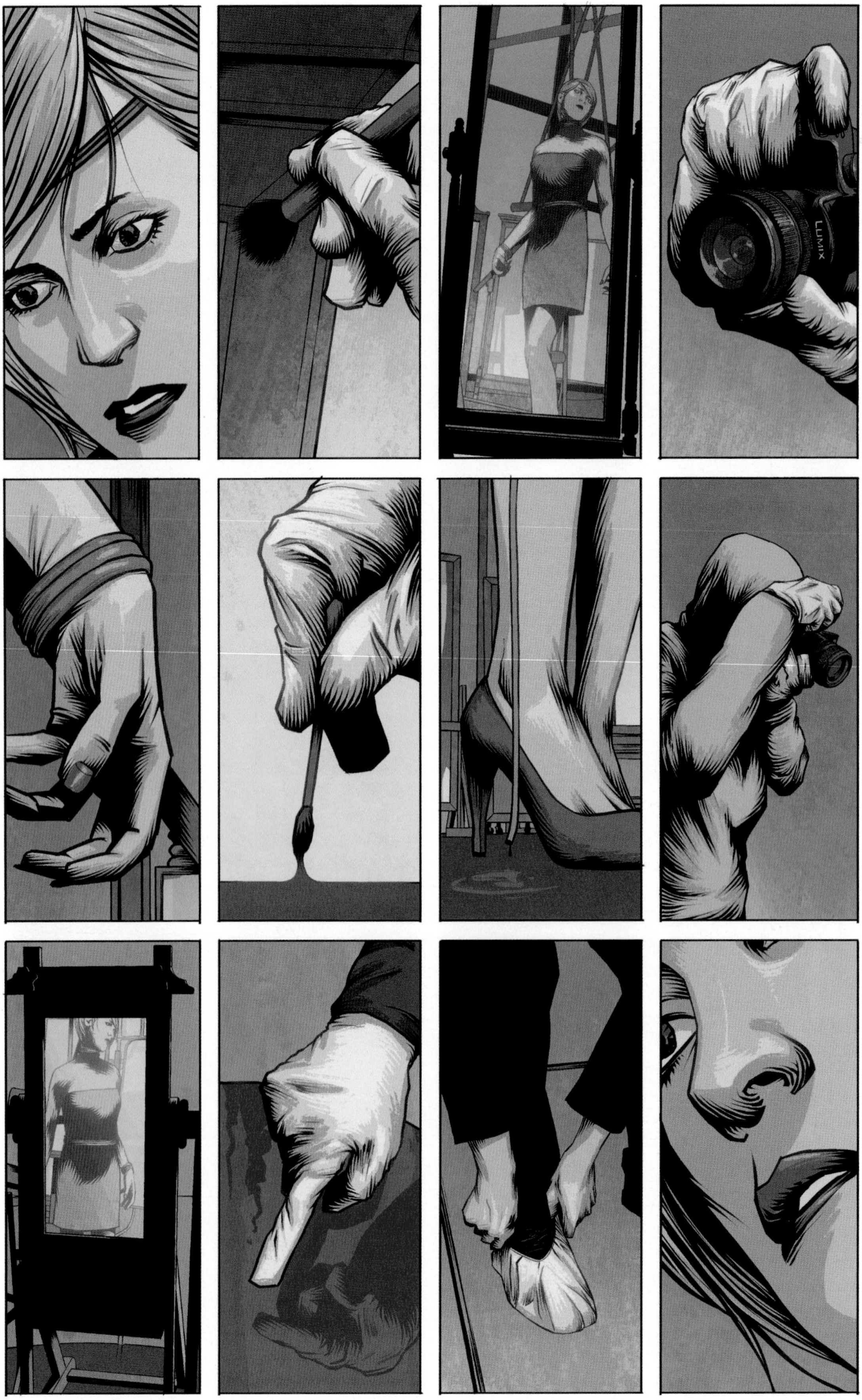
LUMIX

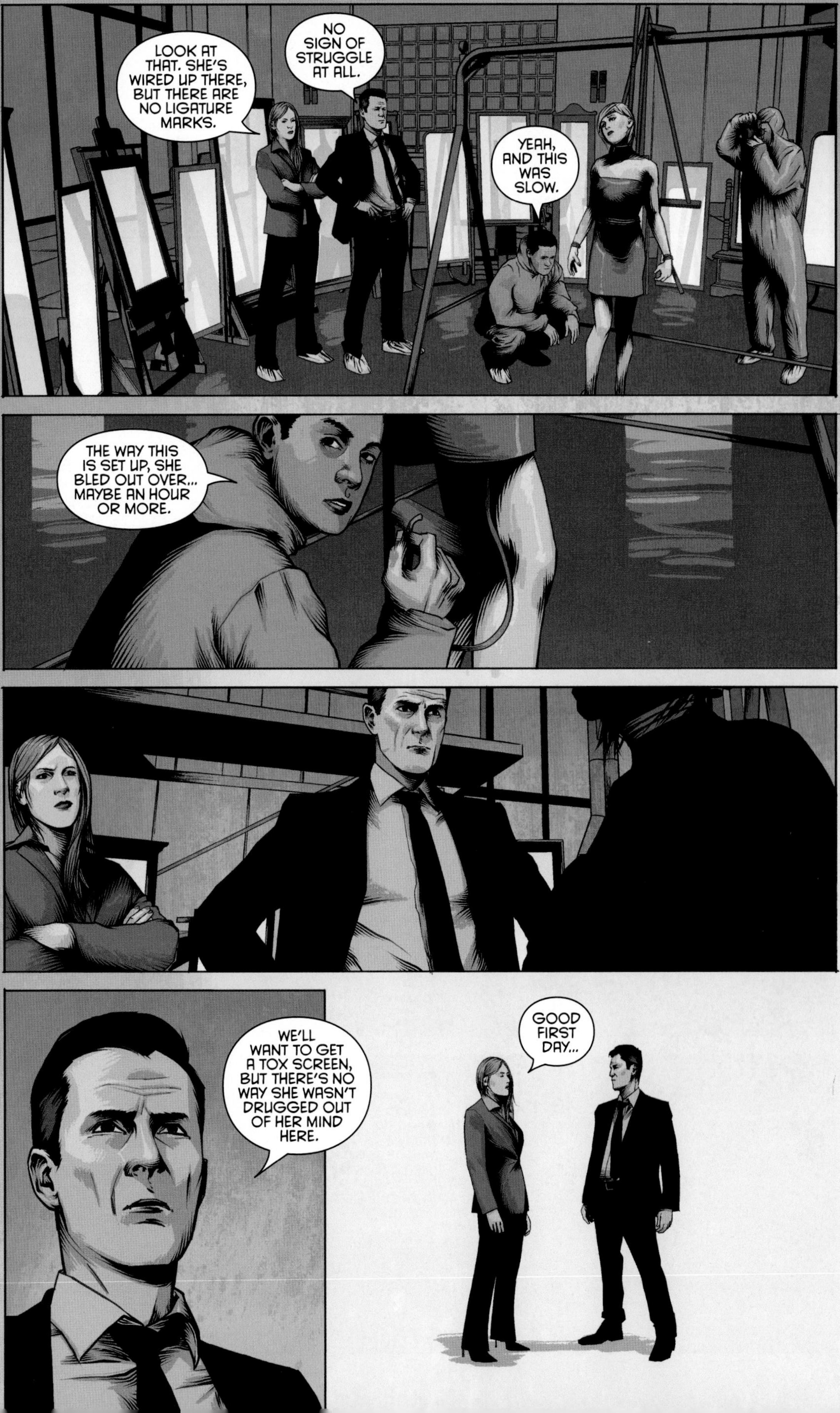
LOOK AT THAT. SHE'S WIRED UP THERE, BUT THERE ARE NO LIGATURE MARKS.
NO SIGN OF STRUGGLE AT ALL.
YEAH, AND THIS WAS SLOW.
THE WAY THIS IS SET UP, SHE BLED OUT OVER... MAYBE AN HOUR OR MORE.
WE'LL WANT TO GET A TOX SCREEN, BUT THERE'S NO WAY SHE WASN'T DRUGGED OUT OF HER MIND HERE.
GOOD FIRST DAY...

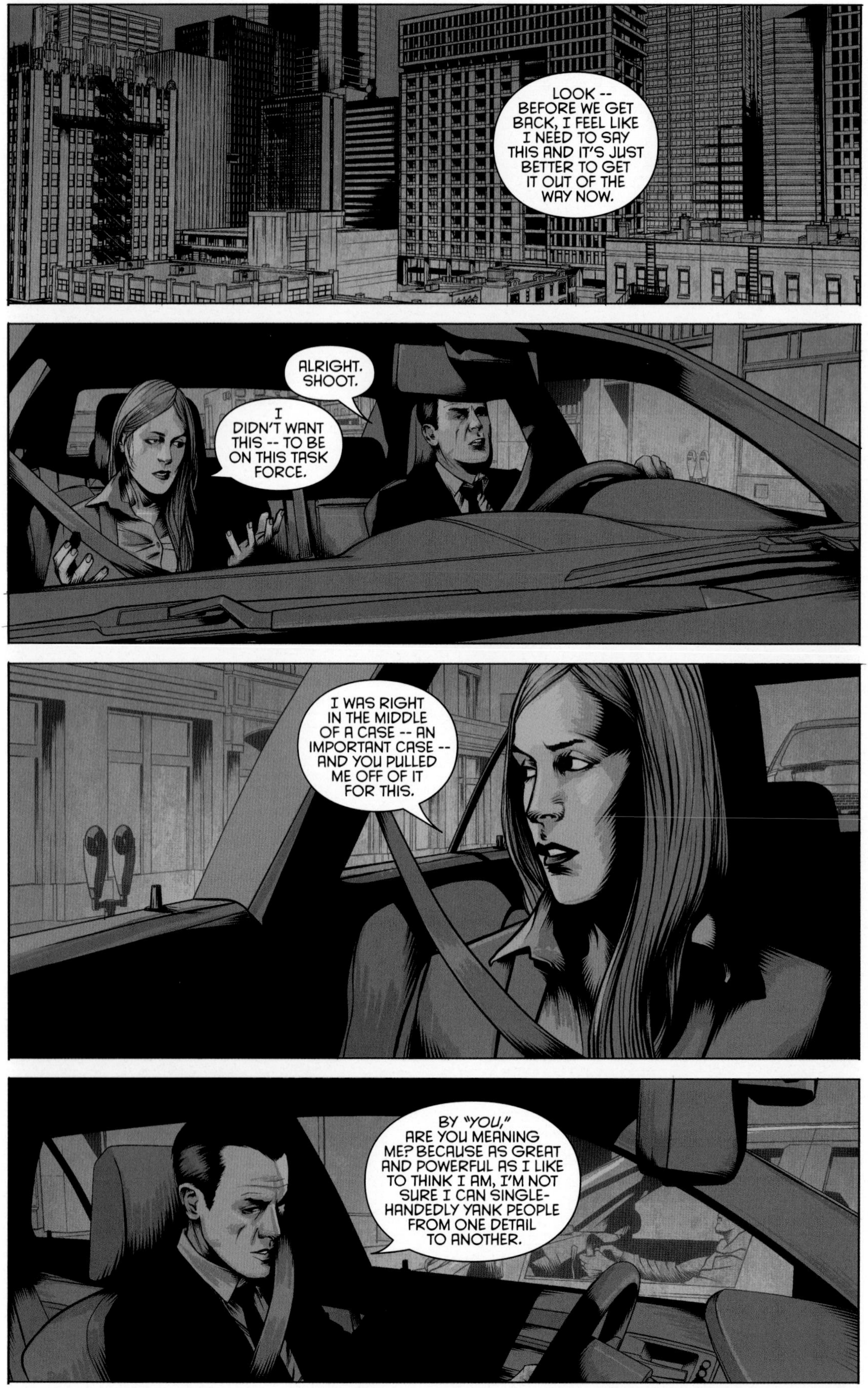
LOOK -- BEFORE WE GET BACK, I FEEL LIKE I NEED TO SAY THIS AND IT'S JUST BETTER TO GET IT OUT OF THE WAY NOW.
ALRIGHT. SHOOT.
I DIDN'T WANT THIS -- TO BE ON THIS TASK FORCE.
I WAS RIGHT IN THE MIDDLE OF A CASE -- AN IMPORTANT CASE -- AND YOU PULLED ME OFF OF IT FOR THIS.
BY "YOU," ARE YOU MEANING ME? BECAUSE AS GREAT AND POWERFUL AS I LIKE TO THINK I AM, I'M NOT SURE I CAN SINGLE-HANDEDLY YANK PEOPLE FROM ONE DETAIL TO ANOTHER.

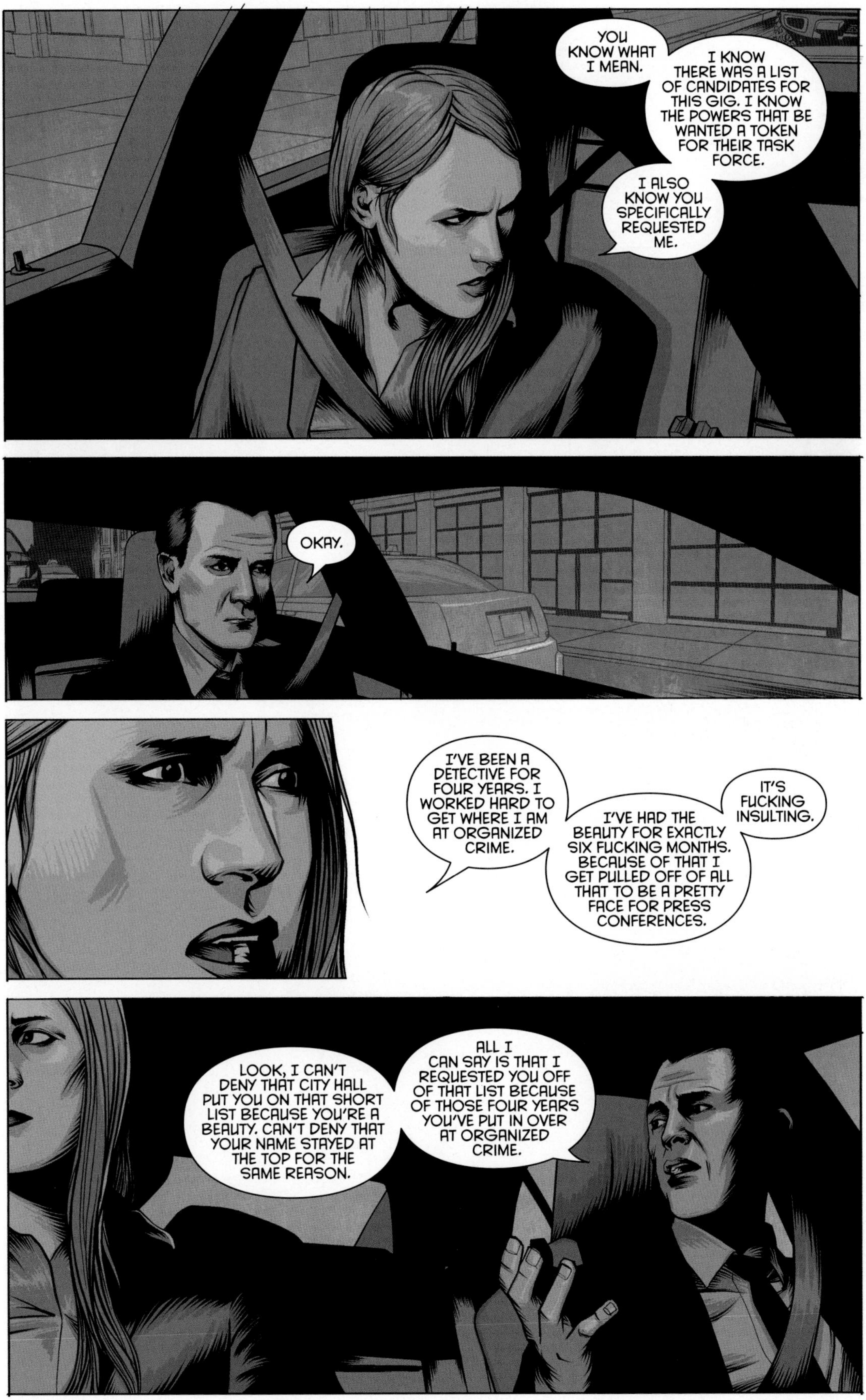
YOU KNOW WHAT I MEAN.
I KNOW THERE WAS A LIST OF CANDIDATES FOR THIS GIG. I KNOW THE POWERS THAT BE WANTED A TOKEN FOR THEIR TASK FORCE.
I ALSO KNOW YOU SPECIFICALLY REQUESTED ME.
OKAY.
I'VE BEEN A DETECTIVE FOR FOUR YEARS. I WORKED HARD TO GET WHERE I AM AT ORGANIZED CRIME.
I'VE HAD THE BEAUTY FOR EXACTLY SIX FUCKING MONTHS. BECAUSE OF THAT I GET PULLED OFF OF ALL THAT TO BE A PRETTY FACE FOR PRESS CONFERENCES.
IT'S FUCKING INSULTING.
LOOK, I CAN'T DENY THAT CITY HALL PUT YOU ON THAT SHORT LIST BECAUSE YOU'RE A BEAUTY. CAN'T DENY THAT YOUR NAME STAYED AT THE TOP FOR THE SAME REASON.
ALL I CAN SAY IS THAT I REQUESTED YOU OFF OF THAT LIST BECAUSE OF THOSE FOUR YEARS YOU'VE PUT IN OVER AT ORGANIZED CRIME.

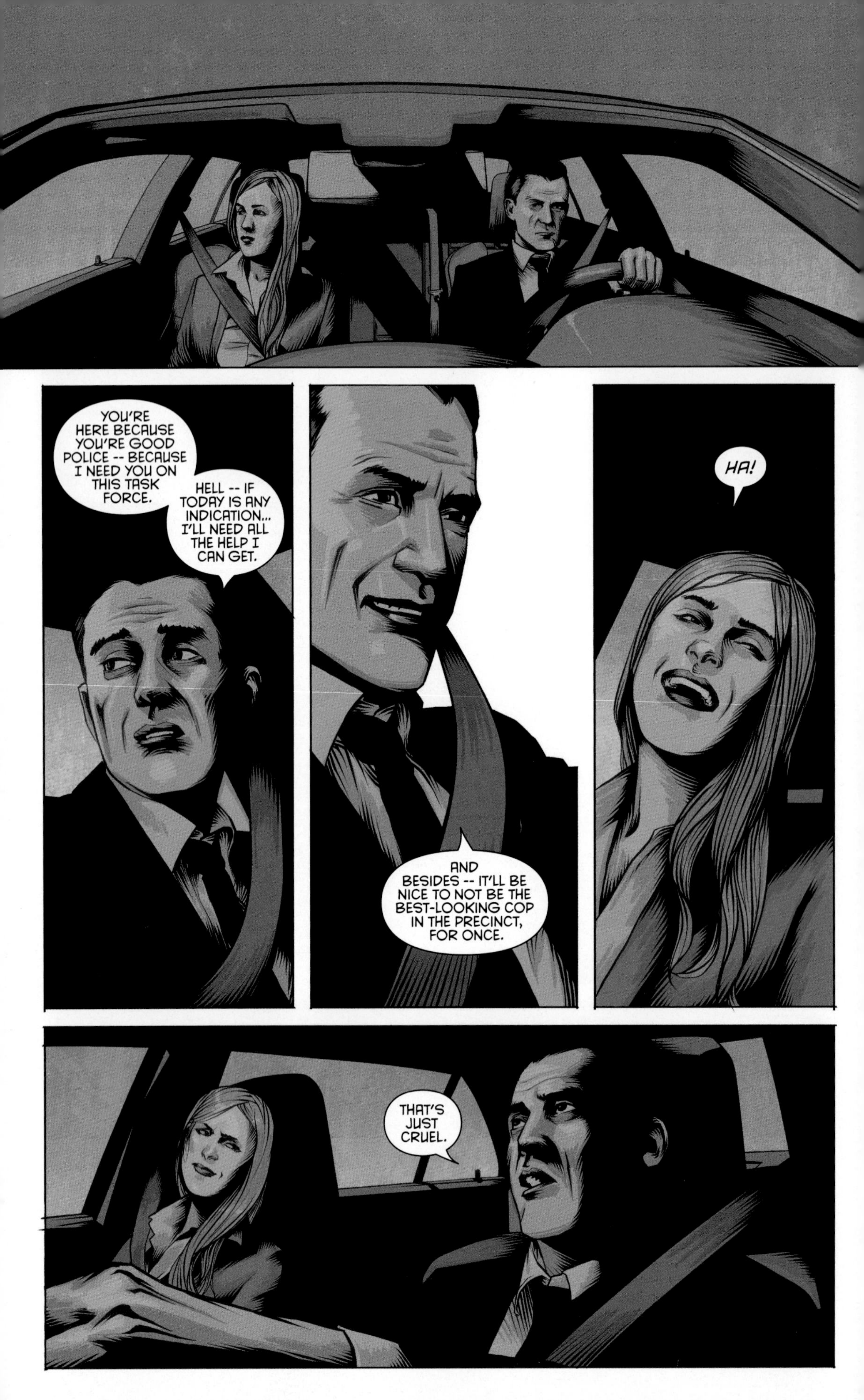
YOU'RE HERE BECAUSE YOU'RE GOOD POLICE -- BECAUSE I NEED YOU ON THIS TASK FORCE.
HELL -- IF TODAY IS ANY INDICATION... I'LL NEED ALL THE HELP I CAN GET.
AND BESIDES -- IT'LL BE NICE TO NOT BE THE BEST-LOOKING COP IN THE PRECINCT, FOR ONCE.
HA!
THAT'S JUST CRUEL.

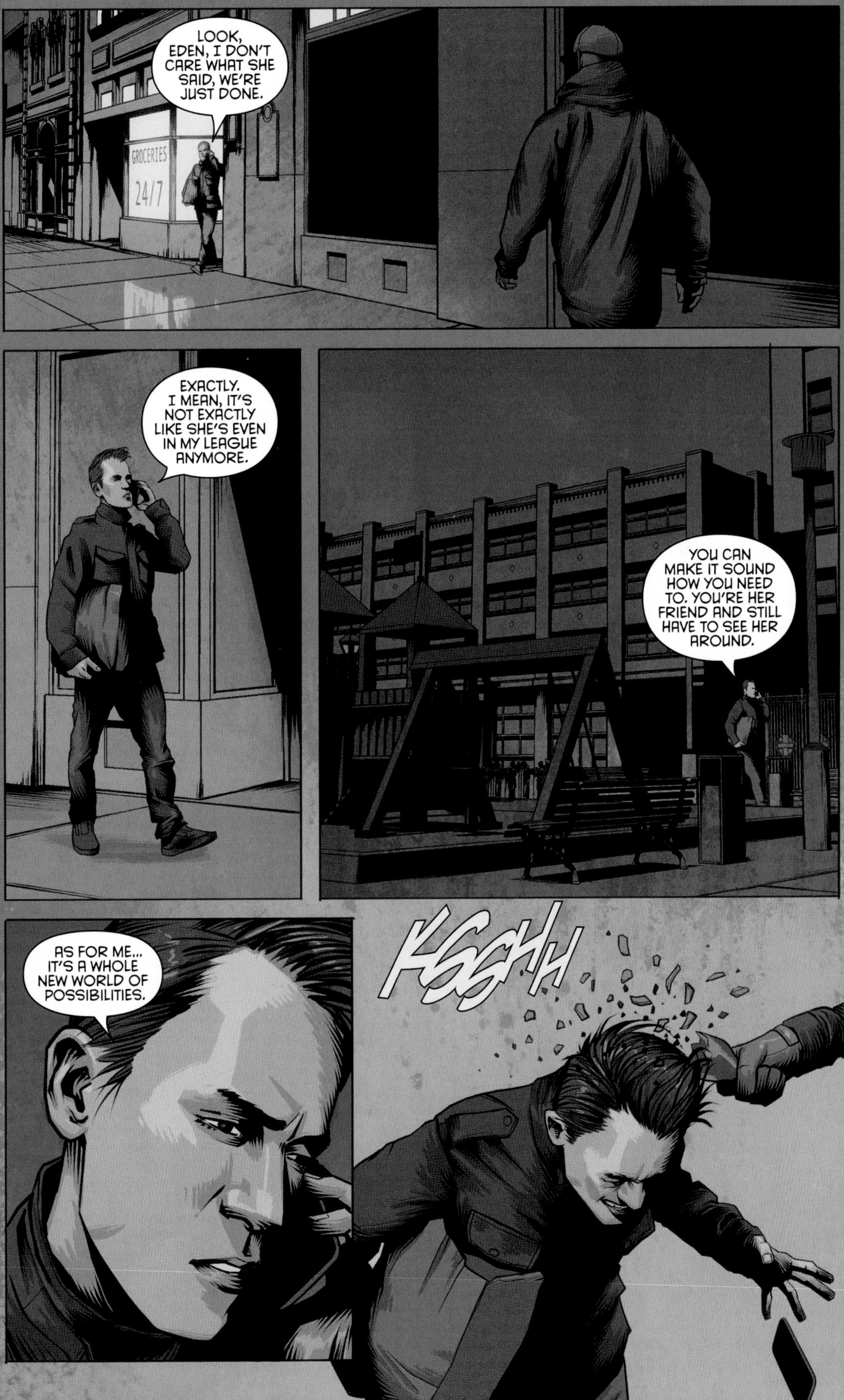
LOOK, EDEN, I DON'T CARE WHAT SHE SAID, WE'RE JUST DONE.
GROCERIES 24/7
EXACTLY. I MEAN, IT'S NOT EXACTLY LIKE SHE'S EVEN IN MY LEAGUE ANYMORE.
YOU CAN MAKE IT SOUND HOW YOU NEED TO. YOU'RE HER FRIEND AND STILL HAVE TO SEE HER AROUND.
AS FOR ME... IT'S A WHOLE NEW WORLD OF POSSIBILITIES.
KSSHH

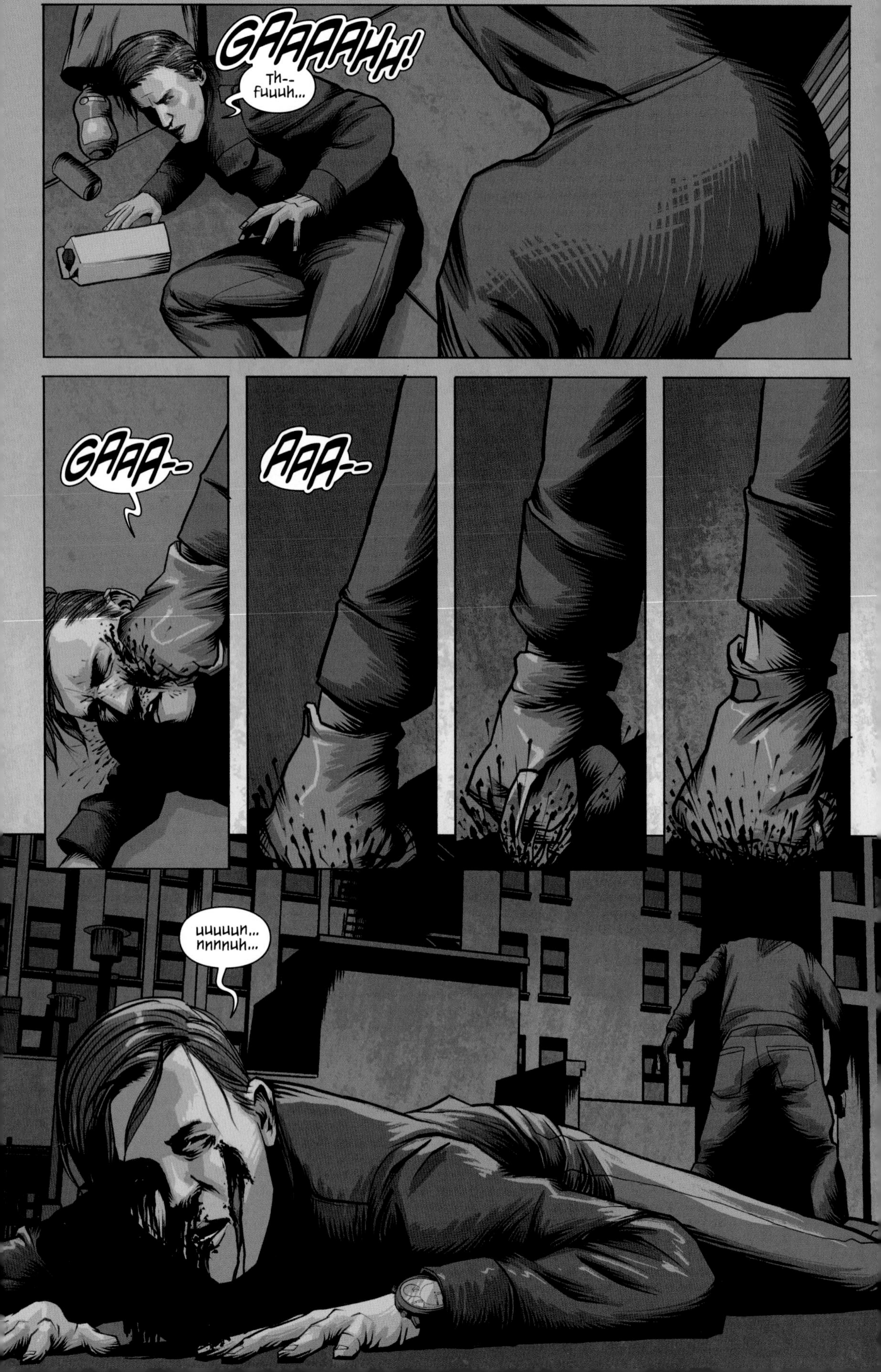
GAAAAAHH!
Th--
fuuuh...
GAAA--
AAA--
uuuuun...
nnnnuh...

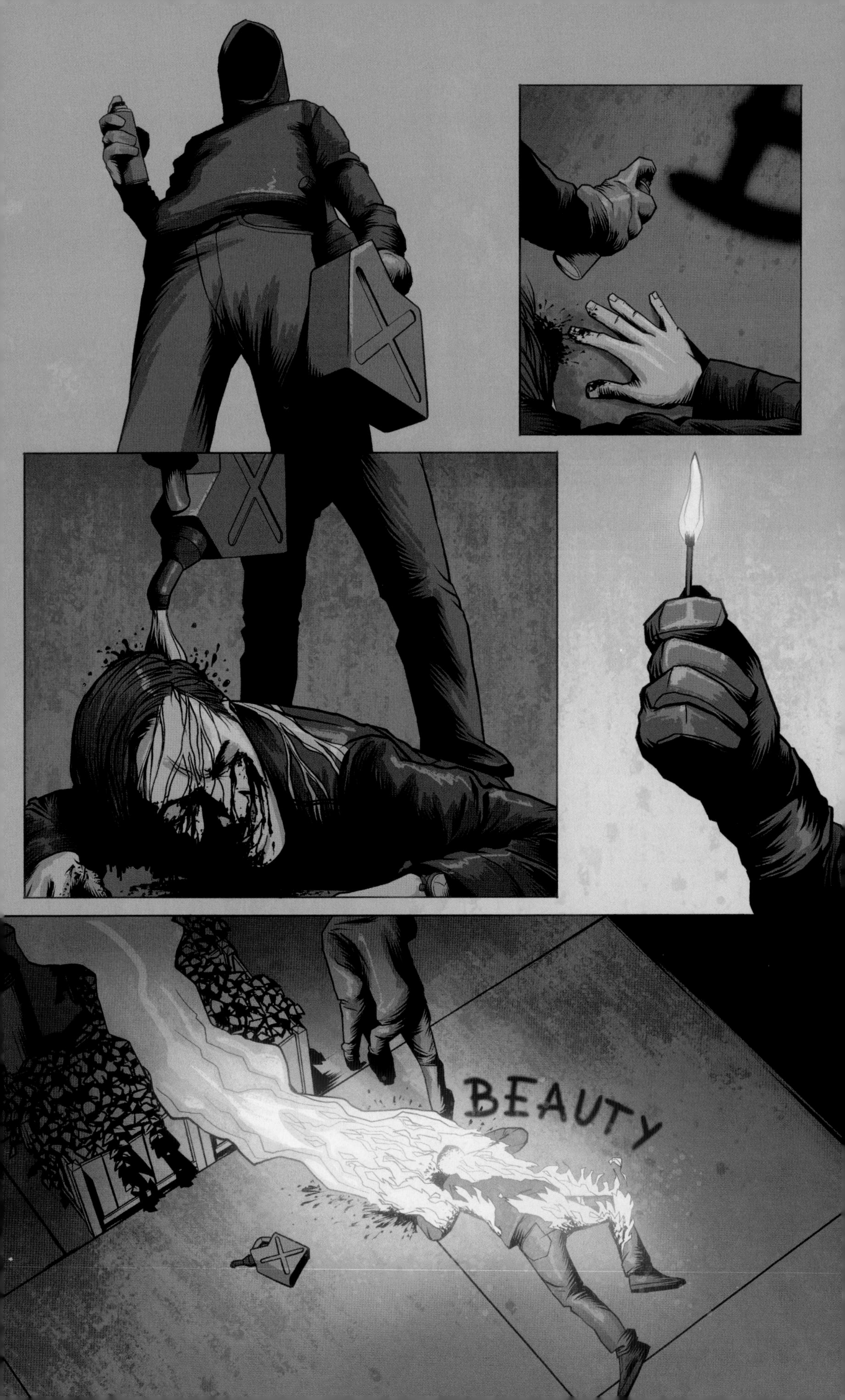
BEAUTY

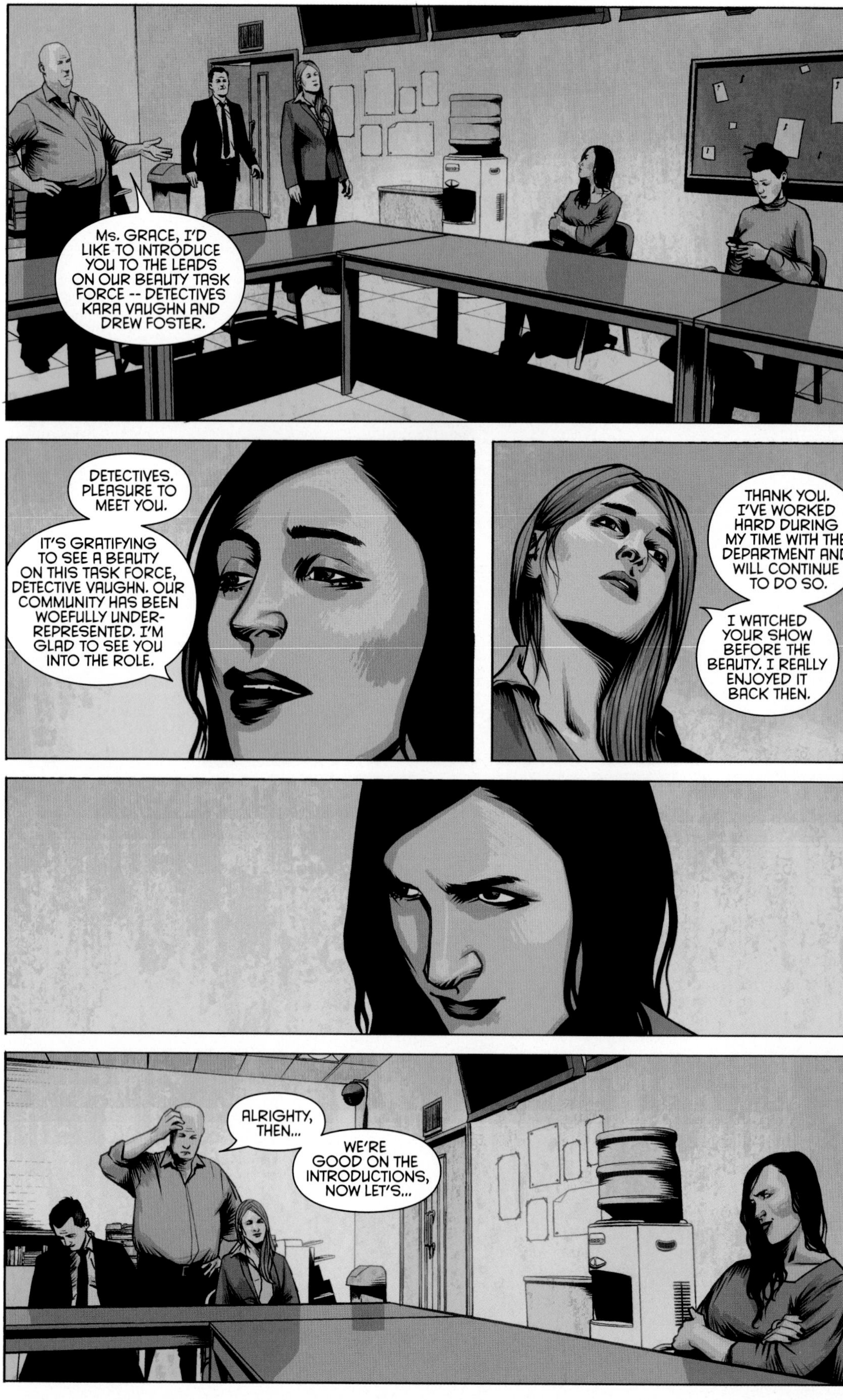
Ms. GRACE, I'D LIKE TO INTRODUCE YOU TO THE LEADS ON OUR BEAUTY TASK FORCE -- DETECTIVES KARA VAUGHN AND DREW FOSTER.
DETECTIVES. PLEASURE TO MEET YOU.
IT'S GRATIFYING TO SEE A BEAUTY ON THIS TASK FORCE, DETECTIVE VAUGHN. OUR COMMUNITY HAS BEEN WOEFULLY UNDER-REPRESENTED. I'M GLAD TO SEE YOU INTO THE ROLE.
THANK YOU. I'VE WORKED HARD DURING MY TIME WITH THE DEPARTMENT AND WILL CONTINUE TO DO SO.
I WATCHED YOUR SHOW BEFORE THE BEAUTY. I REALLY ENJOYED IT BACK THEN.
ALRIGHTY, THEN...
WE'RE GOOD ON THE INTRODUCTIONS, NOW LET'S...

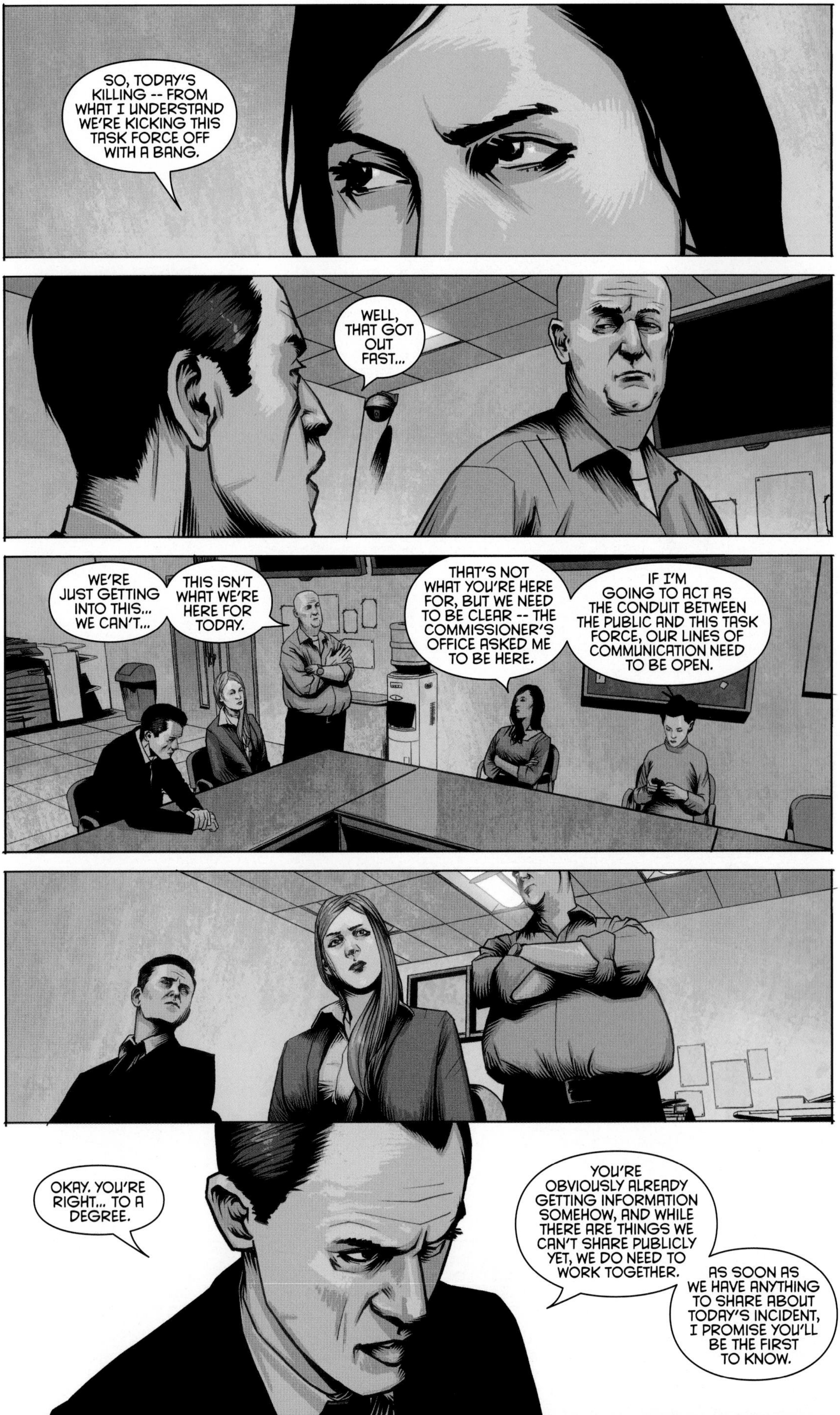
SO, TODAY'S KILLING -- FROM WHAT I UNDERSTAND WE'RE KICKING THIS TASK FORCE OFF WITH A BANG.
WELL, THAT GOT OUT FAST...
WE'RE JUST GETTING INTO THIS... WE CAN'T...
THIS ISN'T WHAT WE'RE HERE FOR TODAY.
THAT'S NOT WHAT YOU'RE HERE FOR, BUT WE NEED TO BE CLEAR -- THE COMMISSIONER'S OFFICE ASKED ME TO BE HERE.
IF I'M GOING TO ACT AS THE CONDUIT BETWEEN THE PUBLIC AND THIS TASK FORCE, OUR LINES OF COMMUNICATION NEED TO BE OPEN.
OKAY. YOU'RE RIGHT... TO A DEGREE.
YOU'RE OBVIOUSLY ALREADY GETTING INFORMATION SOMEHOW, AND WHILE THERE ARE THINGS WE CAN'T SHARE PUBLICLY YET, WE DO NEED TO WORK TOGETHER.
AS SOON AS WE HAVE ANYTHING TO SHARE ABOUT TODAY'S INCIDENT, I PROMISE YOU'LL BE THE FIRST TO KNOW.

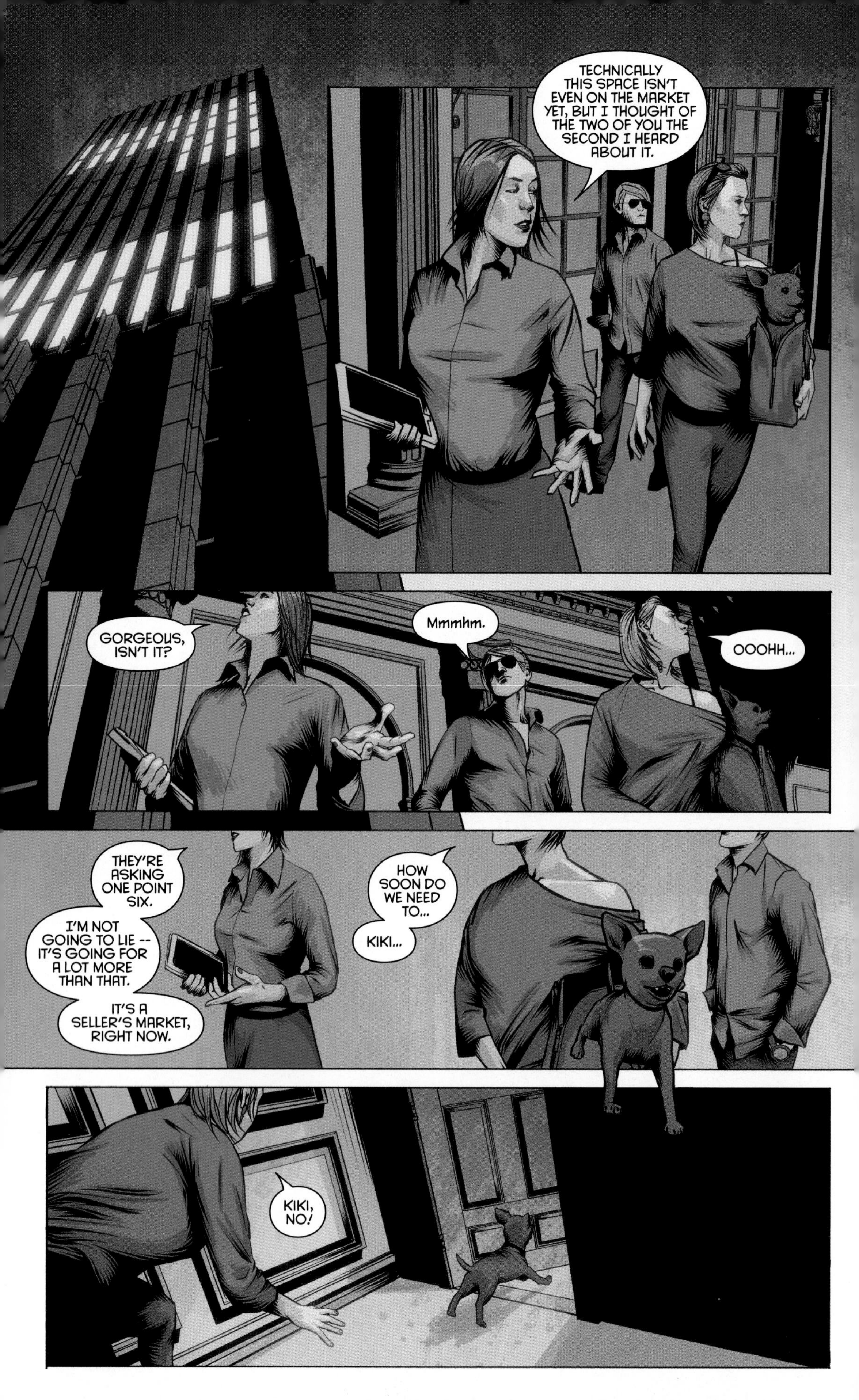
TECHNICALLY THIS SPACE ISN'T EVEN ON THE MARKET YET, BUT I THOUGHT OF THE TWO OF YOU THE SECOND I HEARD ABOUT IT.
GORGEOUS, ISN'T IT?
Mmmhm.
OOOHH...
THEY'RE ASKING ONE POINT SIX.
I'M NOT GOING TO LIE -- IT'S GOING FOR A LOT MORE THAN THAT.
IT'S A SELLER'S MARKET, RIGHT NOW.
HOW SOON DO WE NEED TO...
KIKI...
KIKI, NO!

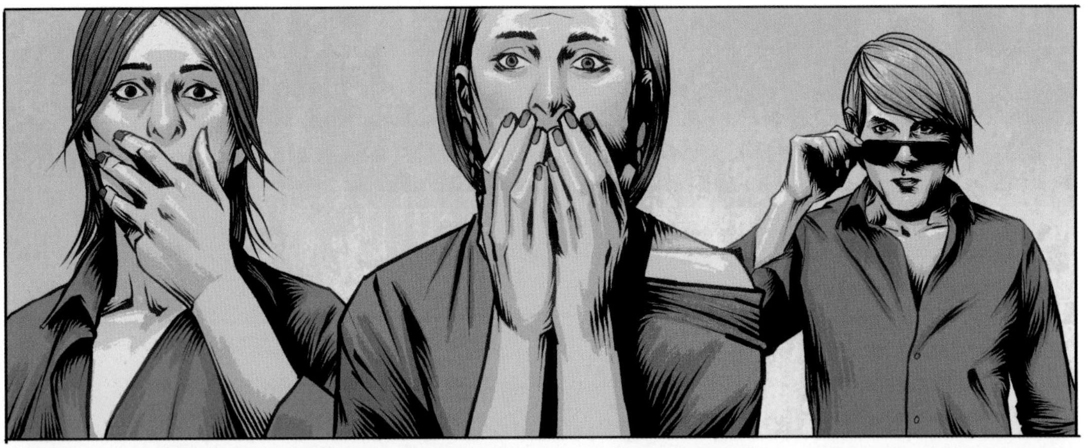
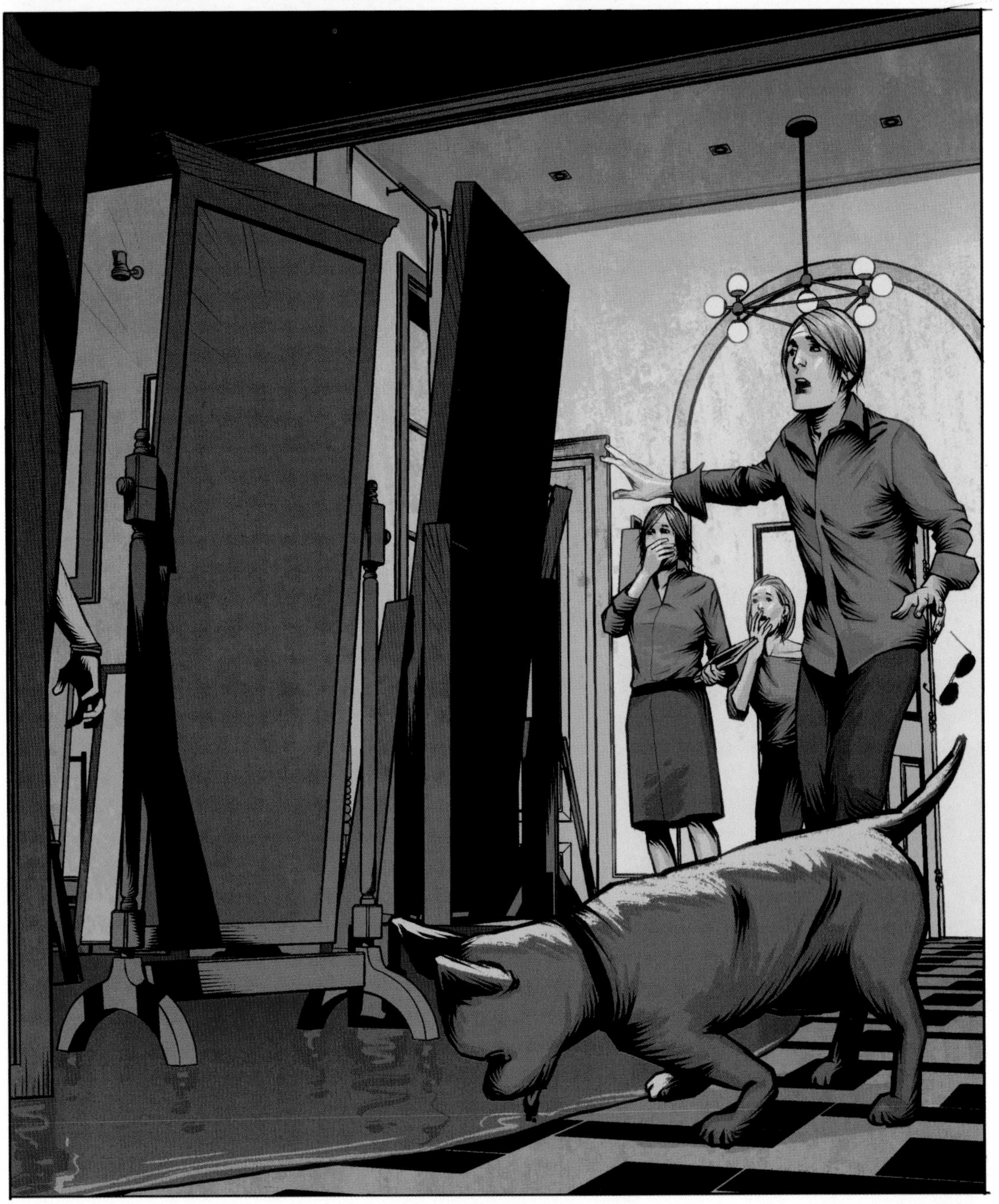

CHAPTER

12

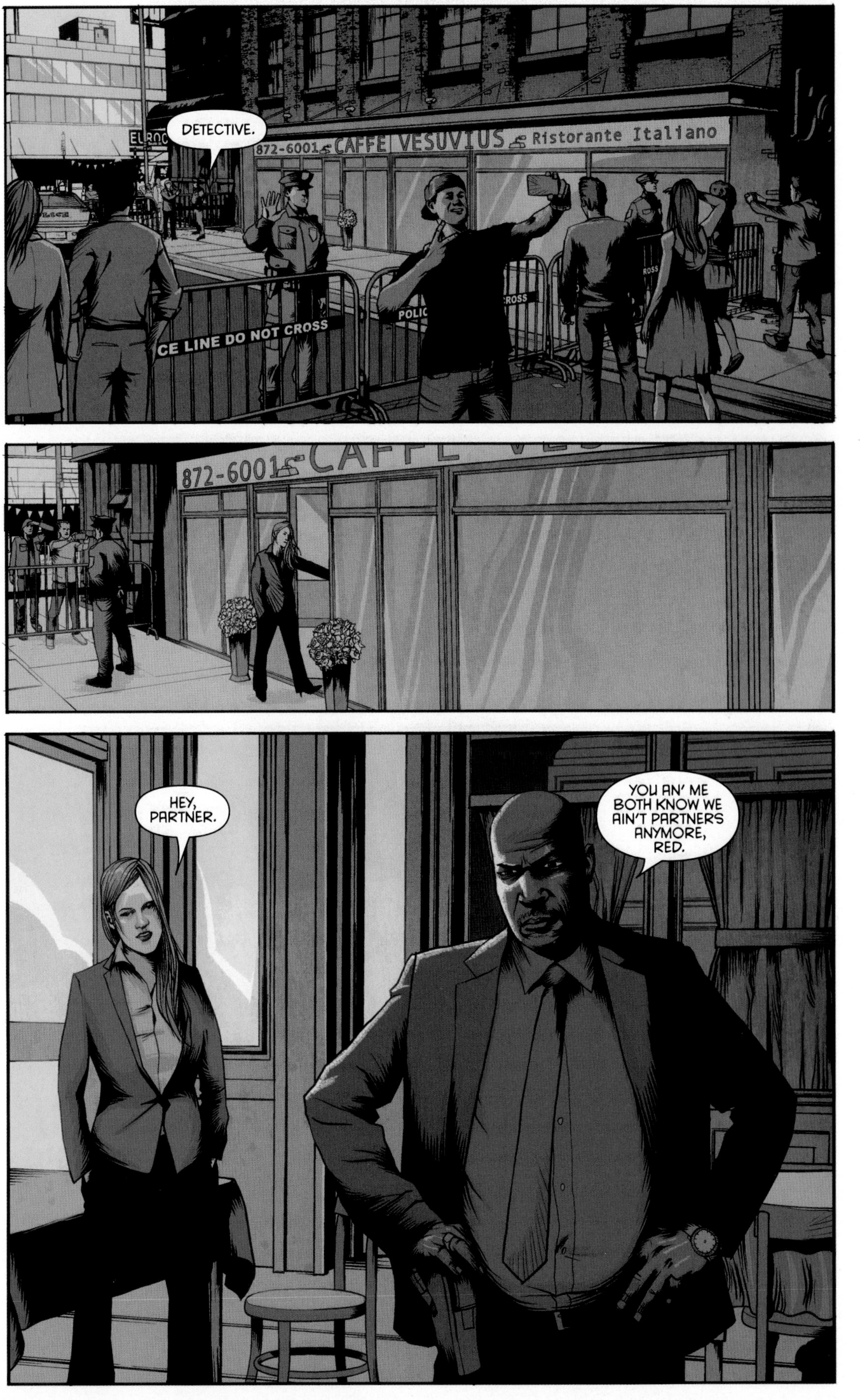
DETECTIVE.
872-6001 CAFFE VESUVIUS Ristorante Italiano
CE LINE DO NOT CROSS
872-6001
HEY, PARTNER.
YOU AN' ME BOTH KNOW WE AIN'T PARTNERS ANYMORE, RED.

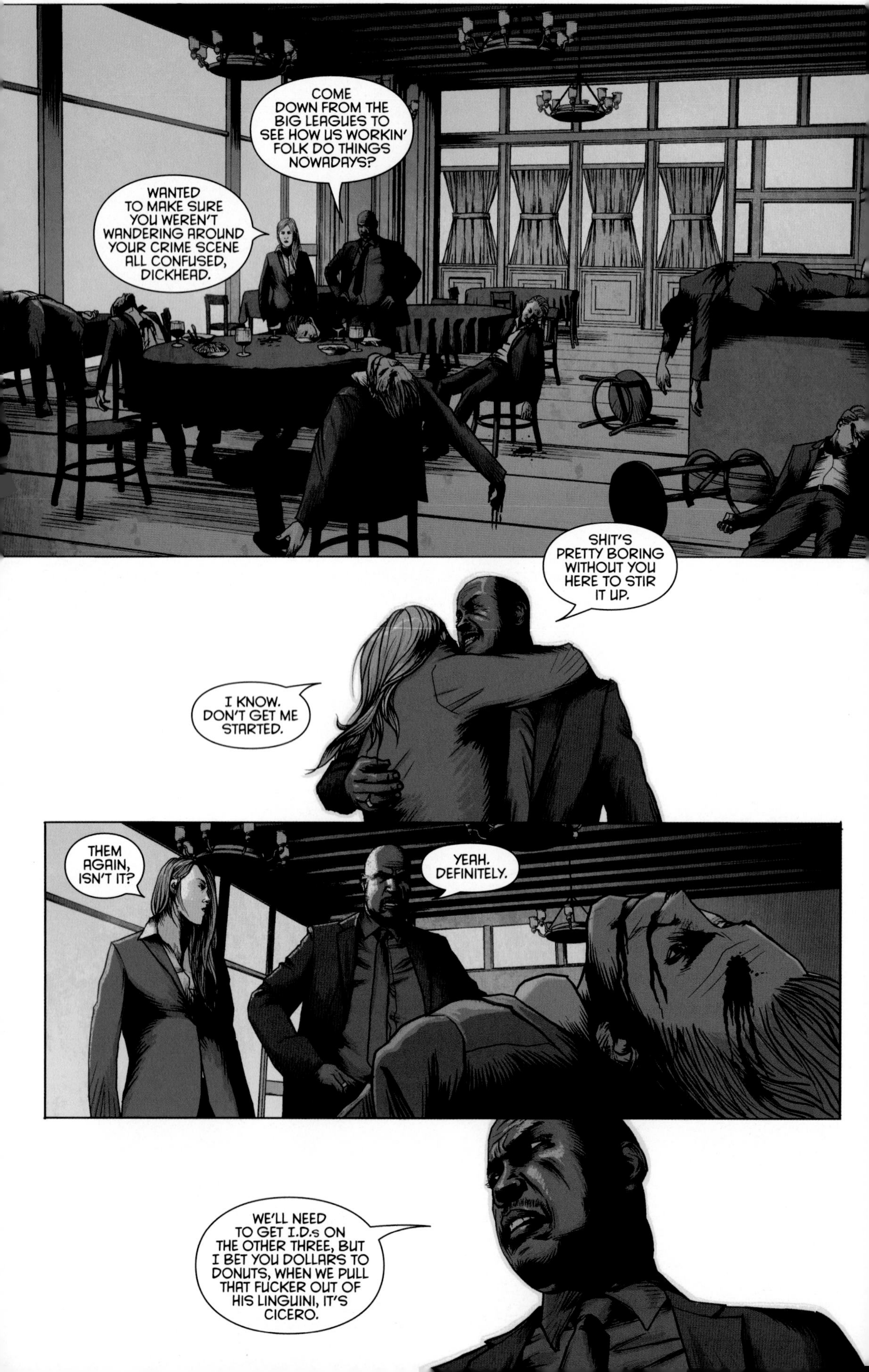
COME DOWN FROM THE BIG LEAGUES TO SEE HOW US WORKIN' FOLK DO THINGS NOWADAYS?
WANTED TO MAKE SURE YOU WEREN'T WANDERING AROUND YOUR CRIME SCENE ALL CONFUSED, DICKHEAD.
SHIT'S PRETTY BORING WITHOUT YOU HERE TO STIR IT UP.
I KNOW. DON'T GET ME STARTED.
THEM AGAIN, ISN'T IT?
YEAH. DEFINITELY.
WE'LL NEED TO GET I.D.s ON THE OTHER THREE, BUT I BET YOU DOLLARS TO DONUTS, WHEN WE PULL THAT FUCKER OUT OF HIS LINGUINI, IT'S CICERO.

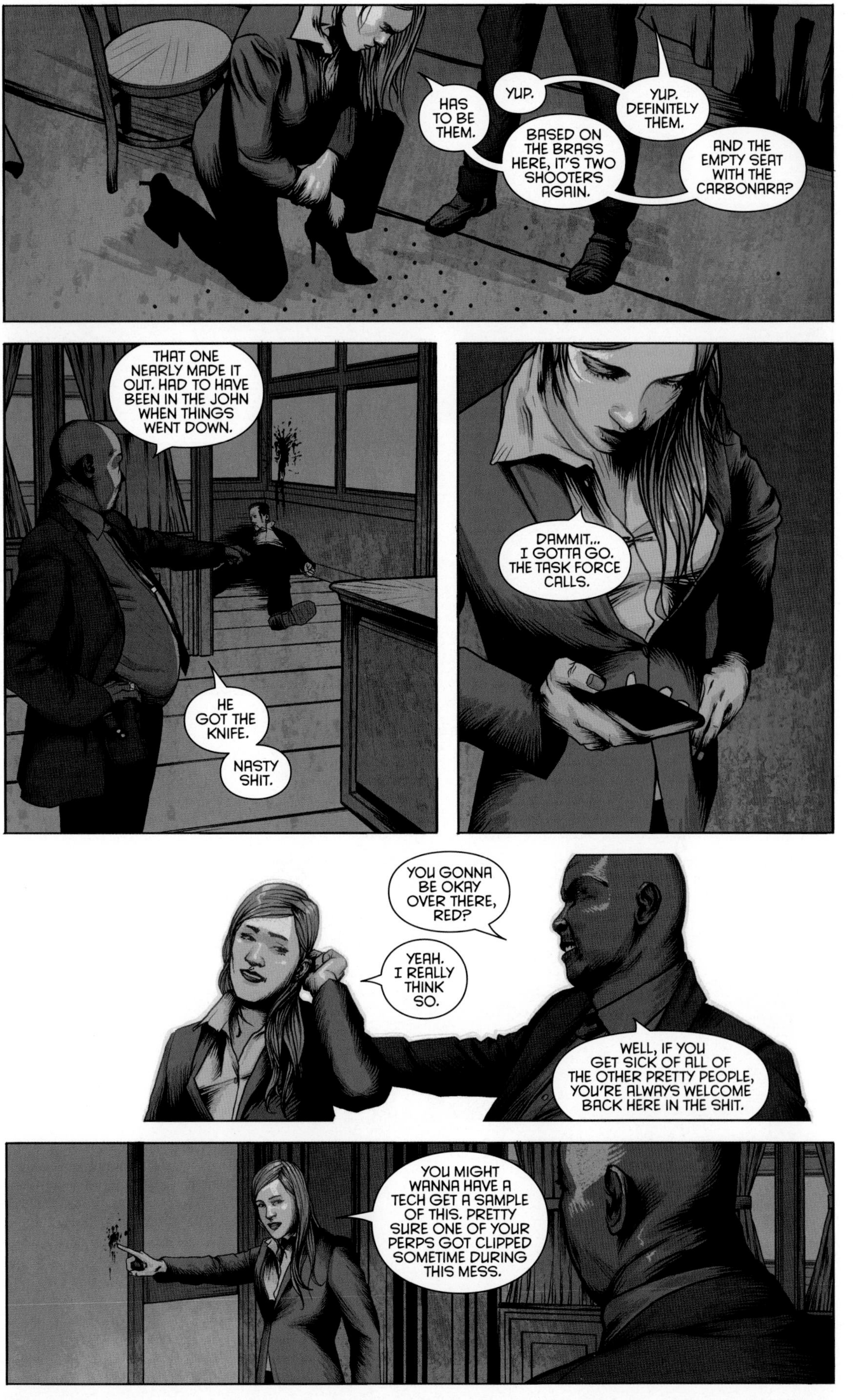
HAS TO BE THEM.
YUP.
YUP. DEFINITELY THEM.
BASED ON THE BRASS HERE, IT'S TWO SHOOTERS AGAIN.
AND THE EMPTY SEAT WITH THE CARBONARA?
THAT ONE NEARLY MADE IT OUT. HAD TO HAVE BEEN IN THE JOHN WHEN THINGS WENT DOWN.
HE GOT THE KNIFE.
NASTY SHIT.
DAMMIT... I GOTTA GO. THE TASK FORCE CALLS.
YOU GONNA BE OKAY OVER THERE, RED?
YEAH. I REALLY THINK SO.
WELL, IF YOU GET SICK OF ALL OF THE OTHER PRETTY PEOPLE, YOU'RE ALWAYS WELCOME BACK HERE IN THE SHIT.
YOU MIGHT WANNA HAVE A TECH GET A SAMPLE OF THIS. PRETTY SURE ONE OF YOUR PERPS GOT CLIPPED SOMETIME DURING THIS MESS.

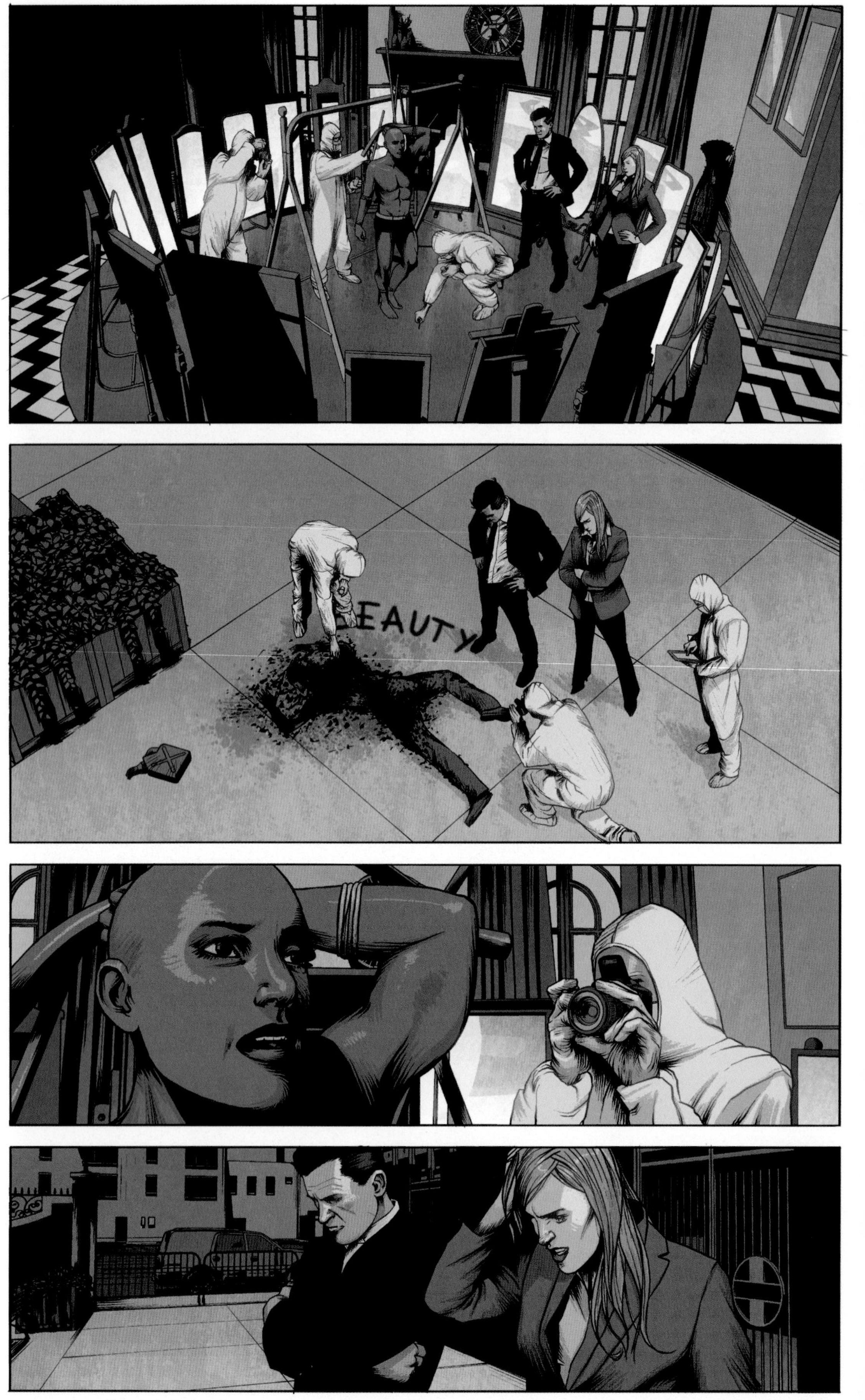
EAUTY

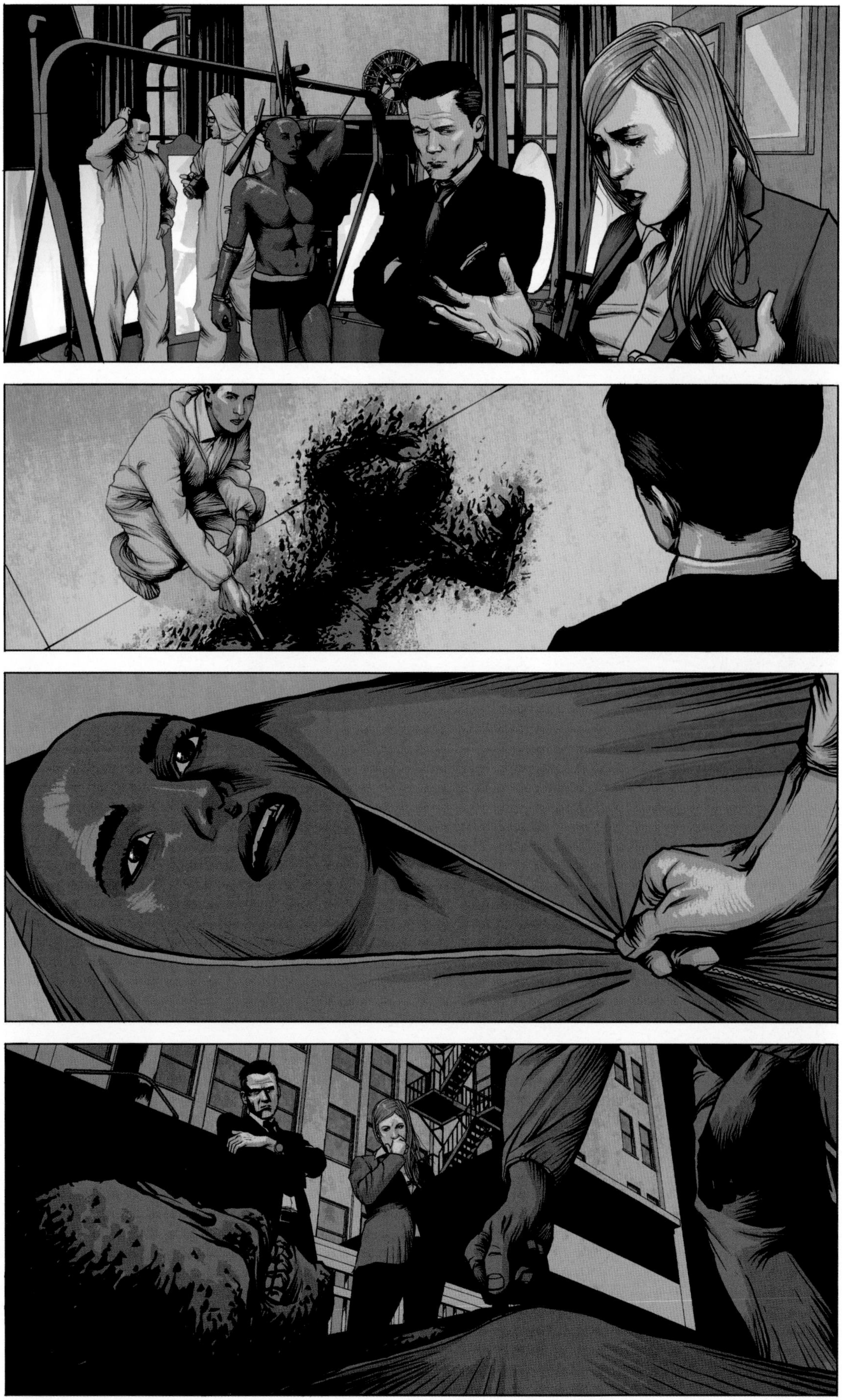

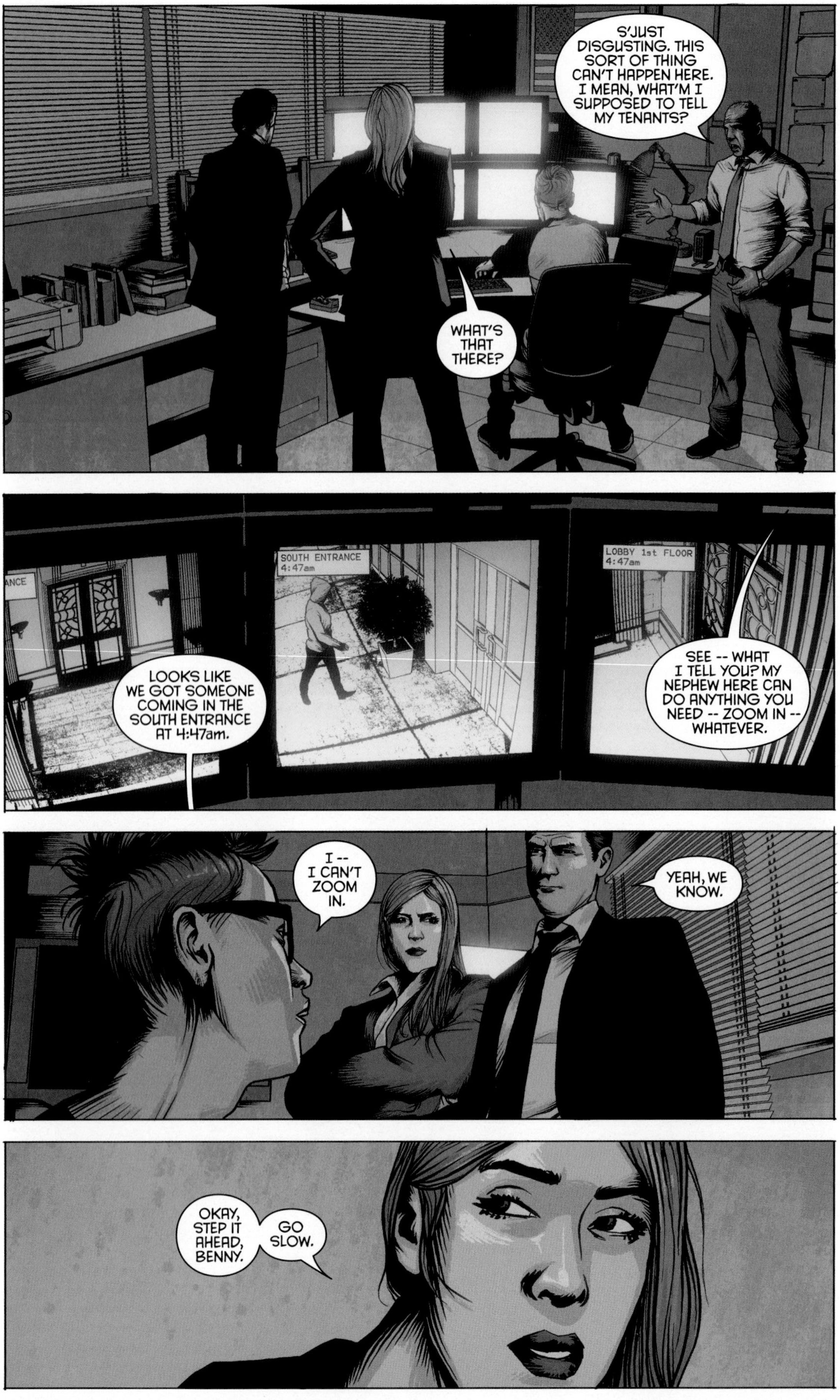
S'JUST DISGUSTING. THIS SORT OF THING CAN'T HAPPEN HERE. I MEAN, WHAT'M I SUPPOSED TO TELL MY TENANTS?
WHAT'S THAT THERE?
SOUTH ENTRANCE 4:47am
LOBBY 1st FLOOR 4:47am
LOOKS LIKE WE GOT SOMEONE COMING IN THE SOUTH ENTRANCE AT 4:47am.
SEE -- WHAT I TELL YOU? MY NEPHEW HERE CAN DO ANYTHING YOU NEED -- ZOOM IN -- WHATEVER.
I -- I CAN'T ZOOM IN.
YEAH, WE KNOW.
OKAY, STEP IT AHEAD, BENNY.
GO SLOW.

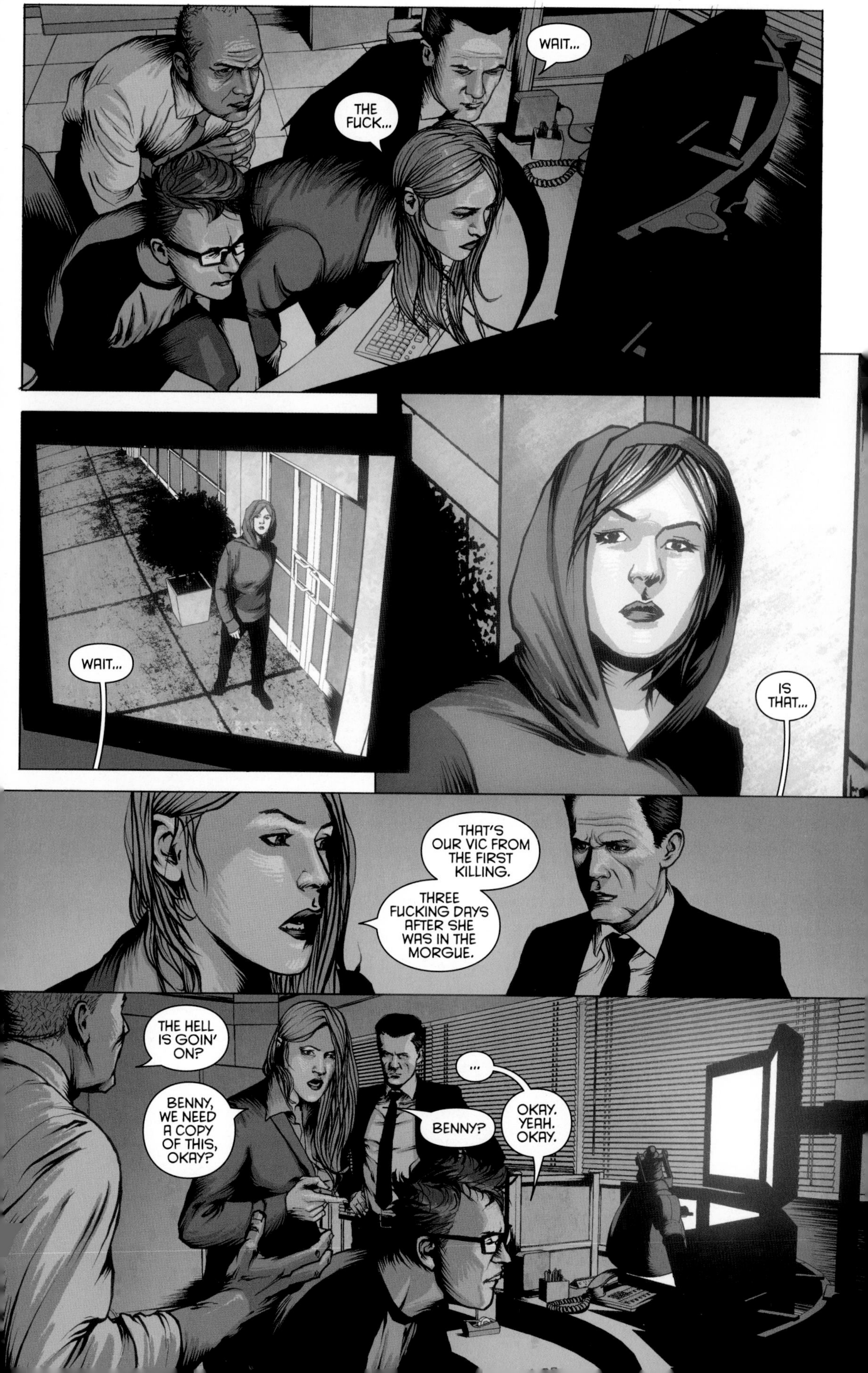
WAIT...
THE FUCK...
WAIT...
IS THAT...
THAT'S OUR VIC FROM THE FIRST KILLING.
THREE FUCKING DAYS AFTER SHE WAS IN THE MORGUE.
THE HELL IS GOIN' ON?
BENNY, WE NEED A COPY OF THIS, OKAY?
BENNY?
...
OKAY. YEAH. OKAY.

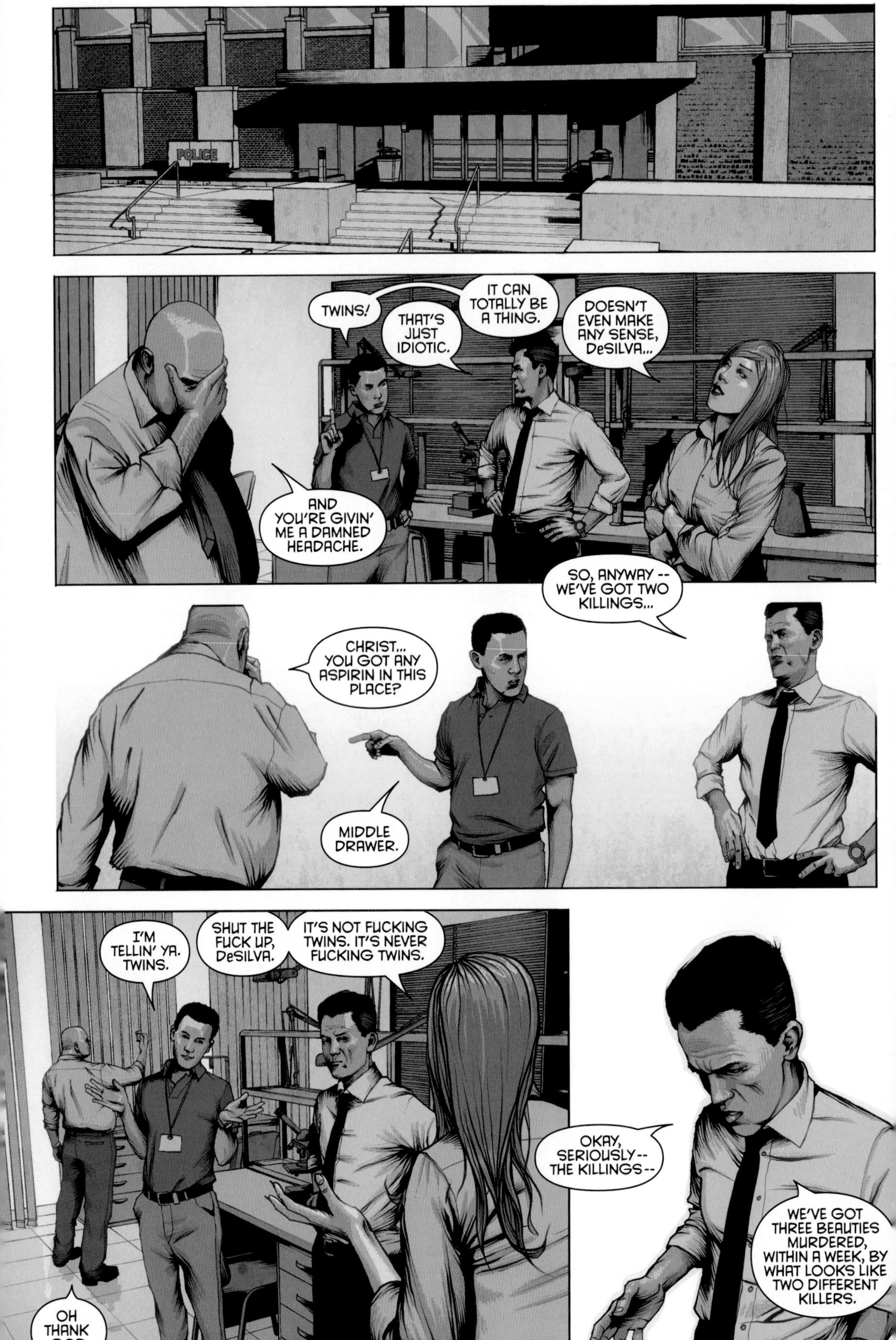
POLICE
TWINS!
IT CAN TOTALLY BE A THING.
THAT'S JUST IDIOTIC.
DOESN'T EVEN MAKE ANY SENSE, DeSILVA...
AND YOU'RE GIVIN' ME A DAMNED HEADACHE.
SO, ANYWAY -- WE'VE GOT TWO KILLINGS...
CHRIST... YOU GOT ANY ASPIRIN IN THIS PLACE?
MIDDLE DRAWER.
I'M TELLIN' YA. TWINS.
SHUT THE FUCK UP, DeSILVA.
IT'S NOT FUCKING TWINS. IT'S NEVER FUCKING TWINS.
OH THANK GOD...
OKAY, SERIOUSLY-- THE KILLINGS--
WE'VE GOT THREE BEAUTIES MURDERED, WITHIN A WEEK, BY WHAT LOOKS LIKE TWO DIFFERENT KILLERS.

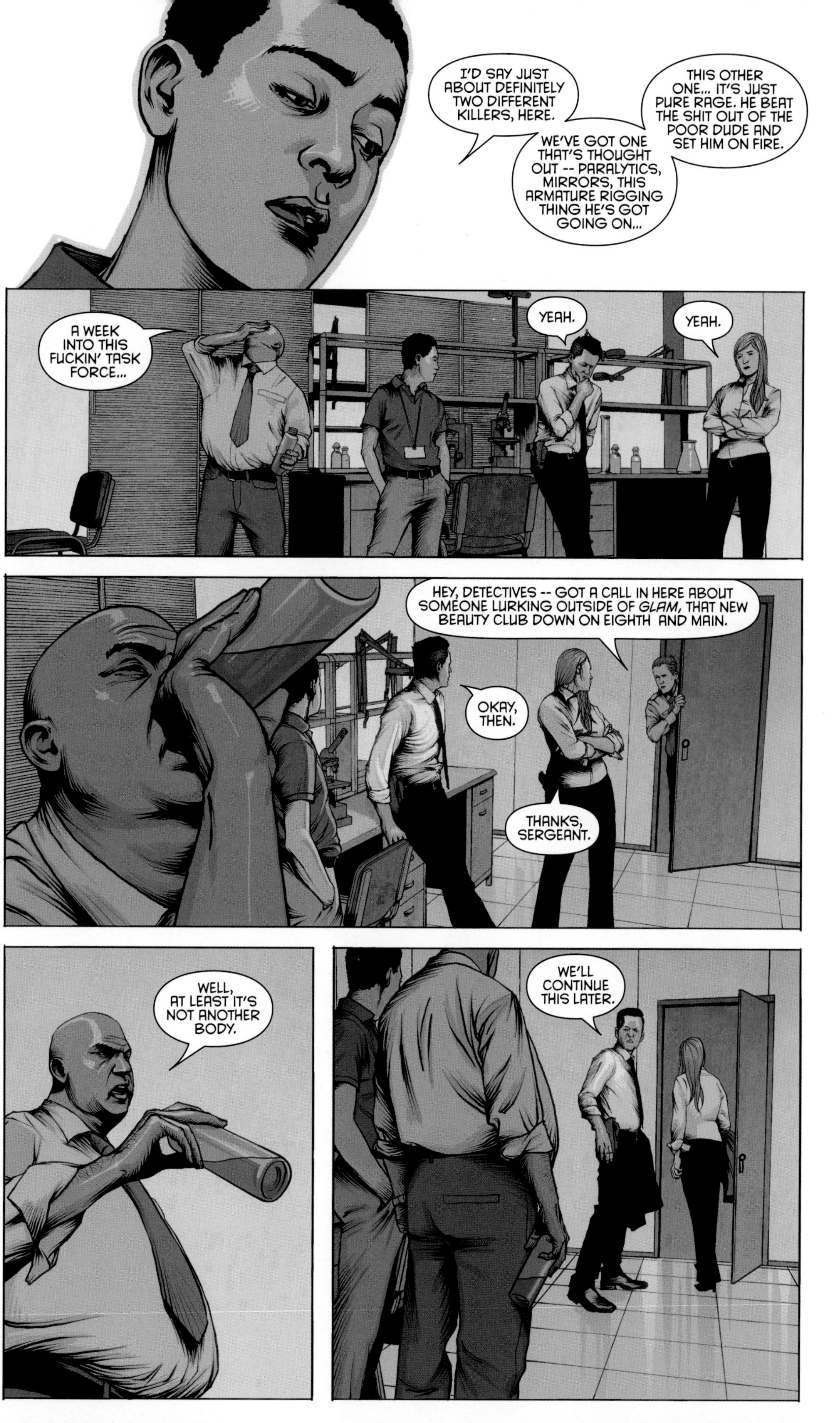
I'D SAY JUST ABOUT DEFINITELY TWO DIFFERENT KILLERS, HERE.
WE'VE GOT ONE THAT'S THOUGHT OUT -- PARALYTICS, MIRRORS, THIS ARMATURE RIGGING THING HE'S GOT GOING ON...
THIS OTHER ONE... IT'S JUST PURE RAGE. HE BEAT THE SHIT OUT OF THE POOR DUDE AND SET HIM ON FIRE.
A WEEK INTO THIS FUCKIN' TASK FORCE...
YEAH.
YEAH.
HEY, DETECTIVES -- GOT A CALL IN HERE ABOUT SOMEONE LURKING OUTSIDE OF GLAM, THAT NEW BEAUTY CLUB DOWN ON EIGHTH AND MAIN.
OKAY, THEN.
THANKS, SERGEANT.
WELL, AT LEAST IT'S NOT ANOTHER BODY.
WE'LL CONTINUE THIS LATER.

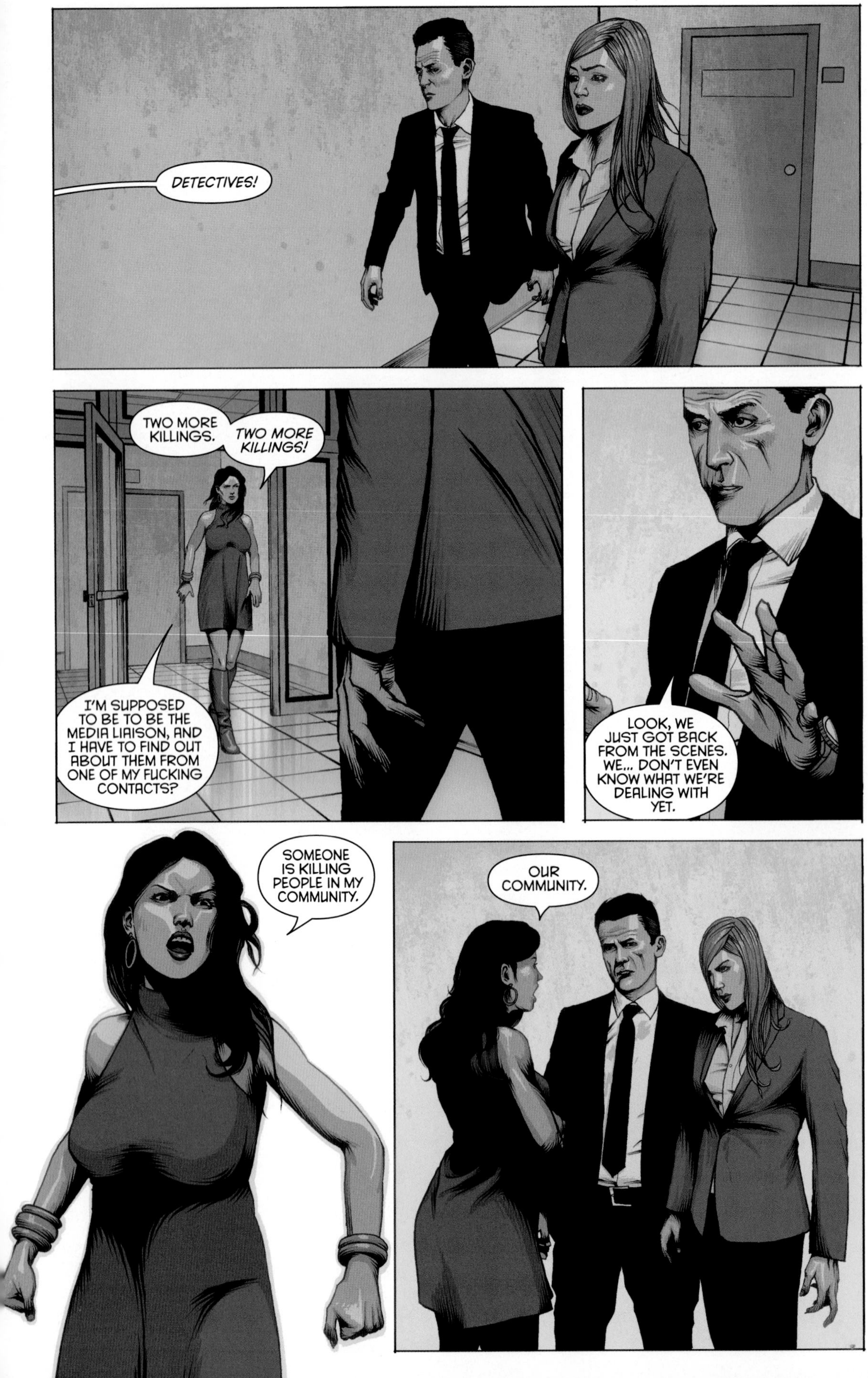
DETECTIVES!
TWO MORE KILLINGS.
TWO MORE KILLINGS!
I'M SUPPOSED TO BE TO BE THE MEDIA LIAISON, AND I HAVE TO FIND OUT ABOUT THEM FROM ONE OF MY FUCKING CONTACTS?
LOOK, WE JUST GOT BACK FROM THE SCENES. WE... DON'T EVEN KNOW WHAT WE'RE DEALING WITH YET.
SOMEONE IS KILLING PEOPLE IN MY COMMUNITY.
OUR COMMUNITY.

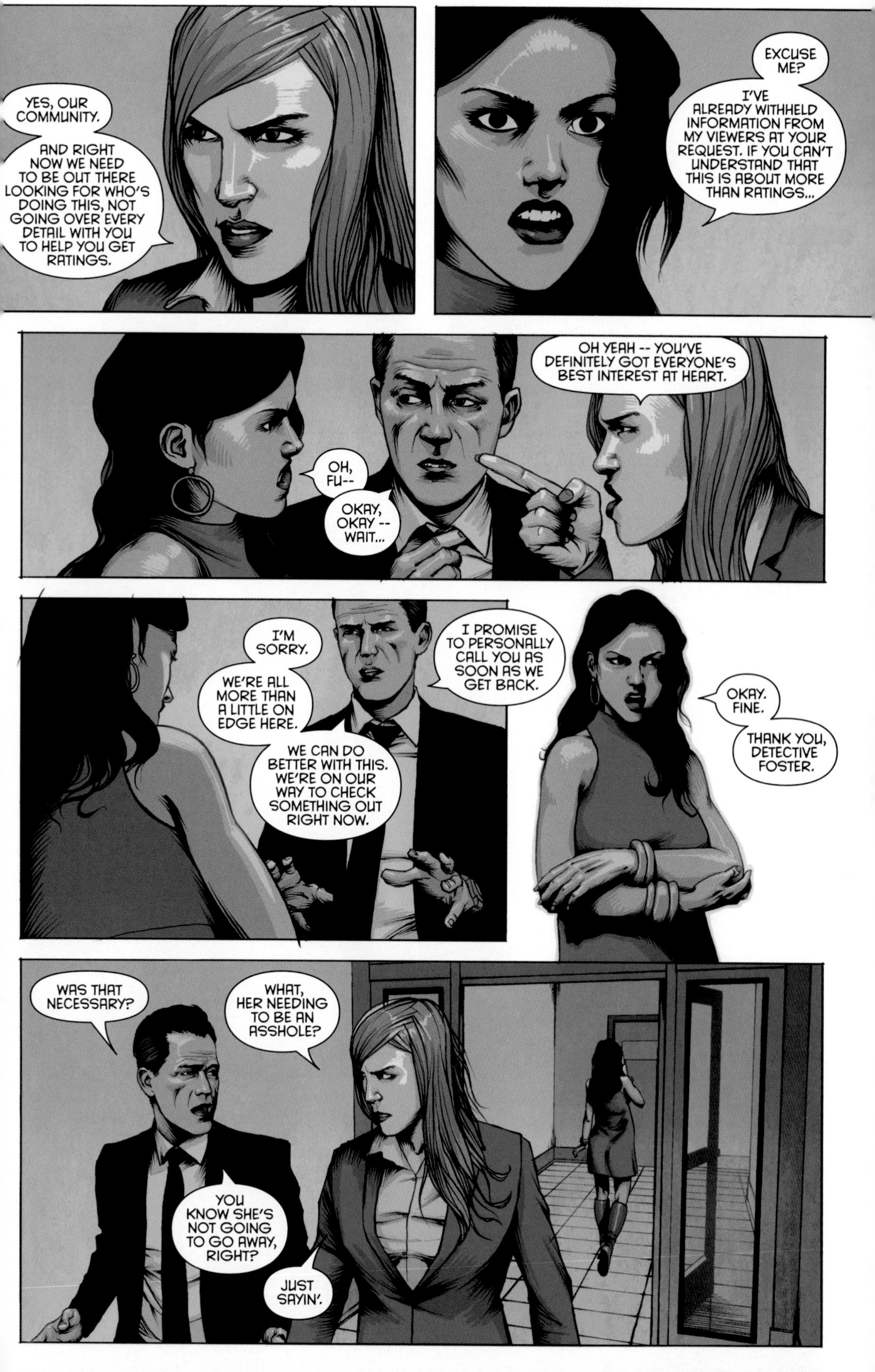
YES, OUR COMMUNITY.
AND RIGHT NOW WE NEED TO BE OUT THERE LOOKING FOR WHO'S DOING THIS, NOT GOING OVER EVERY DETAIL WITH YOU TO HELP YOU GET RATINGS.
EXCUSE ME?
I'VE ALREADY WITHHELD INFORMATION FROM MY VIEWERS AT YOUR REQUEST. IF YOU CAN'T UNDERSTAND THAT THIS IS ABOUT MORE THAN RATINGS...
OH YEAH -- YOU'VE DEFINITELY GOT EVERYONE'S BEST INTEREST AT HEART.
OH, FU--
OKAY, OKAY -- WAIT...
I'M SORRY.
WE'RE ALL MORE THAN A LITTLE ON EDGE HERE.
WE CAN DO BETTER WITH THIS. WE'RE ON OUR WAY TO CHECK SOMETHING OUT RIGHT NOW.
I PROMISE TO PERSONALLY CALL YOU AS SOON AS WE GET BACK.
OKAY. FINE.
THANK YOU, DETECTIVE FOSTER.
WAS THAT NECESSARY?
WHAT, HER NEEDING TO BE AN ASSHOLE?
YOU KNOW SHE'S NOT GOING TO GO AWAY, RIGHT?
JUST SAYIN'.

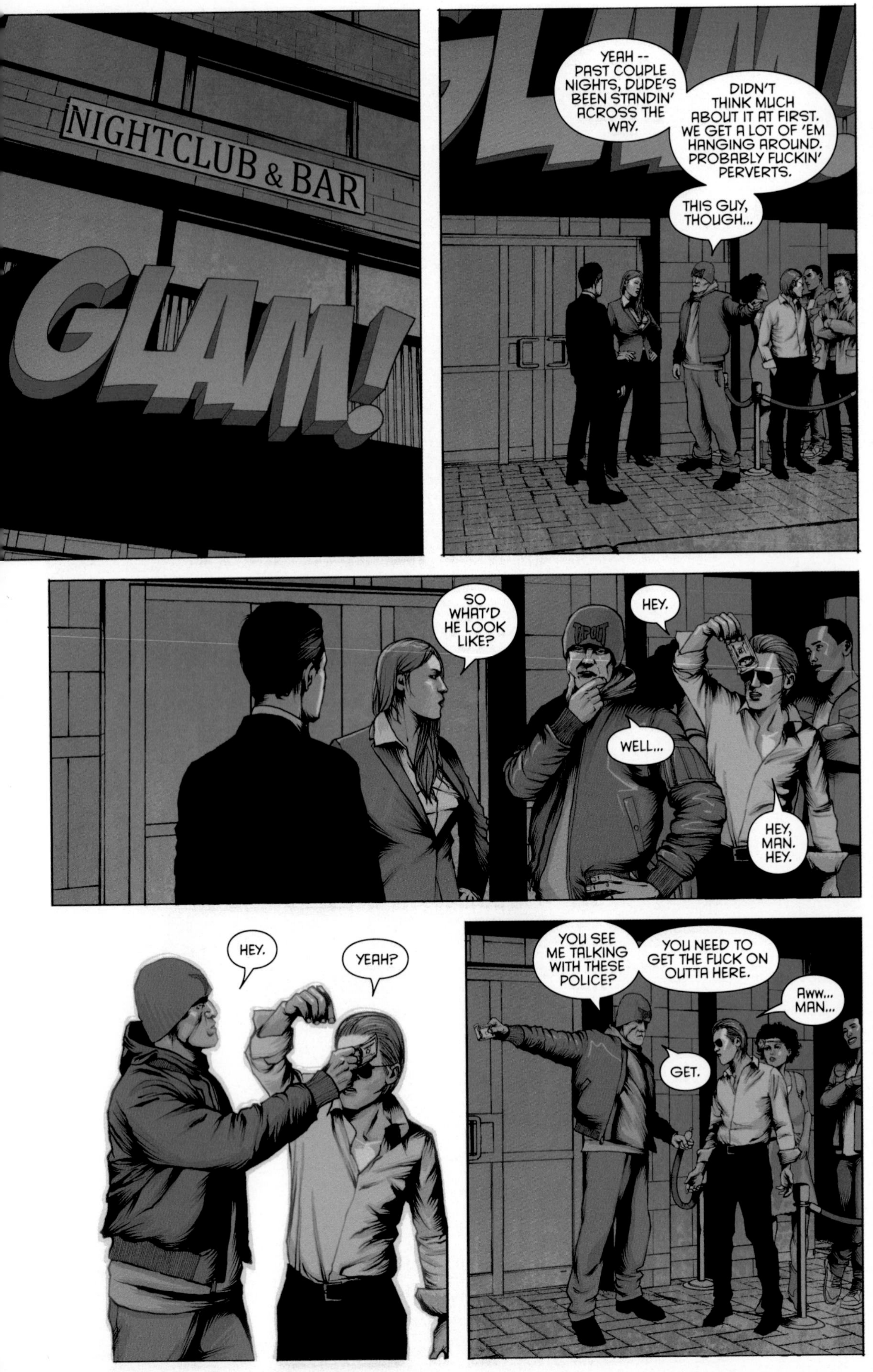
NIGHTCLUB & BAR
GLAM!
YEAH -- PAST COUPLE NIGHTS, DUDE'S BEEN STANDIN' ACROSS THE WAY.
DIDN'T THINK MUCH ABOUT IT AT FIRST. WE GET A LOT OF 'EM HANGING AROUND. PROBABLY FUCKIN' PERVERTS.
THIS GUY, THOUGH...
SO WHAT'D HE LOOK LIKE?
HEY.
WELL...
HEY, MAN. HEY.
HEY.
YEAH?
YOU SEE ME TALKING WITH THESE POLICE?
YOU NEED TO GET THE FUCK ON OUTTA HERE.
AWW... MAN...
GET.

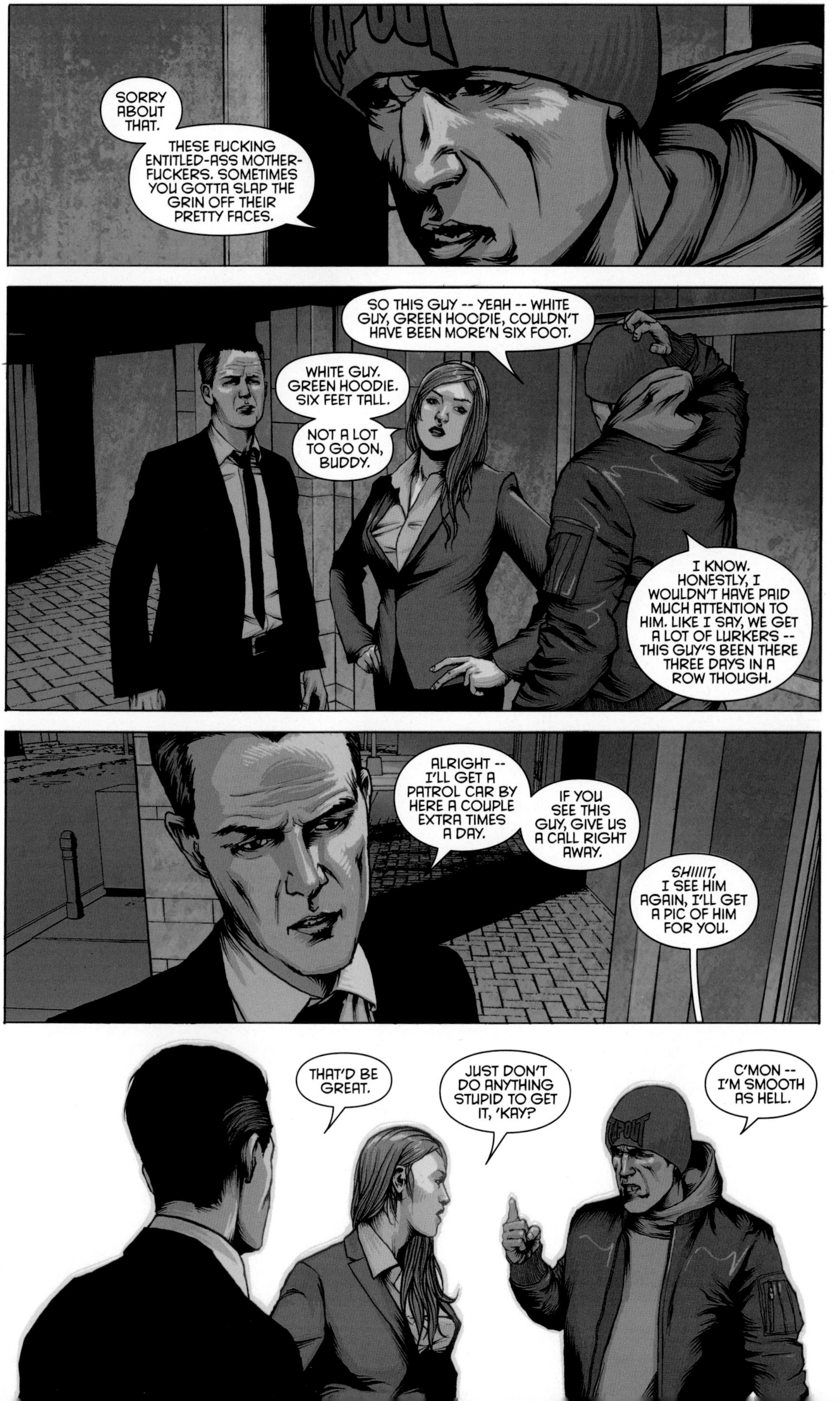
SORRY ABOUT THAT.
THESE FUCKING ENTITLED-ASS MOTHER-FUCKERS. SOMETIMES YOU GOTTA SLAP THE GRIN OFF THEIR PRETTY FACES.
SO THIS GUY -- YEAH -- WHITE GUY, GREEN HOODIE, COULDN'T HAVE BEEN MORE'N SIX FOOT.
WHITE GUY. GREEN HOODIE. SIX FEET TALL.
NOT A LOT TO GO ON, BUDDY.
I KNOW. HONESTLY, I WOULDN'T HAVE PAID MUCH ATTENTION TO HIM. LIKE I SAY, WE GET A LOT OF LURKERS -- THIS GUY'S BEEN THERE THREE DAYS IN A ROW THOUGH.
ALRIGHT -- I'LL GET A PATROL CAR BY HERE A COUPLE EXTRA TIMES A DAY.
IF YOU SEE THIS GUY, GIVE US A CALL RIGHT AWAY.
SHIIIIT, I SEE HIM AGAIN, I'LL GET A PIC OF HIM FOR YOU.
THAT'D BE GREAT.
JUST DON'T DO ANYTHING STUPID TO GET IT, 'KAY?
C'MON -- I'M SMOOTH AS HELL.

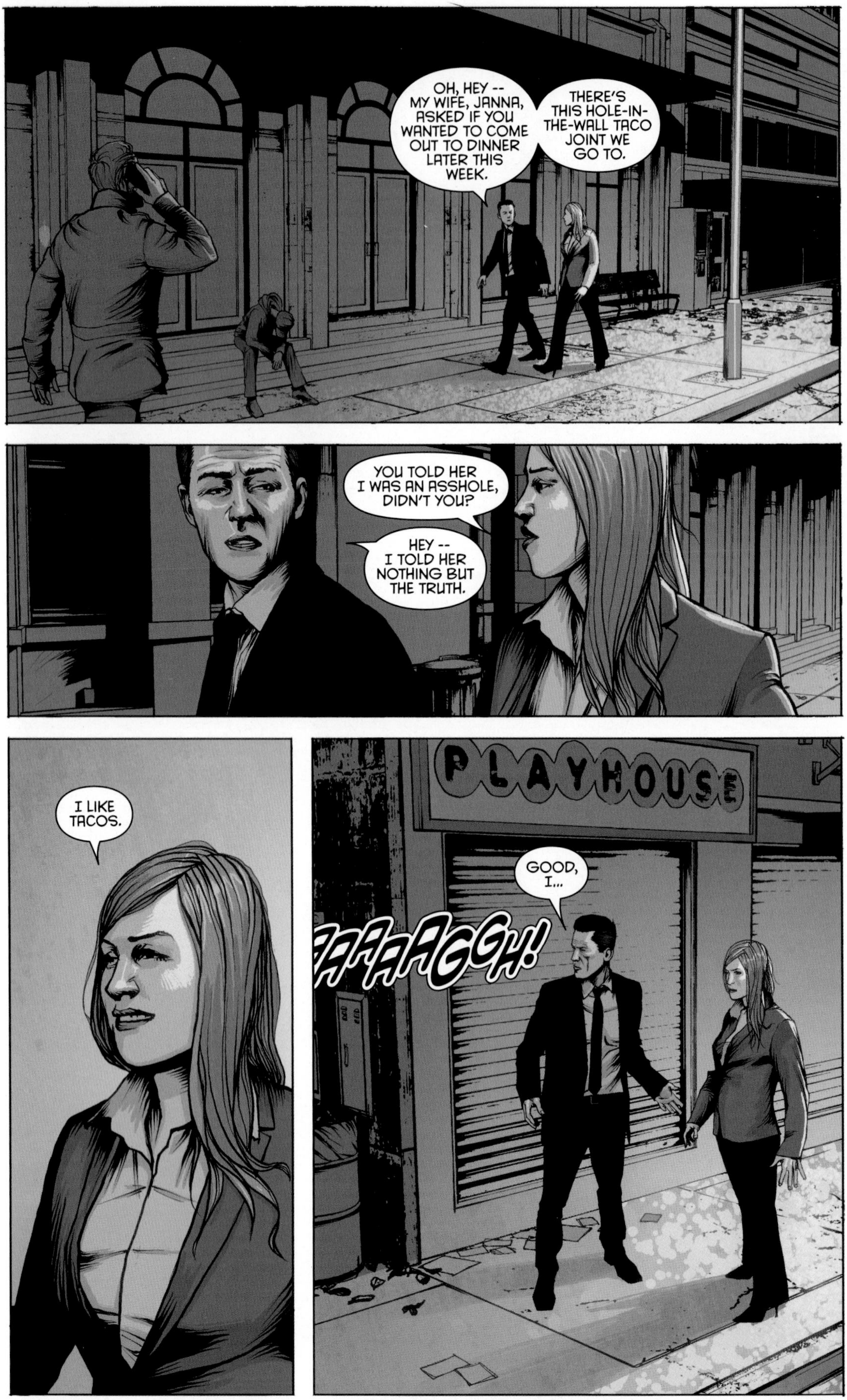
OH, HEY -- MY WIFE, JANNA, ASKED IF YOU WANTED TO COME OUT TO DINNER LATER THIS WEEK.
THERE'S THIS HOLE-IN-THE-WALL TACO JOINT WE GO TO.
YOU TOLD HER I WAS AN ASSHOLE, DIDN'T YOU?
HEY -- I TOLD HER NOTHING BUT THE TRUTH.
I LIKE TACOS.
PLAYHOUSE
GOOD, I...
AAAAAAGGH!

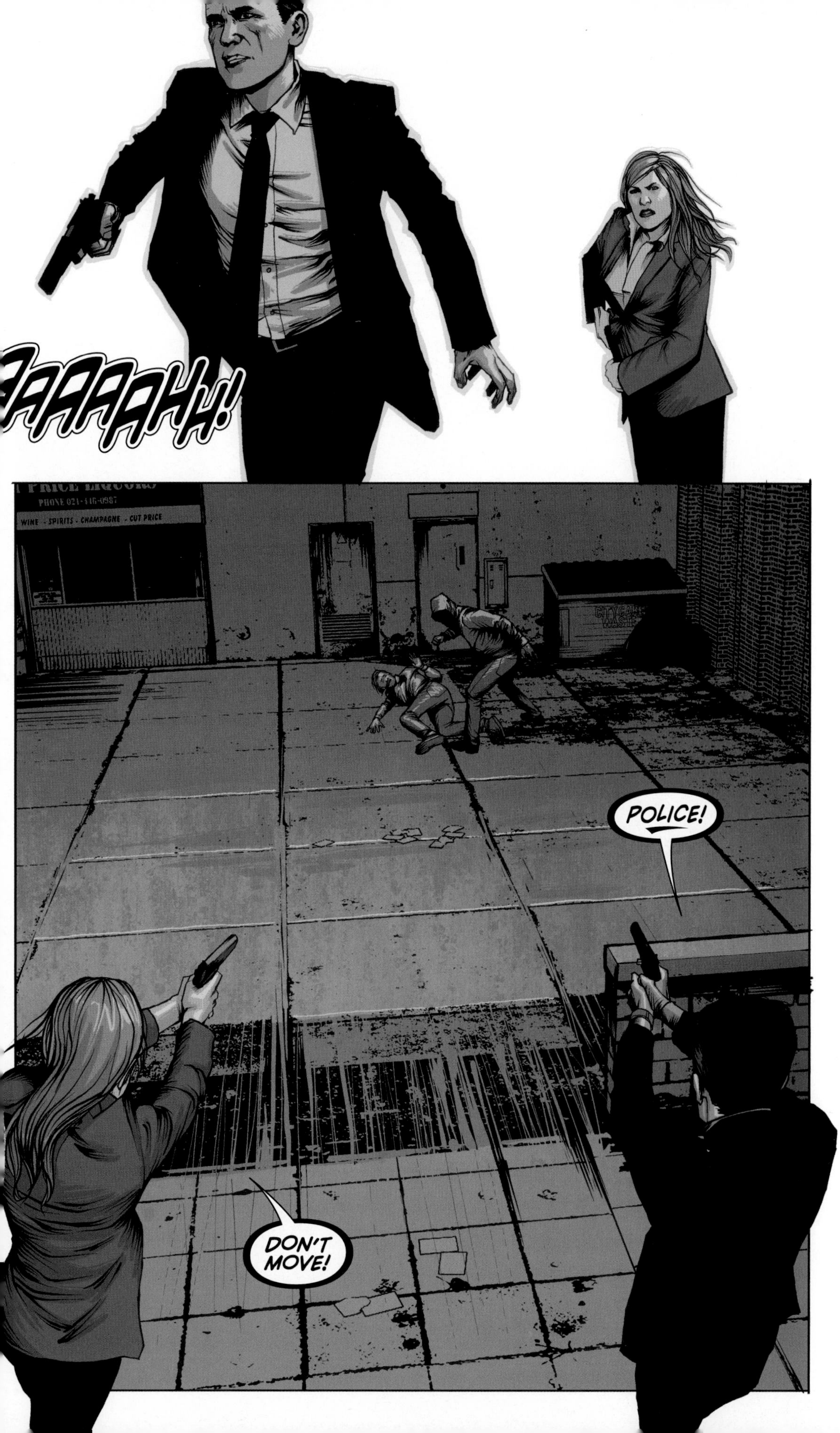
AAAAAHH!
WINE - SPIRITS - CHAMPAGNE - CUT PRICE
POLICE!
DON'T MOVE!

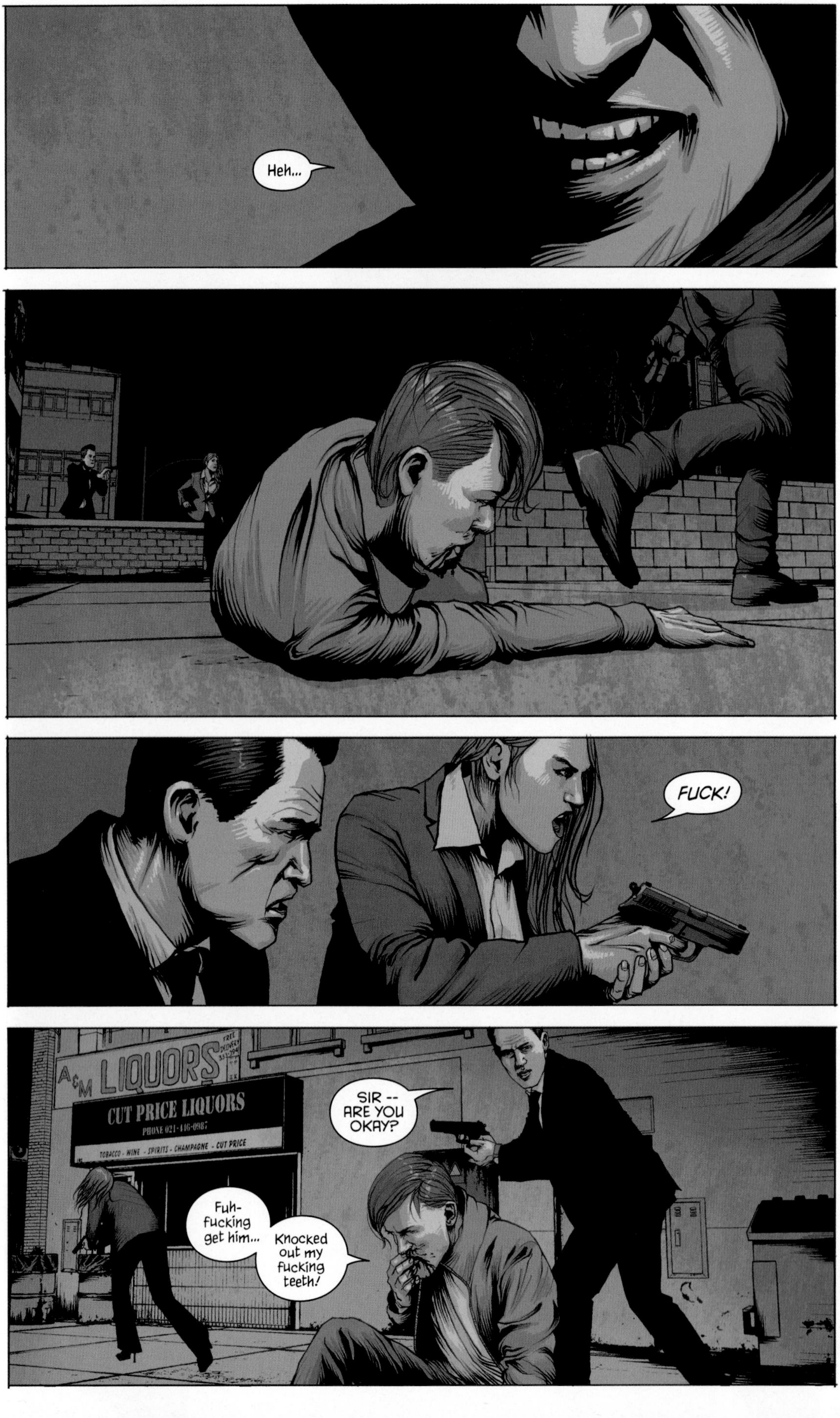
Heh...
FUCK!
A&M LIQUORS
CUT PRICE LIQUORS
PHONE 021-446-0987
TOBACCO - WINE - SPIRITS - CHAMPAGNE - CUT PRICE
SIR -- ARE YOU OKAY?
Fuh- fucking get him...
Knocked out my fucking teeth!

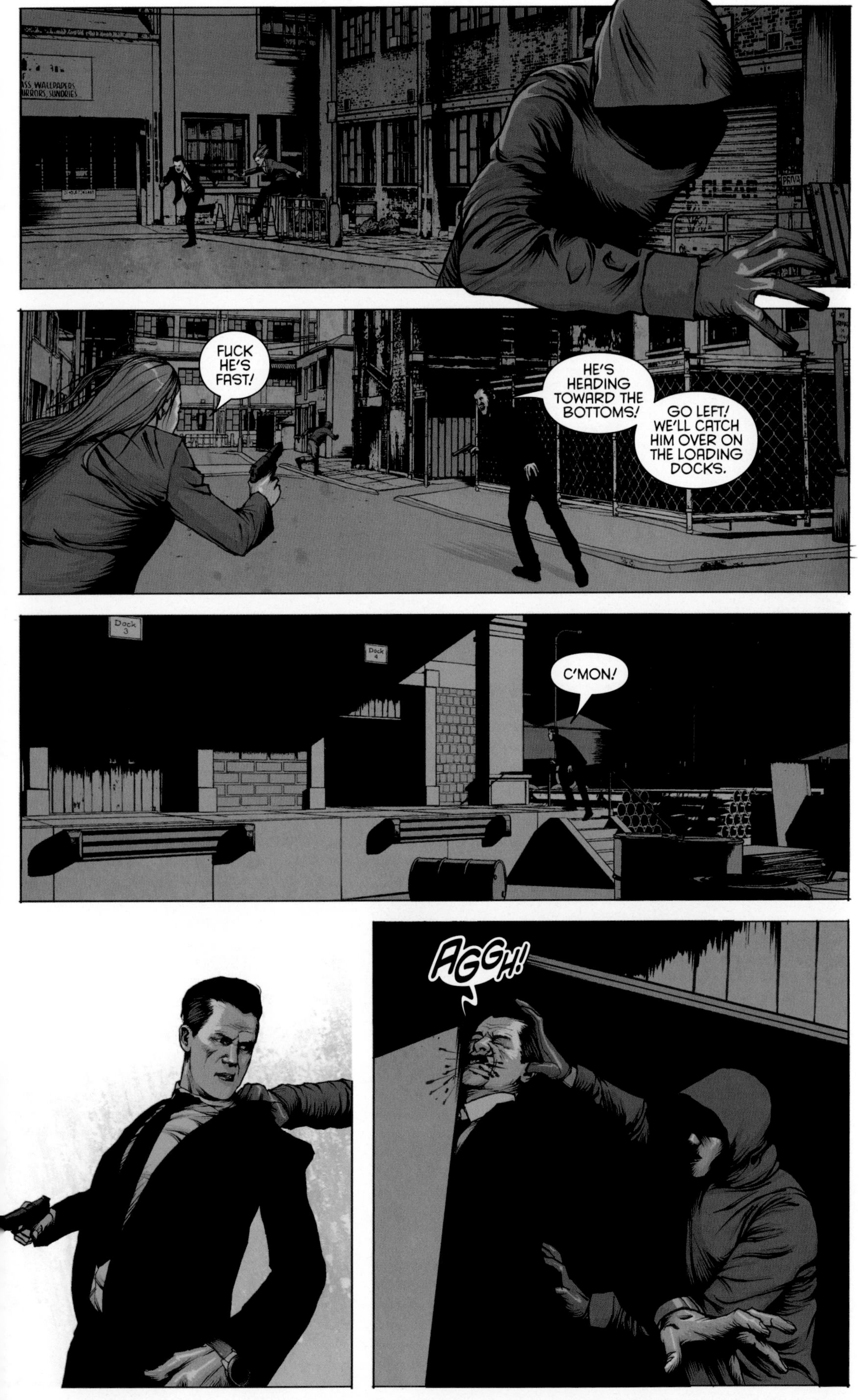
FUCK HE'S FAST!
HE'S HEADING TOWARD THE BOTTOMS!
GO LEFT! WE'LL CATCH HIM OVER ON THE LOADING DOCKS.
C'MON!
AGGH!

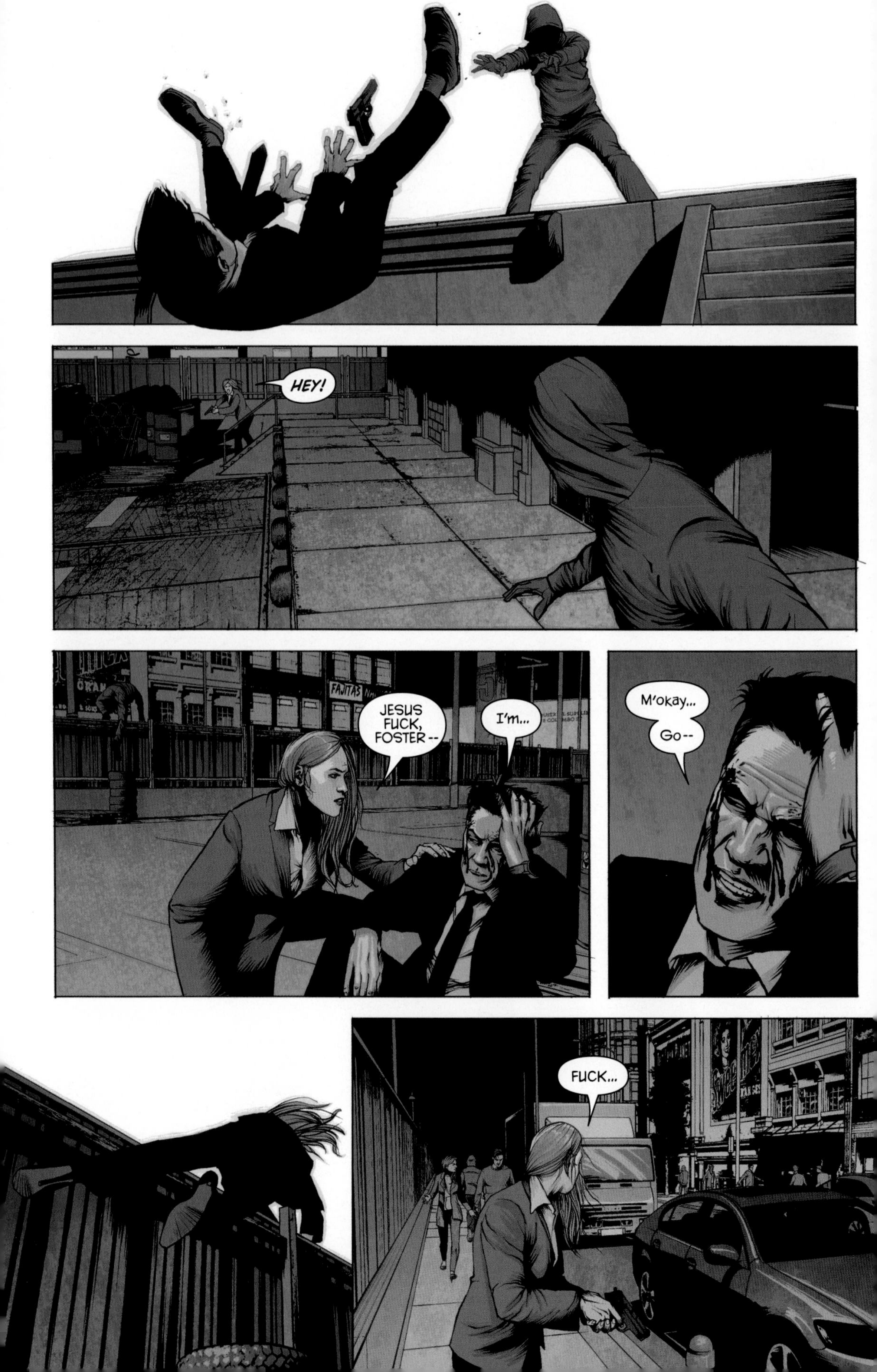
HEY!
FAJITAS
JESUS FUCK, FOSTER --
I'm...
M'okay...
Go--
FUCK...

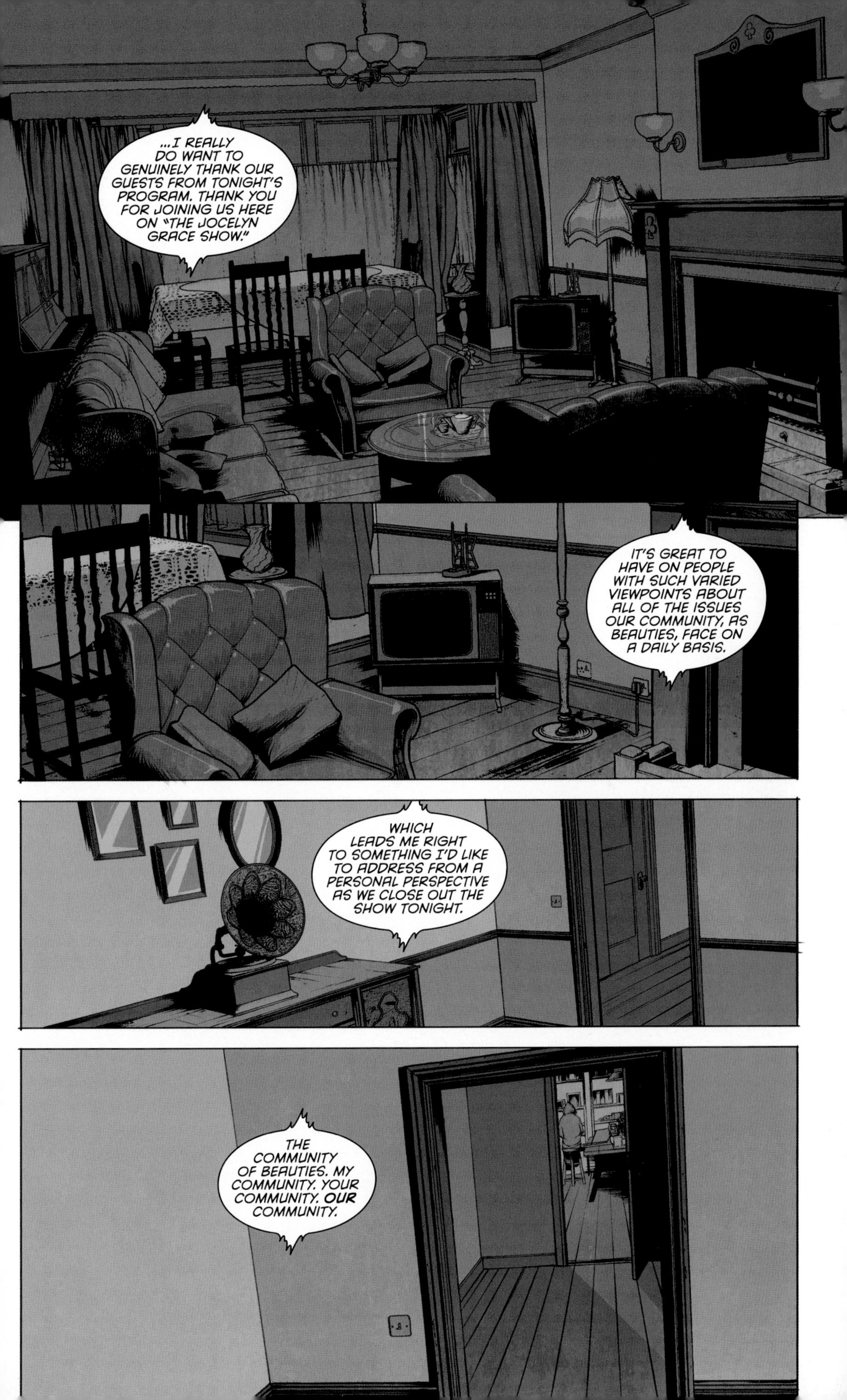
...I REALLY DO WANT TO GENUINELY THANK OUR GUESTS FROM TONIGHT'S PROGRAM. THANK YOU FOR JOINING US HERE ON "THE JOCELYN GRACE SHOW."
IT'S GREAT TO HAVE ON PEOPLE WITH SUCH VARIED VIEWPOINTS ABOUT ALL OF THE ISSUES OUR COMMUNITY, AS BEAUTIES, FACE ON A DAILY BASIS.
WHICH LEADS ME RIGHT TO SOMETHING I'D LIKE TO ADDRESS FROM A PERSONAL PERSPECTIVE AS WE CLOSE OUT THE SHOW TONIGHT.
THE COMMUNITY OF BEAUTIES. MY COMMUNITY. YOUR COMMUNITY. **OUR** COMMUNITY.

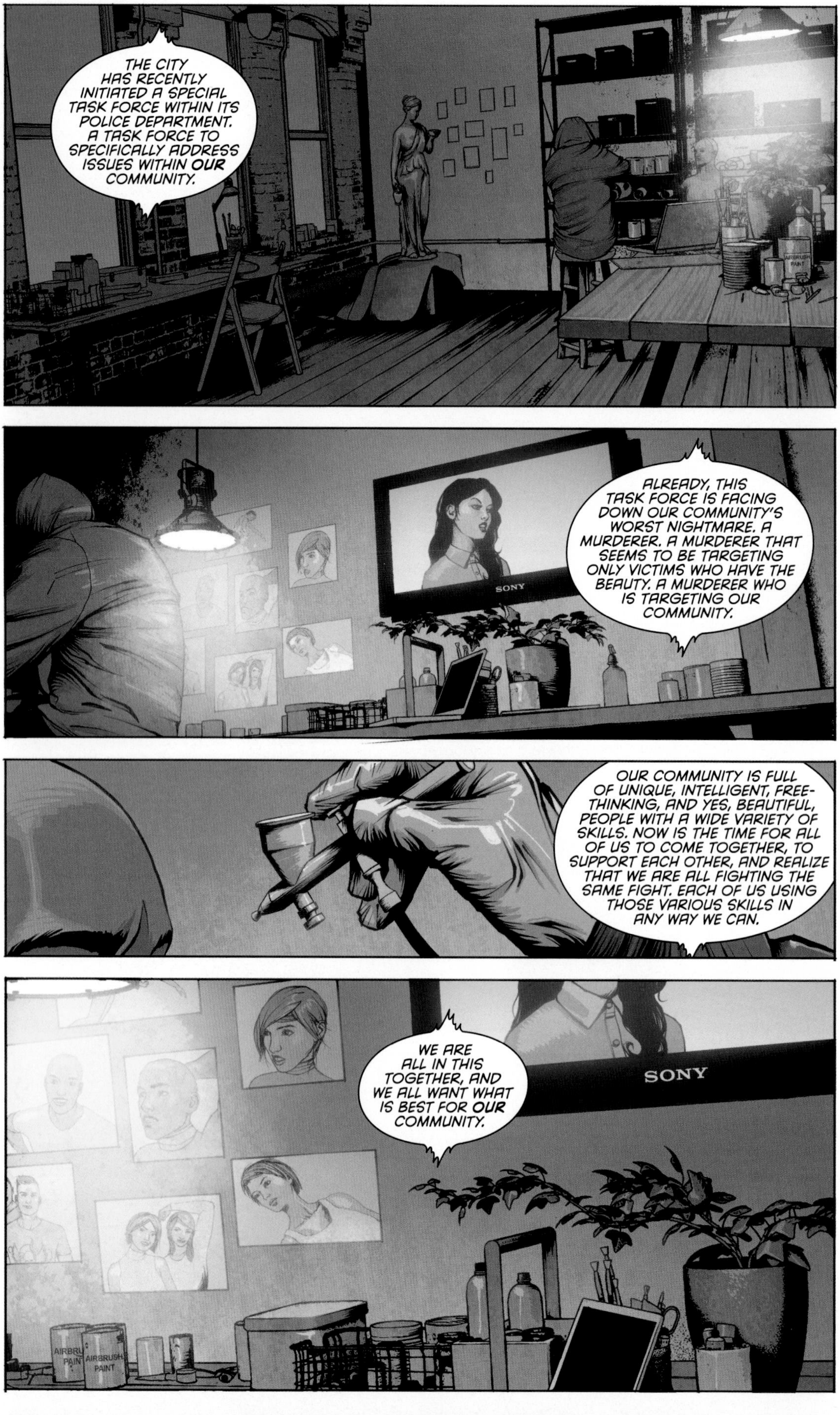
THE CITY HAS RECENTLY INITIATED A SPECIAL TASK FORCE WITHIN ITS POLICE DEPARTMENT. A TASK FORCE TO SPECIFICALLY ADDRESS ISSUES WITHIN **OUR** COMMUNITY.
ALREADY, THIS TASK FORCE IS FACING DOWN OUR COMMUNITY'S WORST NIGHTMARE. A MURDERER. A MURDERER THAT SEEMS TO BE TARGETING ONLY VICTIMS WHO HAVE THE BEAUTY. A MURDERER WHO IS TARGETING OUR COMMUNITY.
SONY
OUR COMMUNITY IS FULL OF UNIQUE, INTELLIGENT, FREE-THINKING, AND YES, BEAUTIFUL, PEOPLE WITH A WIDE VARIETY OF SKILLS. NOW IS THE TIME FOR ALL OF US TO COME TOGETHER, TO SUPPORT EACH OTHER, AND REALIZE THAT WE ARE ALL FIGHTING THE SAME FIGHT. EACH OF US USING THOSE VARIOUS SKILLS IN ANY WAY WE CAN.
WE ARE ALL IN THIS TOGETHER, AND WE ALL WANT WHAT IS BEST FOR **OUR** COMMUNITY.
SONY
AIRBRUSH PAINT

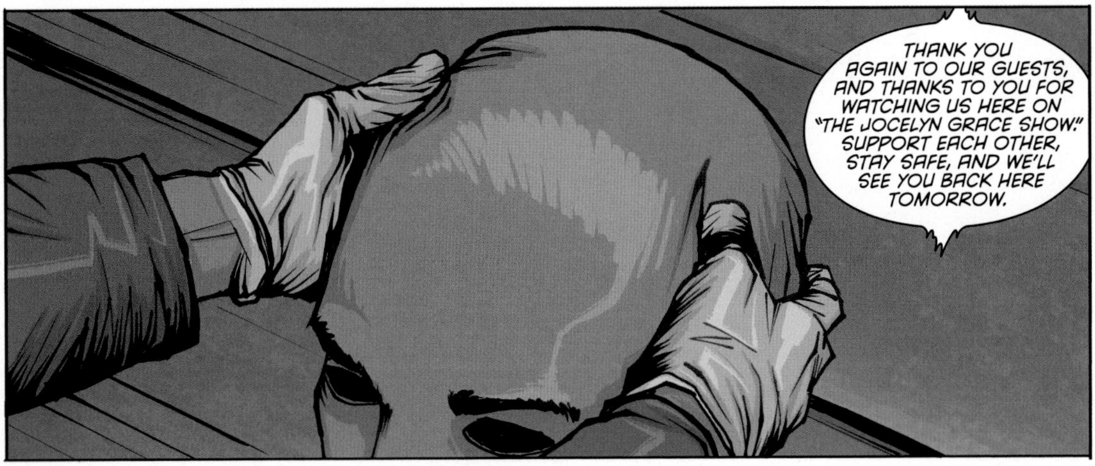
THANK YOU AGAIN TO OUR GUESTS, AND THANKS TO YOU FOR WATCHING US HERE ON "THE JOCELYN GRACE SHOW." SUPPORT EACH OTHER, STAY SAFE, AND WE'LL SEE YOU BACK HERE TOMORROW.

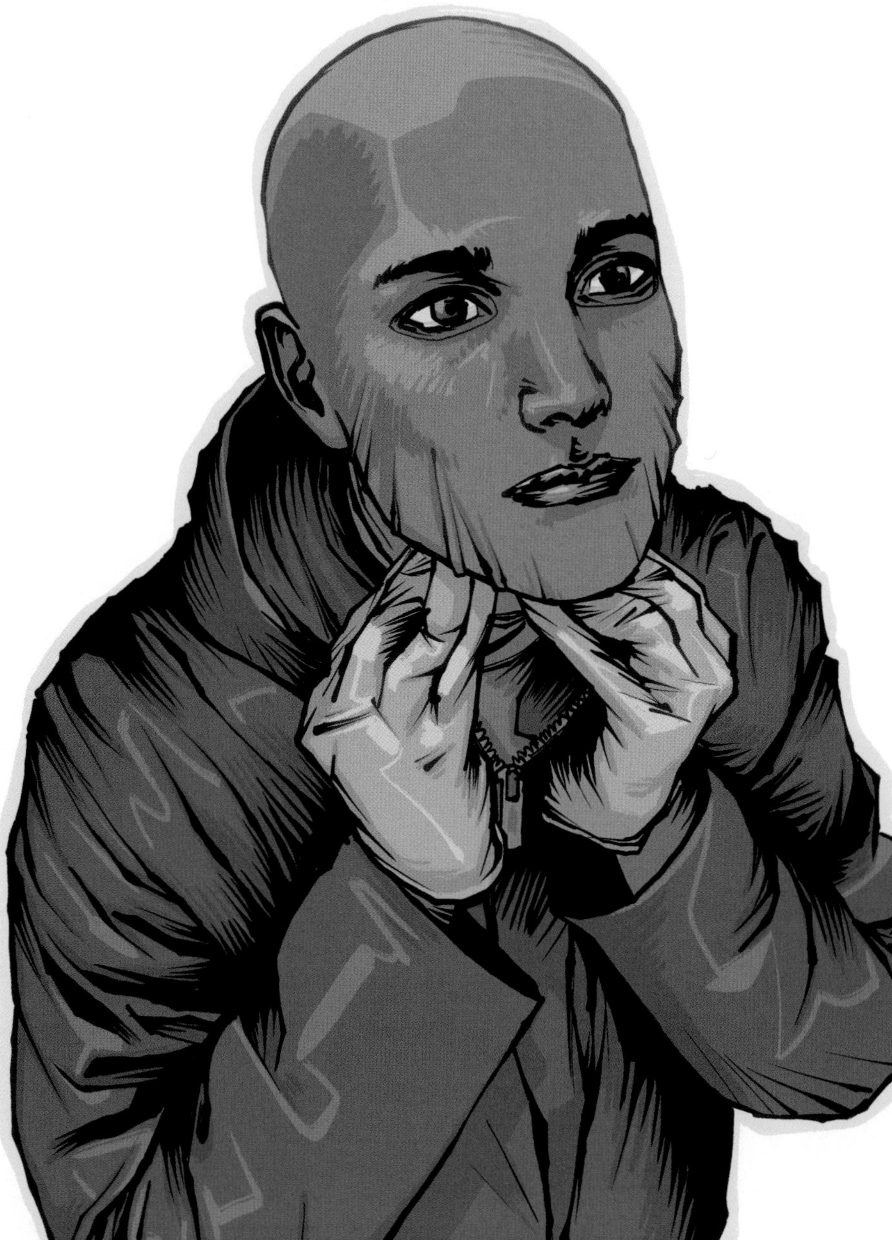

CHAPTER

15

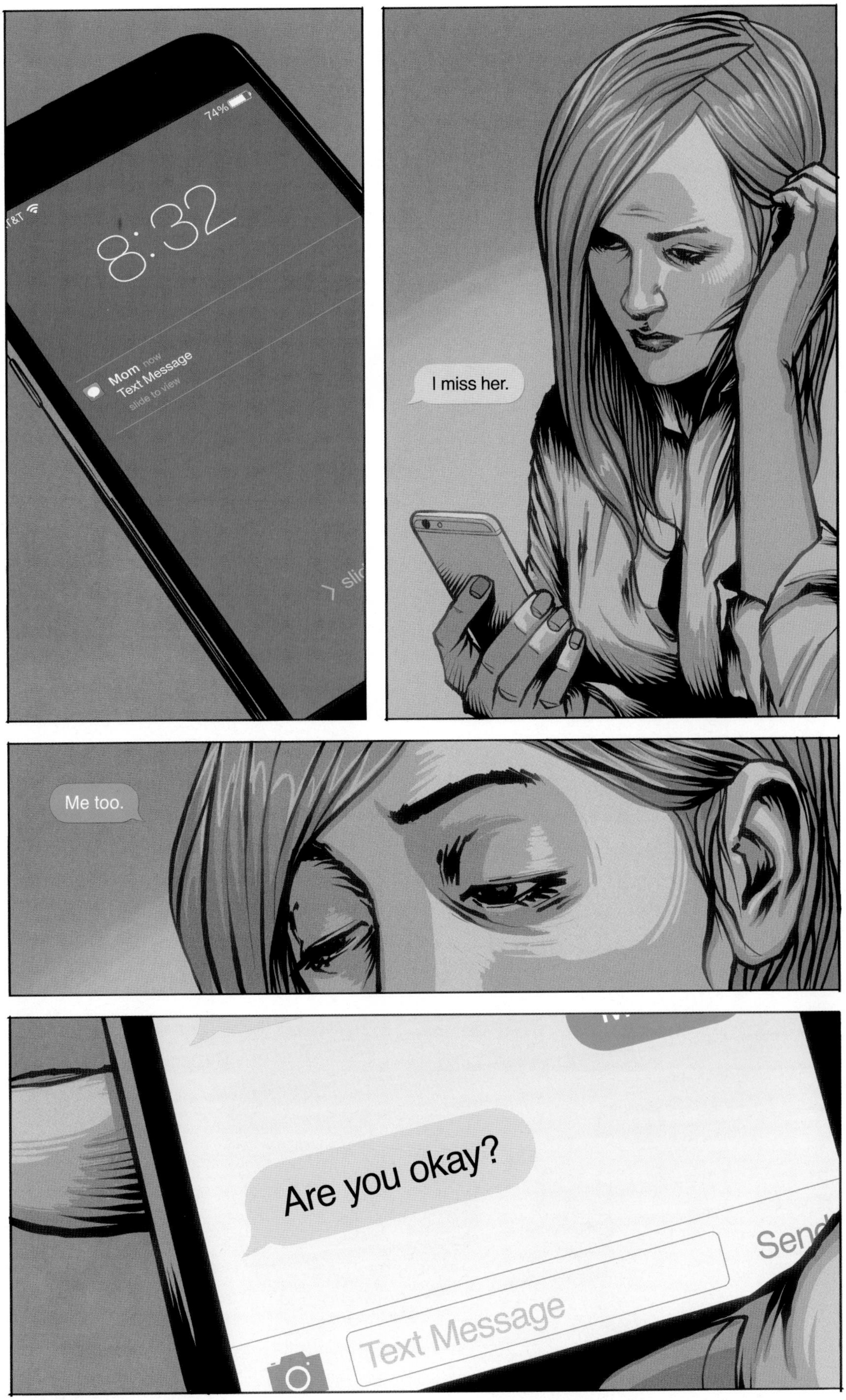
74%
8:32
Mom now
Text Message
slide to view
I miss her.
Me too.
Are you okay?
Text Message

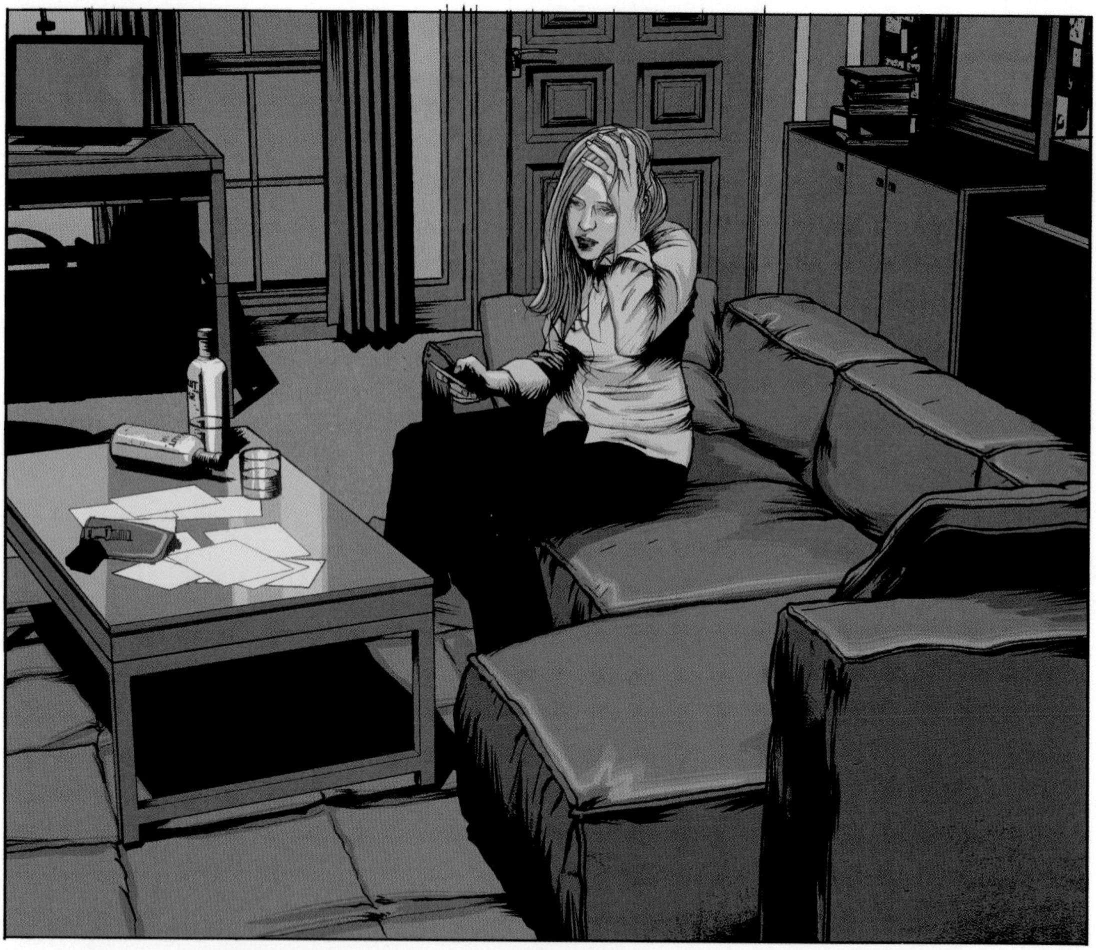

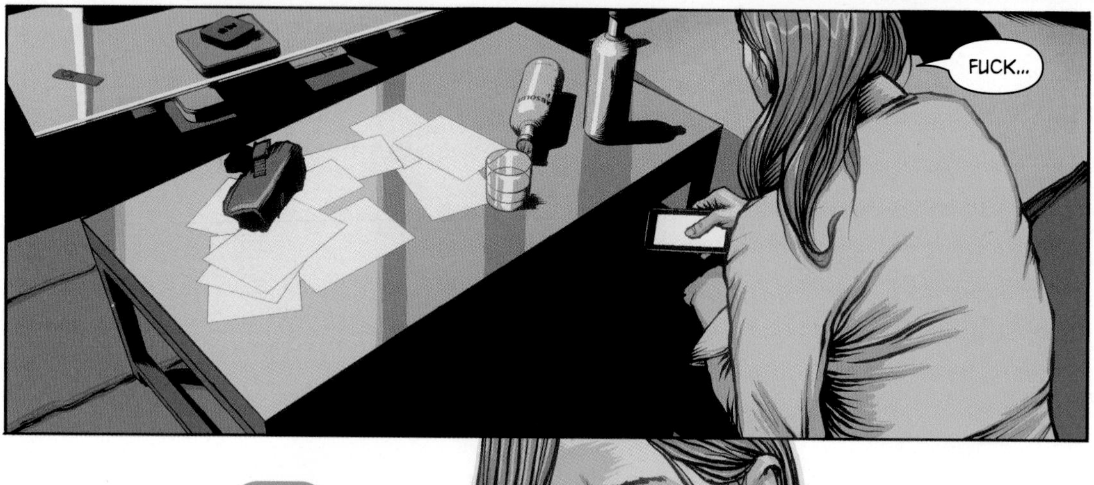
FUCK...

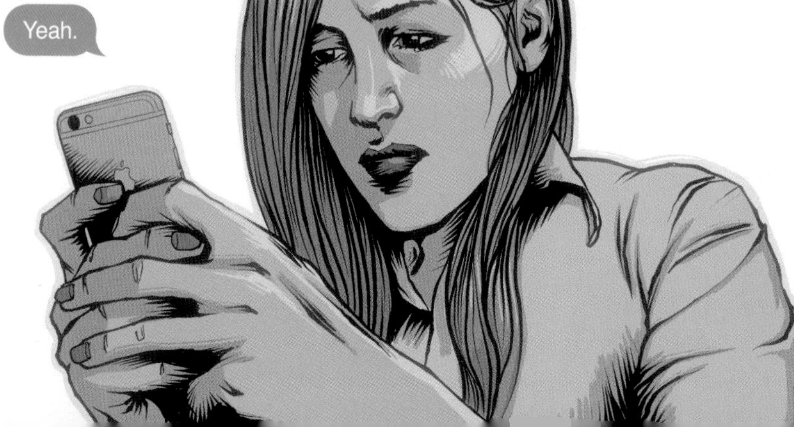
Yeah.

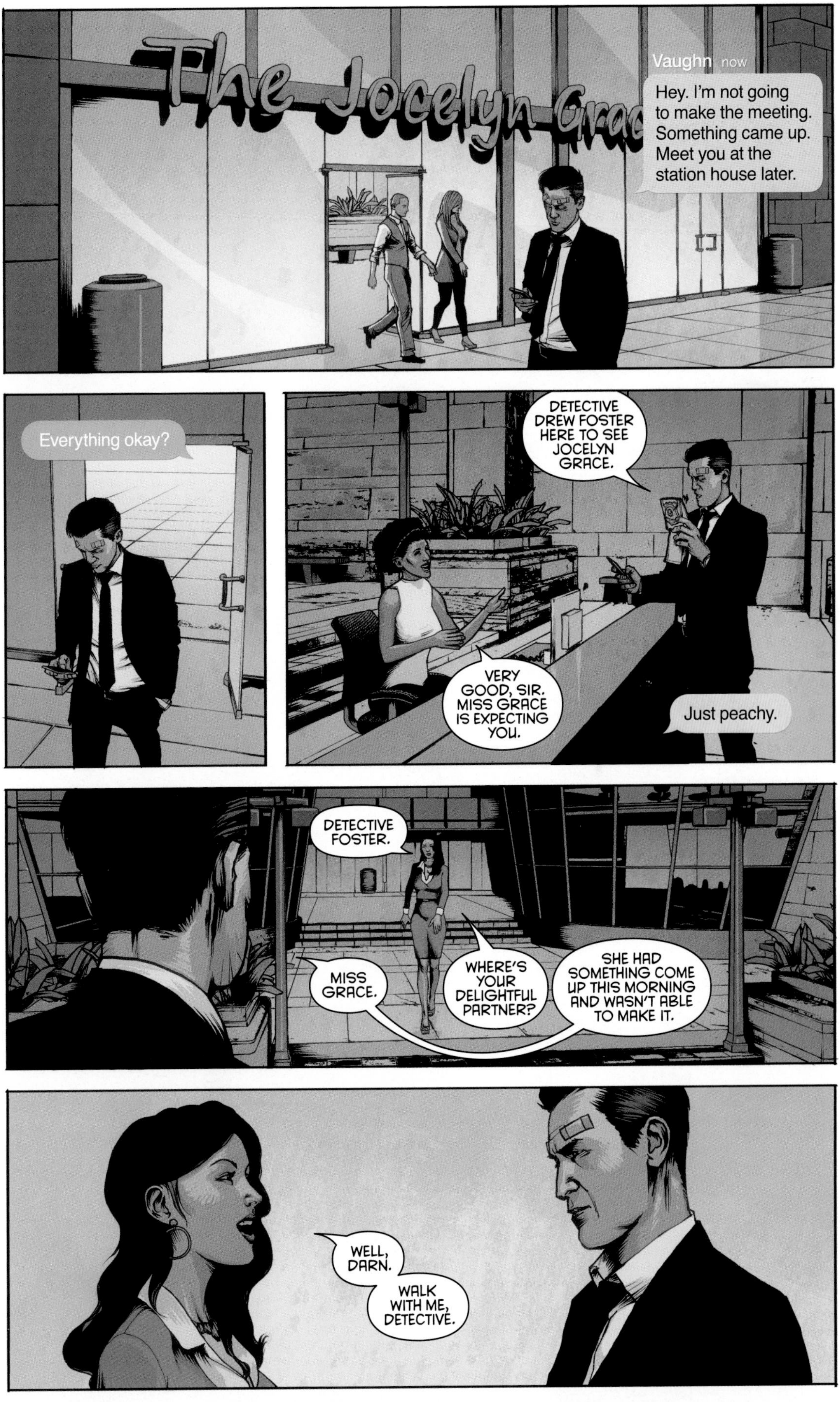
The Jocelyn Grac
Vaughn now
Hey. I'm not going to make the meeting. Something came up. Meet you at the station house later.
Everything okay?
DETECTIVE DREW FOSTER HERE TO SEE JOCELYN GRACE.
VERY GOOD, SIR. MISS GRACE IS EXPECTING YOU.
Just peachy.
DETECTIVE FOSTER.
MISS GRACE.
WHERE'S YOUR DELIGHTFUL PARTNER?
SHE HAD SOMETHING COME UP THIS MORNING AND WASN'T ABLE TO MAKE IT.
WELL, DARN.
WALK WITH ME, DETECTIVE.

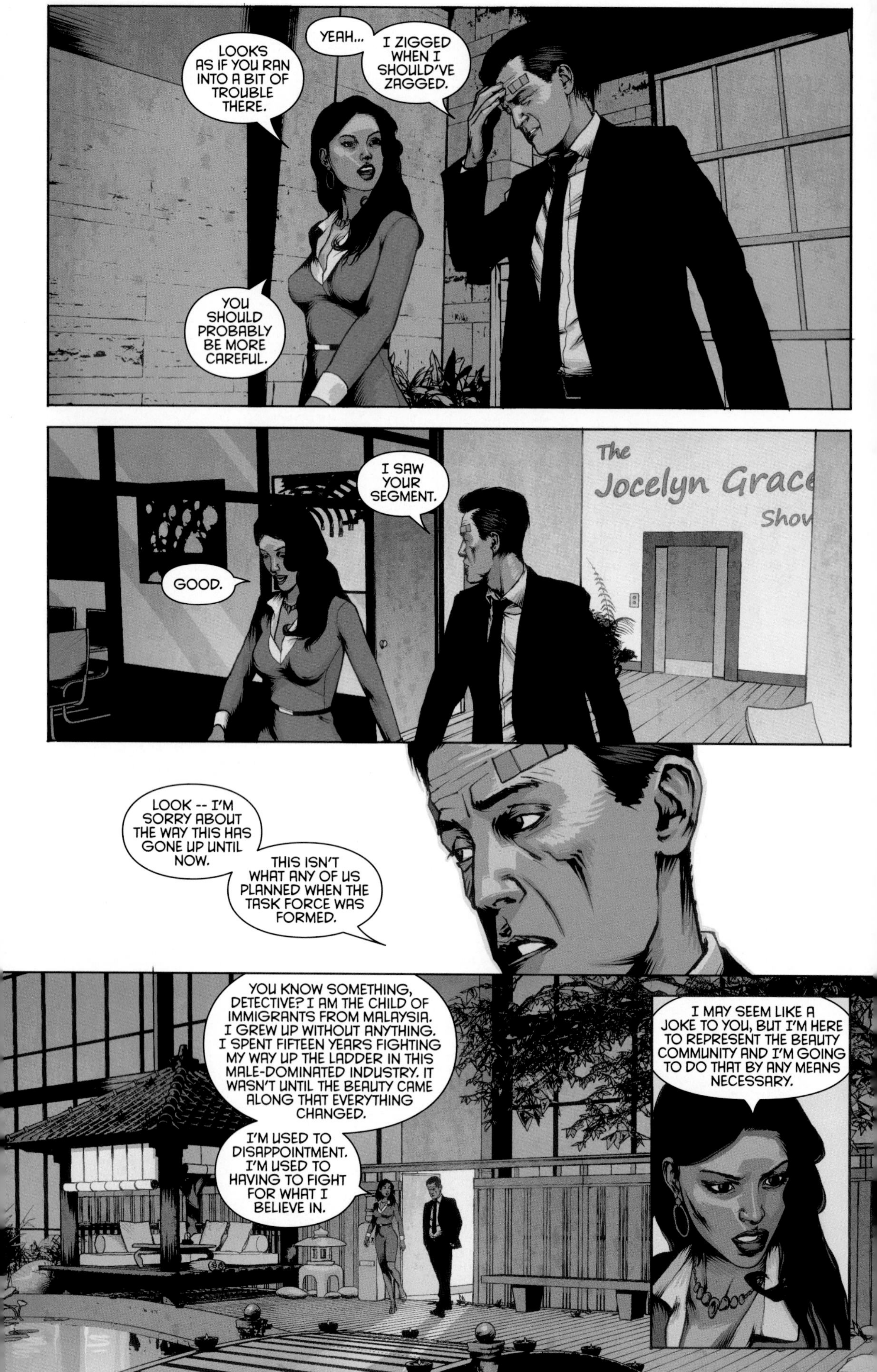
LOOKS AS IF YOU RAN INTO A BIT OF TROUBLE THERE.
YEAH...
I ZIGGED WHEN I SHOULD'VE ZAGGED.
YOU SHOULD PROBABLY BE MORE CAREFUL.
The Jocelyn Grace Show
I SAW YOUR SEGMENT.
GOOD.
LOOK -- I'M SORRY ABOUT THE WAY THIS HAS GONE UP UNTIL NOW.
THIS ISN'T WHAT ANY OF US PLANNED WHEN THE TASK FORCE WAS FORMED.
YOU KNOW SOMETHING, DETECTIVE? I AM THE CHILD OF IMMIGRANTS FROM MALAYSIA. I GREW UP WITHOUT ANYTHING. I SPENT FIFTEEN YEARS FIGHTING MY WAY UP THE LADDER IN THIS MALE-DOMINATED INDUSTRY. IT WASN'T UNTIL THE BEAUTY CAME ALONG THAT EVERYTHING CHANGED.
I'M USED TO DISAPPOINTMENT. I'M USED TO HAVING TO FIGHT FOR WHAT I BELIEVE IN.
I MAY SEEM LIKE A JOKE TO YOU, BUT I'M HERE TO REPRESENT THE BEAUTY COMMUNITY AND I'M GOING TO DO THAT BY ANY MEANS NECESSARY.

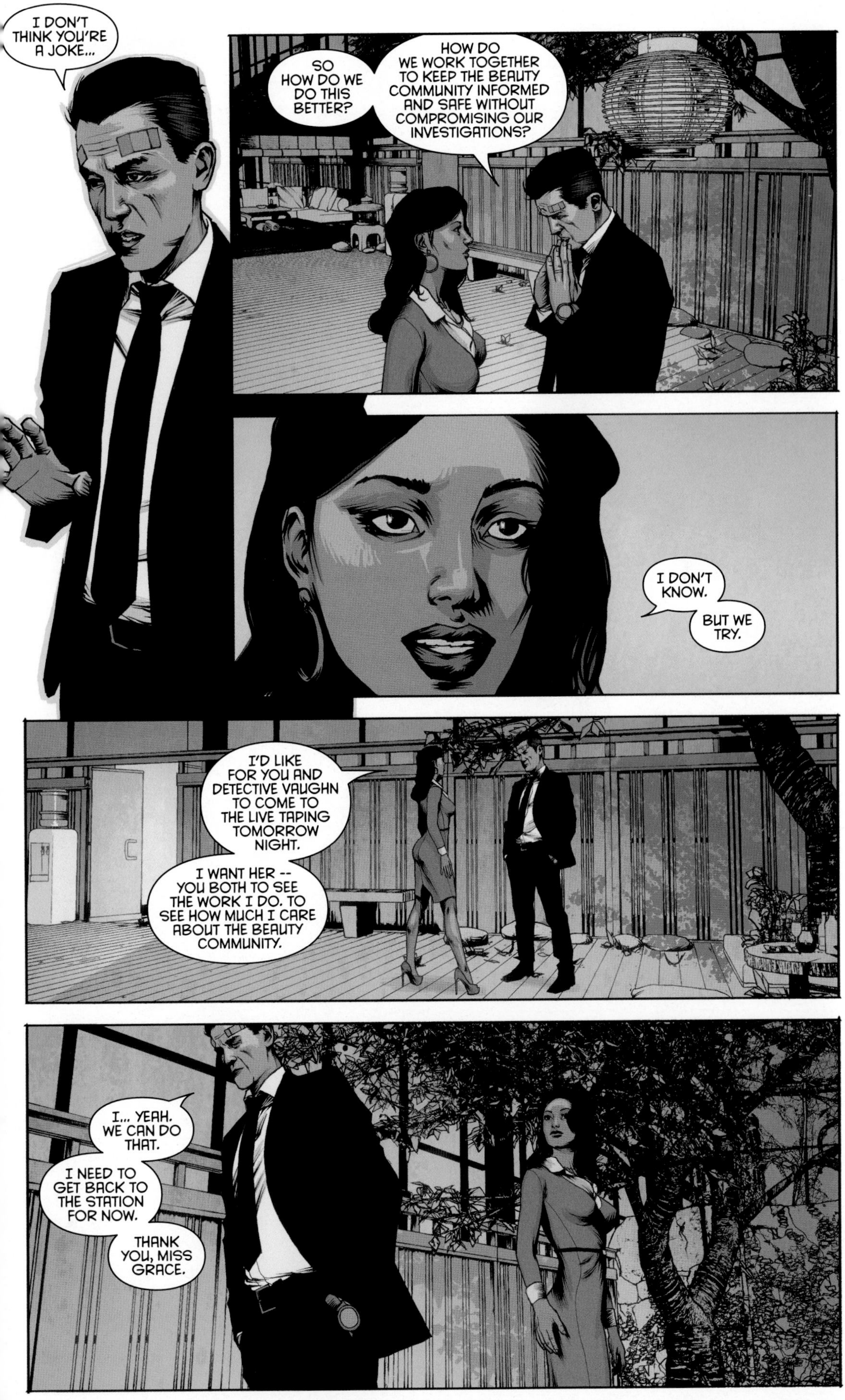
I DON'T THINK YOU'RE A JOKE...
SO HOW DO WE DO THIS BETTER?
HOW DO WE WORK TOGETHER TO KEEP THE BEAUTY COMMUNITY INFORMED AND SAFE WITHOUT COMPROMISING OUR INVESTIGATIONS?
I DON'T KNOW.
BUT WE TRY.
I'D LIKE FOR YOU AND DETECTIVE VAUGHN TO COME TO THE LIVE TAPING TOMORROW NIGHT.
I WANT HER -- YOU BOTH TO SEE THE WORK I DO. TO SEE HOW MUCH I CARE ABOUT THE BEAUTY COMMUNITY.
I... YEAH. WE CAN DO THAT.
I NEED TO GET BACK TO THE STATION FOR NOW.
THANK YOU, MISS GRACE.

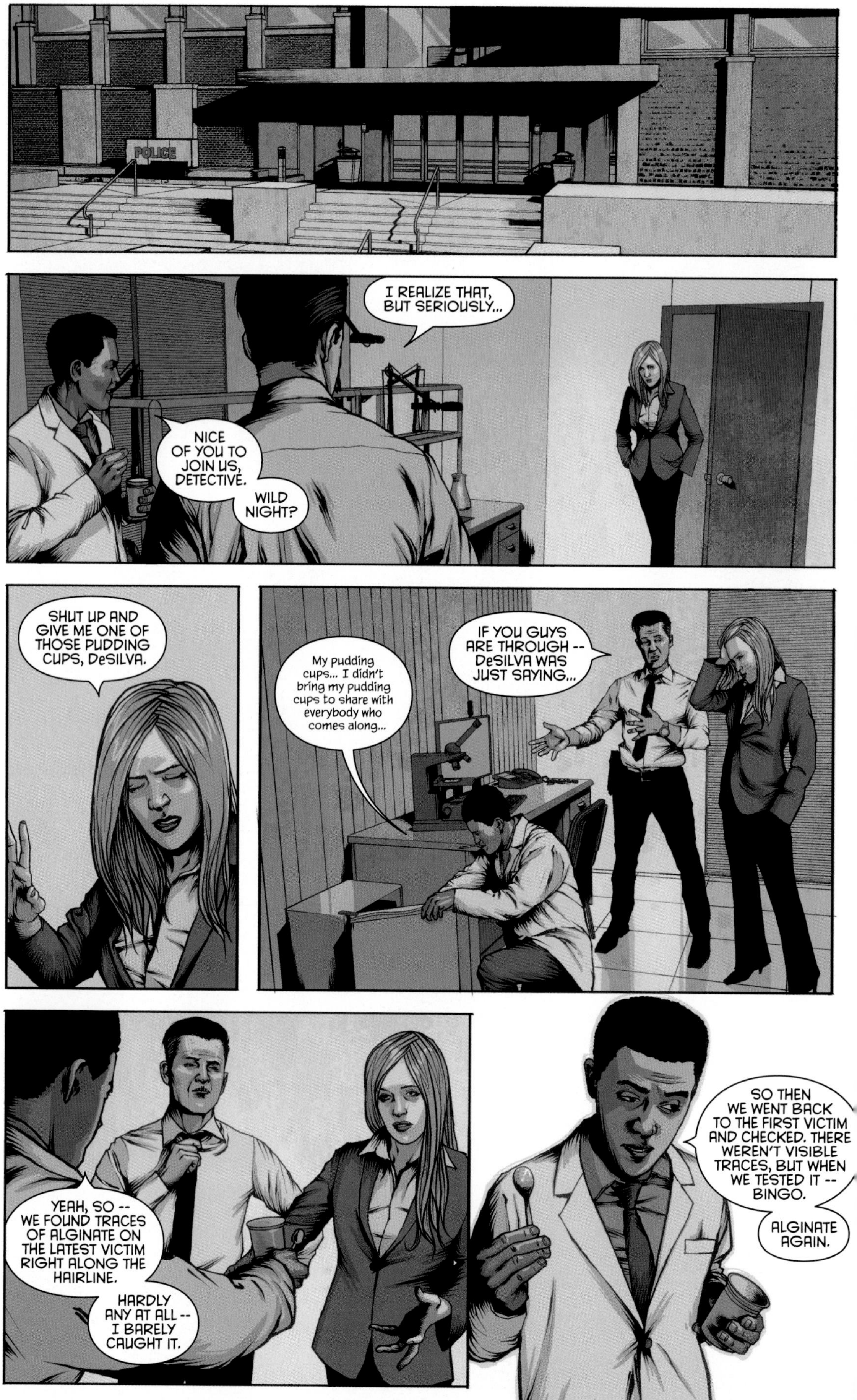
POLICE
I REALIZE THAT, BUT SERIOUSLY...
NICE OF YOU TO JOIN US, DETECTIVE.
WILD NIGHT?
SHUT UP AND GIVE ME ONE OF THOSE PUDDING CUPS, DeSILVA.
My pudding cups... I didn't bring my pudding cups to share with everybody who comes along...
IF YOU GUYS ARE THROUGH -- DeSILVA WAS JUST SAYING...
YEAH, SO -- WE FOUND TRACES OF ALGINATE ON THE LATEST VICTIM RIGHT ALONG THE HAIRLINE.
HARDLY ANY AT ALL -- I BARELY CAUGHT IT.
SO THEN WE WENT BACK TO THE FIRST VICTIM AND CHECKED. THERE WEREN'T VISIBLE TRACES, BUT WHEN WE TESTED IT -- BINGO.
ALGINATE AGAIN.

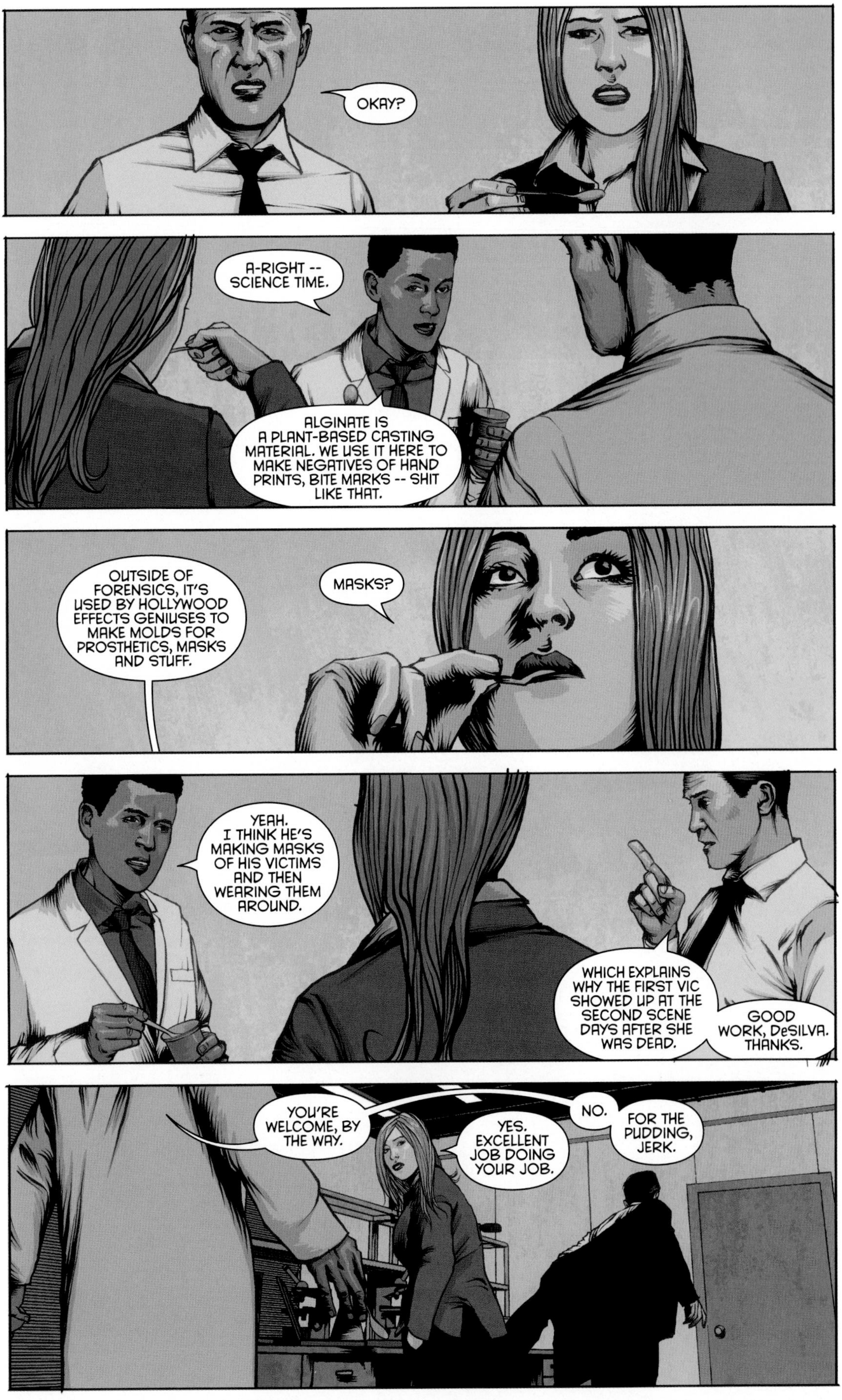
OKAY?
A-RIGHT -- SCIENCE TIME.
ALGINATE IS A PLANT-BASED CASTING MATERIAL. WE USE IT HERE TO MAKE NEGATIVES OF HAND PRINTS, BITE MARKS -- SHIT LIKE THAT.
OUTSIDE OF FORENSICS, IT'S USED BY HOLLYWOOD EFFECTS GENIUSES TO MAKE MOLDS FOR PROSTHETICS, MASKS AND STUFF.
MASKS?
YEAH. I THINK HE'S MAKING MASKS OF HIS VICTIMS AND THEN WEARING THEM AROUND.
WHICH EXPLAINS WHY THE FIRST VIC SHOWED UP AT THE SECOND SCENE DAYS AFTER SHE WAS DEAD.
GOOD WORK, DeSILVA. THANKS.
YOU'RE WELCOME, BY THE WAY.
YES. EXCELLENT JOB DOING YOUR JOB.
NO.
FOR THE PUDDING, JERK.

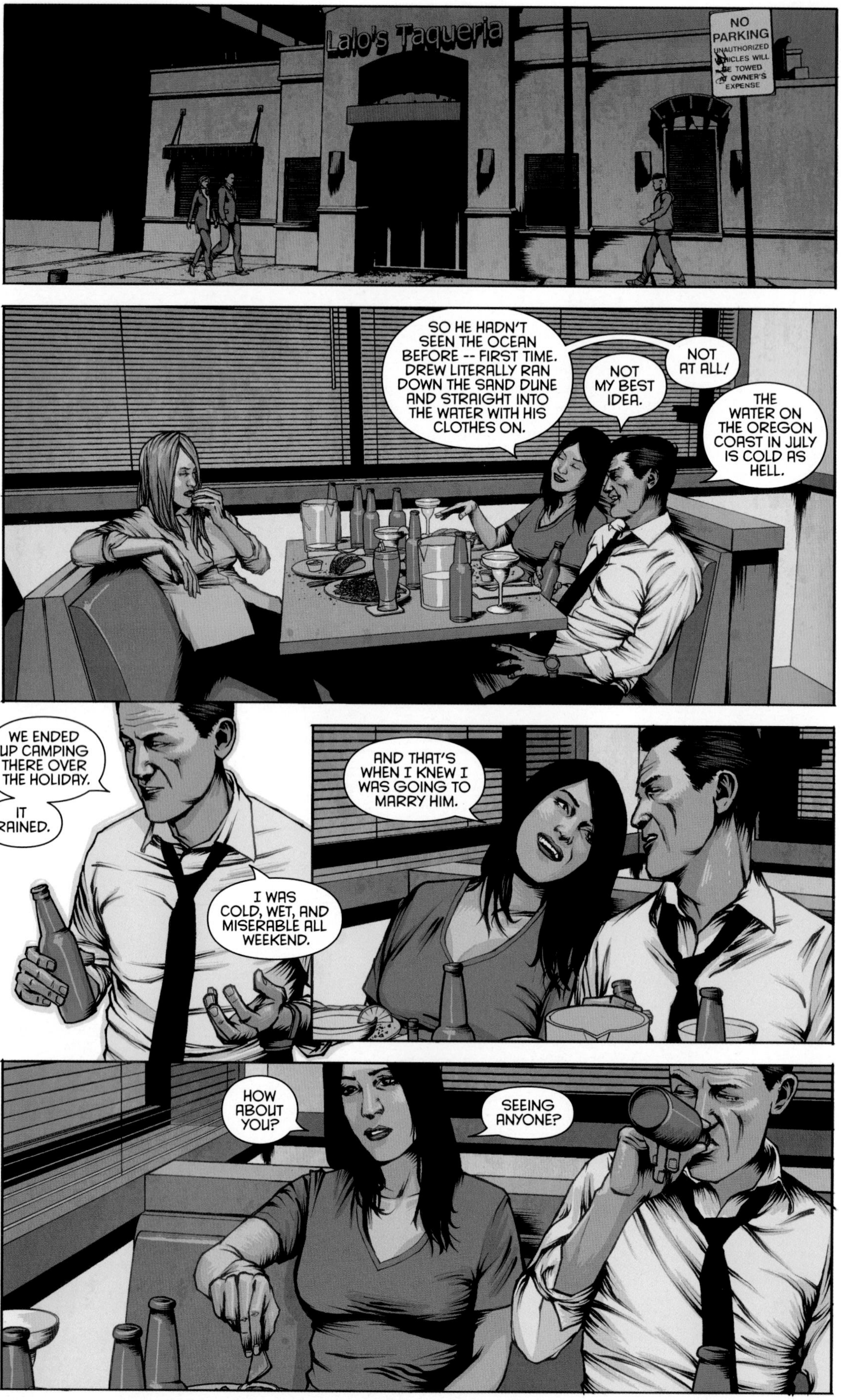
Lalo's Taqueria
NO PARKING UNAUTHORIZED VEHICLES WILL BE TOWED AT OWNER'S EXPENSE
SO HE HADN'T SEEN THE OCEAN BEFORE -- FIRST TIME. DREW LITERALLY RAN DOWN THE SAND DUNE AND STRAIGHT INTO THE WATER WITH HIS CLOTHES ON.
NOT MY BEST IDEA.
NOT AT ALL!
THE WATER ON THE OREGON COAST IN JULY IS COLD AS HELL.
WE ENDED UP CAMPING THERE OVER THE HOLIDAY.
IT RAINED.
I WAS COLD, WET, AND MISERABLE ALL WEEKEND.
AND THAT'S WHEN I KNEW I WAS GOING TO MARRY HIM.
HOW ABOUT YOU?
SEEING ANYONE?

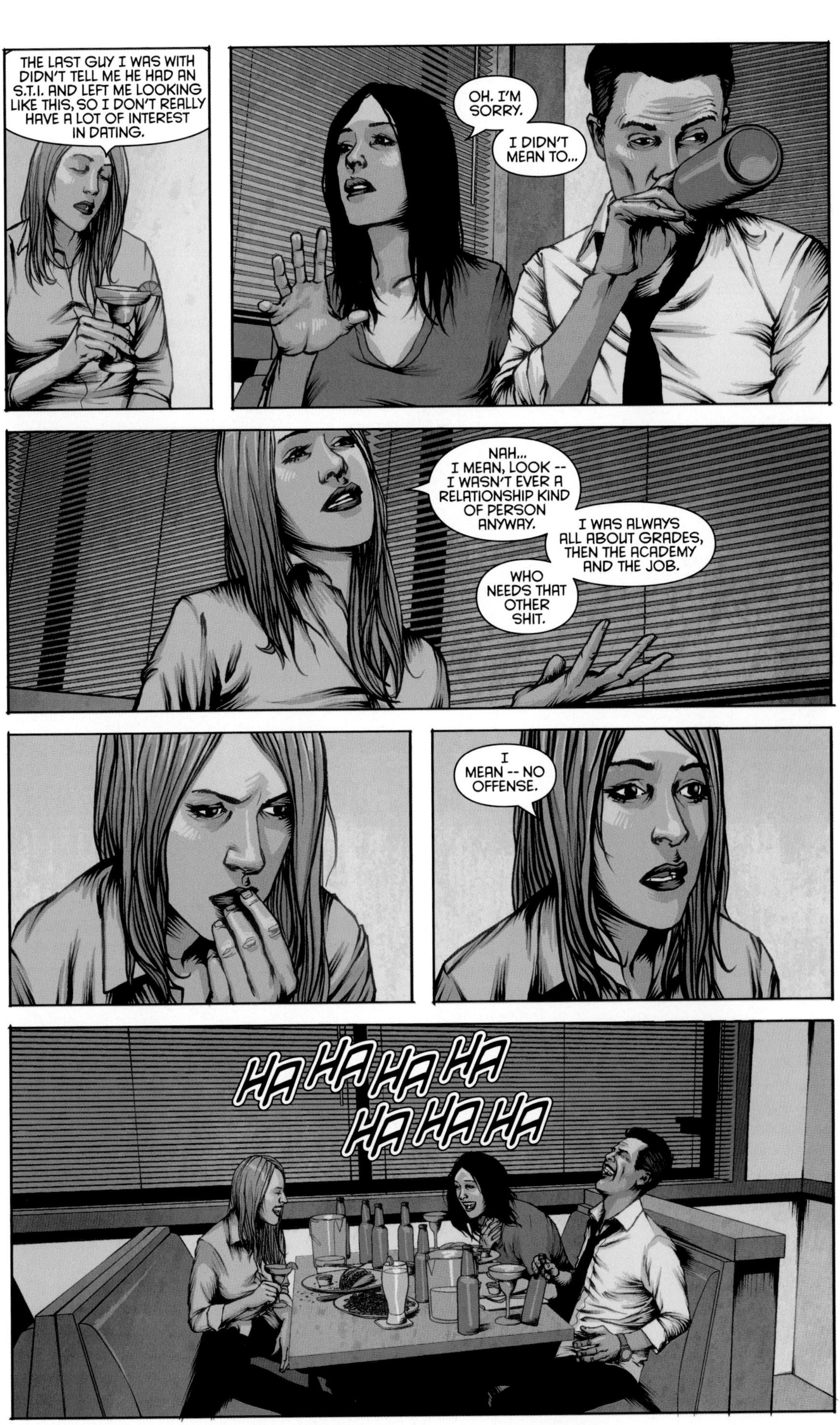
THE LAST GUY I WAS WITH DIDN'T TELL ME HE HAD AN S.T.I. AND LEFT ME LOOKING LIKE THIS, SO I DON'T REALLY HAVE A LOT OF INTEREST IN DATING.
OH. I'M SORRY.
I DIDN'T MEAN TO...
NAH... I MEAN, LOOK -- I WASN'T EVER A RELATIONSHIP KIND OF PERSON ANYWAY.
I WAS ALWAYS ALL ABOUT GRADES, THEN THE ACADEMY AND THE JOB.
WHO NEEDS THAT OTHER SHIT.
I MEAN -- NO OFFENSE.
HA HA HA HA HA
HA HA HA HA

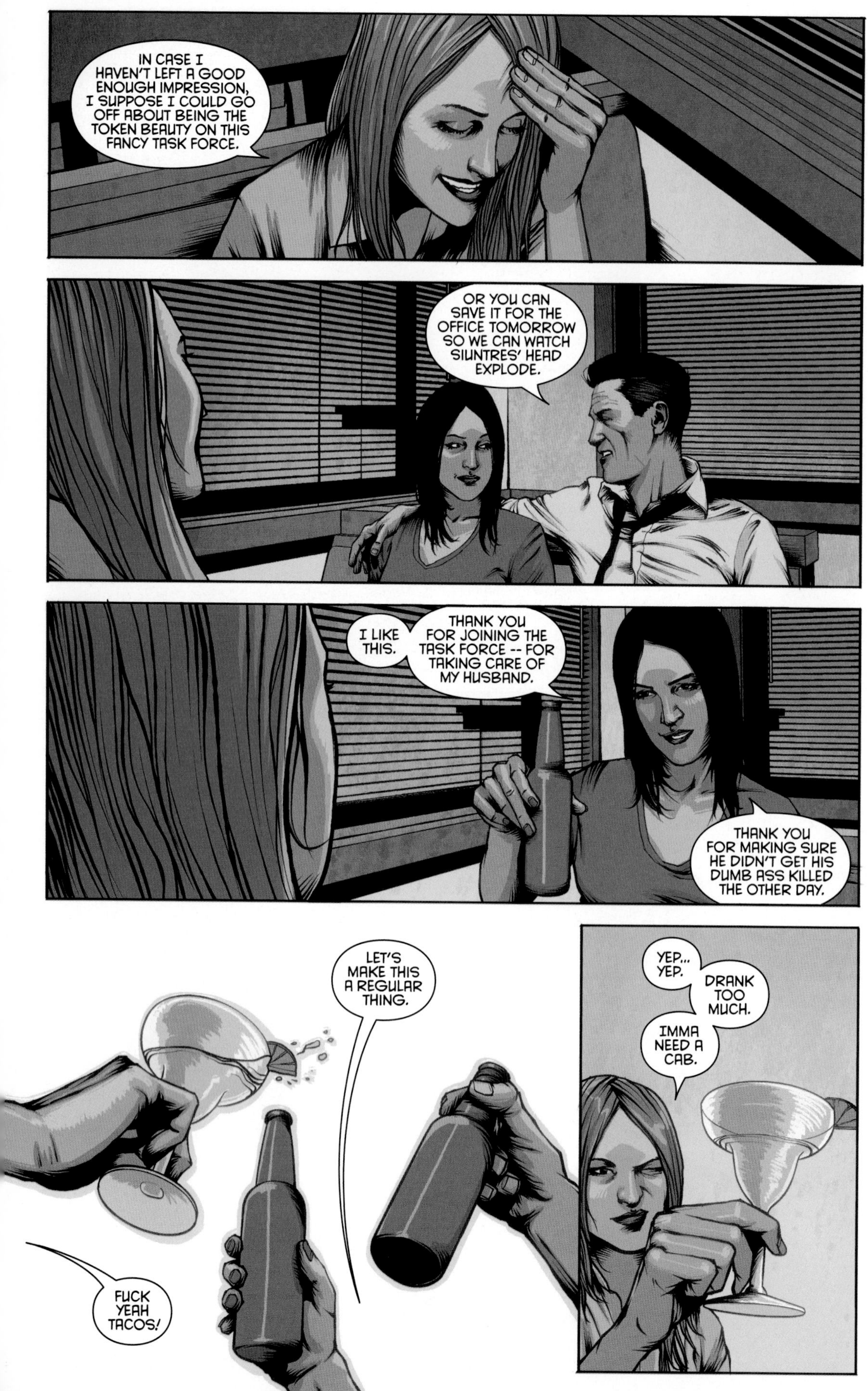
IN CASE I HAVEN'T LEFT A GOOD ENOUGH IMPRESSION, I SUPPOSE I COULD GO OFF ABOUT BEING THE TOKEN BEAUTY ON THIS FANCY TASK FORCE.
OR YOU CAN SAVE IT FOR THE OFFICE TOMORROW SO WE CAN WATCH SIUNTRES' HEAD EXPLODE.
I LIKE THIS.
THANK YOU FOR JOINING THE TASK FORCE -- FOR TAKING CARE OF MY HUSBAND.
THANK YOU FOR MAKING SURE HE DIDN'T GET HIS DUMB ASS KILLED THE OTHER DAY.
LET'S MAKE THIS A REGULAR THING.
FUCK YEAH TACOS!
YEP... YEP.
DRANK TOO MUCH.
IMMA NEED A CAB.

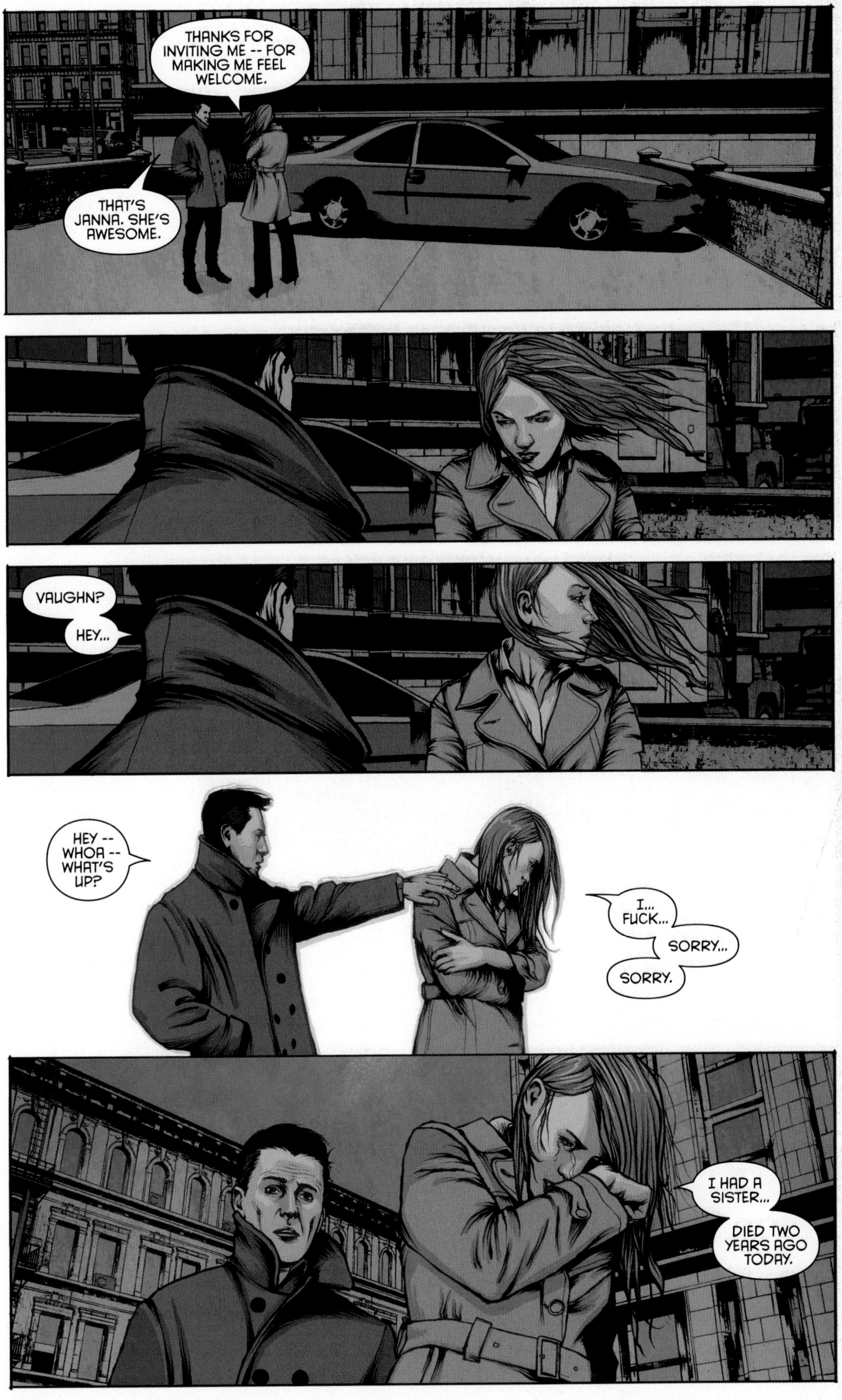
THANKS FOR INVITING ME -- FOR MAKING ME FEEL WELCOME.
THAT'S JANNA. SHE'S AWESOME.
VAUGHN?
HEY...
HEY -- WHOA -- WHAT'S UP?
I... FUCK...
SORRY...
SORRY.
I HAD A SISTER...
DIED TWO YEARS AGO TODAY.

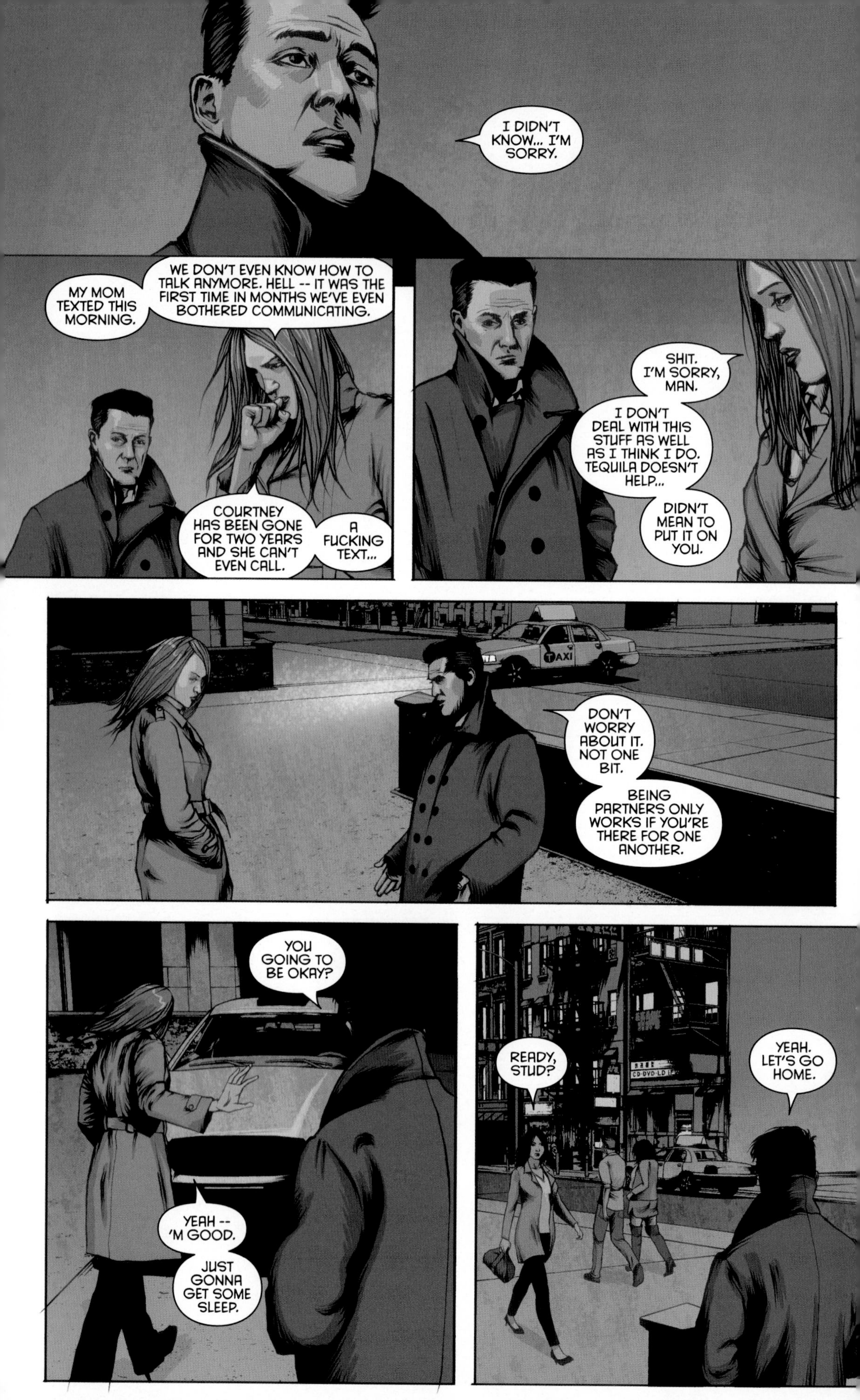
I DIDN'T KNOW... I'M SORRY.
MY MOM TEXTED THIS MORNING.
WE DON'T EVEN KNOW HOW TO TALK ANYMORE. HELL -- IT WAS THE FIRST TIME IN MONTHS WE'VE EVEN BOTHERED COMMUNICATING.
COURTNEY HAS BEEN GONE FOR TWO YEARS AND SHE CAN'T EVEN CALL.
A FUCKING TEXT...
SHIT. I'M SORRY, MAN.
I DON'T DEAL WITH THIS STUFF AS WELL AS I THINK I DO. TEQUILA DOESN'T HELP...
DIDN'T MEAN TO PUT IT ON YOU.
TAXI
DON'T WORRY ABOUT IT. NOT ONE BIT.
BEING PARTNERS ONLY WORKS IF YOU'RE THERE FOR ONE ANOTHER.
YOU GOING TO BE OKAY?
YEAH -- 'M GOOD.
JUST GONNA GET SOME SLEEP.
READY, STUD?
YEAH. LET'S GO HOME.
CD·DVD·LD

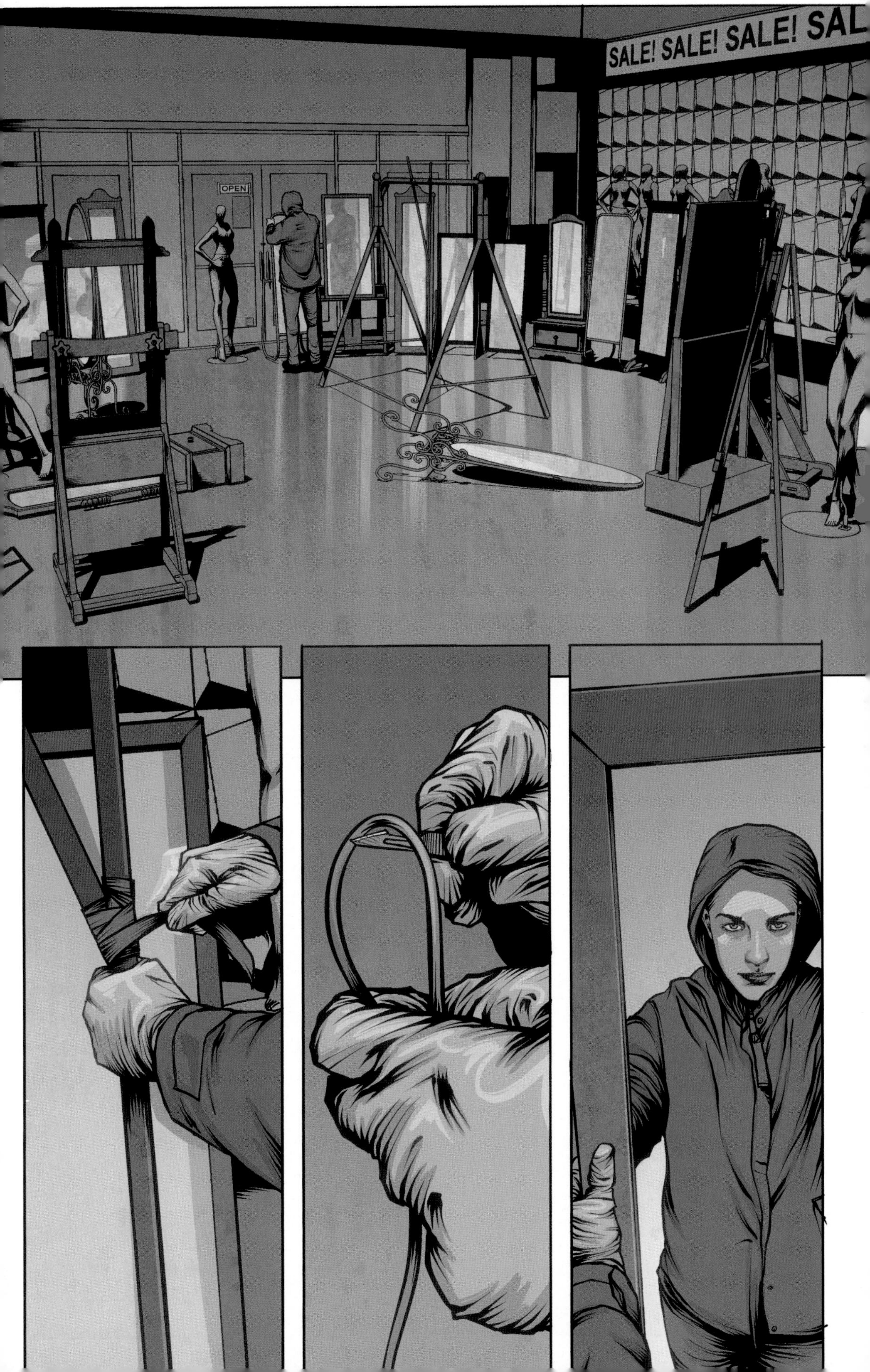
SALE! SALE! SALE! SAL
OPEN

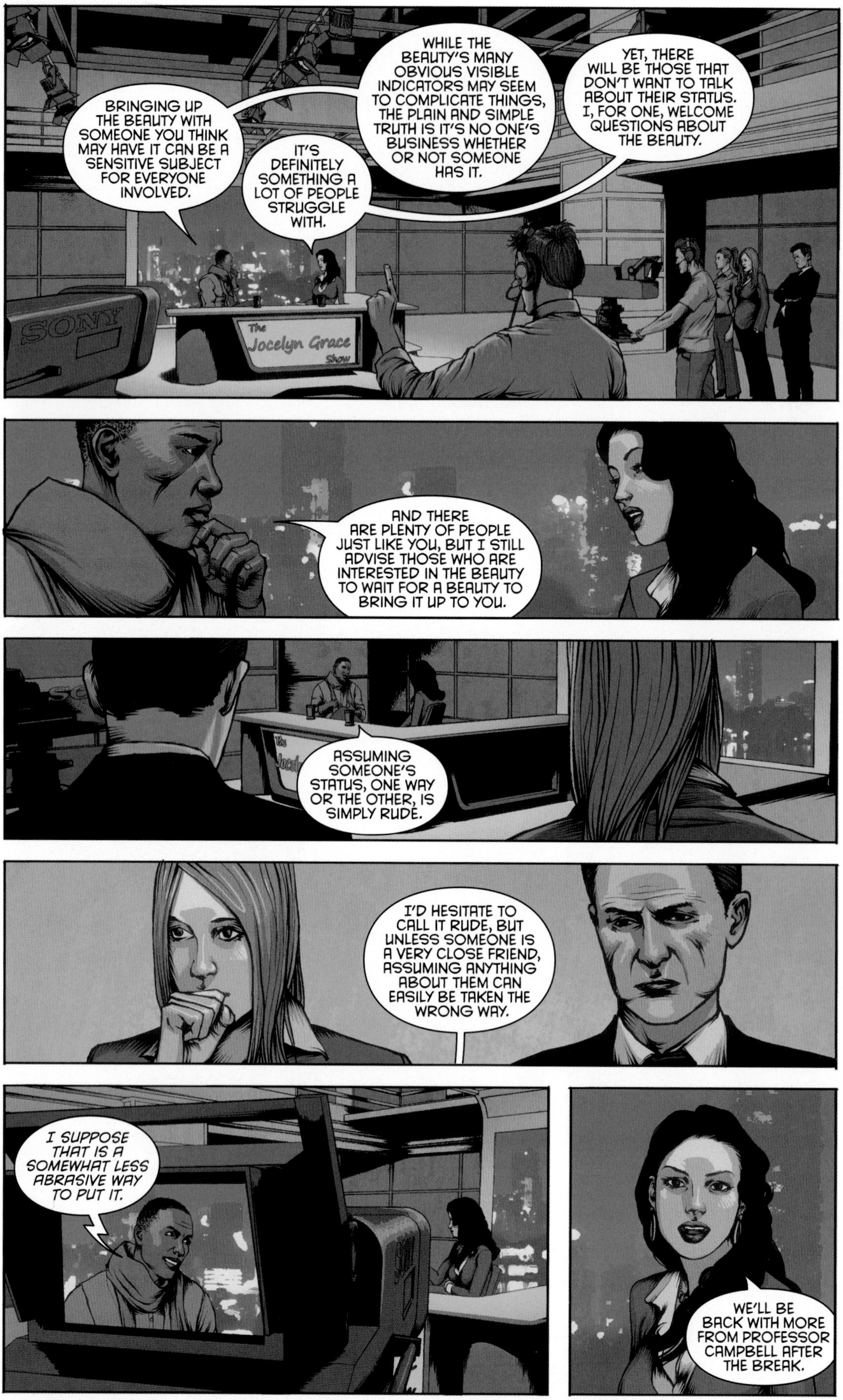
BRINGING UP THE BEAUTY WITH SOMEONE YOU THINK MAY HAVE IT CAN BE A SENSITIVE SUBJECT FOR EVERYONE INVOLVED.
IT'S DEFINITELY SOMETHING A LOT OF PEOPLE STRUGGLE WITH.
WHILE THE BEAUTY'S MANY OBVIOUS VISIBLE INDICATORS MAY SEEM TO COMPLICATE THINGS, THE PLAIN AND SIMPLE TRUTH IS IT'S NO ONE'S BUSINESS WHETHER OR NOT SOMEONE HAS IT.
YET, THERE WILL BE THOSE THAT DON'T WANT TO TALK ABOUT THEIR STATUS. I, FOR ONE, WELCOME QUESTIONS ABOUT THE BEAUTY.
SONY
The Jocelyn Grace Show
AND THERE ARE PLENTY OF PEOPLE JUST LIKE YOU, BUT I STILL ADVISE THOSE WHO ARE INTERESTED IN THE BEAUTY TO WAIT FOR A BEAUTY TO BRING IT UP TO YOU.
ASSUMING SOMEONE'S STATUS, ONE WAY OR THE OTHER, IS SIMPLY RUDE.
I'D HESITATE TO CALL IT RUDE, BUT UNLESS SOMEONE IS A VERY CLOSE FRIEND, ASSUMING ANYTHING ABOUT THEM CAN EASILY BE TAKEN THE WRONG WAY.
I SUPPOSE THAT IS A SOMEWHAT LESS ABRASIVE WAY TO PUT IT.
WE'LL BE BACK WITH MORE FROM PROFESSOR CAMPBELL AFTER THE BREAK.

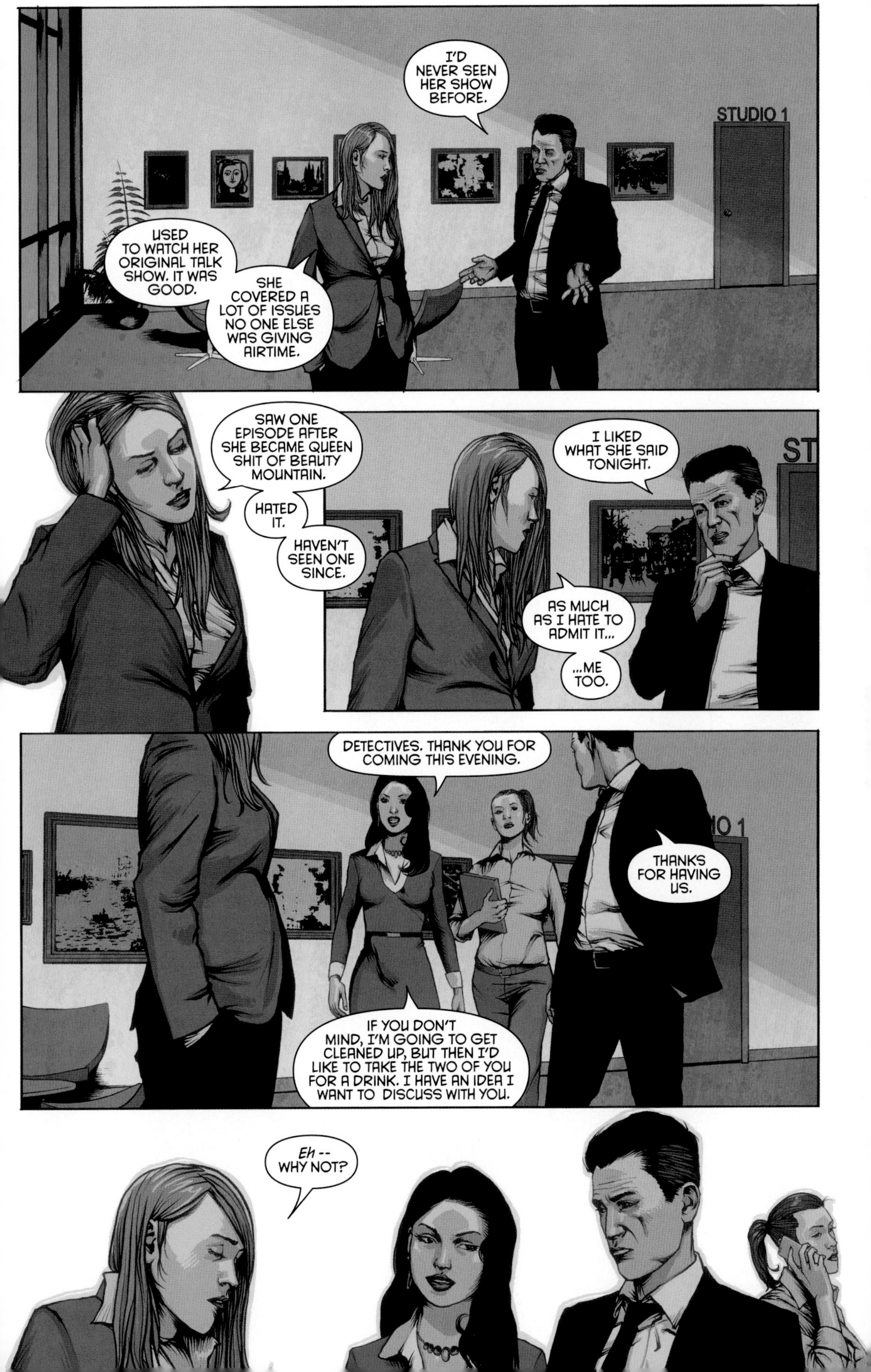
I'D NEVER SEEN HER SHOW BEFORE.
STUDIO 1
USED TO WATCH HER ORIGINAL TALK SHOW. IT WAS GOOD.
SHE COVERED A LOT OF ISSUES NO ONE ELSE WAS GIVING AIRTIME.
SAW ONE EPISODE AFTER SHE BECAME QUEEN SHIT OF BEAUTY MOUNTAIN.
HATED IT.
HAVEN'T SEEN ONE SINCE.
I LIKED WHAT SHE SAID TONIGHT.
AS MUCH AS I HATE TO ADMIT IT...
...ME TOO.
DETECTIVES. THANK YOU FOR COMING THIS EVENING.
THANKS FOR HAVING US.
IF YOU DON'T MIND, I'M GOING TO GET CLEANED UP, BUT THEN I'D LIKE TO TAKE THE TWO OF YOU FOR A DRINK. I HAVE AN IDEA I WANT TO DISCUSS WITH YOU.
Eh -- WHY NOT?

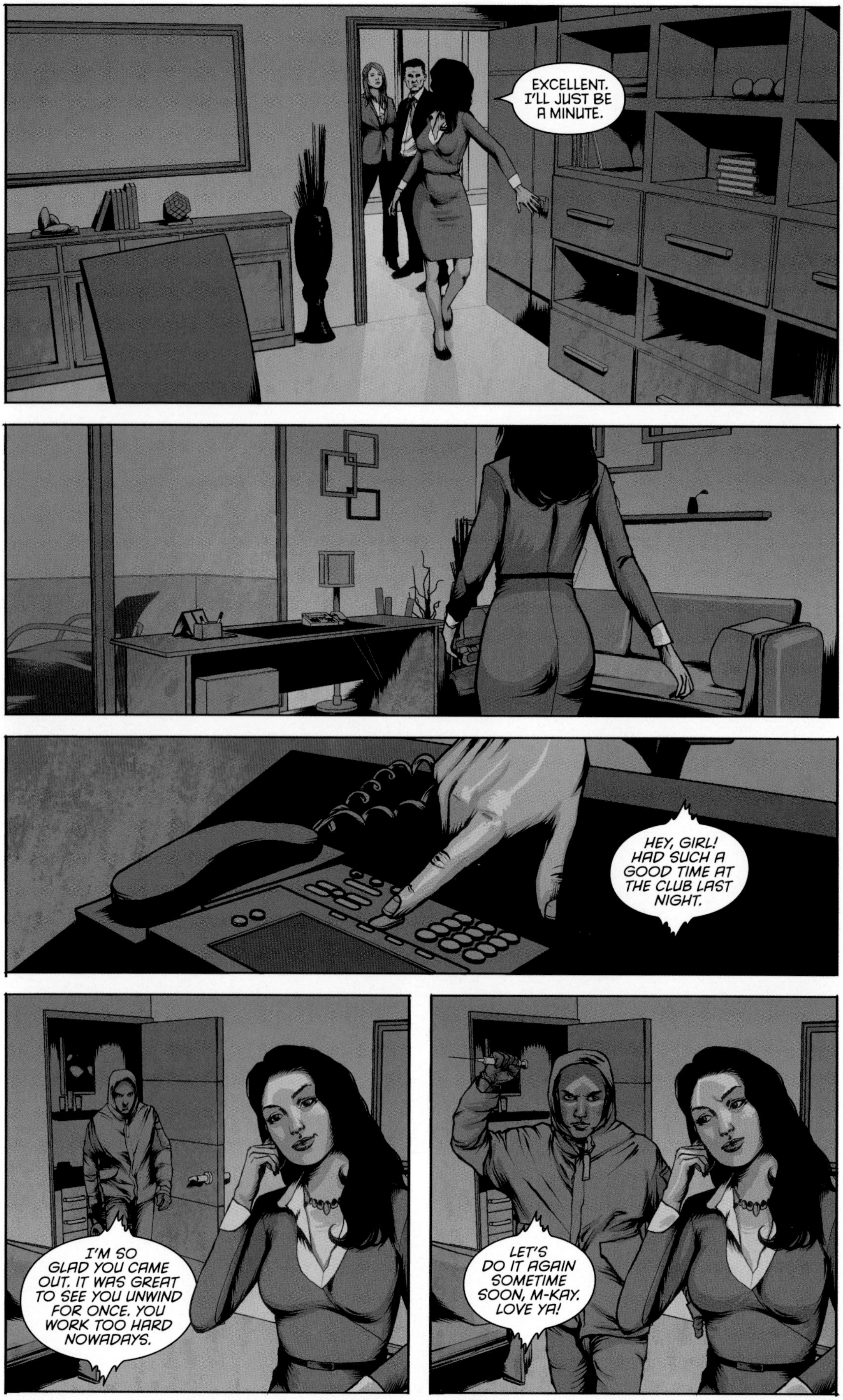
EXCELLENT. I'LL JUST BE A MINUTE.
HEY, GIRL! HAD SUCH A GOOD TIME AT THE CLUB LAST NIGHT.
I'M SO GLAD YOU CAME OUT. IT WAS GREAT TO SEE YOU UNWIND FOR ONCE. YOU WORK TOO HARD NOWADAYS.
LET'S DO IT AGAIN SOMETIME SOON, M-KAY. LOVE YA!

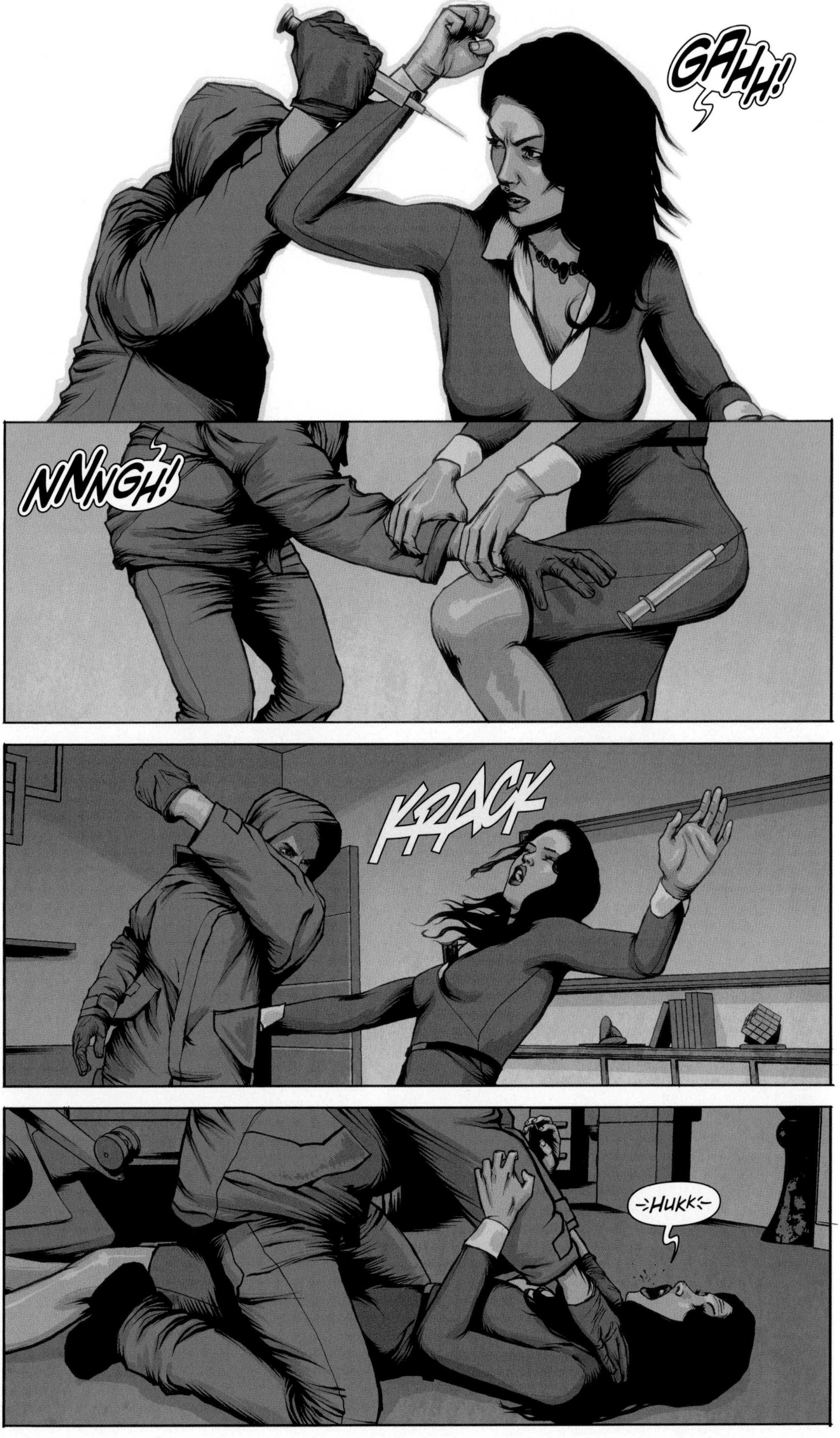
GAHH!
NNNGH!
KRACK
HUKK

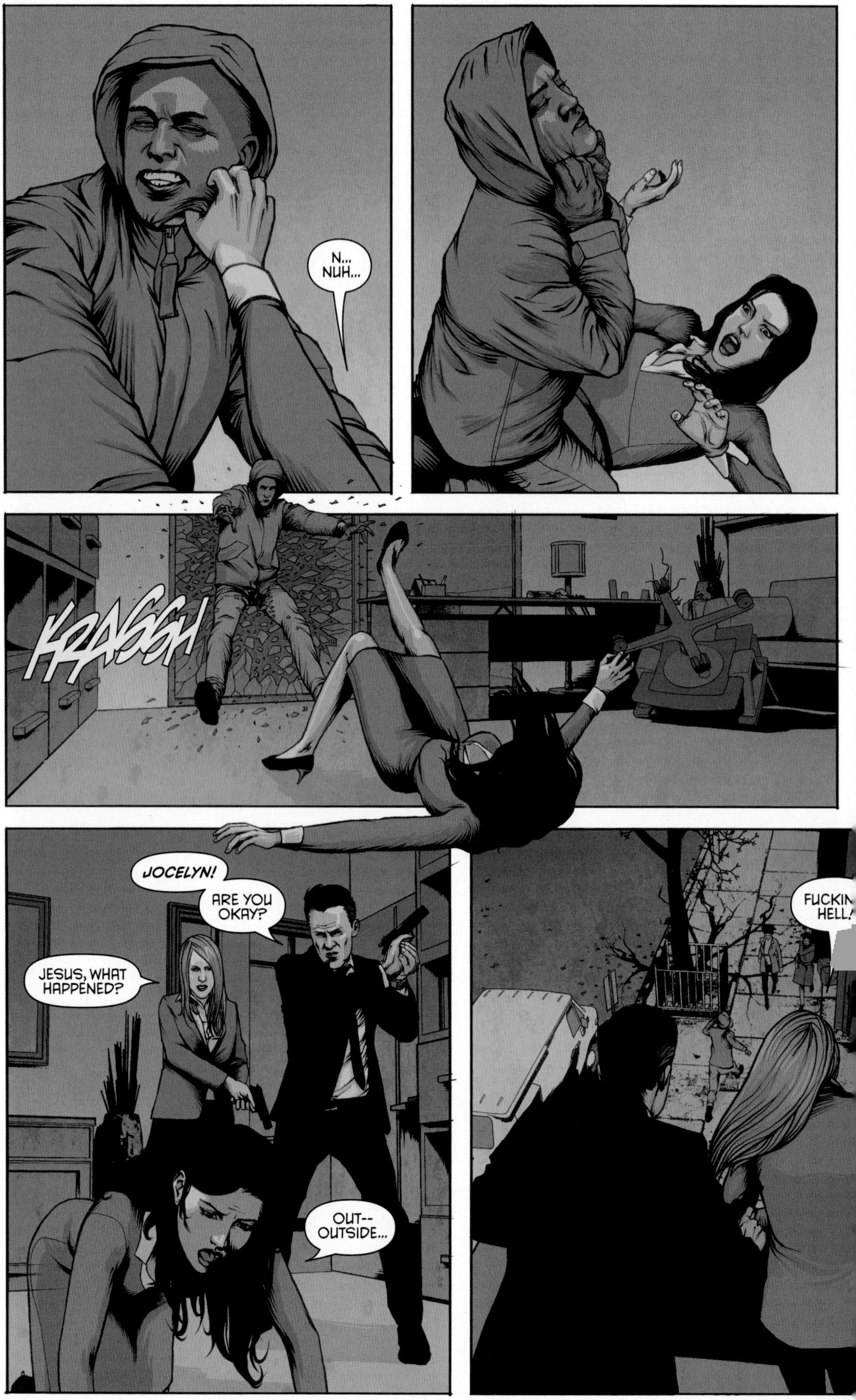
N... NUH...
KRASSH
JOCELYN!
ARE YOU OKAY?
JESUS, WHAT HAPPENED?
OUT-- OUTSIDE...
FUCKIN HELL!

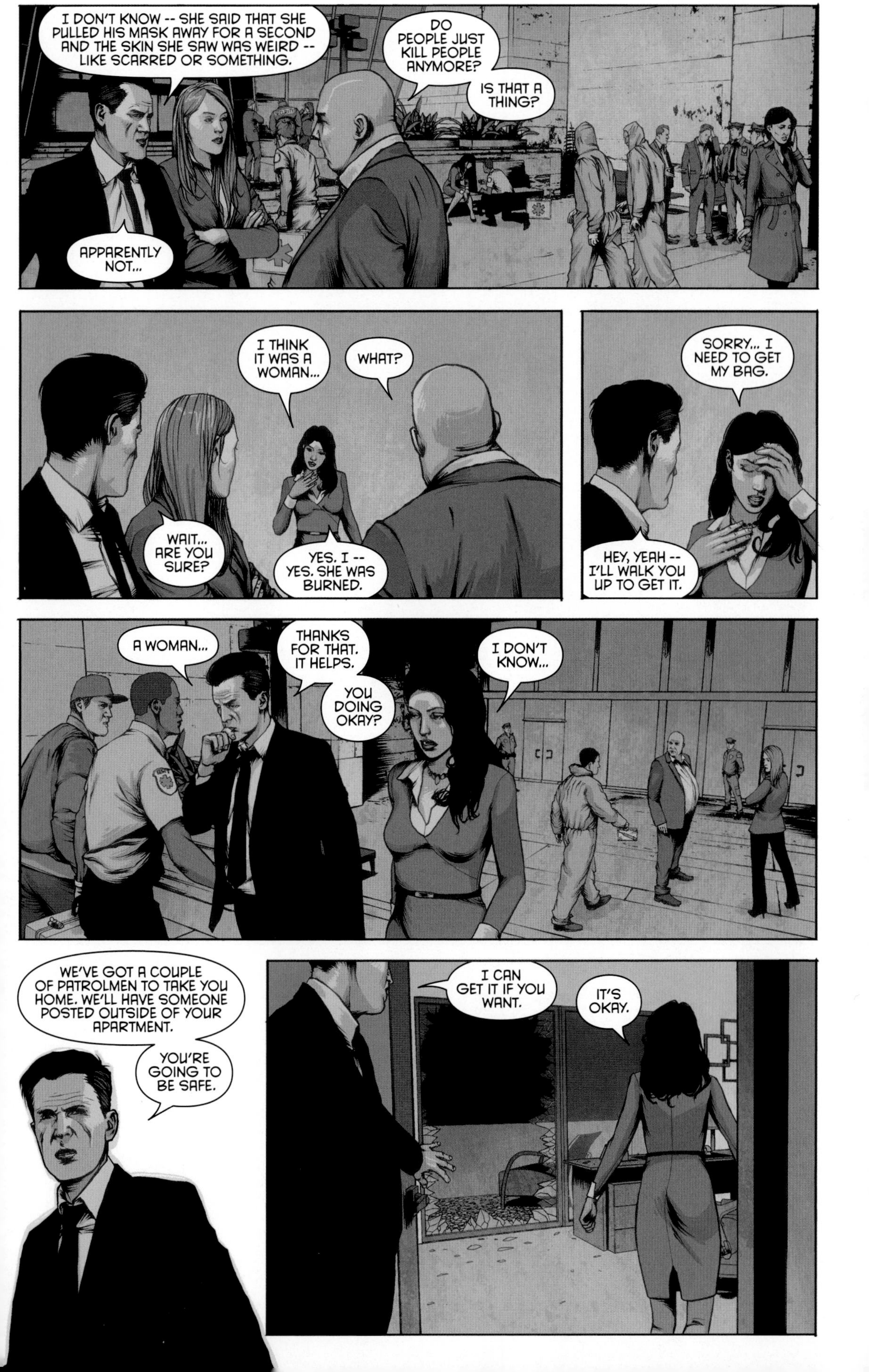
I DON'T KNOW -- SHE SAID THAT SHE PULLED HIS MASK AWAY FOR A SECOND AND THE SKIN SHE SAW WAS WEIRD -- LIKE SCARRED OR SOMETHING.
DO PEOPLE JUST KILL PEOPLE ANYMORE?
IS THAT A THING?
APPARENTLY NOT...
I THINK IT WAS A WOMAN...
WHAT?
WAIT... ARE YOU SURE?
YES. I -- YES. SHE WAS BURNED.
SORRY... I NEED TO GET MY BAG.
HEY, YEAH -- I'LL WALK YOU UP TO GET IT.
A WOMAN...
THANKS FOR THAT. IT HELPS.
YOU DOING OKAY?
I DON'T KNOW...
WE'VE GOT A COUPLE OF PATROLMEN TO TAKE YOU HOME. WE'LL HAVE SOMEONE POSTED OUTSIDE OF YOUR APARTMENT.
YOU'RE GOING TO BE SAFE.
I CAN GET IT IF YOU WANT.
IT'S OKAY.

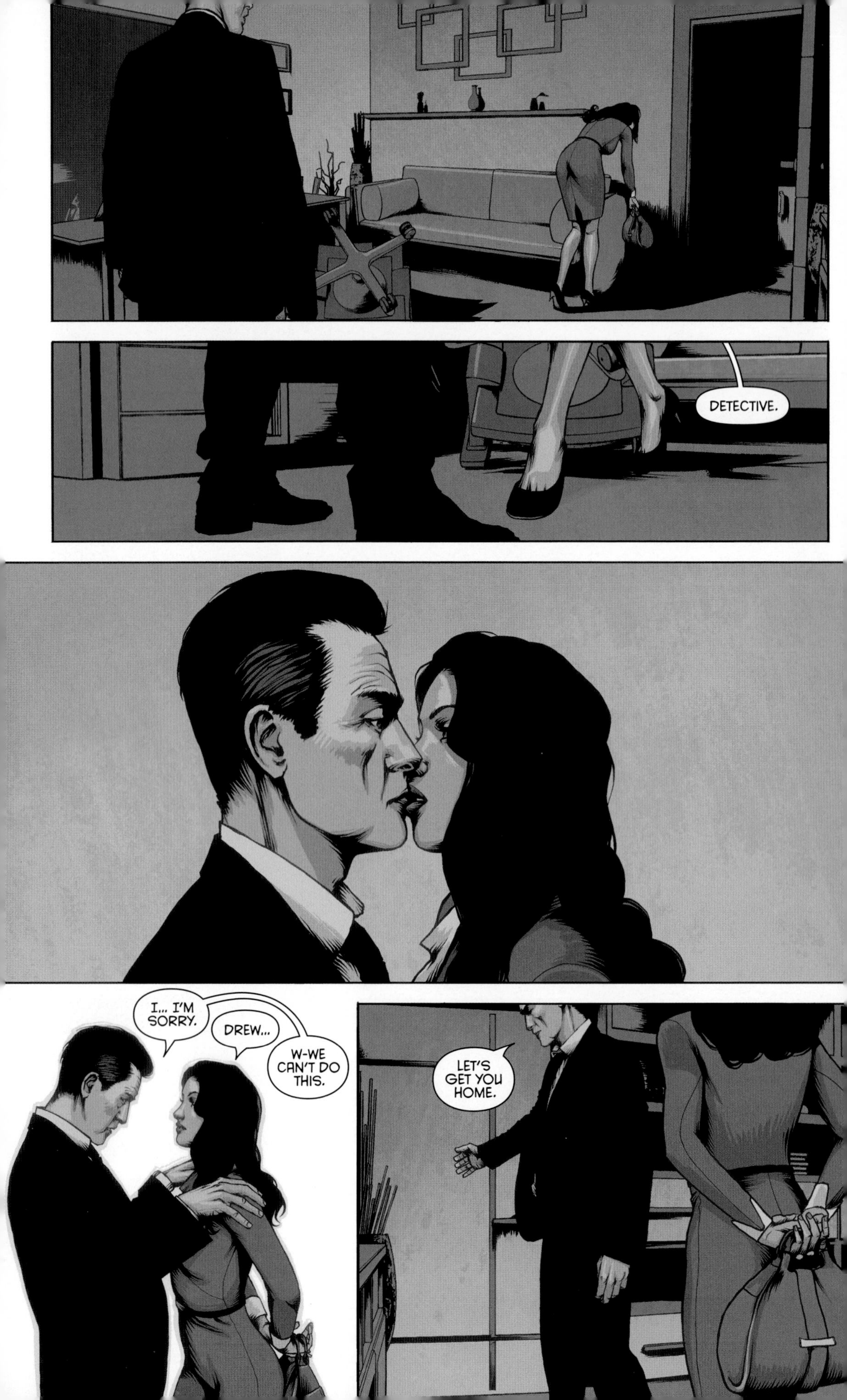
DETECTIVE.
I... I'M SORRY.
DREW...
W-WE CAN'T DO THIS.
LET'S GET YOU HOME.

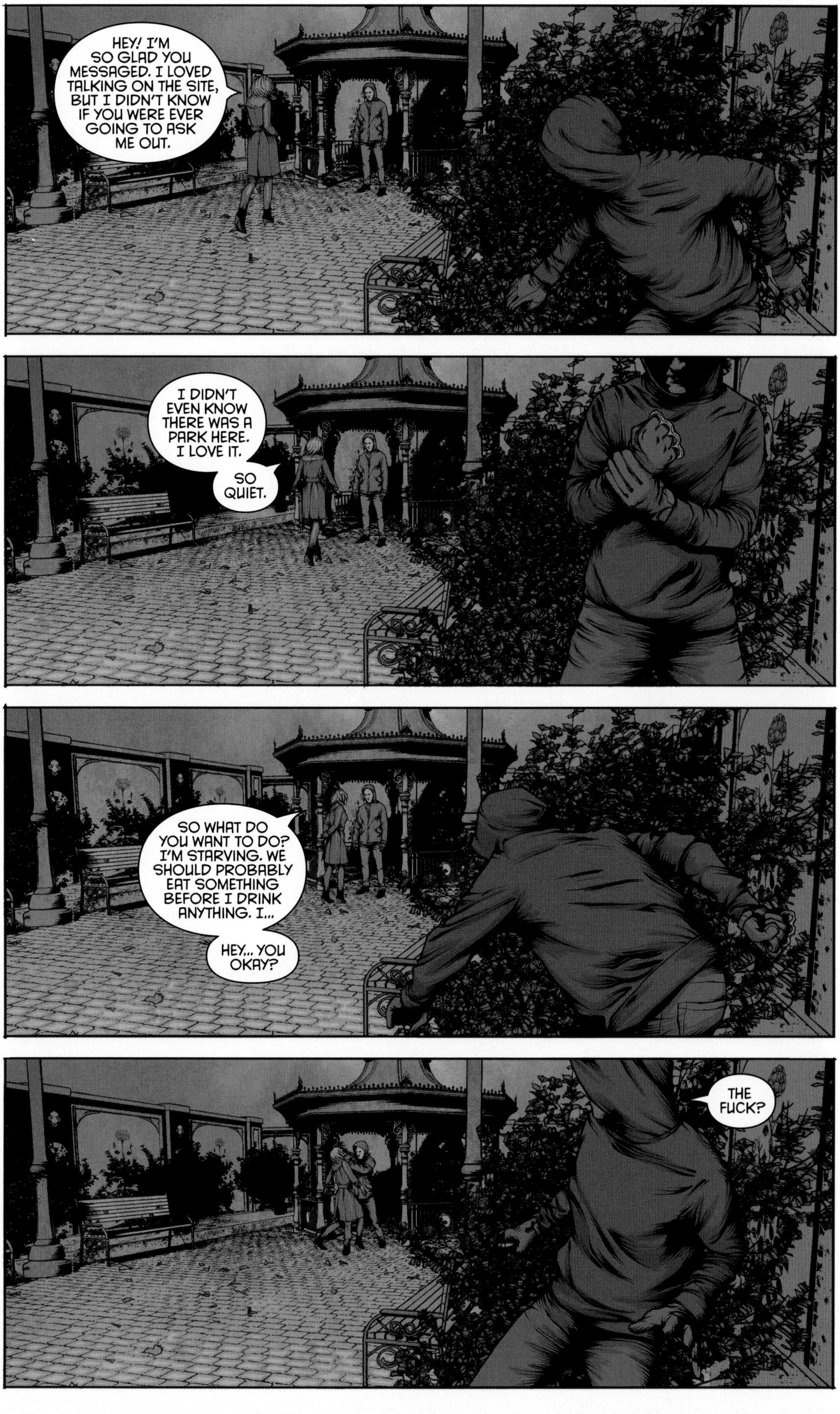
HEY! I'M SO GLAD YOU MESSAGED. I LOVED TALKING ON THE SITE, BUT I DIDN'T KNOW IF YOU WERE EVER GOING TO ASK ME OUT.
I DIDN'T EVEN KNOW THERE WAS A PARK HERE. I LOVE IT.
SO QUIET.
SO WHAT DO YOU WANT TO DO? I'M STARVING. WE SHOULD PROBABLY EAT SOMETHING BEFORE I DRINK ANYTHING. I...
HEY... YOU OKAY?
THE FUCK?

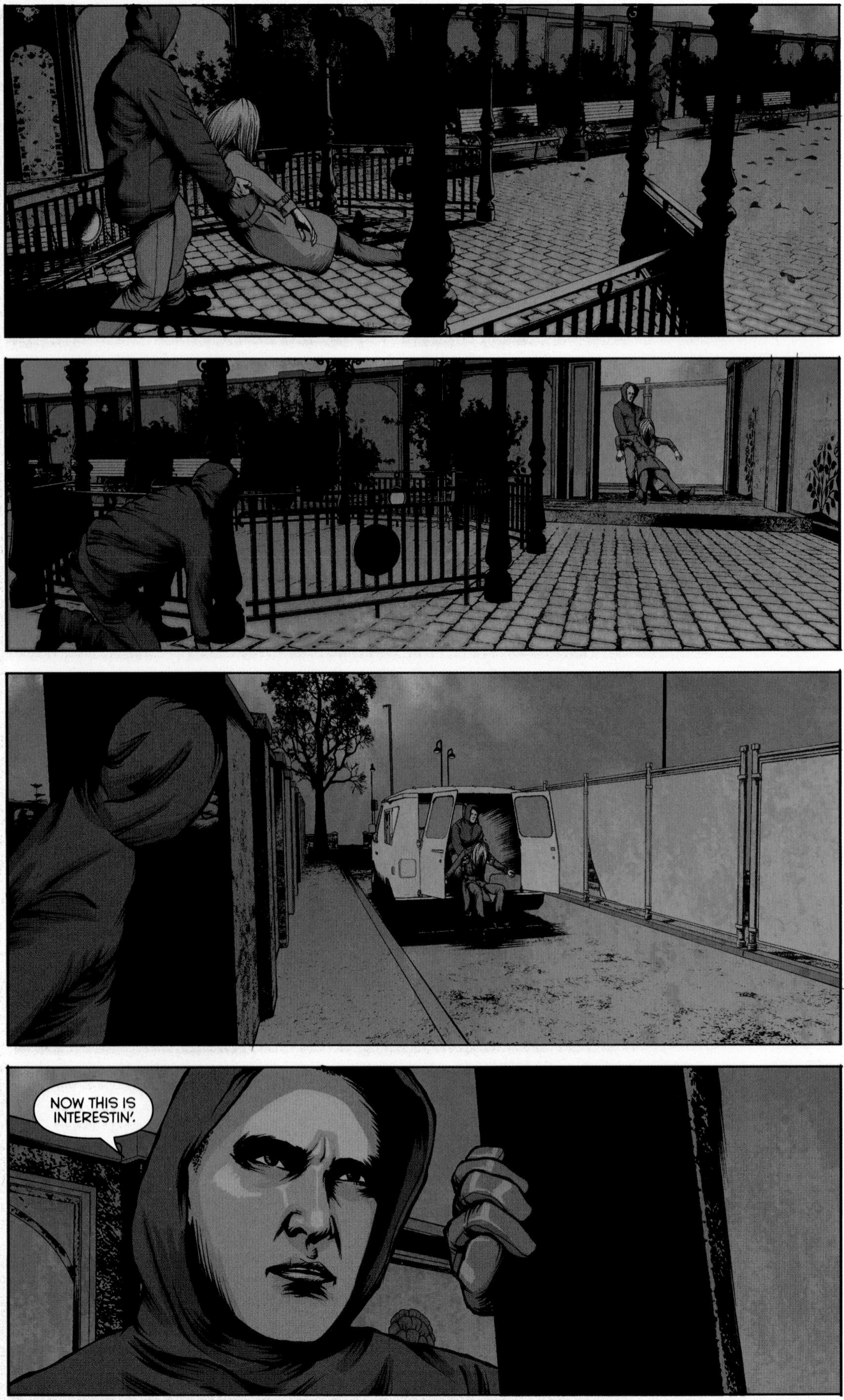
NOW THIS IS INTERESTIN'.

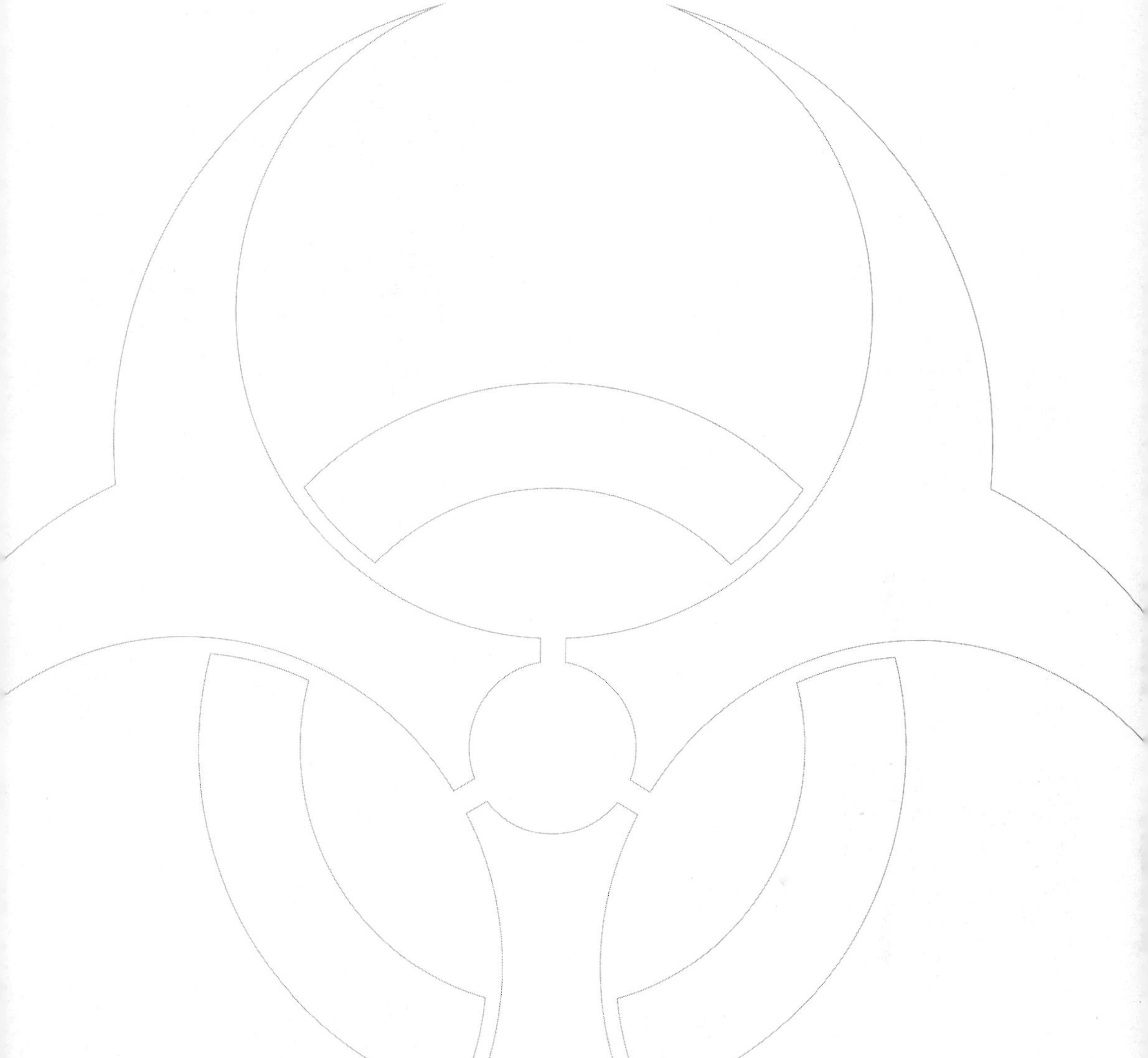

CHAPTER

16

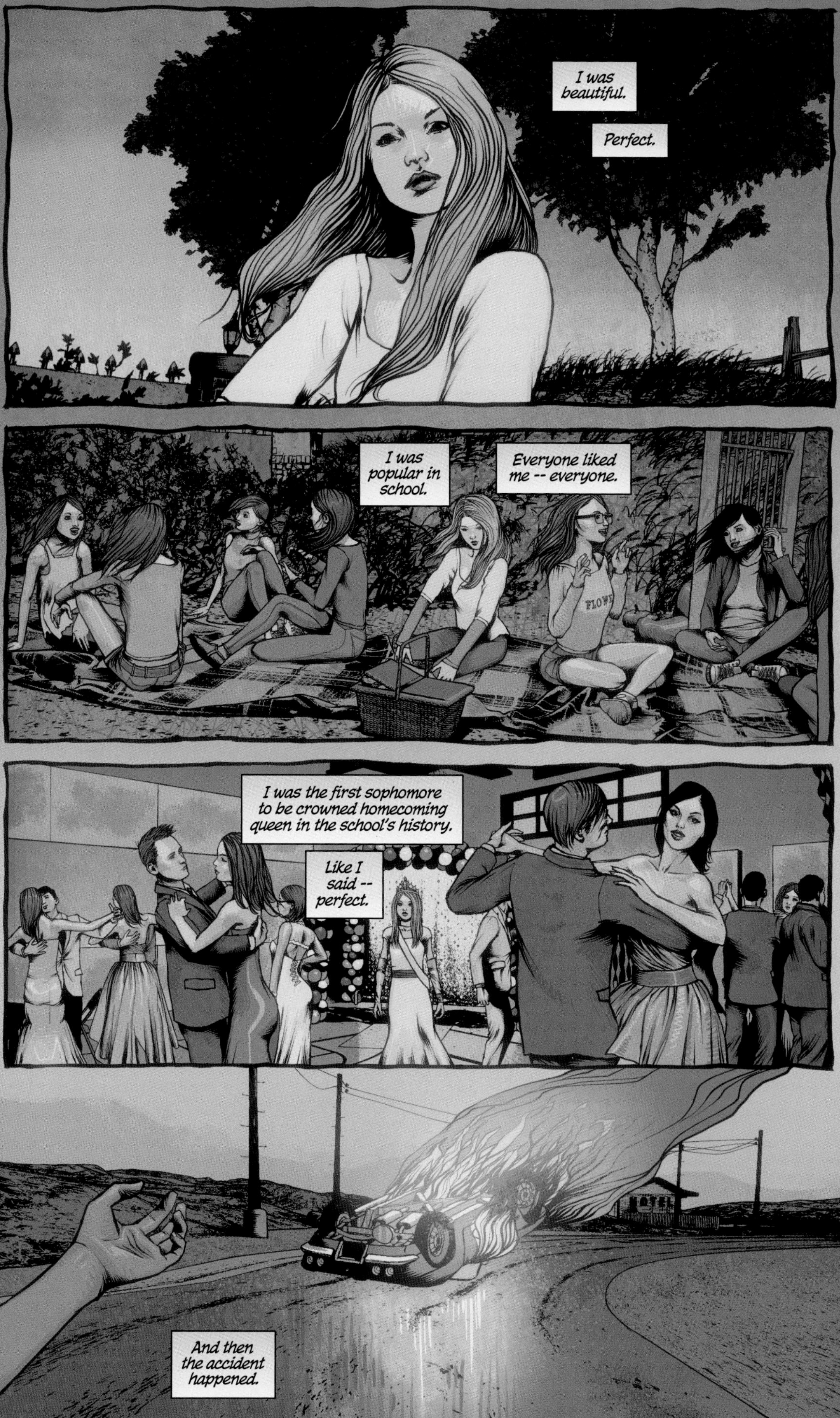
I was beautiful.
Perfect.
I was popular in school.
Everyone liked me -- everyone.
I was the first sophomore to be crowned homecoming queen in the school's history.
Like I said -- perfect.
And then the accident happened.

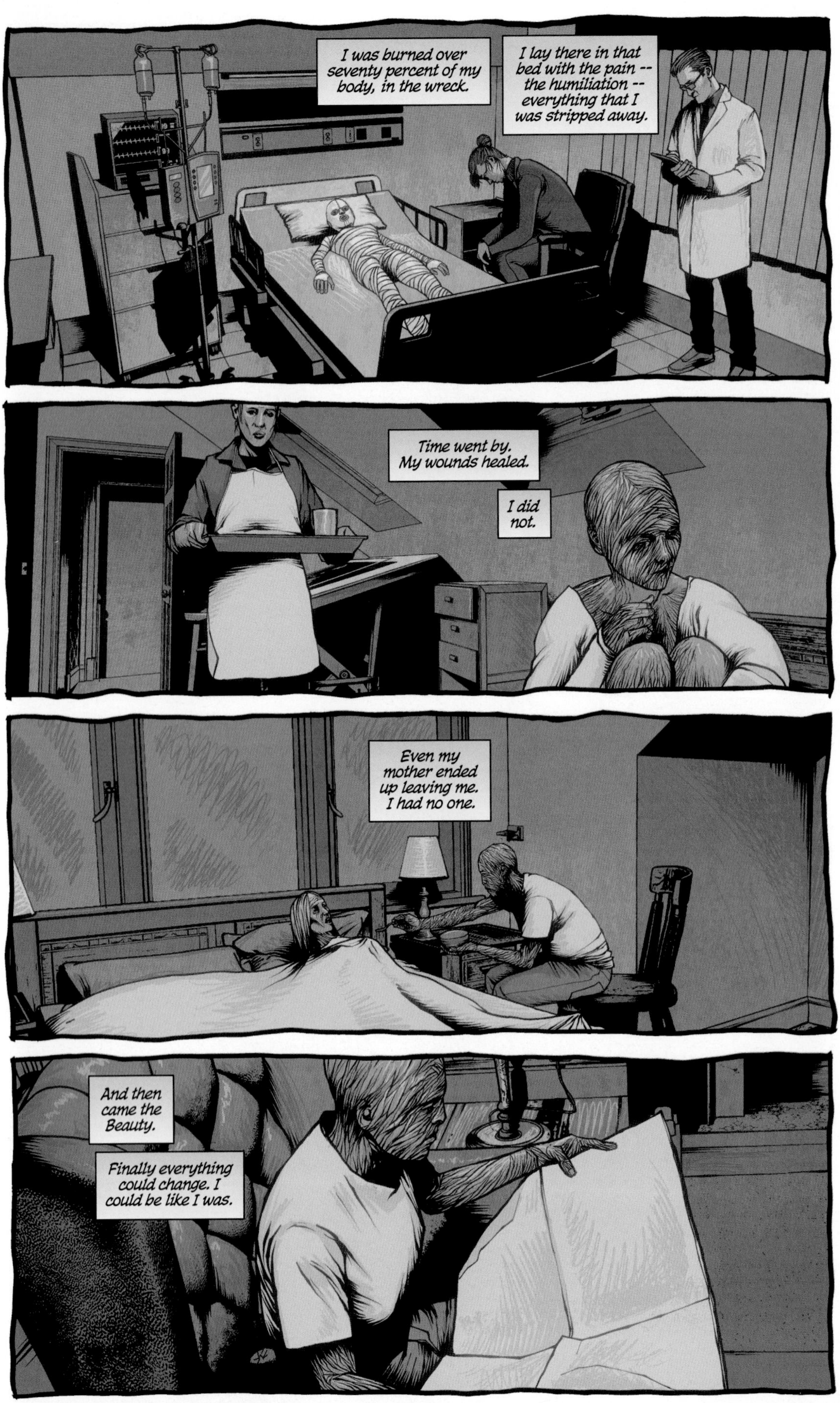
I was burned over seventy percent of my body, in the wreck.
I lay there in that bed with the pain -- the humiliation -- everything that I was stripped away.
Time went by. My wounds healed.
I did not.
Even my mother ended up leaving me. I had no one.
And then came the Beauty.
Finally everything could change. I could be like I was.

I COULD BE PERFECT AGAIN.
GGGGG...
BUT...
YOU CAN'T FIX THIS.
AND YOU... SO PERFECT. JUST LIKE I USED TO BE. YOU DON'T EVEN BEGIN TO APPRECIATE WHA--
WELL LOOKIT YOU.

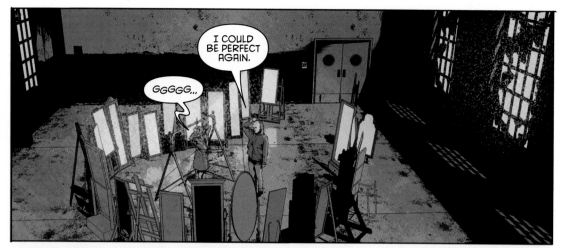

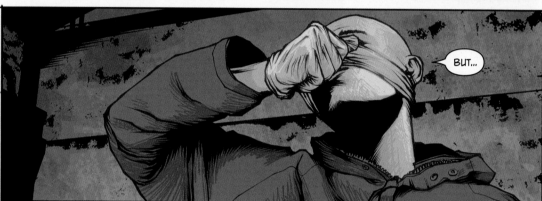

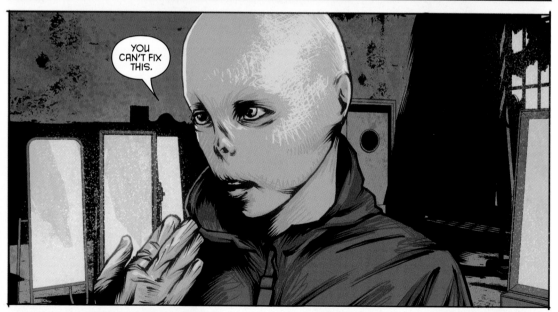

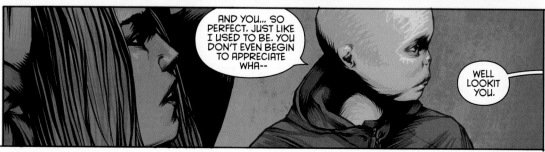

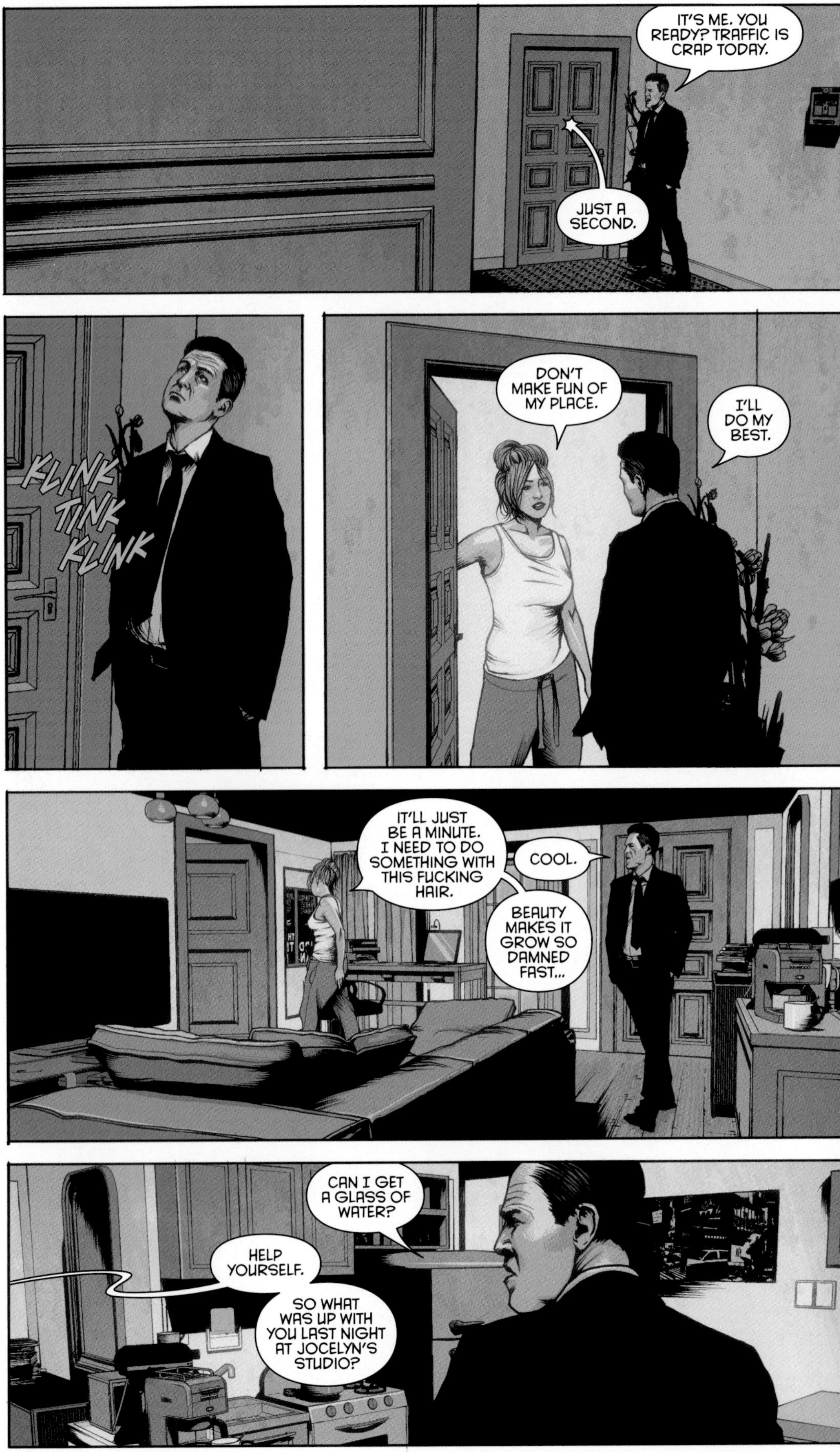
IT'S ME. YOU READY? TRAFFIC IS CRAP TODAY.
JUST A SECOND.
KLINK
TINK
KLINK
DON'T MAKE FUN OF MY PLACE.
I'LL DO MY BEST.
IT'LL JUST BE A MINUTE. I NEED TO DO SOMETHING WITH THIS FUCKING HAIR.
COOL.
BEAUTY MAKES IT GROW SO DAMNED FAST...
CAN I GET A GLASS OF WATER?
HELP YOURSELF.
SO WHAT WAS UP WITH YOU LAST NIGHT AT JOCELYN'S STUDIO?

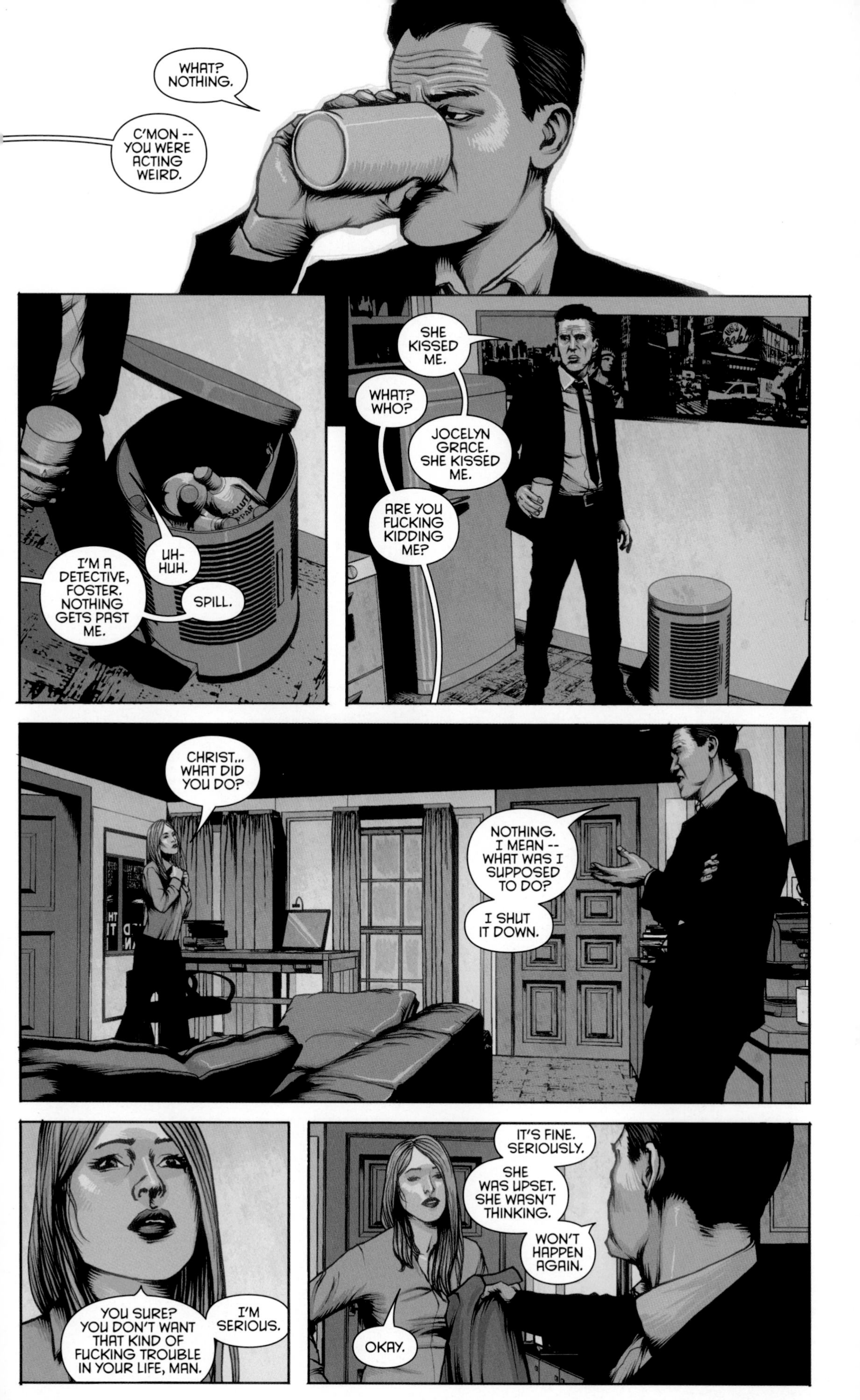
WHAT? NOTHING.
C'MON -- YOU WERE ACTING WEIRD.
I'M A DETECTIVE, FOSTER. NOTHING GETS PAST ME.
UH-HUH.
SPILL.
SHE KISSED ME.
WHAT? WHO?
JOCELYN GRACE. SHE KISSED ME.
ARE YOU FUCKING KIDDING ME?
CHRIST... WHAT DID YOU DO?
NOTHING. I MEAN -- WHAT WAS I SUPPOSED TO DO?
I SHUT IT DOWN.
YOU SURE? YOU DON'T WANT THAT KIND OF FUCKING TROUBLE IN YOUR LIFE, MAN.
I'M SERIOUS.
IT'S FINE. SERIOUSLY.
SHE WAS UPSET. SHE WASN'T THINKING.
WON'T HAPPEN AGAIN.
OKAY.

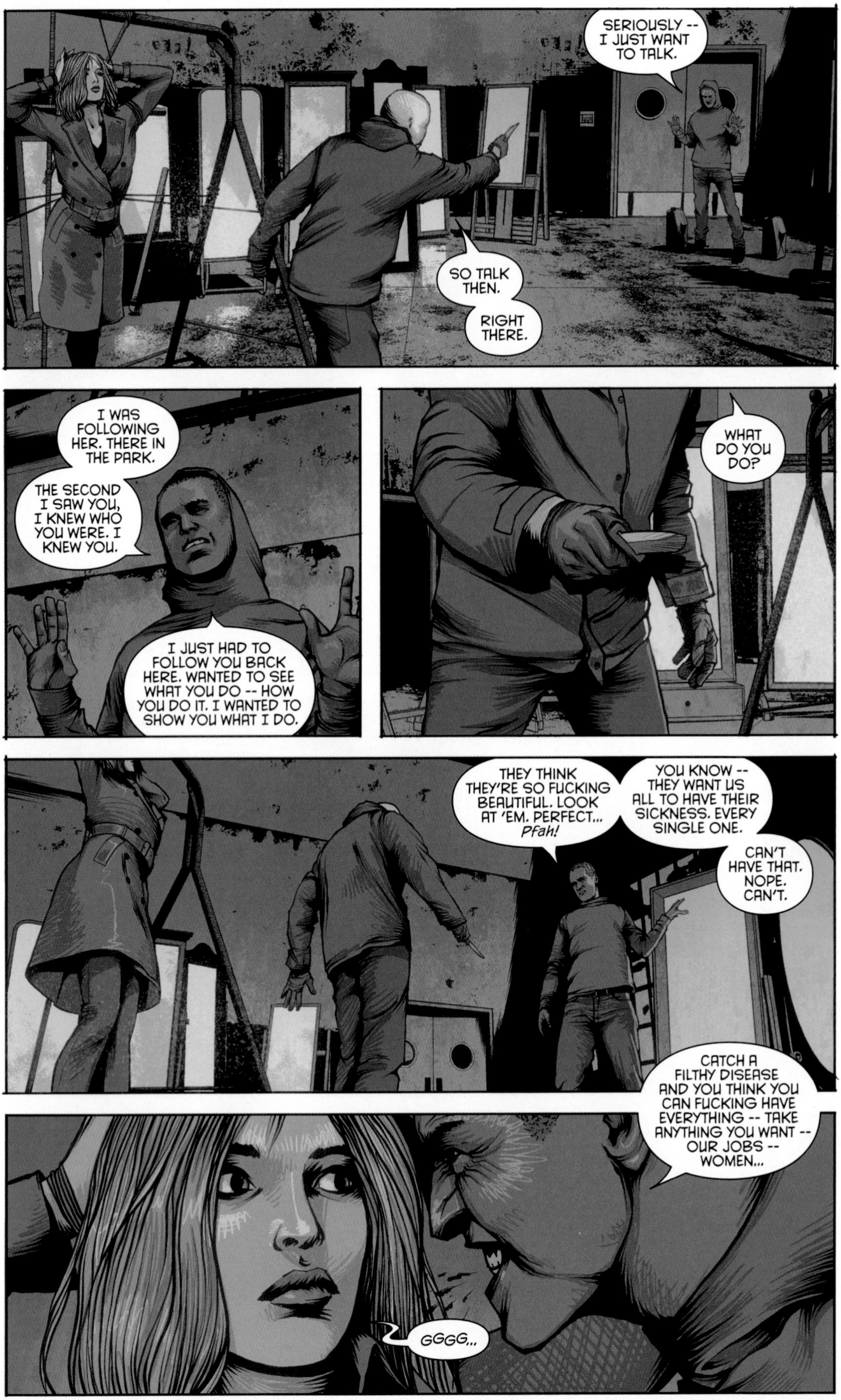
SERIOUSLY -- I JUST WANT TO TALK.
SO TALK THEN.
RIGHT THERE.
I WAS FOLLOWING HER. THERE IN THE PARK.
THE SECOND I SAW YOU, I KNEW WHO YOU WERE. I KNEW YOU.
I JUST HAD TO FOLLOW YOU BACK HERE. WANTED TO SEE WHAT YOU DO -- HOW YOU DO IT. I WANTED TO SHOW YOU WHAT I DO.
WHAT DO YOU DO?
THEY THINK THEY'RE SO FUCKING BEAUTIFUL. LOOK AT 'EM. PERFECT... *Pfah!*
YOU KNOW -- THEY WANT US ALL TO HAVE THEIR SICKNESS. EVERY SINGLE ONE.
CAN'T HAVE THAT. NOPE. CAN'T.
CATCH A FILTHY DISEASE AND YOU THINK YOU CAN FUCKING HAVE EVERYTHING -- TAKE ANYTHING YOU WANT -- OUR JOBS -- WOMEN...
GGGG...

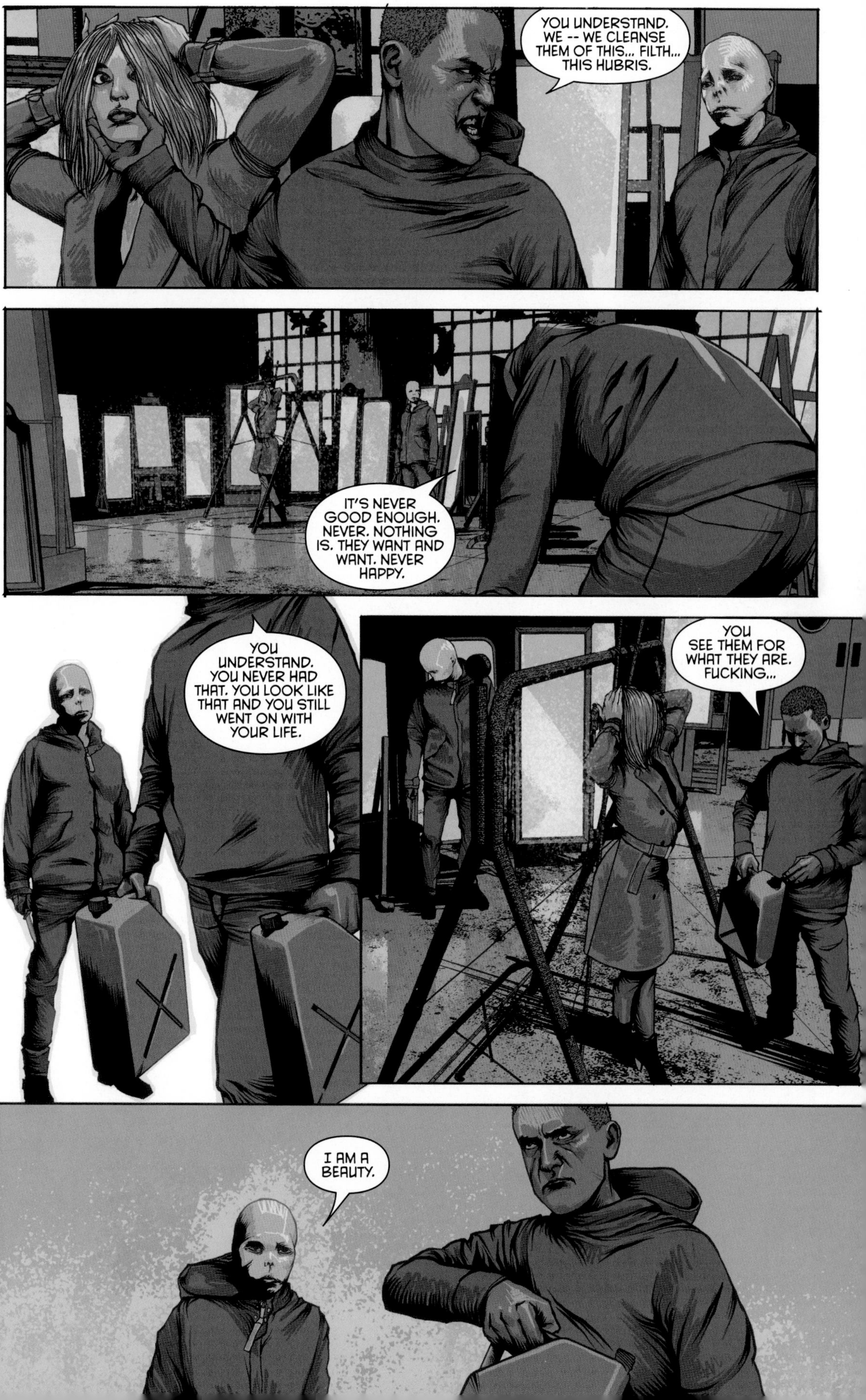
YOU UNDERSTAND. WE -- WE CLEANSE THEM OF THIS... FILTH... THIS HUBRIS.
IT'S NEVER GOOD ENOUGH. NEVER. NOTHING IS. THEY WANT AND WANT. NEVER HAPPY.
YOU UNDERSTAND. YOU NEVER HAD THAT. YOU LOOK LIKE THAT AND YOU STILL WENT ON WITH YOUR LIFE.
YOU SEE THEM FOR WHAT THEY ARE. FUCKING...
I AM A BEAUTY.

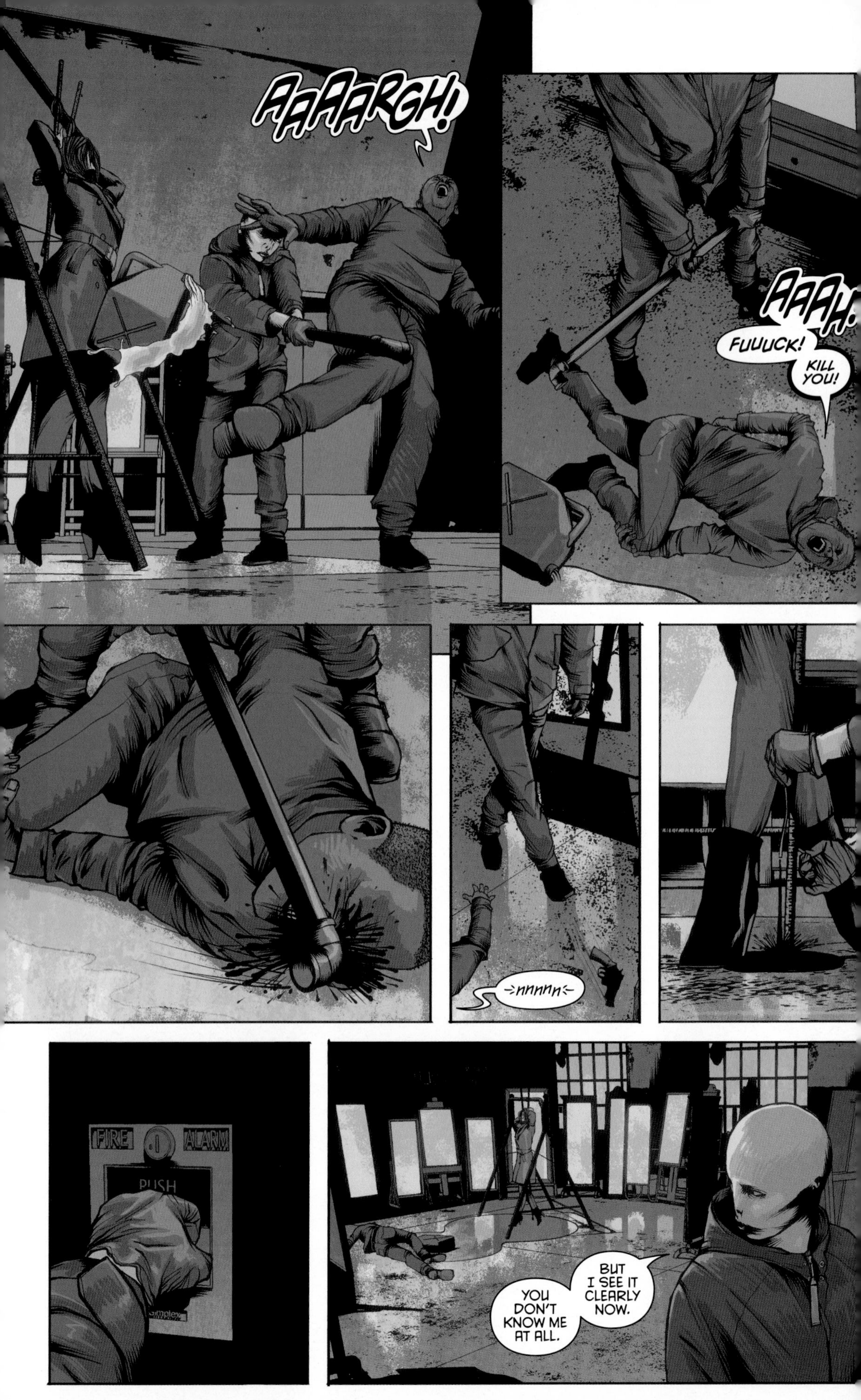
AAAARGH!
AAAH!
FUUUCK!
KILL YOU!
nnnnn
FIRE
ALARM
PUSH
YOU DON'T KNOW ME AT ALL.
BUT I SEE IT CLEARLY NOW.

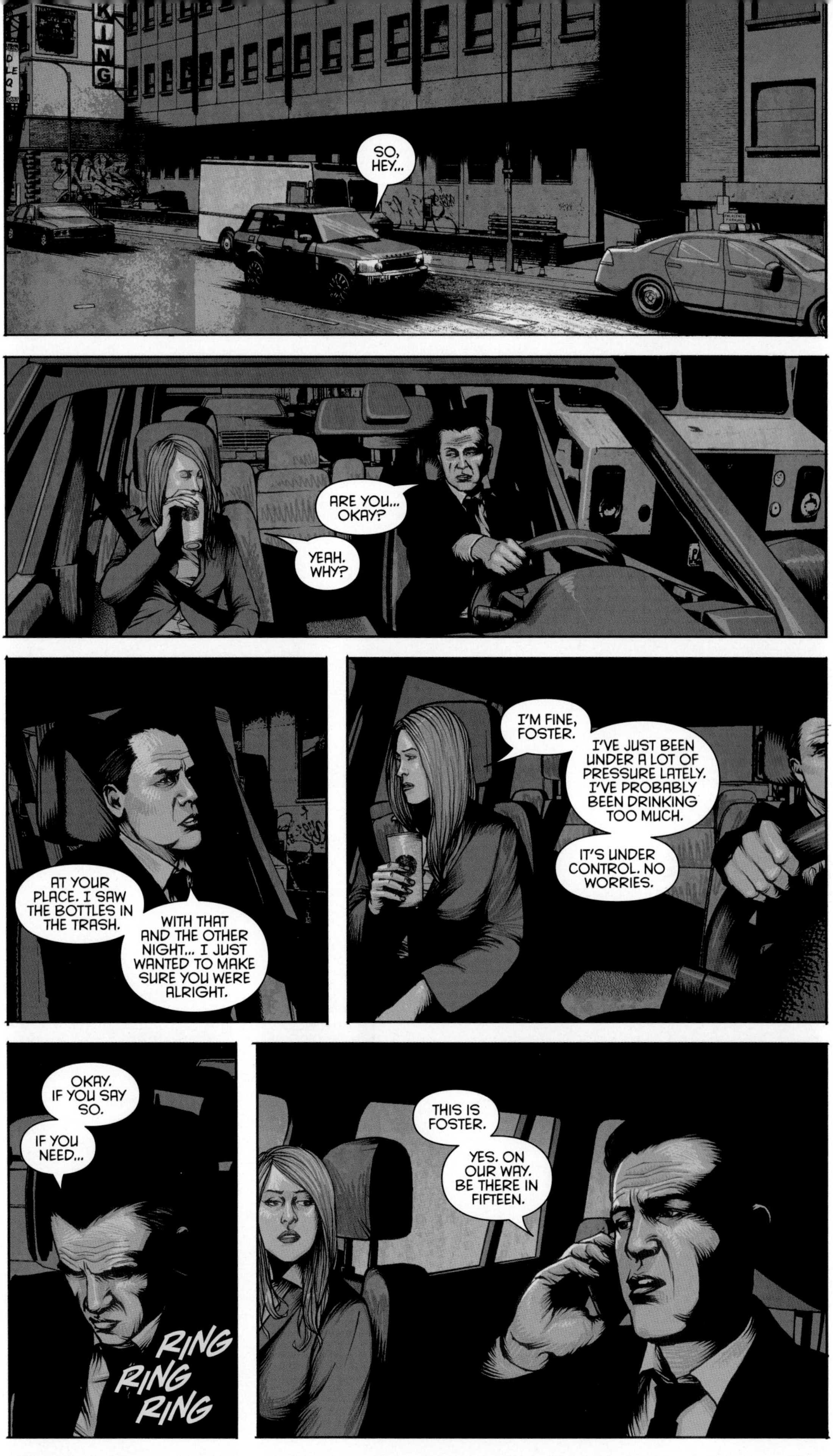
SO, HEY...
ARE YOU... OKAY?
YEAH. WHY?
AT YOUR PLACE. I SAW THE BOTTLES IN THE TRASH.
WITH THAT AND THE OTHER NIGHT... I JUST WANTED TO MAKE SURE YOU WERE ALRIGHT.
I'M FINE, FOSTER.
I'VE JUST BEEN UNDER A LOT OF PRESSURE LATELY. I'VE PROBABLY BEEN DRINKING TOO MUCH.
IT'S UNDER CONTROL. NO WORRIES.
OKAY. IF YOU SAY SO.
IF YOU NEED...
RING RING RING
THIS IS FOSTER.
YES. ON OUR WAY. BE THERE IN FIFTEEN.

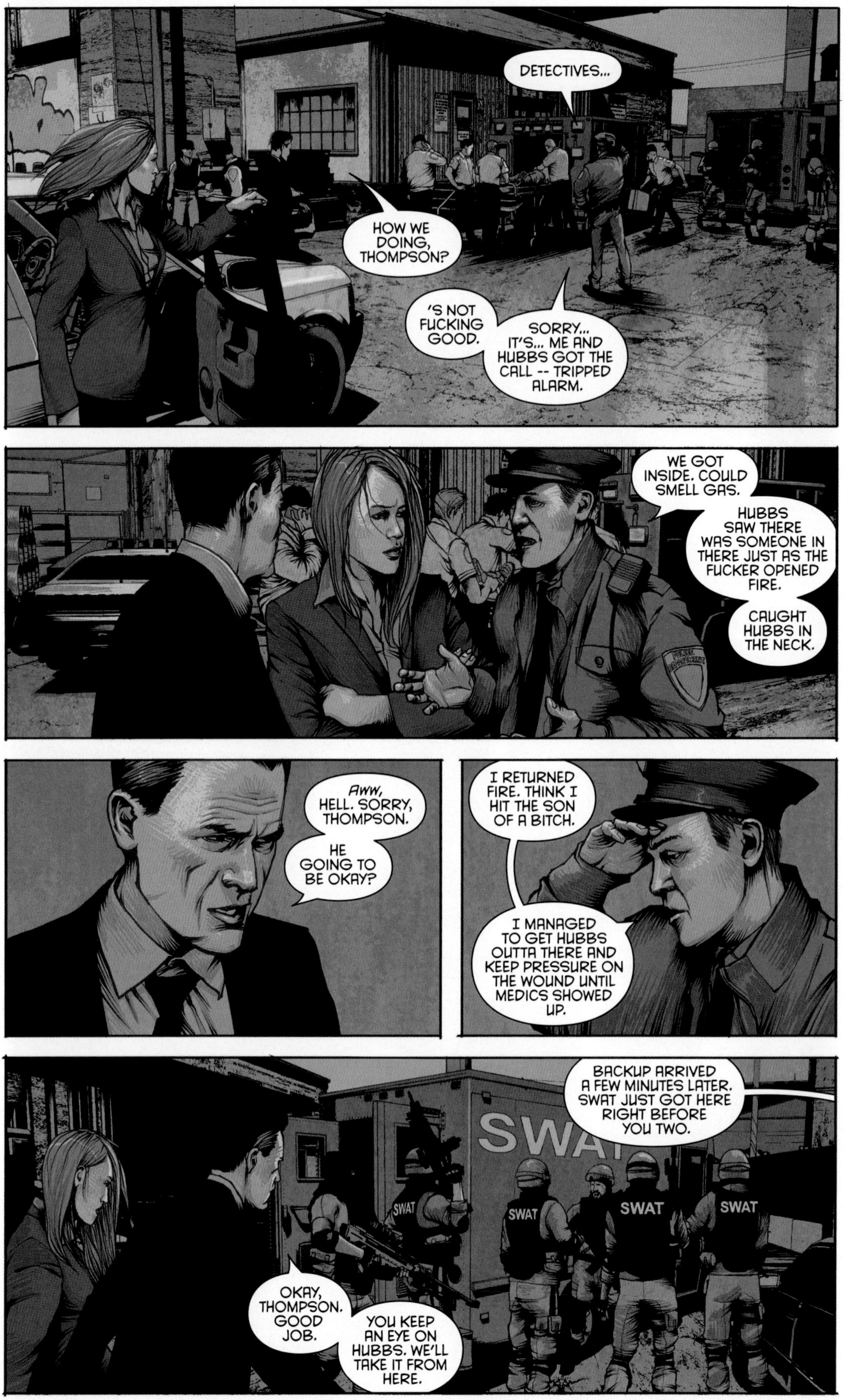
DETECTIVES...
HOW WE DOING, THOMPSON?
'S NOT FUCKING GOOD.
SORRY... IT'S... ME AND HUBBS GOT THE CALL -- TRIPPED ALARM.
WE GOT INSIDE. COULD SMELL GAS.
HUBBS SAW THERE WAS SOMEONE IN THERE JUST AS THE FUCKER OPENED FIRE.
CAUGHT HUBBS IN THE NECK.
Aww, HELL. SORRY, THOMPSON.
HE GOING TO BE OKAY?
I RETURNED FIRE. THINK I HIT THE SON OF A BITCH.
I MANAGED TO GET HUBBS OUTTA THERE AND KEEP PRESSURE ON THE WOUND UNTIL MEDICS SHOWED UP.
BACKUP ARRIVED A FEW MINUTES LATER. SWAT JUST GOT HERE RIGHT BEFORE YOU TWO.
SWAT
OKAY, THOMPSON. GOOD JOB.
YOU KEEP AN EYE ON HUBBS. WE'LL TAKE IT FROM HERE.

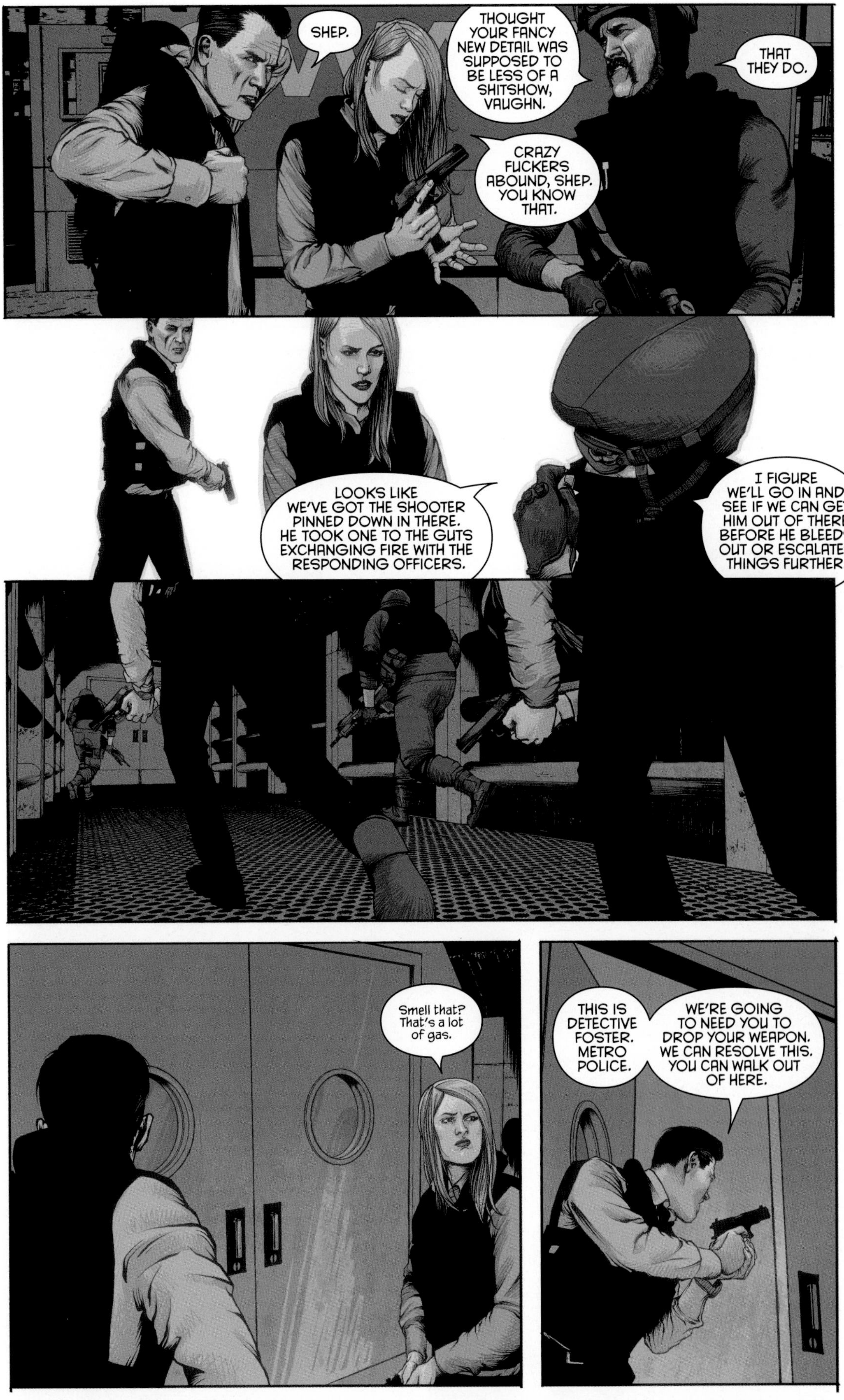
SHEP.
THOUGHT YOUR FANCY NEW DETAIL WAS SUPPOSED TO BE LESS OF A SHITSHOW, VAUGHN.
THAT THEY DO.
CRAZY FUCKERS ABOUND, SHEP. YOU KNOW THAT.
LOOKS LIKE WE'VE GOT THE SHOOTER PINNED DOWN IN THERE. HE TOOK ONE TO THE GUTS EXCHANGING FIRE WITH THE RESPONDING OFFICERS.
I FIGURE WE'LL GO IN AND SEE IF WE CAN GET HIM OUT OF THERE BEFORE HE BLEEDS OUT OR ESCALATES THINGS FURTHER.
Smell that? That's a lot of gas.
THIS IS DETECTIVE FOSTER. METRO POLICE.
WE'RE GOING TO NEED YOU TO DROP YOUR WEAPON. WE CAN RESOLVE THIS. YOU CAN WALK OUT OF HERE.

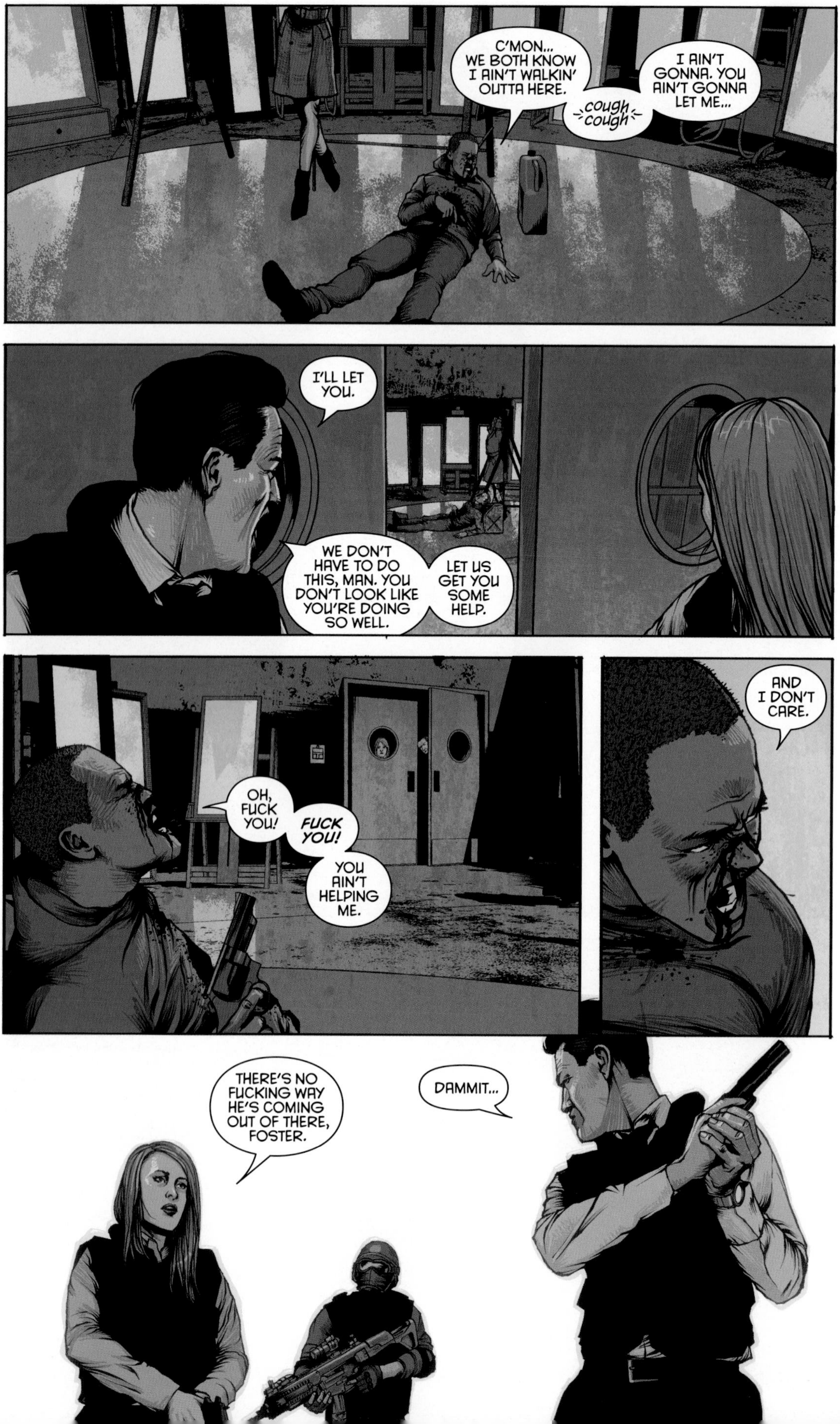
C'MON... WE BOTH KNOW I AIN'T WALKIN' OUTTA HERE.
cough cough
I AIN'T GONNA. YOU AIN'T GONNA LET ME...
I'LL LET YOU.
WE DON'T HAVE TO DO THIS, MAN. YOU DON'T LOOK LIKE YOU'RE DOING SO WELL.
LET US GET YOU SOME HELP.
OH, FUCK YOU!
FUCK YOU!
YOU AIN'T HELPING ME.
AND I DON'T CARE.
THERE'S NO FUCKING WAY HE'S COMING OUT OF THERE, FOSTER.
DAMMIT...

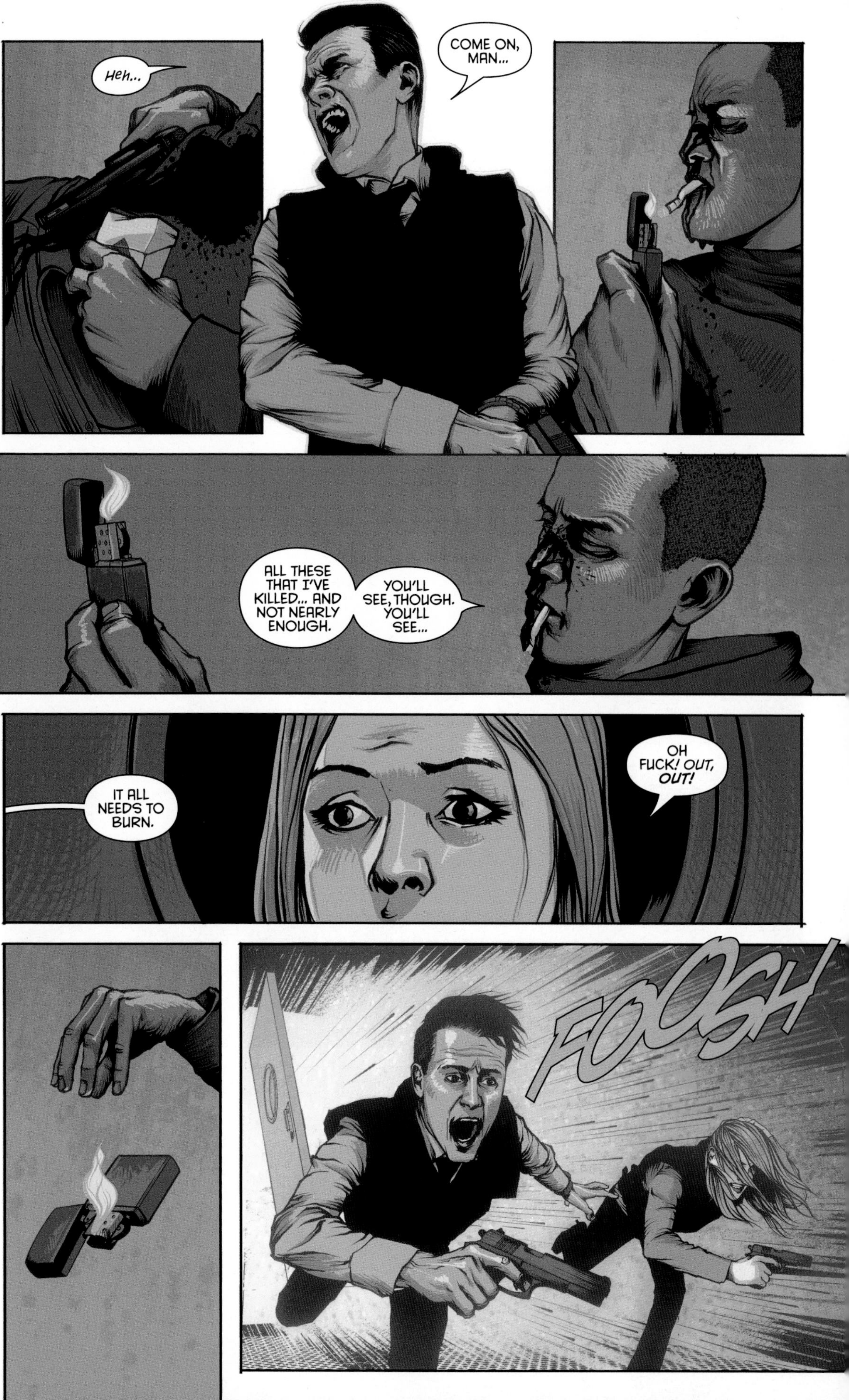
Heh...
COME ON, MAN...
ALL THESE THAT I'VE KILLED... AND NOT NEARLY ENOUGH.
YOU'LL SEE, THOUGH. YOU'LL SEE...
IT ALL NEEDS TO BURN.
OH FUCK! OUT, OUT!
FOOSH

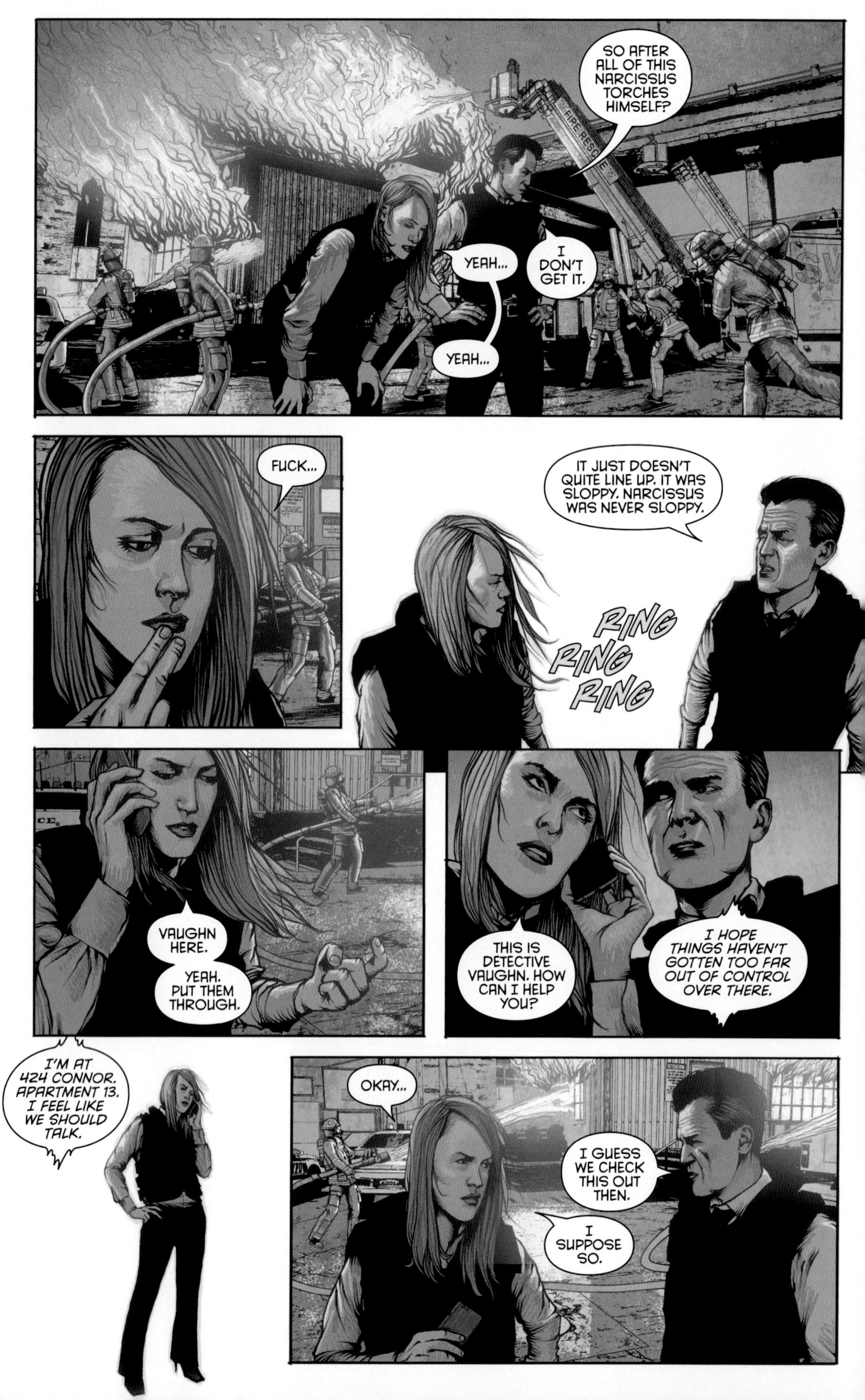
SO AFTER ALL OF THIS NARCISSUS TORCHES HIMSELF?
YEAH...
I DON'T GET IT.
YEAH...
FIRE RESCUE
FUCK...
IT JUST DOESN'T QUITE LINE UP. IT WAS SLOPPY. NARCISSUS WAS NEVER SLOPPY.
RING RING RING
VAUGHN HERE.
YEAH. PUT THEM THROUGH.
THIS IS DETECTIVE VAUGHN. HOW CAN I HELP YOU?
I HOPE THINGS HAVEN'T GOTTEN TOO FAR OUT OF CONTROL OVER THERE.
I'M AT 424 CONNOR. APARTMENT 13. I FEEL LIKE WE SHOULD TALK.
OKAY...
I GUESS WE CHECK THIS OUT THEN.
I SUPPOSE SO.

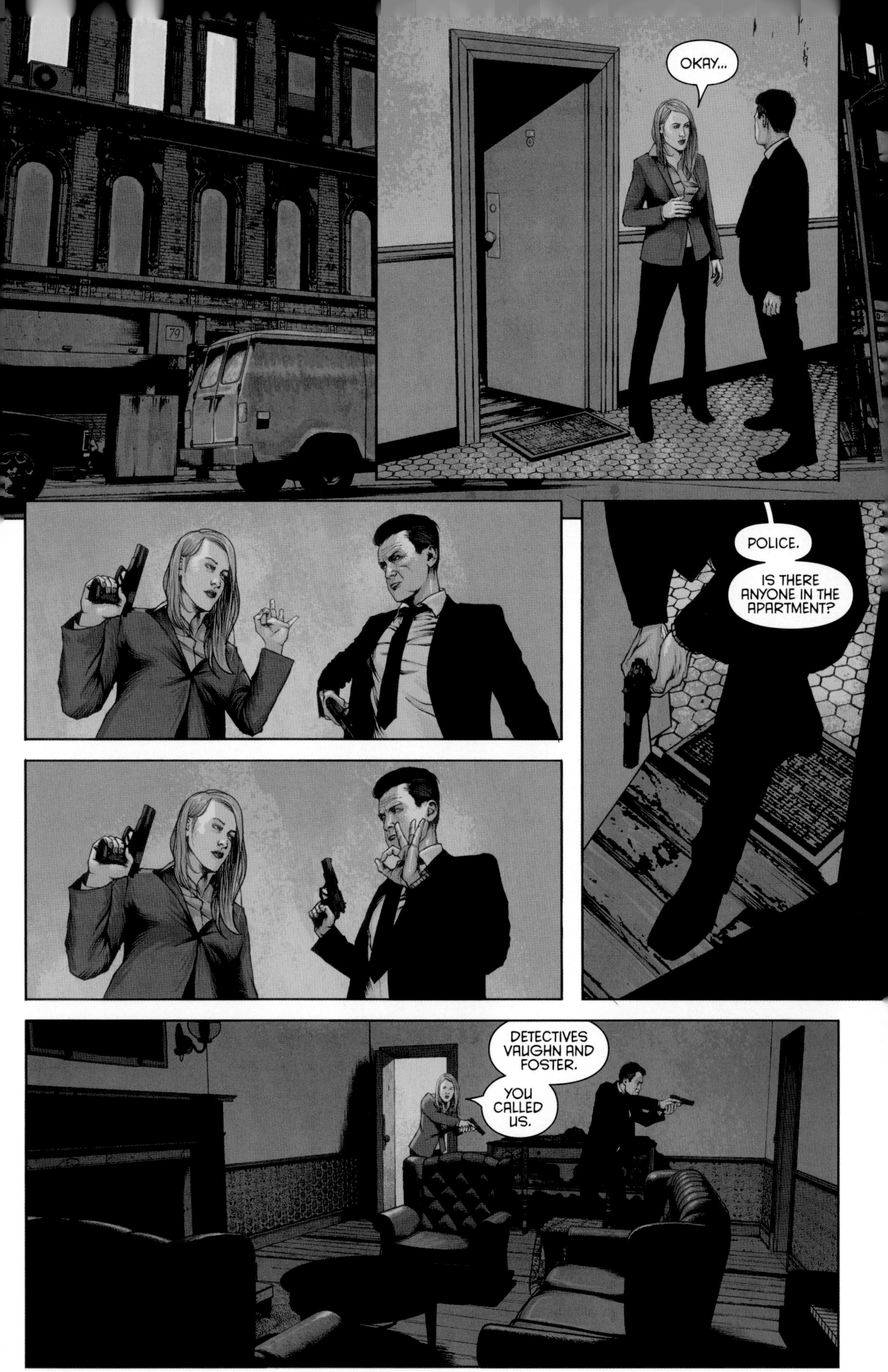
OKAY...
POLICE.
IS THERE ANYONE IN THE APARTMENT?
DETECTIVES VAUGHN AND FOSTER.
YOU CALLED US.

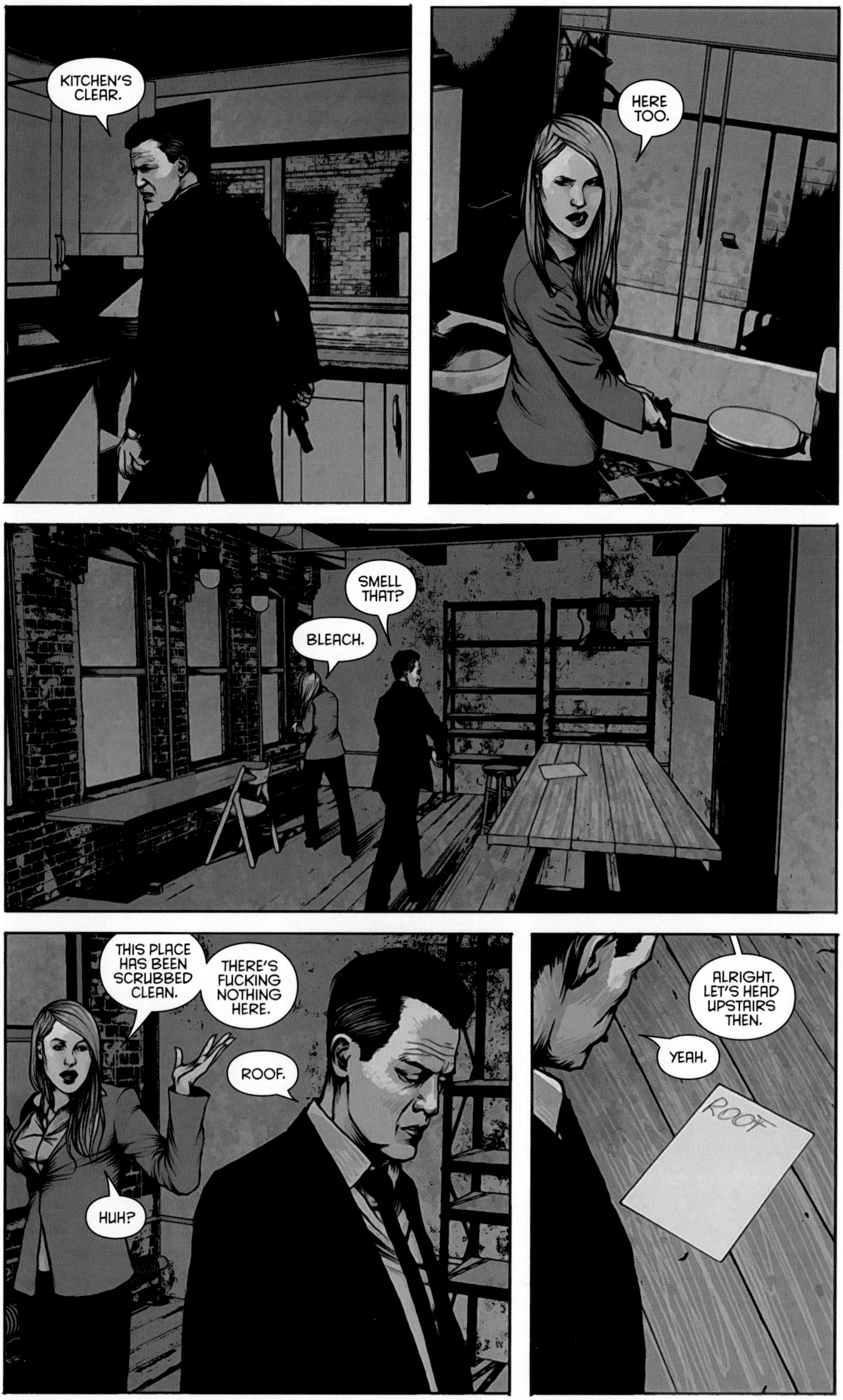
KITCHEN'S CLEAR.
HERE TOO.
SMELL THAT?
BLEACH.
THIS PLACE HAS BEEN SCRUBBED CLEAN.
THERE'S FUCKING NOTHING HERE.
ROOF.
HUH?
ALRIGHT. LET'S HEAD UPSTAIRS THEN.
YEAH.
ROOF

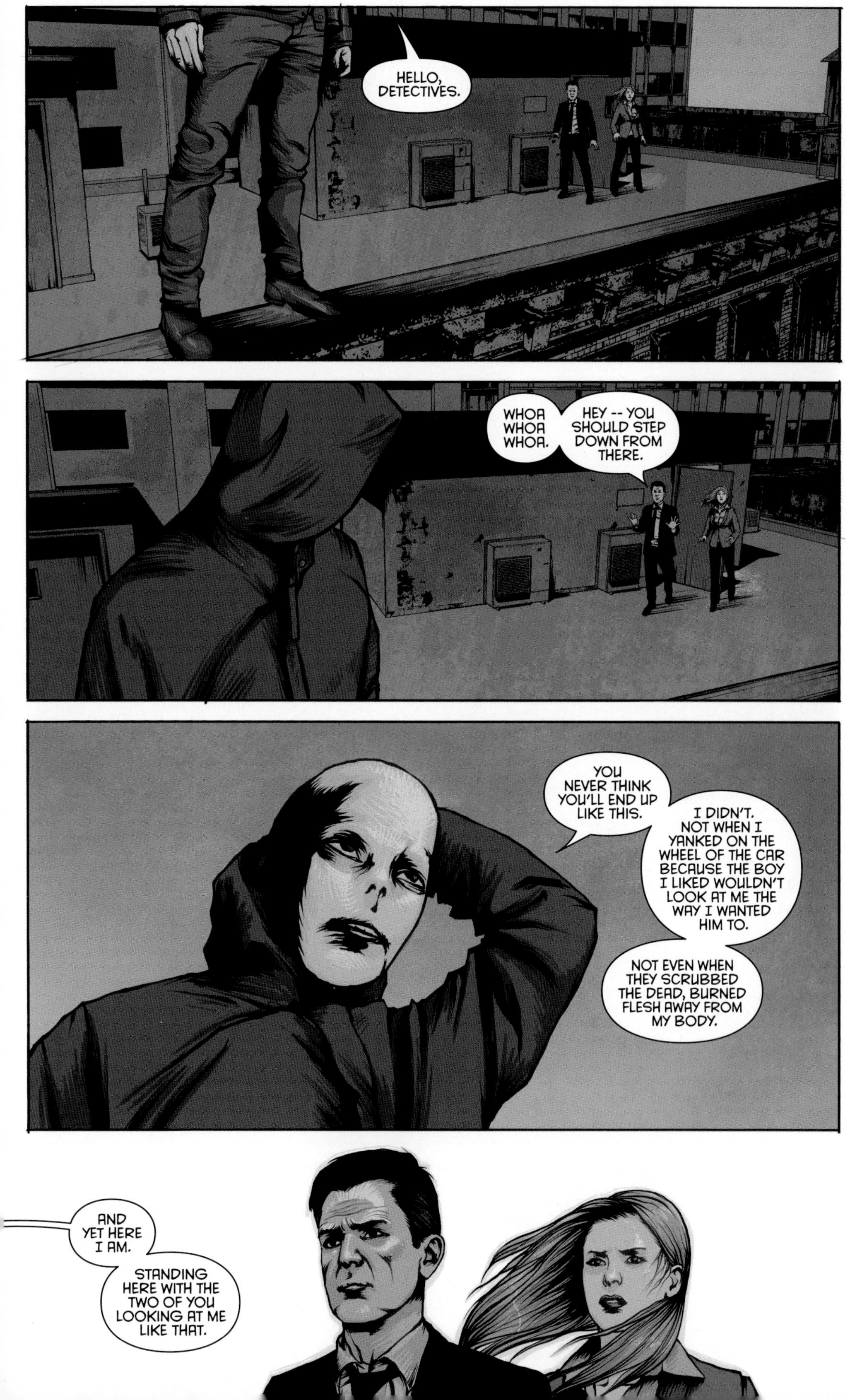
HELLO, DETECTIVES.
WHOA WHOA WHOA.
HEY -- YOU SHOULD STEP DOWN FROM THERE.
YOU NEVER THINK YOU'LL END UP LIKE THIS.
I DIDN'T. NOT WHEN I YANKED ON THE WHEEL OF THE CAR BECAUSE THE BOY I LIKED WOULDN'T LOOK AT ME THE WAY I WANTED HIM TO.
NOT EVEN WHEN THEY SCRUBBED THE DEAD, BURNED FLESH AWAY FROM MY BODY.
AND YET HERE I AM.
STANDING HERE WITH THE TWO OF YOU LOOKING AT ME LIKE THAT.

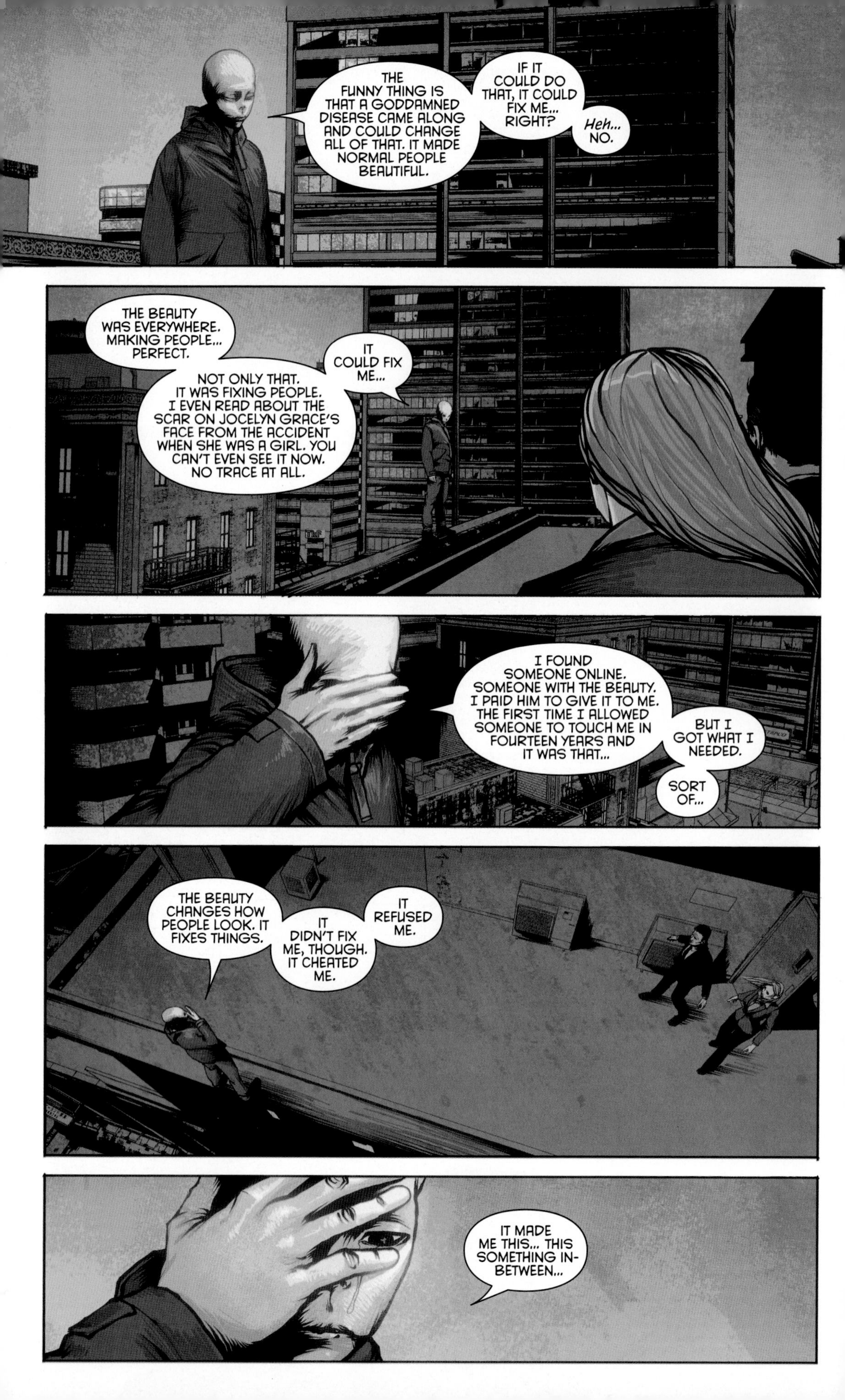
THE FUNNY THING IS THAT A GODDAMNED DISEASE CAME ALONG AND COULD CHANGE ALL OF THAT. IT MADE NORMAL PEOPLE BEAUTIFUL.
IF IT COULD DO THAT, IT COULD FIX ME... RIGHT?
Heh... NO.
THE BEAUTY WAS EVERYWHERE. MAKING PEOPLE... PERFECT.
NOT ONLY THAT. IT WAS FIXING PEOPLE. I EVEN READ ABOUT THE SCAR ON JOCELYN GRACE'S FACE FROM THE ACCIDENT WHEN SHE WAS A GIRL. YOU CAN'T EVEN SEE IT NOW. NO TRACE AT ALL.
IT COULD FIX ME...
I FOUND SOMEONE ONLINE. SOMEONE WITH THE BEAUTY. I PAID HIM TO GIVE IT TO ME. THE FIRST TIME I ALLOWED SOMEONE TO TOUCH ME IN FOURTEEN YEARS AND IT WAS THAT...
BUT I GOT WHAT I NEEDED.
SORT OF...
THE BEAUTY CHANGES HOW PEOPLE LOOK. IT FIXES THINGS.
IT DIDN'T FIX ME, THOUGH. IT CHEATED ME.
IT REFUSED ME.
IT MADE ME THIS... THIS SOMETHING IN-BETWEEN...

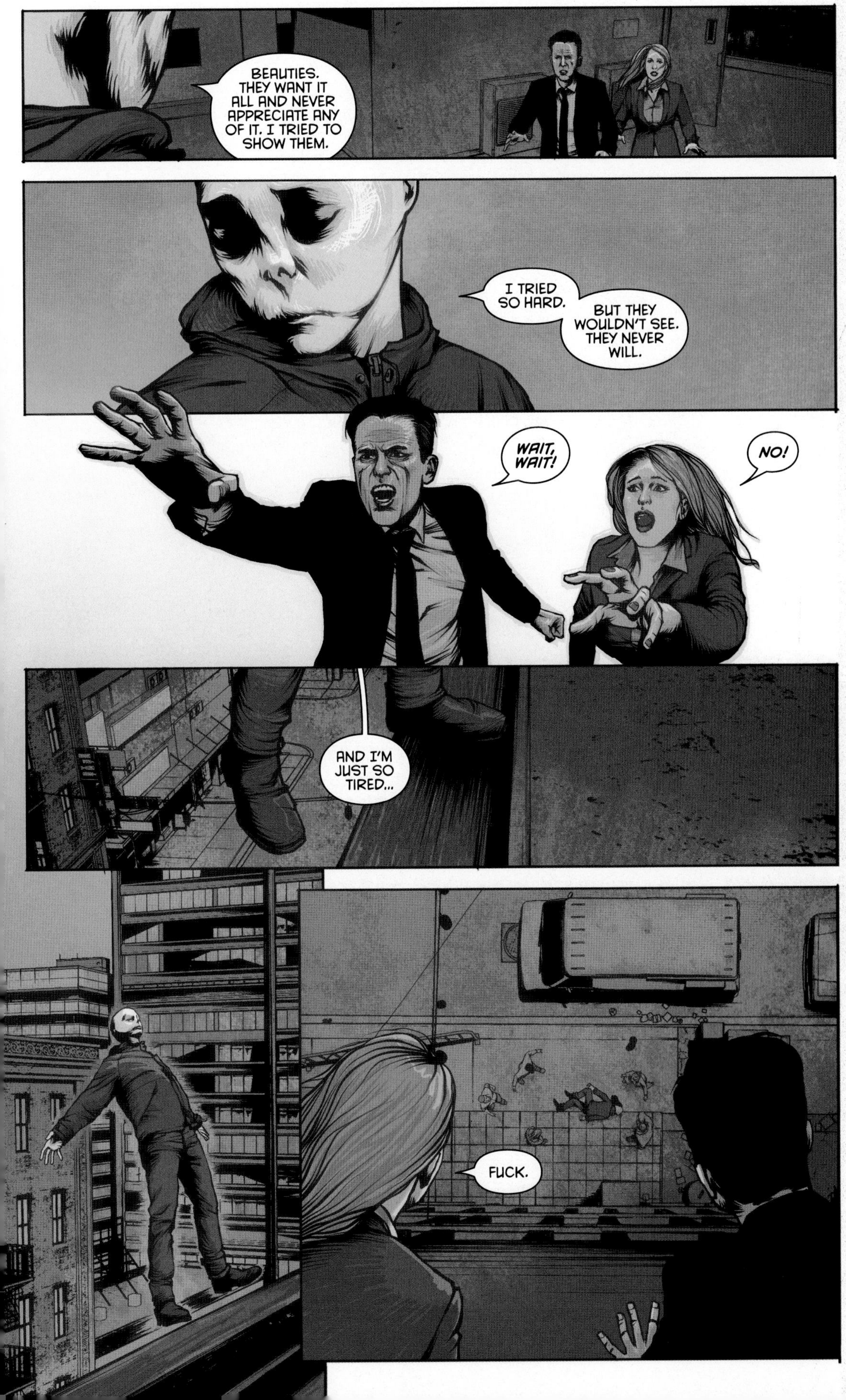
BEAUTIES. THEY WANT IT ALL AND NEVER APPRECIATE ANY OF IT. I TRIED TO SHOW THEM.
I TRIED SO HARD.
BUT THEY WOULDN'T SEE. THEY NEVER WILL.
WAIT, WAIT!
NO!
AND I'M JUST SO TIRED...
FUCK.

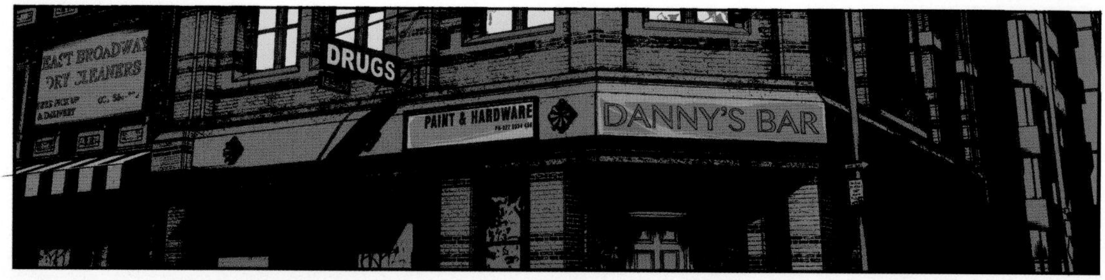
EAST BROADWAY
DRY CLEANERS
DRUGS
PAINT & HARDWARE
DANNY'S BAR

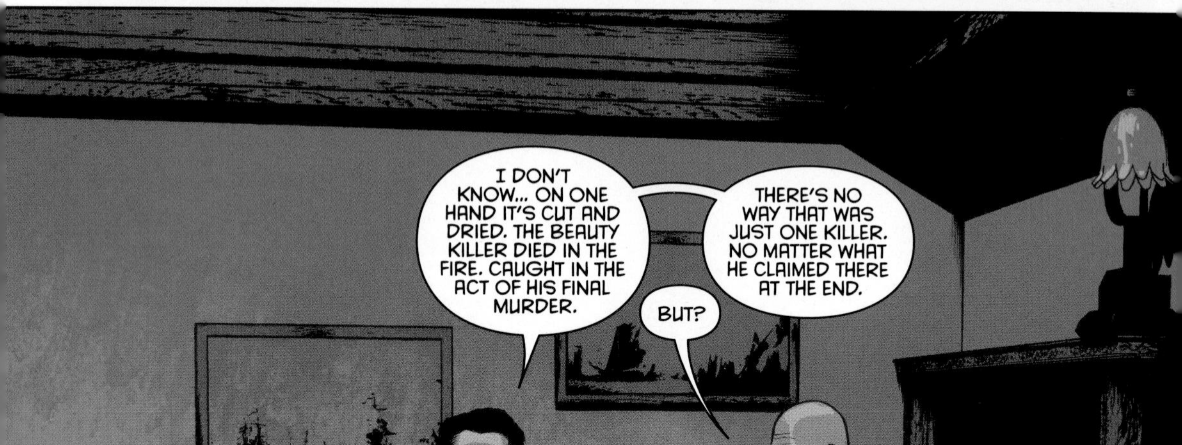
I DON'T KNOW... ON ONE HAND IT'S CUT AND DRIED. THE BEAUTY KILLER DIED IN THE FIRE. CAUGHT IN THE ACT OF HIS FINAL MURDER.
BUT?
THERE'S NO WAY THAT WAS JUST ONE KILLER. NO MATTER WHAT HE CLAIMED THERE AT THE END.

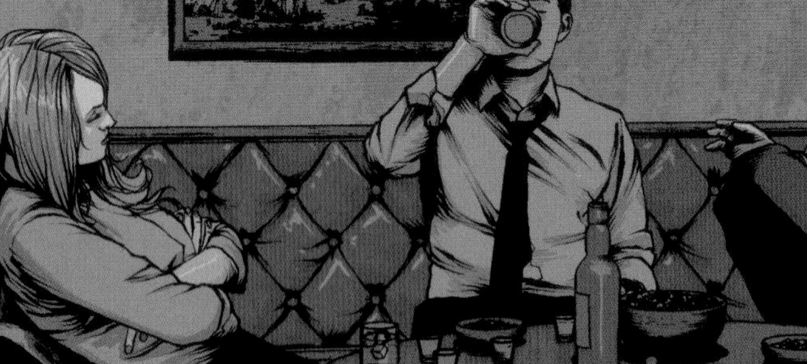
BUT THE KILLINGS HAVE STOPPED. ALL OF THEM.
AND NO MATTER WHAT WE MIGHT THINK, THERE'S NO EVIDENCE AT ALL CONNECTING AMY McDONOUGH TO ANY OF THIS. WHATEVER TRUTH THERE IS... DIED WITH HER WHEN SHE JUMPED OFF THAT ROOF.

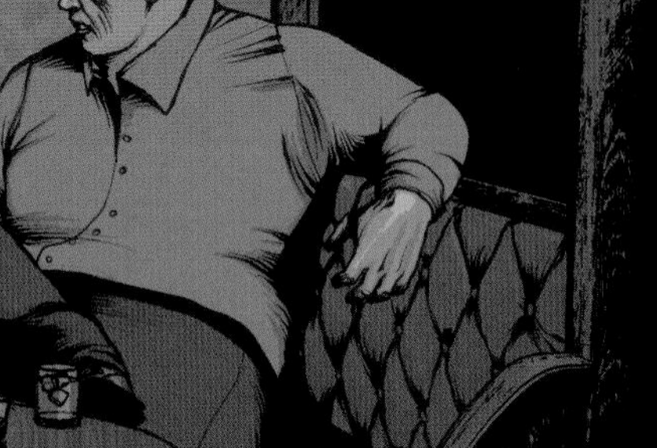
WE HAVE TO CLOSE IT.

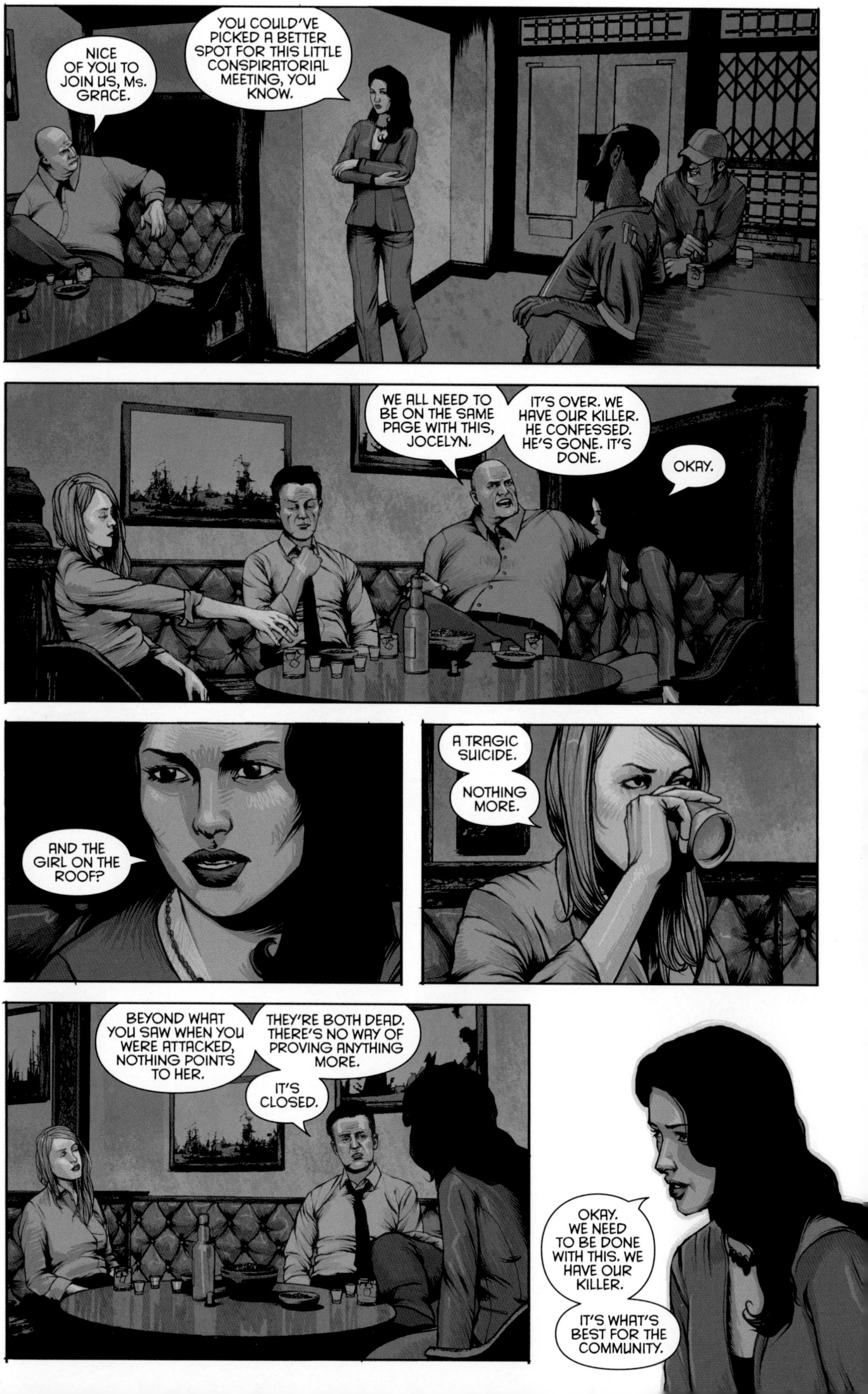
NICE OF YOU TO JOIN US, Ms. GRACE.
YOU COULD'VE PICKED A BETTER SPOT FOR THIS LITTLE CONSPIRATORIAL MEETING, YOU KNOW.
WE ALL NEED TO BE ON THE SAME PAGE WITH THIS, JOCELYN.
IT'S OVER. WE HAVE OUR KILLER. HE CONFESSED. HE'S GONE. IT'S DONE.
OKAY.
AND THE GIRL ON THE ROOF?
A TRAGIC SUICIDE.
NOTHING MORE.
BEYOND WHAT YOU SAW WHEN YOU WERE ATTACKED, NOTHING POINTS TO HER.
THEY'RE BOTH DEAD. THERE'S NO WAY OF PROVING ANYTHING MORE.
IT'S CLOSED.
OKAY. WE NEED TO BE DONE WITH THIS. WE HAVE OUR KILLER.
IT'S WHAT'S BEST FOR THE COMMUNITY.

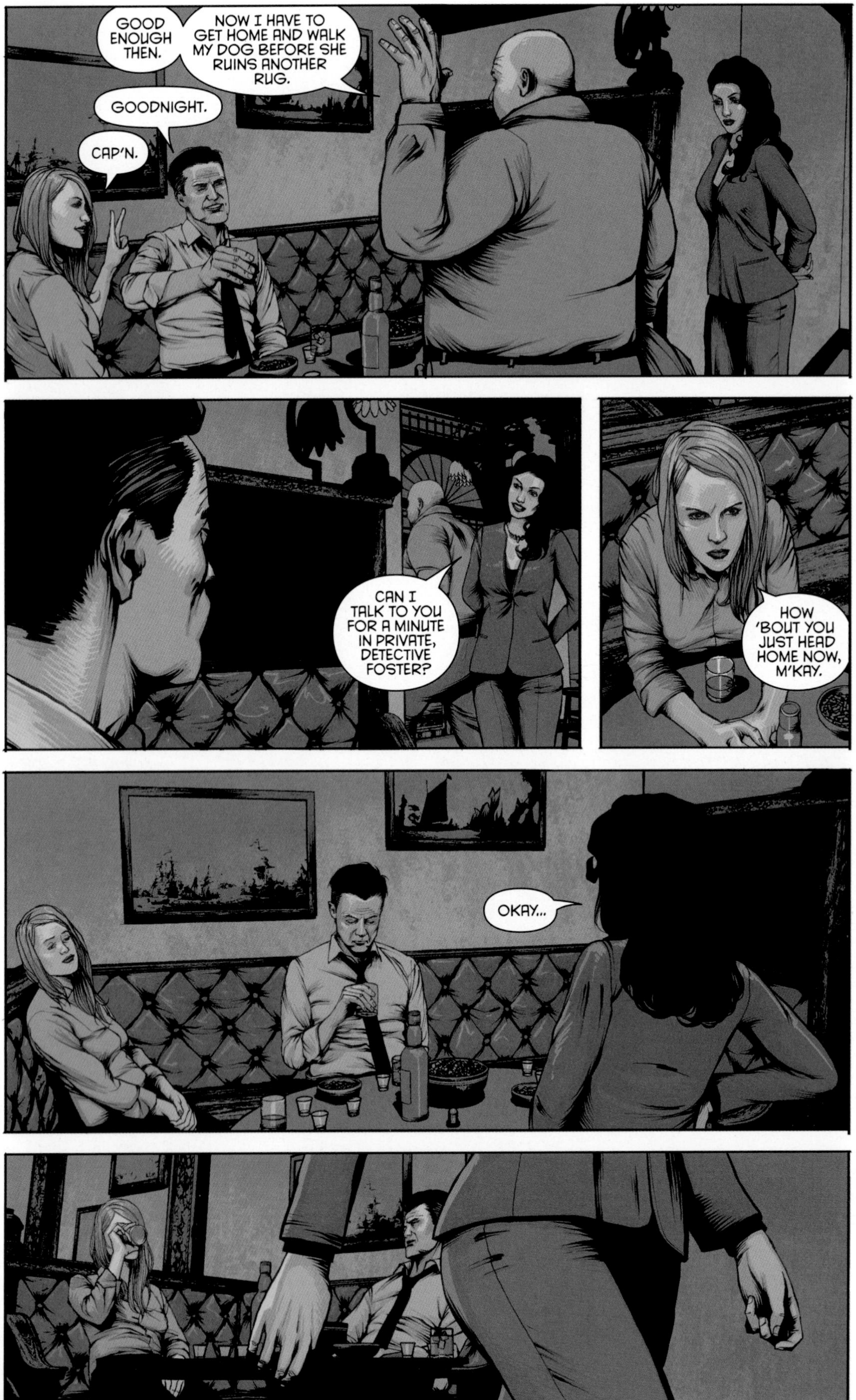
GOOD ENOUGH THEN.
NOW I HAVE TO GET HOME AND WALK MY DOG BEFORE SHE RUINS ANOTHER RUG.
GOODNIGHT.
CAP'N.
CAN I TALK TO YOU FOR A MINUTE IN PRIVATE, DETECTIVE FOSTER?
HOW 'BOUT YOU JUST HEAD HOME NOW, M'KAY.
OKAY...

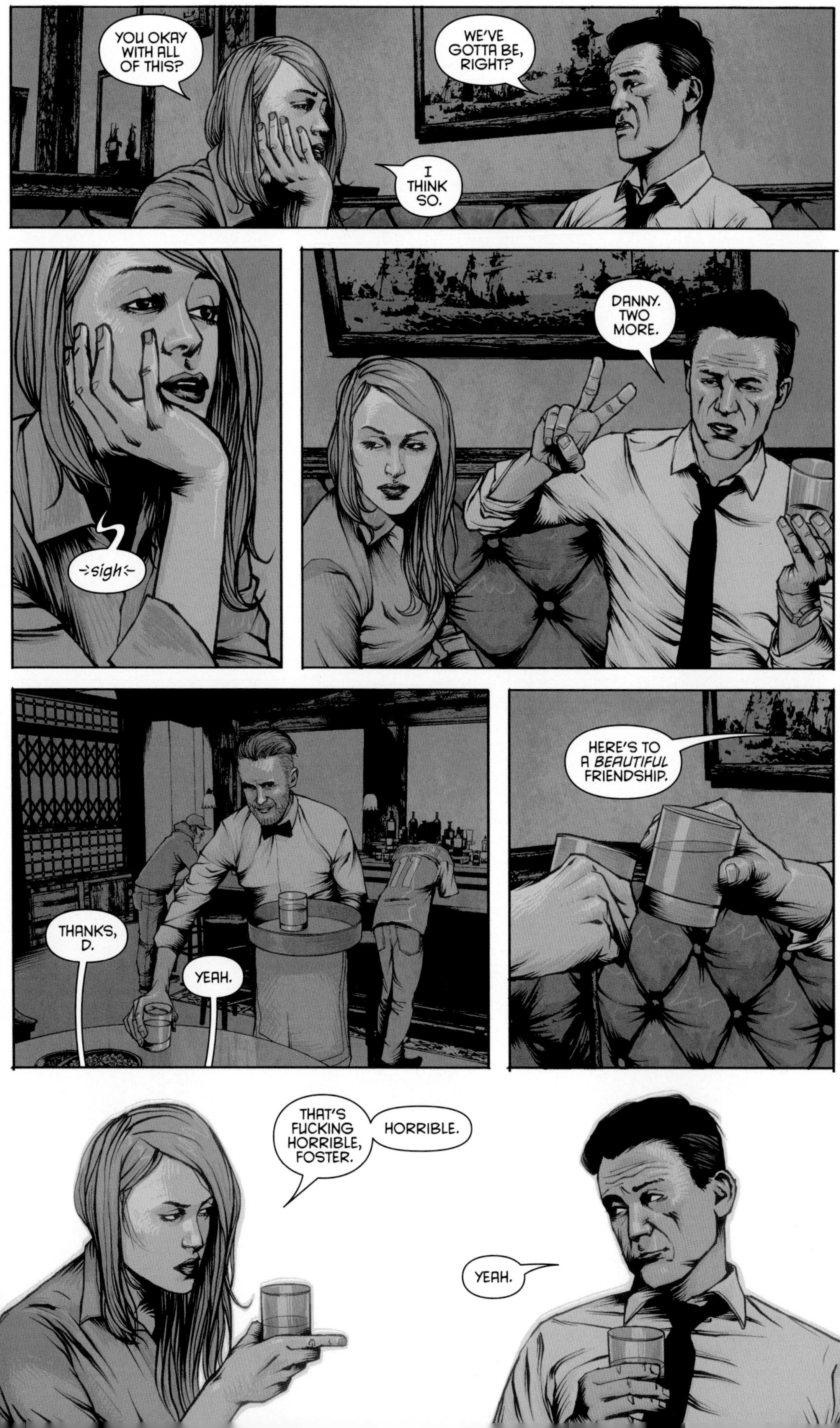
YOU OKAY WITH ALL OF THIS?
WE'VE GOTTA BE, RIGHT?
I THINK SO.
sigh
DANNY. TWO MORE.
THANKS, D.
YEAH.
HERE'S TO A *BEAUTIFUL* FRIENDSHIP.
THAT'S FUCKING HORRIBLE, FOSTER.
HORRIBLE.
YEAH.

C O V E R S

BEAUTY
12
$3.99

ISSUE #12
Cover A
Jeremy Haun
& John Rauch

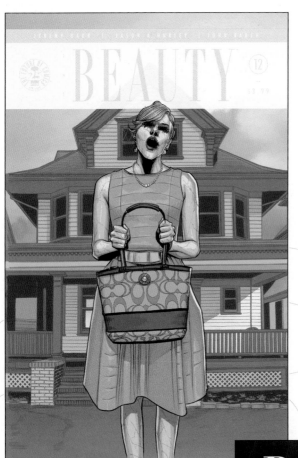

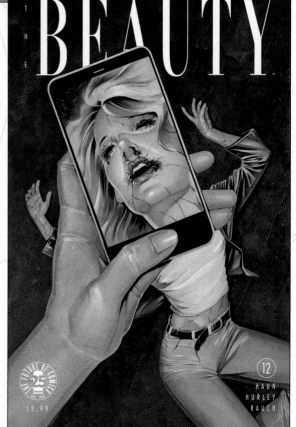

ISSUE #12
Cover B
Yunfan Zhou

THE BEAUTY
12
HAUN
HURLEY
RAUCH
$3.99

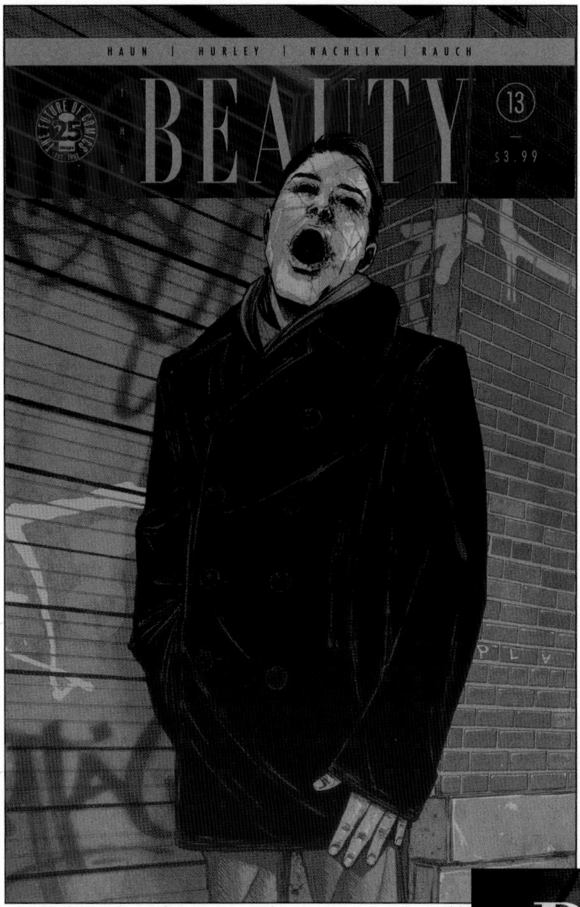
HAUN | HURLEY | NACHLIK | RAUCH
THE BEAUTY
13
$3.99

ISSUE #13
Cover A
Jeremy Haun
& John Rauch

ISSUE #13
Cover B
Laura Tolton

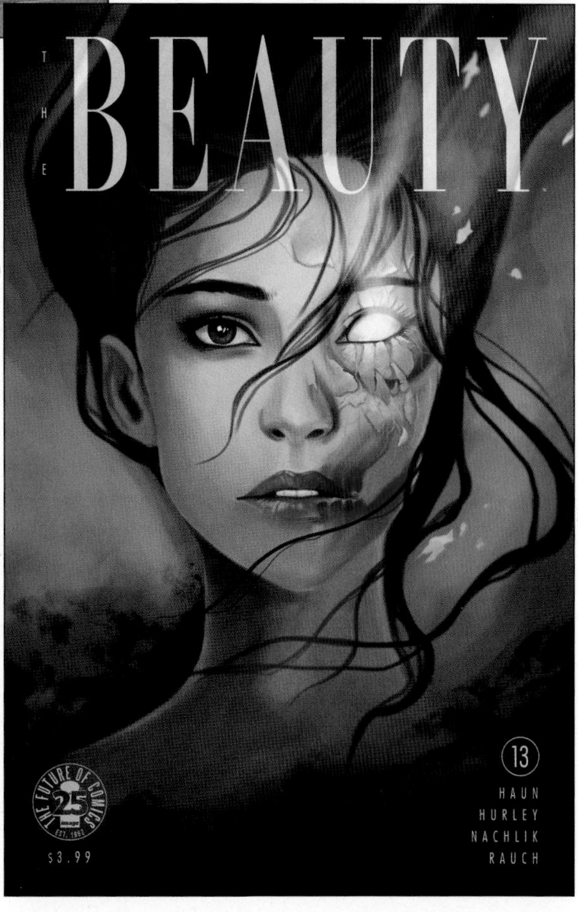
THE BEAUTY
13
HAUN
HURLEY
NACHLIK
RAUCH
$3.99

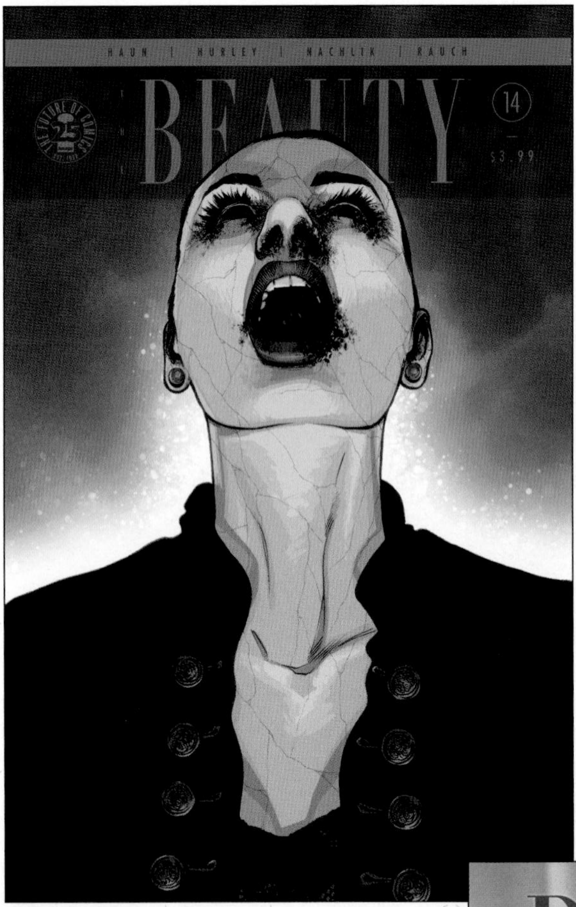
HAUN | HURLEY | NACHLIK | RAUCH
BEAUTY
14
$3.99

ISSUE #14
Cover B
Aaron Lee Kafton

ISSUE #14
Cover A
Jeremy Haun
& John Rauch

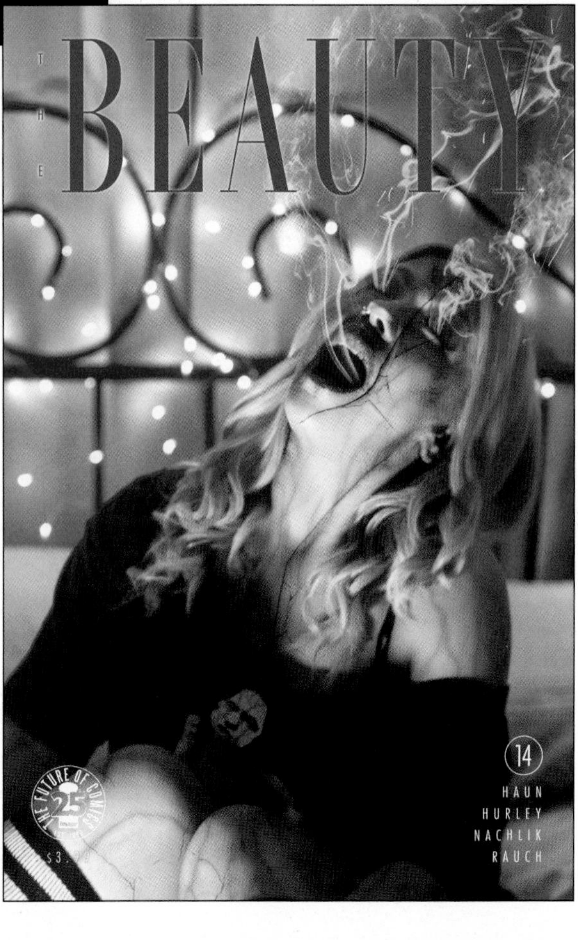
THE BEAUTY
14
HAUN
HURLEY
NACHLIK
RAUCH

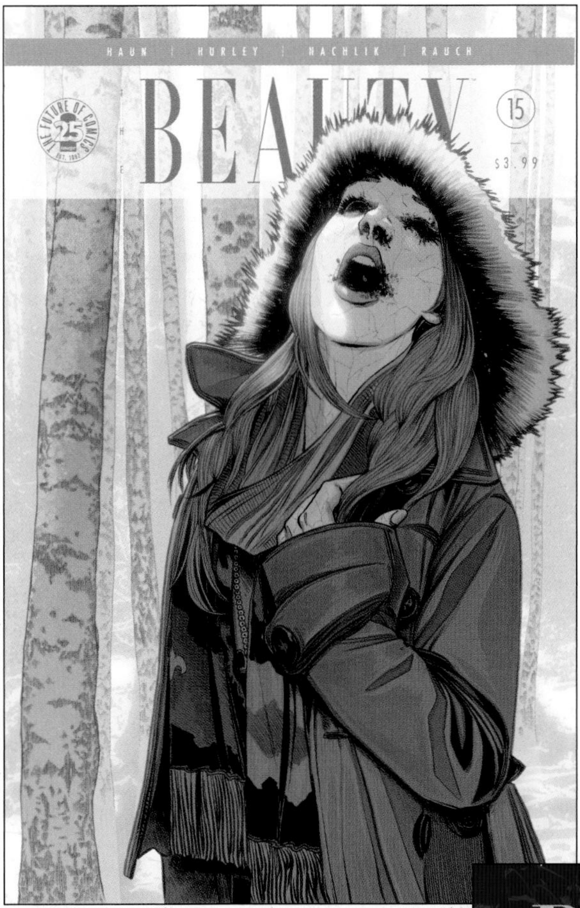
HAUN | HURLEY | NACHLIK | RAUCH
THE BEAUTY
15
$3.99

ISSUE #15

Cover A

Jeremy Haun
& John Rauch

ISSUE #15

Cover B

Christopher Mitten

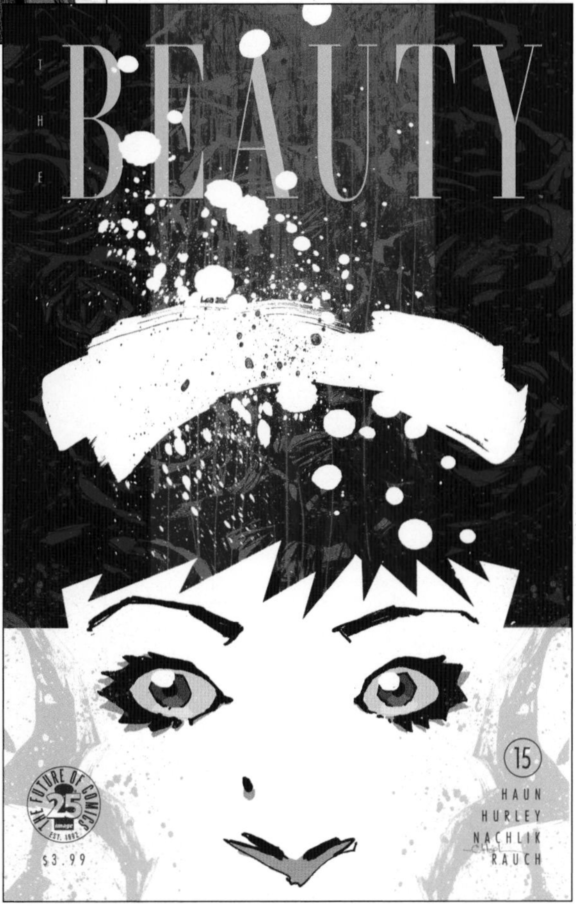
THE BEAUTY
15
HAUN
HURLEY
NACHLIK
RAUCH
$3.99

HAUN | HURLEY | NACHLIK | RAUCH
16
$3.99

ISSUE #16
Cover A
Jeremy Haun
& John Rauch

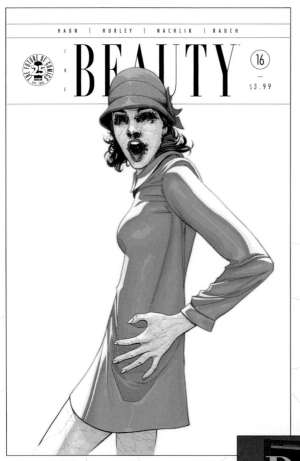

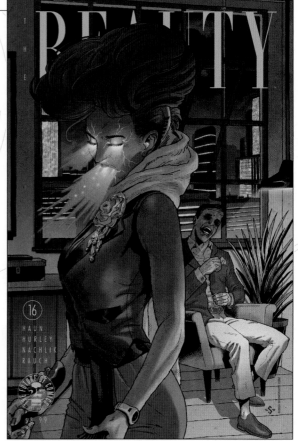

ISSUE #16
Cover B
Shane White

16
HAUN
HURLEY
NACHLIK
RAUCH

PROCESS

"Some of my very early Foster and Vaughn sketches. Both characters were already designed. I just had to get used to drawing them in various poses that I imagined would be relevant in the book."

Thomas Nachlik

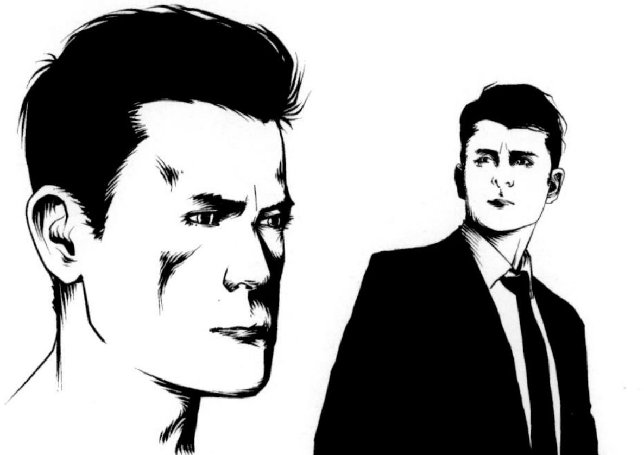

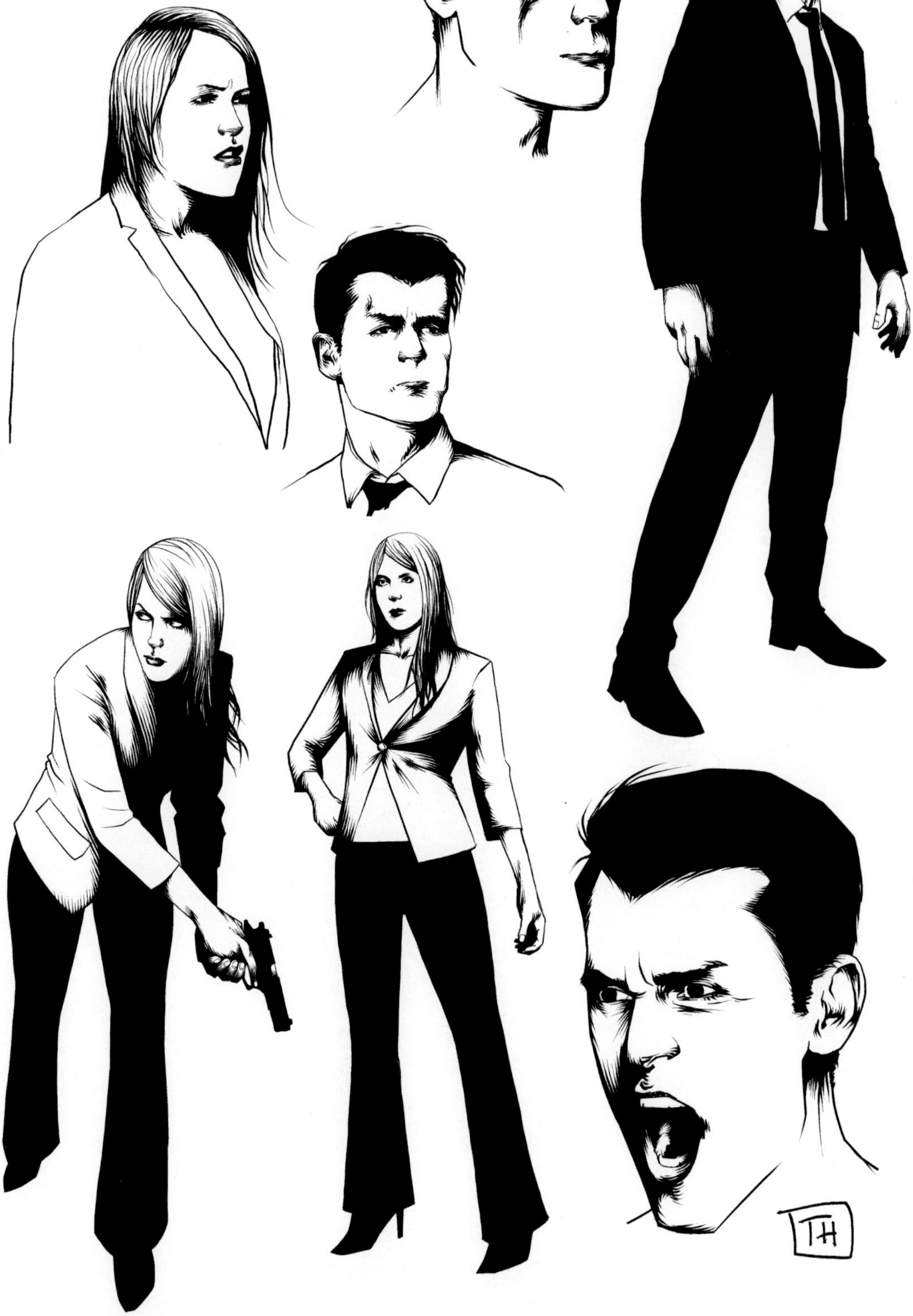
TH

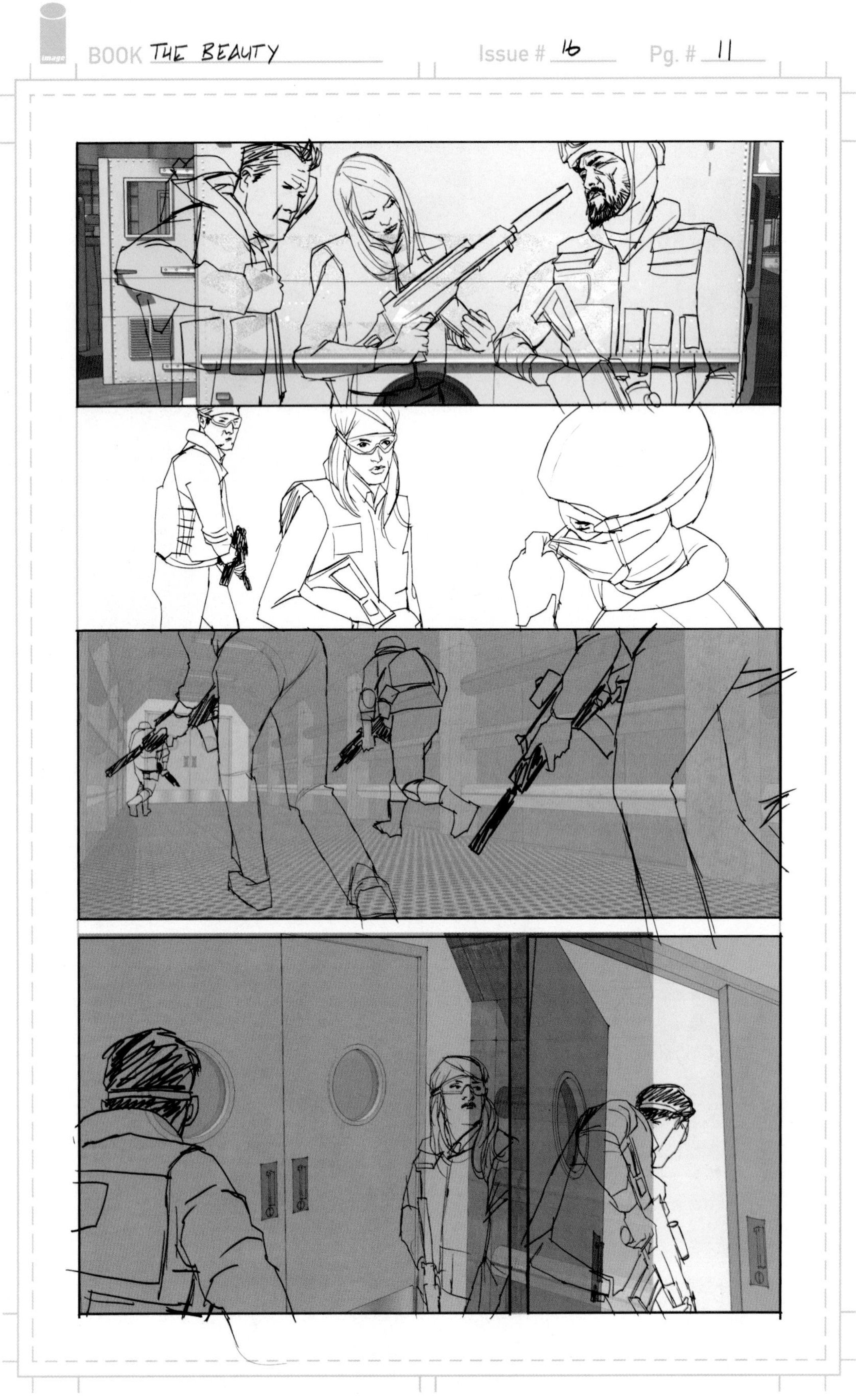
BOOK THE BEAUTY
Issue # 16
Pg. # 11

"My steps from layouts/rough pencils to inks. In this particular scene, influenced by unrealistic cop movies, I gave Foster and Vaughn automatic rifles and goggles that I assumed was standard procedure for

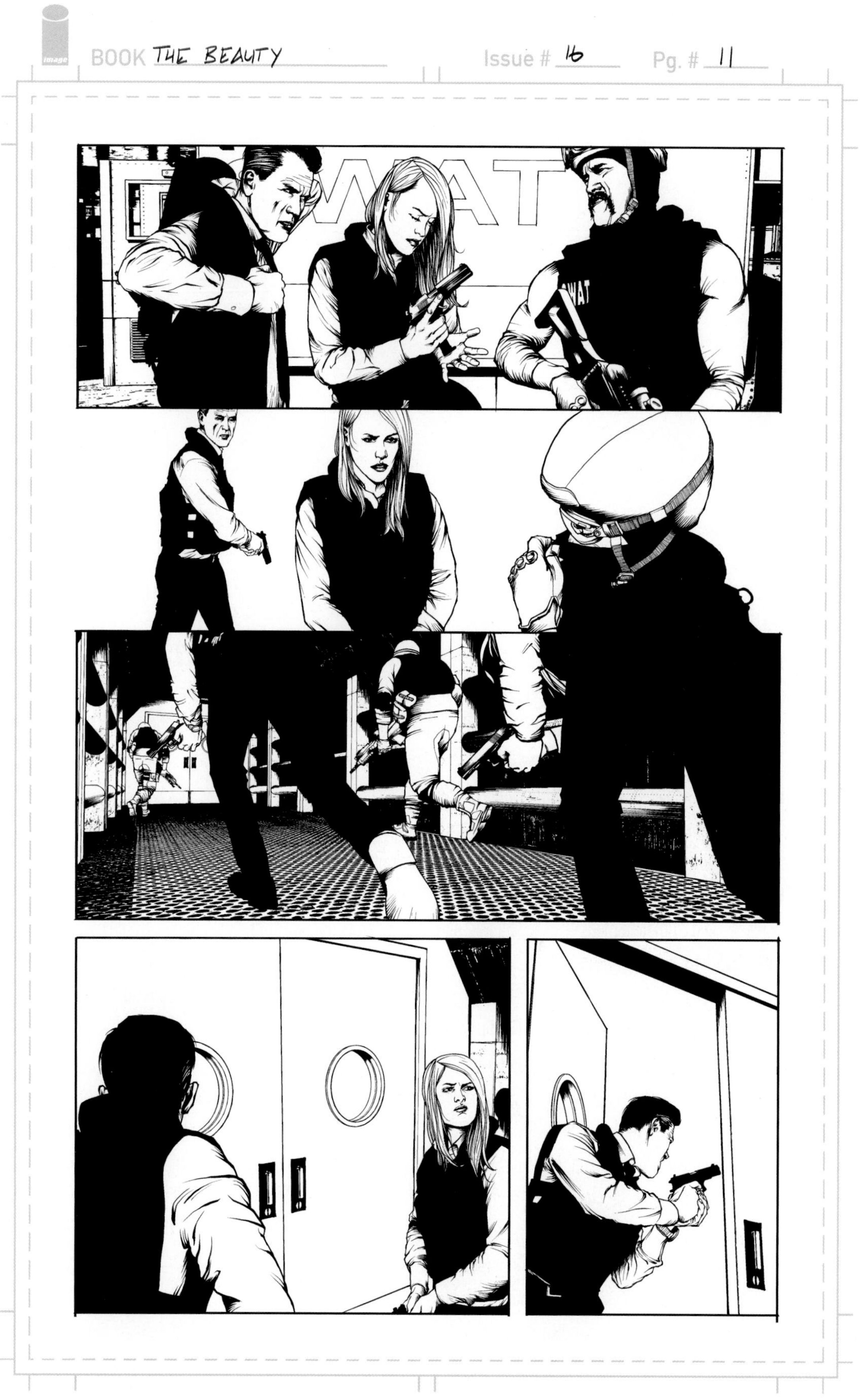
BOOK THE BEAUTY
Issue # 16
Pg. # 11

detectives handling hostage situations. But they got edited out and I ended up re-drawing both characters using their regular guns and not wearing eye protection." **Thomas Nachlik**

BIOGRAPHIES

Jeremy Haun, co-writer, co-creator, and often artist of THE BEAUTY, has also worked on *Wolf Moon* from Vertigo, and *Constantine* and *Batwoman* from DC. Over the past decade plus, along with wearing calluses on his fingers doing work for DC, Marvel, Image, and others, he has created and written several projects. Some you might know are the graphic novel *Narcoleptic Sunday, The Leading Man,* and *Dino Day.* He is a part of the Bad Karma Creative group, whose *Bad Karma Volume One* debuted at NYCC 2013, thanks to Kickstarter funding.

Jeremy resides in a crumbling mansion in Joplin, Missouri, with his wife and two superheroes-in-training.

Jason A. Hurley has been in the comic book game for over fifteen years. However, none of you have ever heard of him because, until recently, he's been almost completely exclusive to the retail sector. In addition to comic books, he loves pro wrestling, bad horror movies, Freddy Mercury, hummingbirds, his parents, and pizza. While he's never actually tried it, he also thinks curling looks like a hell of a lot of fun. Hurley claims his personal heroes are Earl Bassett and Valentine McKee, because they live a life of adventure on their own terms. He also claims that he would brain anyone who showed even the most remote signs of becoming a cannibalistic undead bastard, including his own brother, without a second thought. He's lived in Joplin, Missouri, for most of his life, and never plans to leave.

Thomas Nachlik is a Polish-born illustrator, living in Germany with his wife and two cats. His client list includes Top Cow, Boom, Amazon Studios, and DC Comics.

John Rauch is an American comic book colorist whose credits include: THE DARKNESS, INVINCIBLE, *Teen Titans: Year One, Patsy Walker: Hellcat,* and a bunch of other stuff not worth bragging about. He enjoys speaking about himself in the third person and pretending he is more talented and relevant than he really is to fight off bouts of depression.

Fonografiks The banner name for the comics work of designer Steven Finch, "Fonografiks" has provided lettering and design to a number of Image Comics titles, including NOWHERE MEN, INJECTION, TREES, THEY'RE NOT LIKE US, WE STAND ON GUARD, and the multi-award winning SAGA.

Joel Enos is a writer and editor of comics and stories. Recent editing projects include the graphic novel THE RATTLER and the collected edition of THE SAVIORS, both published by Image Comics.